MATKA

SARAH HANLEY

This book is a work of fiction. Any references to historical events, real people, or real places are used fictitiously. Other names, characters, places and events are the products of the author's imagination, and any resemblance to actual events or places or persons, living or dead, is entirely coincidental.

First paperback and e-book edition August 2018

ISBN 978-1-7324442-0-1 (paperback)
ISBN 978-1-7324442-1-8 (e-book)

Library of Congress Control Number: 2018906778

Published by Edward Wayne Publishing
Maple Grove, Minnesota
www.edwardwaynepublishing.com
www.sarahhanleybooks.com

To Baba and Papa, and their
daughter, my mama, Janina.

PRONUNCIATIONS

Zosia	ZO-sha
Minsk Mazowiecki	meensk mazo-VYET-ski
Dziewczynka	jef-CHEEN-ka
Tadeusz	ta-DE-oosh
Wildflecken	VEELD-fleck-en
Durzyn	DOUR-zyn
Czeslaw	CHES-lawf

MATKA

CHAPTER ONE

August, 1943: Morning.

Turn.

Turn.

Please turn.

The knob didn't move. Silence hovered in the alley, but Zosia Wilusz knew the regulars were gathered, like every other morning. She kept her eyes on the tarnished doorknob. If it so much as quivered, she would be first. She had to be first. Her children were starving.

She knew the knob wouldn't turn. It didn't yesterday and it wouldn't today. Still, she had to be ready. She would endure another broom to the head, even welcome it, for one more try at the trash thrown from the back door of the deli.

A dozen or so other Poles in similar states of starvation rustled the quiet around her, each tucked behind a brick corner or under wooden steps. Her countrymen, there to fight for the few salvageable pieces of food that the Jews would discard and hiding so they wouldn't be chased away before the bounty was tossed. Not long ago the scavengers were her trusted neighbors. Now they were only rivals, united against each other in hunger.

Most of the Jews were already taken from Minsk Mazowiecki. A few hung on, able to avoid the Gestapo. Some even dared to keep businesses open under assumed names, knowing they had targets on their backs. It was only a matter of time.

Along with her envy and resentment of the Jews there was now a new, uneasy pity festering within Zosia. The whispers around town assured her that the Jews were being lead to their deaths. At least she was alive. That maybe wouldn't last, either.

The pattern of the doorknob's patina burned into her retinas as she concentrated all her thoughts toward the back door. She felt the lines around her eyes deepen. Another chisel crack in a once sculpted face. The years had not been kind.

Maybe she could will the knob to turn with her mind. The transient gypsies sometimes had such powers. Maybe there was some gypsy in her blood that she could call upon. That might explain her inky black hair. It could also explain why her father left them. It was years ago, but she still searched for excuses.

So many holes to fill within her, but her priorities were the empty stomachs at home.

Without a sound, she commanded the last Jew left in town to open the door. She took a deep breath to relax her nerves but choked on the sour smell of week-old trash that filled the alley. She and everyone else had already rummaged through it, time and again. They all needed fresh trash. She pressed her nose into her sleeve to block out the lingering stench of molded cabbage and fermented fish that lay rejected on the ground.

"Zosia." A raspy voice floated from a few feet away. Zosia looked and saw half of Ignasja's face and much of her belly peeking from behind the cinder block wall of the deserted bank.

Zosia didn't acknowledge her. She refocused on the deli's back door. Ignasja only came every morning for the gossip and was usually the one to spread it.

"They're all gone, Zosia. It's over."

"Shht." Zosia put her finger to her lips and shook her head as if she were reprimanding her children at Good Friday services.

"It doesn't matter, they're gone. Dead." Ignasja's many chins wobbled while she spoke. It made Zosia's guts churn—from contempt because Ignasja had no business being there with the starved and from hunger because her neighbor's face looked like fatty chicken skin. "I saw it myself," Ignasja proudly allowed her voice to rise. Nothing pleased the woman more than having information that others didn't, even if she had to make it up. "Dirty shits. They deserve it."

"Watch your mouth, Ignasja. Or you're next."

"Not as long as I pray to the Virgin Mother."

"You think the Gestapo cares about that?" Zosia stopped. She wouldn't engage. Ignasja couldn't be trusted.

There was a pause before Ignasja spoke again. "I'm surprised you're defending them, given what they did to Wiktor."

A deep ache gripped Zosia's empty stomach at the mention of her dead husband. Jittery, she shifted her weight. The rancid air threatened to suffocate her.

"They won't even let us have their rotten trash," Ignasja went on. "We have to hide, waiting to battle the rats and each other for it. Then they come out and chase us away with their brooms and shovels, like their garbage is even too good for us." She loudly cleared her throat and spat on the ground. "Let the pigs be slaughtered."

Zosia didn't respond. Bile bubbled inside her.

A train whistle in the distance broke the stillness. It was the eleven forty-five out of Warsaw. A soft groan rose from the alley's hiding spots. It was too late. If the Jews hadn't taken out the morning trash by now, they weren't going to. They were gone.

The hairs on the back of Zosia's neck stood on end. She tied the babushka she had hoped to use as a knapsack under her chin. They would have to depend on Maxim even more now.

Dear daughter, forgive me.

With dropped shoulders, she turned to slink between the buildings toward the main road. She kept a sharp eye out for uniformed Germans hiding in crannies. She didn't know if they were stalking the streets, but there were rumors. With no Jews left to occupy the Gestapo's attention, anyone caught roaming the streets could be vulnerable. She was certain that capture meant death. She'd heard stories, and she believed them.

Luckily, she knew every cobblestone and concrete crack like her own palm. She took her first baby steps here on the streets of Minsk Mazowiecki. This was where she learned to love, and it was where her heart eventually shattered. She smuggled toward home like a moth blending with the leaves, making the sign of the cross in front of the Church of St. Michael the Archangel out of habit and not hope.

She reached into her pocket for a cigarette before remembering she'd smoked her last one the previous day. It would be a long walk home without the taste of tobacco to distract from the want of meat. In the place of breakfast, anxiety filled her stomach and pushed her forward, holding flames to her heels as they clicked against the bricks.

Wincing, she silently cursed her brown suede pumps; her work loafers were still soaked from yesterday's rain. Everything else unneeded had been sold months ago, exchanged for a zloty or two to put toward dinner. She kept a pair of work shoes and a pair of dress shoes for church or other special occasions—if occasions were ever allowed to be special again.

As she made the final turn to her house, Zosia spotted Marisha sitting on the opposite curb. Her daughter's thick black hair matched her own. The young woman wore a blue-flowered dress that sagged on her flat body, lean not from the youth of her seventeen years but from starvation. She rested her elbows on her knees, her hands covering her face.

"Marisha," Zosia called out.

The girl peeked out between her fingers, scurried to her feet, and rushed away down the cobblestones.

"Wait," Zosia said and darted across the street toward her.

Still moving at a determined speed-walk, Marisha glanced over her shoulder at her mother. "Leave me alone."

"Marisha, what happened?"

"I said, leave me alone. I hate you."

"I know." Zosia caught up and touched her daughter's thin arm, stopping her. "Tell me. What happened?" She put just enough pressure on Marisha's shoulder to turn the girl. When she did, she was met with sad eyes, one of which was dark and swollen. Zosia caressed the distorted skin. "Is this Maxim?" she asked, her voice filled with worry.

Marisha nodded. "He's a brute. He says he loves me, but then he does this. I hate him, and I hate that you keep sending me to him."

"Marisha, you—"

"That's not even the worst of it this time," Marisha cut her off. She reached into the pocket of her dress, pulled out a folded piece of paper and handed it to her mother. Zosia recognized the stationery. She had received a similar letter last week.

Zosia let go of her daughter's shoulder and sighed. "You wrote to Aunt Brygida?"

Marisha nodded. "Read it."

She didn't need to, but she unfolded it anyway to appease her daughter.

Dearest Marisha,

Thank you for the letter, sweet girl. I regret to say that we're unable to help you. As I told your

> *mother just last week when she wrote to ask the same, Bronek and I cannot harbor anyone here at the house. The war has hit England hard, and we've had to say goodbye to our housekeeper. We may have to let our cook go, too. Please take care of yourself, and give your brothers each a big kiss from their auntie and uncle.*
>
> *Always, Brygida*

Unsurprised, Zosia folded the letter and handed it to Marisha. Her daughter's naiveté worried her more than Brygida's response. "You asked Auntie if you could go live with her?"

Marisha nodded, her eyes welling again. "And you asked the same. How could you abandon us?" She pushed her limp black hair behind both ears and wiped at her face with her wrists. She stared at the ground to avoid Zosia's concerned eyes.

Zosia watched the young woman fume. *Such is youth*, Zosia supposed. She was probably the same at that age. In fact, she knew she was.

An image of a young, smiling Wiktor, barely twenty years old, slipped into Zosia's head. Passion clouded her judgment at the time, but she had been right to allow it. She hadn't yet been debilitated by years of worry and mistrust.

"No." Zosia shook her head. "I asked if *you* could live with her. You and your brothers. I hoped Brygida would be a better option than Maxim. I only want to keep you safe." She reached out and nudged Marisha's chin up so she could look her straight in the eye. "You know I would never go and live with her. We barely made it through childhood without killing each other." She smiled.

Marisha's eyes darkened and Zosia watched despair fall over her daughter. "I can't keep seeing Maxim. What do I do?"

"You will stay with him for now. He will keep you alive. You and your brothers."

"Matka, he beats me."

"I know." It broke Zosia's heart, but with war raging around them there were few choices. Marisha was almost a woman, but in Zosia's eyes she was still her *dziewczynka*—her little girl. The most important thing was survival, and Zosia would do anything to ensure that her children lived, even if it meant convincing Marisha to fake a relationship with an abusive German soldier.

Zosia bristled at the image of Maxim in her head—his harsh blond hair, his crooked front tooth, the little mole under his eye that resembled a tick. Maxim Hirsch didn't treat Marisha well, but he brought her food which Marisha then shared with her younger brothers. With the Jews gone, Maxim's help was crucial for her family. "Stay with him until I can figure something else out. If he offers marriage, accept it. In fact," Zosia paused, her heart skipping as she considered her next words, "the best thing you can do right now is get yourself pregnant."

Marisha's reaction was appropriately horrified. *This should be me,* Zosia thought. *If only I were ten years younger.* Zosia's thirty-three years looked and felt like so many more. Her skin sagged, creasing around her lips and across her forehead.

"So you want me to be a whore?" Marisha said, sobbing.

Zosia squared her chin. She'd given birth to Marisha when she was sixteen. Marisha was now a year older than that, but she was only beginning to learn the hard lessons of life. Zosia wished she could keep the girl innocent, but the hostile world resisted her hopes. Marisha needed to understand the desperation of their situation. "Love in return for your survival." Zosia's tone was stern, unfaltering. "Trust me, my love. Give him whatever he asks. You will at least live to deal with him later. Divorce isn't an option if you're dead."

Marisha's eyes grew huge. "Divorce?"

Zosia caught her error. She and Wiktor raised their children to be Catholic, and even though Zosia's own faith had waned over the years she could never allow herself to completely abandon her religion. The question still hung in the back of her mind: *What if they're right?*

"Not an ideal solution, of course," Zosia recanted, "But divorce is still better than death. Right now, Maxim is your best chance."

Marisha nodded, still wiping her eyes. She motioned to Zosia's empty hands, changing the subject. "No luck at the deli? Did the Jews go after you with shovels again?"

Zosia shook her head. "They're gone."

Any color left in Marisha's face seeped away down her neck. "So now what? Maxim won't be back until next week."

Zosia studied each of the houses along the street, searching every window shutter and chimney brick for answers. Her body jolted. "Where's Kolec?" She arched her eyebrow at her daughter.

Marisha looked toward Mr. Guzinski's house. No one stood next to their neighbor's property for that long without answering to the bloodthirsty Doberman on guard outside. Kolec was the monster that perpetuated Zosia's irrational fear of dogs. She'd seen him nearly tear the legs off of a young boy who dared chase his ball up the walk.

Both women stood motionless and searched the shabby, stucco-sided house. Knots tightened in Zosia's stomach. Something was wrong. She surveyed the sparse vegetable bed. It was mostly dug up and still muddy from the previous day's rain. An ominous shiver raced up her spine.

"Marisha, here," she untied the babushka from around her hair and gave it to her daughter. "Gather up whatever is left in the garden. Dig deep if you have to. There has to be something there."

"Where are you going?" Marisha took the scarf.

Zosia didn't answer. As if crossing a tightrope, she tiptoed up the brick walk toward the house until she could reach her hand out and feel the stucco against her palm. She held her breath and peered in the window. Nothing seemed out of place. The front door was closed, the curtains open. Everything appeared normal.

It was after she exhaled that she spotted a small plate of potatoes and a spindly chicken drumstick on the kitchen table. A glass of milk was tipped over and a fork was on the floor.

Zosia's sight closed to a dark tunnel. She stumbled away from the window and into a hedge that lined the front of the house. Her momentum stopped abruptly when the heel of her shoe sank into a large, firm mound: the carcass of a dead Doberman. Gaping wounds ran along its neck and side as if it had been sliced open and its organs harvested. A pool of scarlet painted the grass below. Zosia's brown suede shoes were blackened by blood.

Sweat sprouted from her pores, and she forgot her pains of hunger. She ran down the walk toward the street where her daughter was on her knees digging into the ground with her fingernails. "Marisha, come quickly," Zosia could barely speak the words.

Agitated by her mother's fear, Marisha collected a small pile of muddy potatoes into the babushka and pushed herself up to standing. "What is it?"

"Quickly!" Zosia was already on the street and halfway between the houses, leaving a trail of bloody footprints behind her.

"Matka, wait! Where did this blood come from? Is Mr. Guzinski all right?"

Zosia didn't stop running until she threw herself against her own front door. The doorknob turned and she flung herself inside.

"Stefek! Antoni!"

"Matka!" Stefek, her youngest son, ran from the bedroom.

Zosia fell to her knees and hugged the nine-year-old boy

before holding him at arms length to focus on him. He was pale, his eyes like bagels. "Thank God you're safe."

Marisha caught up and burst into the room with her armload of potatoes. "What's going on?"

"Where's Antoni? Is he all right?" Zosia ignored Marisha and scanned the darkened hallway for her elder son, who was struggling with the same tuberculosis that killed his father. Stefek didn't answer. Zosia's stomach lurched. "Where is your brother, Stefek?"

Stefek melted into tears. "They took him, Matka."

All of Zosia's remaining strength drained from her body at once. Blood pulled away from her lips, ears, and fingertips, leaving a tingling numbness behind. Her body shook.

"Who? Who took him?" Marisha dropped to her knees beside Stefek and let the potatoes roll onto the floor this way and that, leaving trails of mud in their wake. "Stefek, what happened?"

"We hid under our beds," his tiny voice shook with terror. "The soldiers were coming. I told Antoni to get out of his bed and climb underneath it, just like you said. He did. I promise he did." Stefek's body heaved and quaked. He tried to get the words out between sobs. "Then I hid under my bed. I crawled way into the corner and covered myself with a blanket. I heard the door open and the men started yelling. I was scared. I was so scared, Matka."

"But they found Antoni?" Marisha continued for him.

Stefek nodded. "He coughed, Matka. He tried not to, I know he did. But he was coughing all morning." Stefek cried harder. "I didn't make a sound, but I was so scared. They pulled him out and took him away. I heard him screaming. I'm sorry. I'm so sorry." Stefek dissolved into a puddle next to Zosia.

Zosia's body coiled into a ball on the floor. She should have never left her two boys, only nine and twelve, alone. Not with Antoni as sick as he was and Marisha out forming a bridge with the enemy. Zosia should have been there with them instead of trying to steal food she knew was already gone. She covered her face with her hands and moaned.

"The Gestapo." Marisha's voice fell to a whisper.

"Matka, I'm sorry," Stefek said through his tears.

Zosia looked at her son. Through his fear she saw guilt, too; something she knew all too well. It tore her apart that her youngest child felt such a dangerous emotion.

It was all her fault.

Still on her knees, Zosia straightened her back and wrapped her arms around Stefek again. "Stefek, you did everything you were supposed to." The words stung like cheap vodka on her throat. "You were a good boy and very brave. I'm proud of you."

Kneeling helplessly on the floor, rage burned within her. They took her son. She would not roll over and give up. She had to fight.

"I don't understand," Marisha's voice elevated to hysterics. "What do they want with him? He's not Jewish. They're only taking Jews, aren't they?" Marisha put her hand on her mother's shoulder and squeezed, shaking her. "Aren't they? What do they want with a twelve-year-old Catholic boy?"

With a thousand kilos of weight pulling her down, Zosia dragged herself to her feet, her eyes burning with fury. She stared out the open door toward the street. "They don't care, Marisha. Has Maxim told you nothing about his duties? The boy is ill, and he's Polish." Zosia felt heavy, yet jumpy. She couldn't move, but she couldn't stand still.

She had to do something. Anything.

A whisper caught in her throat. "The trains." Zosia willed herself to move. "Stay here, watch Stefek," she said to Marisha and stepped toward the door. She was in a dream where her feet were held to the ground with thick molasses as the walls closed in. She didn't trust her legs, yet she pulled one foot in front of the other and found she could move faster than she thought. In an instant she was out the door and into the street.

Marisha's voice warbled after her, "You mean they'll kill him? Why? Matka, wait!"

Zosia, who was already as far as Mr. Guzinski's house, didn't answer. She had to get to the train station.

"Matka! Matka!" Stefek and Marisha's voices melded together. Zosia could barely hear them, and could hardly see in front of her. She only knew she was moving by the click of her heels meeting the cobblestones.

"Matka, wait." Marisha caught up and grabbed her sleeve, pulling her mother to a stop. Stefek was close behind. He grabbed his mother around her waist in a desperate embrace.

Marisha's mind was working more clearly than Zosia's. "Would they bother with the train station here in town? Service has been unsteady since the Germans came. I've heard the Gestapo take Jews to the trains in Warsaw. Do you think they took Antoni into the city?"

It seemed like Marisha was speaking a different language. Zosia searched her daughter's face until the words sank into her head. "You're right. I have to get to Warsaw." She stared up the street, her vision pulled in swirls and waves through her tears. They had no car. "How—?" Her stare returned to Marisha, who only reflected Zosia's distress. "Maybe Maxim?"

Marisha shook her head, but then pointed toward their neighbor's house. "Does Mr. Guzinski have a car?" The two women scanned the man's property, and without a word they ran to the rear of the house with Stefek trailing behind them. They pulled open the wooden doors that sealed his garage and were greeted by the grill of a black Ford Eifel.

Zosia pulled open the driver's door but Marisha stopped her. "Matka, you don't drive."

"I do today." She couldn't let fear stop her. She hated cars, and, like most housewives, never learned to drive. She was convinced she would end up splattered across the road somewhere. Details about those kinds of accidents frequented the *Nowiny* newspaper. She'd sold Wiktor's Fiat only days after he died, wanting nothing to do with it.

She climbed behind the steering wheel and grabbed the key that hung from a string around the rearview mirror. She rolled down the window and gave Stefek a kiss on the top of his head. "Stefek, be a good boy for Marisha, I'll return as soon as I can. Marisha," she paused for breath, "watch yourself and Stefek. Be aware." She looked into her daughter's eyes. Marisha nodded. She understood. Zosia could not lose another child.

Zosia slipped the key into the ignition, but her fingers froze before she could turn it.

Her father's laugh echoed in her head. He'd been a happy drunk until that day. A friend's borrowed sedan, an afternoon drive. Zosia and Brygida were so little. They were giddy, bouncing and giggling in the back seat, too young for the bitterness that would come between them later. Her mother sat in the front holding Oskar, still so much a baby that he still needed help sitting up.

The thunder of crunching metal and blackness silenced her father's laughter. When Zosia awoke, she was on the floor of the car's backseat, her nose gushing blood. Brygida was crying. So was their mother. The last thing Zosia remembered seeing before she'd blacked out was a rag doll crashing through the windshield and catapulting through the air. She didn't know whose doll it was, since neither she nor Brygida brought their dollies with them. Her mother's screams hinted that it wasn't a doll at all.

For months afterward, she'd often ask her mother where her baby brother had gone, but her mother had only sobbed and pushed her away. Nothing was ever the same.

Her fingers trembled on the key, still poised uselessly in

the ignition.

"Move over," Marisha opened the driver's door and climbed in, forcing Zosia to scoot across the bench seat. She turned the key, and the engine roared to life.

"No! Let me come!" Stefek grabbed the steering wheel through the window and jumped up and down.

"Marisha, we can't leave Stefek alone." Zosia reached for the passenger door, but Marisha grabbed her mother's arm before she could open it.

"We can't bring him with us. Maxim sometimes talks about the chaos at the station. Stefek will get lost for sure. He'll be captured and end up on his own train to God knows where. He'll be safer here." Both women fell silent. They stared at each other, searching for the right thing to say or do or think while Stefek howled beside them.

"But Matka, what if they take you away, too?"

Valuable time was slipping away. Zosia swallowed her doubt. "They won't," her voice soothed. "Run down the street to Ignasja's house, the big blue one. Stay with her until I come and get you. I promise we won't be gone long." Zosia's words were automatic—in her heart she didn't trust her own promise.

"The fat lady?" Stefek's bottom lip quivered. "But what if the German soldiers come back? She's too—"

"Ignasja will keep you safe." Zosia didn't let her own uncertainty show. She kissed her fingers and waved them toward her son. "Remember, you are a strong and brave boy. Matka loves you." She paused. "I'll be home soon."

Stefek nodded and stepped away from the car, his eyes wide with fear. Marisha pushed the Eifel into gear and sped out of the garage. The wheels clipped the curb as she pulled onto the street, sending bile into Zosia's throat.

Zosia moaned and pressed her face into her hands. She had to believe that she would find her son somewhere in the sprawling metropolis of Warsaw. It was unlikely, but she had to trust in something.

When the road smoothed and their speed steadied, Marisha glanced at her mother. "Do you know where the train station is?"

Zosia didn't. She pried her eyelids open and forced herself to not look out the window at the road whizzing past. She unlatched the glove compartment to dig for a map of the city. There wasn't one.

Marisha was quiet for a few minutes. "We could follow the signs." Then she said under her breath, "I hope there are signs."

"I suppose we could ask someone," Zosia said, though she knew that was impossible. The city was crawling with Gestapo waiting for any excuse to gather up Poles and get rid of them. If they were lucky enough to come across a Varsovian to question, he'd most likely hurry along with his head down, offering neither a smile nor eye contact. It's what Zosia would do.

"I'm turning here," Marisha pulled into the far right lane by a sign that read *Aleksandrowka 0.2.*

"Why on earth? Leave the highway? The back roads will take so much longer." Zosia hoped they were at least still headed east.

"See up ahead? There's a train crossing sign. This road should take us right along the tracks. It could lead us straight into the station in Warsaw."

Zosia nodded. Logic was something her mind couldn't grasp at that moment. "Who taught you to drive? Surely not your father?"

Marisha stretched her lips into a grimace. "Maxim. Turns out he's good for something."

Zosia didn't remind Marisha of the stale loaves of bread and dried meats that Maxim brought them week after week.

The car sped along. When Marisha spoke again, her voice was filled with a desperate heaviness that crowded the car's interior and threatened to smother them. "Matka, Maxim told me if I'm ever captured, the best way to survive is to be chosen for a work assignment. He said to stay out of the camps at all costs, but he wouldn't say why. He even wanted me to volunteer to work in Germany. Slave labor, he said, but at least I would go of my own free will." Marisha took a deep, trembling breath. "Antoni can't work. He can barely walk, he's so ill. They'll kill him right away, won't they?" She let out a sob and brought her hand to her mouth. "Say they won't. Please say they won't kill him."

Zosia stayed silent, unable to truthfully give Marisha the answer they both wanted, unable to even think about the possibility of her son's execution. Marisha leaned her foot harder onto the gas pedal.

The Eifel entered Warsaw, and the two women found their way to the station with the help of city signage. Marisha fought the car through the crowds and stopped as close as she could. "Go find him. I'll park and come after you."

Zosia jumped out of the Eifel like a snapped rubber band and hurried toward the platform. There were several trains staged. Mobs of people clamored in every direction. Most were there against their wills.

"Antoni! Antoni!" Confusion and disorder surrounded her. A little girl stood crying next to a train until a soldier smashed the butt of his rifle into her face. A group of men tried to overtake their captors, only to be shot in the head by the Germans' shiny pistols. Screams, cries, and gunshots pierced the thick, rumbling black exhaust of the idling trains.

Zosia turned around and around in her blood-splattered pumps. "Antoni, please!" Her voice blended into the turmoil. Dread scraped behind her eyes. Hopelessness swept over her, but she resolved to stand there and yell his name until every person on the platform had boarded a train and the trains were all gone.

Fingers closed around Zosia's arm. She nearly screamed until she saw it was Marisha. Her eyes were red and panicked.

Zosia imagined her own were much the same. "Matka, I heard some men talking. This isn't the only train station in Warsaw. He could have been taken to the other one." A tear trickled out onto Marisha's cheek. "What do we do?"

Zosia spun around, the whirl of commotion and people making her dizzy. She reached for every guard that passed her, even though she knew it could mean her own demise. Though she wasn't a prime target since she wasn't young or old, educated or ill, she was still no different than the prisoners surrounding her. "Sir, please, I'm looking for my son. Sir, my son, he's twelve. Sir, have you seen a boy, Antoni? He's been taken by mistake. Sir . . ."

Above the clanging, banging, shouting and screaming around her, along with the hollow ringing of terror that ricocheted between Zosia's ears, came a weak voice.

"Matka?"

She wasn't sure she'd even heard it, or if it was only her mind projecting the boy's sweet, familiar sound into her ears. Frantic, she focused on every child in the crowd. She searched for his dark hair, his pointed nose.

"Matka," the voice said again.

"Antoni?"

"Matka!" Like the end of a dream that slowly fades to reality, the sound took shape and became the voice she knew, tinged with illness and trepidation. She swung around to find her boy, pale and weak, struggling in the grip of a German soldier.

"Antoni!" Zosia ran to her son and lunged to scoop him into her arms, but the guard grabbed her shoulder.

"Step back," he said in broken Polish.

"This is my son, let him go."

"He's coming with us." The guard gripped Antoni's arm with one hand and held Zosia back with the other.

"No, please, he's very ill. Let him go."

"That's why we're taking him. There is no room for sick swine in Poland."

"Take me instead." The words spilled from Zosia's lips. Her voice sounded far away as it pleaded, "I can work. He's just a boy. If he's to die, let him do so in peace." Before the soldier could answer, she wrestled her son from the man's grip. "Antoni, go with Marisha." She pointed to her daughter, whose mouth hung open in horror as she watched the guard's hand clamp down on Zosia.

Antoni's wide eyes bulged from his ghost-white face. He paused for a second, then he pushed a sweaty wad of gold fabric into Zosia's palm. She closed her fist around it, barely noticing.

"Matka, what—" Marisha's voice faded.

"Marisha, take him home," she yelled across the sea of people as the guard pulled Zosia toward the boxcars. "Go! I'll come back. I promise."

"No! Matka!" Marisha reached for her mother, but the mob swept along and pulled them away.

As Zosia was dragged to the train she saw Marisha grab Antoni's hand. They turned and disappeared. Zosia was lifted into the boxcar and packed in with the rest of the prisoners. The door slid shut in front of her, revealing only a small window with vertical steel bars that severed her view into narrow slices.

Go. Please, be safe. Zosia's eyes watched the spot where her children disappeared. She watched it until the train pulled away.

CHAPTER TWO

Evening.

Formless blurs of green and gray rushed past in the waning sun of evening. Zosia was numb from the shock of what had happened. She was likely being carried off to her death, and she'd left her three children alone, defenseless, and frightened during a dangerous war. She thought briefly of Maxim helping them, but heaviness set in when she accepted what she had always known—he was the enemy, not to be trusted.

The crowd of people behind her in the cattle car buzzed with apprehension. A few women and several children cried, and someone hacked with pneumonia, tuberculosis, vomit, or all three. Somewhere toward the back a baby bleated like a lamb.

She stared out her little window at Poland. Or, what was once Poland. Her homeland was gone. Even Minsk Mazowiecki, her comfortable little town, had turned into something unrecognizable. Shortly after the occupation started, the Germans ushered most of the Jews into a ghetto similar to Warsaw's, but on a smaller scale. About a year ago, they were taken away, and the few remaining Jews kept the town running. Now they were gone, too.

Zosia grew up indifferent to the Jews. Many of her and

Wiktor's friends held a deep distrust of them, but for the most part, Zosia didn't pay any mind. The Jews were mostly of a higher class—lawyers, doctors, businessmen—but they kept to themselves and didn't bother Zosia.

Then Wiktor became ill.

She could never forgive them. But, she knew without them, her little village would have crumbled. She wondered if she would ever see Minsk Mazowiecki again. Or her children—her babies. She pressed her hands to her ears to block out the anguished infant behind her.

Inhaling deeply, she concentrated on what she *did* have: air. The motion of the train and the swell of people rocked back and forth, but she held her ground in front of the window. She could breathe, and she could see outside. A hand fell on her arm, and she planted her feet. She had no intention of giving up her space.

"Mrs. Wilusz?"

"Mr. Guzinski." Zosia wanted to hug the old man, but she resisted. Her relationship with her neighbor was icy at best, but familiarity was comforting. "What happened? I was at your house, I knew they took you."

"They came before noon," Mr. Guzinski said. He cradled his right hand, which was wrapped in bandages browned with what looked like dried blood. "I was sitting down for lunch. They took me out to a truck and loaded me into the bed with the others, but not before they shattered my hand with a hammer." He held it up and winced. "Then they brought Antoni in, too. Looks like Marisha's little *gówno* Gestapo boyfriend didn't help your family after all." His face bent with annoyance.

Zosia turned away and locked her gaze on the countryside whizzing past. She was aware of her neighbors' distaste for Maxim, but she never cared much about village gossip when her children's lives were at stake. "Mr. Hirsch isn't Gestapo. He's a German soldier, following orders like our own brothers in the

Polish Army." She felt obligated to defend him. He brought her children food.

"Well, I guess it doesn't matter now," Mr. Guzinski said. "What happened to Antoni? Is he here? Did he escape?"

"I took his place." Zosia was too exhausted to explain any more.

He paused. "The only thing a mother could do, I suppose. At least he is safe."

"I don't know if he's safe." Zosia stared at the shapeless landscape flashing past. "Is anyone safe?"

Mr. Guzinski shrugged. "You may have saved his life."

"But I didn't." Zosia's voice trembled. "He's ill. He'll die soon, just like his father." She looked up at the man with hesitation, unsure if he was friend or foe. "All I did was leave my children with no one to protect them. I didn't save anyone." She raised her eyebrows. "And yes, Marisha's *little shit boyfriend* probably won't be much help to them," she said, emphasizing Mr. Guzinski's profane characterization of Maxim.

"If your son is to die," he softened his voice, "He can do it with dignity. He knew his mother was brave and sacrificed herself for him. He can peacefully go to God."

She let his words sink in. She wasn't sure how much peace she felt with her son going to a fickle God. "I borrowed your car," she said through clenched teeth.

He nodded. "I won't need it anymore." They were quiet for a while, which Zosia welcomed. She only wanted to stare out the window into the nothingness.

After a few minutes, Mr. Guzinski spoke again. "Just thank God you're not Jewish. Or worse, Gypsy." He patted the gold diamond pinned to his shirt. There was a purple P centered on the fabric. "As long as you have this, you can maybe buy yourself a day or two."

Zosia turned her head and stared at the diamond. She had

no such thing. Her eyes swelled with horror.

"You didn't get an assignment, did you?" the man noticeably cringed when Zosia shook her head. "They were distributed after we were pushed out of the trucks. The Jews got their stars if they didn't already have them. The rest of us got these."

Shivering from panic, her gaze fell down to her hand, still fisted around a piece of gold fabric. She uncoiled her fingers, stiff and tingling from squeezing the tiny bundle. The wrinkled shape flattened until it presented a gold diamond surrounding a purple P.

She'd saved Antoni, and now he'd saved her.

"Oh, thank God," Mr. Guzinski said. "You need to find a way to pin it to your clothing. They told us to not ever be without it."

Zosia reached inside the collar of her dress and unhooked a safety pin from a seam, letting the small hole it was holding fall open. She attached the P above her left breast.

"Mrs. Wilusz." Mr. Guzinski cleared his throat. "You were at my house. Did you see Kolec?"

Zosia kept her vision fixed out the window. "Yes."

He took a deep breath. "Did he survive?"

She knew her neighbor lived alone and rarely had visitors. He had nothing else in the world besides that demon of a dog. She turned to look at him. "Yes. He ran across the street and was digging in a trashcan. I'm sure he'll be fine."

He smiled and bowed his head.

The journey, wherever they were going, was long. The sun dipped beyond the trees, and the scene outside of her window became black. Mr. Guzinski lit a cigarette for Zosia with his good hand, and she eagerly took it. It helped to cover the putrid smells overwhelming the car, since people had no other option but to relieve themselves inside.

The woman with the baby wrestled her way to the front of

the car, and Zosia stepped to the side to allow the child some air at the window. Both women stayed silent, and Zosia didn't look at the infant. She shuddered when she considered what would happen to the baby once they reached their destination.

She turned her thoughts instead to something comforting. Wiggling her fingers, she concentrated on the very tips. Her mind focused, and she could almost feel the swish of linen and the warmth of flannel flowing through her hands. Her ears transformed the clanking of the rails beneath her feet into the satisfying clatter of her old Singer sewing machine. She visualized it eating the colorful fabric and spitting out something new and beautiful on the other side.

Her beloved sewing machine was a pleasure born of necessity. As a child, the beautiful dresses that hung in the department stores fascinated Zosia. She longed to try every color, to feel every cut of fabric. She loved the way silk flowed, the way tulle crunched. She would lose herself within the racks of garments until her panicked mother pulled her out from under the thick velvet gowns and oblige her with a chosen favorite dress from the sale rack. Zosia had a closet of cheap but beautiful clothes.

By the time Brygida was four, though, the younger sister was skilled at playing their mother against Zosia, especially once their mother was consumed by grief for their brother. Brygida got everything she wanted, and Zosia got what was left, if anything. Zosia spent too many Christmas dinners in scratchy gray wool while Brygida danced in rich green satin and collected compliments from relatives and neighbors. Zosia decided, at ten years old, that if she wanted pretty clothes, she'd have to make her own rather than compete with Brygida.

Sewing became something Zosia savored. She used her mother's machine until she married Wiktor. His wedding gift to her had been her very own Singer.

As she stood in the crowded, fetid cattle car, she thought

only of zigzagged thread making seams as straight and strong as the tracks she was gliding over. The needle in her head worked tirelessly throughout the night.

CHAPTER THREE

The next morning.

Morning illuminated the world outside the window. The train rattled and slowed. It pulled next to a concrete platform where men in black uniforms with bright red armbands paced. Each carried a rifle on his back.

The palms of Zosia's hands dripped with sweat. Her pulse pounded. She wondered when she would die—when the doors opened? After the prisoners were lined up outside? The train heaved a final sigh and the brakes squealed. The doors groaned open. The placidly strolling Gestapo agents switched to shouting at the train and each other, waving their arms and rushing around while large dogs barked at the commotion. Zosia spilled from the car with the others.

Confused chatter rippled across the crowd of prisoners. A megaphone clicked and buzzed, and Polish words with a German accent blasted from it. "Prisoners, line up. Listen for further instruction." Zosia scanned the platform. Gestapo agents created a lethal arc around them. Each rifle was drawn, ready to kill. There was no possibility for escape unless one was to crawl under the train.

Swallowing several times to combat a throat raw from lack of water, Zosia fell into line between an elderly man and a large, beefy woman. She studied the woman out of the corner of her eye. She was built like a man with broad shoulders and a dense neck. A plain, brown dress hung on her straight hips. The muscles in the woman's square jaw flexed: *tighten, relax, tighten, relax.* Zosia's eyes fell to the woman's hands by her sides. Thick, strong fists clenched and unclenched in rhythm with her jaw.

The voice boomed through the megaphone. "You will be given an assignment. You are to either return to the train, or you will stay where you are in line to be taken inside the camp."

To your death, Zosia finished for him in her head. She looked down the line toward the camp gates and the non-descript buildings and watchtowers that stood beyond them. She shivered. No one outside of the Nazi Party knew what happened in any of the camps, but the looming structures beyond the gate were ominous.

"Some of you," the voice continued, "will be chosen as laborers and distributed where needed. If your qualifications match, you will assemble near the rear of the train."

Zosia closed her eyes. *Please let me be chosen as a laborer. Please God, let me live to see my children again.* Her eyes snapped open. Her plea surprised her. She hadn't trusted God since Wiktor died. All of her prayers for him never helped.

A guard slowly made his way down the line, coming her way. She strained her ears to hear his questions so she could have the best possible answers ready at her turn.

"Name?"

"Voytek Guzinski." Zosia's breath seized. It was her neighbor.

"Age?"

"Sixty-four."

"Occupation?"

There was a brief pause. "Factory work. Assembly line."

Zosia knew it was a lie. He was a well-educated mechanical engineer.

"Return to the train."

"But I can—"

"You'll be sent to a more industrial town. Next. Name."

She didn't dare turn her head to watch Mr. Guzinski leave the line and climb into the boxcar. About half of the people in line returned to the train, the other half stayed. Many in either group wore a star, but there were several wearing a purple P, too. A few people, maybe fifteen or twenty, stood in a small group as the chosen laborers. There were children around of all ages, but none held the safety of a work assignment. They were either in line or on the train. Those were the only options for the young and the very old; they were not useful.

The guard approached the woman next to Zosia. "Name?"

"Petronela Kloc."

"Age?"

"Thirty-six."

"Occupation?"

"Farm labor," Petronela said defiantly. The brick wall of a woman towered over the guard. Zosia couldn't be sure, but she thought she saw the guard flinch.

"Join the laborers." Without another question, the guard waved toward the group of men and women off to the side. Petronela nodded and stepped out of line. The guard moved forward.

"Name?"

"Zosia Wilusz." Her vision lifted to meet the most dazzling blue eyes she'd ever seen. Her tongue stumbled over itself.

"Age?"

"Thirty-three."

"Occupation?"

"Farm labor," she said, following Petronela's lead.

The guard dropped his pencil. "*—Sheisse.*" He bent down to retrieve it, and she saw him notice her feet. He rose back to full height. "Your shoes are soaked with blood."

"Yes."

"Why?"

Her throat constricted. She searched her brain for a reason that would make her desirable. "Farm work."

The guard arched his eyebrow. "You work with animals?"

"Yes."

"Caring for them or slaughtering them?"

"Both."

"Interesting that you would be working in such conditions in your high-heeled shoes." The guard sneered at Zosia.

She was careful to look just past him so as not be caught in his chilling blue stare. "I'm never far from my work," she said with feigned confidence. "My shoes do not stop me."

The guard's smirk flattened. He waved behind him, already eyeing the old man in line after Zosia. "Join the laborers. And find some goddamned work shoes."

Without showing the relief that waved over her, she stepped forward and stood next to Petronela Kloc. Petronela nodded at her and took a long drag off of her cigarette. "What's your name?" she asked, her voice growling as smoke curled from her lips.

"Zosia."

"I was hoping we'd both end up here. You look like a tough woman." Petronela held the cigarette out for Zosia who thankfully took it and sucked in the bitter taste of burning tobacco. She didn't answer Petronela. The thought of this grizzly bear of a woman calling her tough was more than she could piece together in her head. As she let the smoke out of her lungs, she assessed the other workers in the small group. All seemed solid and strong, and all had a P pinned to their clothing.

"Who do you know on the inside? Anyone?" a young

man asked. He wore a stylish jacket and had slicked-back hair. "Friends? Brothers?" The man grinned. "Lovers?"

"Inside?" Zosia was confused. Inside what? The camp? The Reich? The Gestapo? She thought for a moment about Maxim and wondered if he would be considered *inside*.

A gunshot rang out, silencing the anxious chatter and rousing a chorus of barking dogs. It was followed by a longer series of gunfire. The chosen workers and all other prisoners remaining on the platform fell to the ground onto their stomachs, a routine learned from years of Nazi occupation.

Zosia covered her head with her hands. This was the end.

After several seconds, the roar of weaponry simmered to only the barking dogs. Zosia looked up. She was alive.

A bullhorn clicked and hissed. "Do not try to escape. You will be killed." Imperfect Polish with a German inflection made the threat sound even more sinister. "Let this be a warning. Now get up, you fucking cowards."

Zosia pulled herself upright with everyone else. A number of lifeless bodies were sprawled on the platform and under the boxcars. Several had tried to escape their fates by scrambling beneath the train. None had made it. Zosia stared in horror at the mangled corpses and bloody concrete. She was frozen, her throat gasping for air that her lungs couldn't draw in.

"If you need different shoes," a gruff voice said in her ear, "you better go now." Petronela calmly leaned over her, nodding in the direction of a dead man nearby.

Up and down the platform the dead were being carefully pillaged. Surviving prisoners pulled pants, jackets, even socks off the bodies. The guards scurried to keep order, swinging their rifles like baseball bats to knock down the looters. Every few minutes the sharp crack of a gun split the air and another prisoner fell to the ground.

Zosia stood motionless with the smoldering cigarette still

dangling between her fingers. She mustered the loudest whisper she could without any air in her lungs. "They'll kill me."

"They'll kill you if you work too slowly, which you'll be forced to do in high heels. Go slow, I'll go with you." Petronela took the cigarette back from Zosia, and, keeping a sharp eye on the guards, nudged Zosia along. Both women slithered toward the body.

As they closed in, one young guard looked in the direction of Zosia and Petronela. He paused and hugged his rifle closer. Petronela stared at him threateningly. She slowly lifted the cigarette to her mouth and took a deep drag, closing her eyes as if she were making love, though the expression was far more menacing than seductive on her harsh features. Then she exhaled the smoke and let her gaze fall back on the guard. Zosia stood frozen next to her, her eyes glued to his weapon.

The young man watched Petronela and her cigarette for only a moment before moving on to shout orders at the people inside the boxcars. A very tiny curve engaged at the corner of Petronela's lips. She seemed to have a certain power over men, but not in the expected, feminine way. It wasn't sexual, it was intimidating.

"Go," Petronela hissed, "Go now. I've got you covered."

Before she could think, Zosia scurried to the dead man. Her face burned hot, and her vision blurred with terror. She dropped to her knees and pulled at the man's boots until they released from his feet.

"Quickly!" Petronela warned. She held the cigarette close to her lips while her eyes darted around furtively.

Zosia stumbled to her feet, the muddy work boots tucked under her arm. She raced back to her new friend, and the two women nonchalantly rejoined the laborers.

Her breath shook but she steadied herself. *I'm fine. I made it.* She bent to switch her footwear, having to tightly bind the man's larger boots onto her small but swollen feet. She kicked the bloody pumps to the side and gulped deep breaths of air to keep from drowning in her terror.

Petronela took another casual drag off of her cigarette. “Thanks.” Her lips stayed in their slight upward curve. “That was fun.”

CHAPTER FOUR

Minutes.

A vast, muddy field welcomed those who had convinced the guards they were worthy of work, and, therefore, mercy. Countless emaciated bodies, hunched and barely moving, already filled the farmland. When the newcomers approached, the existing laborers raised their heads. The hoes and shovels swung faster, the bones and withered muscles flexed visibly beneath the slaves' thin, filthy skin. They were, or at least once were, people.

Zosia trudged along in her stolen work boots, the sticky mud requiring more effort with every step.

"These fields need tending," the guard with the blue eyes called from his Kübelwagen. He climbed out of the vehicle, lit a cigarette, and threw an armful of tools onto the ground. "Anyone caught loitering or resting . . ." He stopped and examined the workers in the field. As he did, a man a few meters away stumbled with his shovel and dropped briefly to one knee. The guard pulled his pistol and pointed it at the man. A splintering crack echoed off of the granite quarries that surrounded them. Dark liquid burst from the man's head, and he dropped to the ground. ". . . will be dealt with accordingly."

Zosia's stomach turned and twisted like sticky dough in a bowl. She looked away without moving her head. Along the edges of her vision, the spindly skeletons in the field moved even faster, their implements heaving in a tense silence only perforated with exaggerated grunts and the sound of metal meeting soil.

Petronela made a move toward the tools first, sneering at the guard as she chose the least broken shovel. Zosia followed her lead and reached for a hoe, but a hand gripped her shoulder. Every nerve in her body constricted. "You," the guard pinched through to her bone, "with the shoes. Come with me." Zosia glanced at Petronela who lifted her chin and gave the tiniest nod. Zosia followed the guard to his vehicle. He climbed behind the wheel but ordered Zosia to walk. "Quickly. Keep up." He stomped on the gas pedal. Zosia took off in a sprint behind the Kübelwagen, coughing from the dust and exhaust it tossed into her face and bending her toes in a way that would keep the oversized boots on her feet.

The Kübelwagen took a hard left in front of a large white farmhouse at the bottom of the hill. The house no longer held a farmer's family. Now a sizeable black swastika consumed the gable where she imagined the family Christmas wreaths once hung. It had been taken over by the Nazis, like everything else. Loudspeakers hung above the swastika at the apex of the roof, and a razor wire fence enshrouded the building. Two long, scabby barracks buildings flanked the farmhouse, and behind one was a cobbled kitchen.

The Kübelwagen sped past the farmhouse and the barracks and aimed for three red barns about eighty meters behind the kitchen. Zosia pushed her legs to keep up. She arrived at the barn only moments after the guard stepped out of the vehicle.

"You claim to be a butcher?"

Zosia's sweating face burned hotter. "Yes," she panted. She felt faint. She'd never slaughtered anything in her life, but if she was given a special assignment, it might be enough to keep her alive. She worked to steady her gasping breath.

He waved his cigarette toward the barn. "You'll come here every morning. Early." He kicked open the door to the first barn. Inside was a flurry of feathers: white, brown, black. Cackling and crowing rang in her ears. "You will slaughter chickens. We need at least fifty carcasses dressed by nine o'clock, in time to be sent to nearby farms. Also for our own lunches. Not yours, of course." He wrinkled his nose, his blond hair flopping into his nearly transparent eyes, "Mine." He pushed his hair off his forehead, "If you fail to have the crates ready when the train stops, or if you touch a chicken for yourself, you will be shot." He gave her a condescending grin.

"Yes, *mein Herr*." When she was a little girl, Zosia once watched her mother slaughter a chicken. The headless bird terrified her as it ran around the yard, its death throes in the form of silently spurting blood from its neck. Zosia hoped it was enough of a lesson to lend her some success.

The guard motioned toward the train tracks near the quarry in the distance. "You will bring the crates to the train and load them. Then you'll join the others in the field for the rest of the day."

Zosia gaped at the fowl inside the barn. *What am I doing? I've never killed a chick—*

Something cold and hard pressed against her temple. Her mind flashed to the man in the field, blood exploding from his head simply because he tripped. She took a tentative step into the barn toward the chickens.

"Sturmbannführer Voss." A young man in uniform ran up behind them. "The director is here."

Herr Voss dropped his firearm into his holster and his cigarette into the dirt. "Get out to the fields. Start the chickens tomorrow." He climbed into the Kübelwagen with the young man and sped toward the farmhouse.

Zosia lugged herself back up the hill toward the fields. She needed to become a skilled chicken butcher by sunrise. She knew by nine o'clock the next morning she'd be dead.

CHAPTER FIVE

July, 1944.

"You're wrong." Tadeusz's voice was a screeching red against the backdrop of blue sky and gray people. The light breeze did nothing to stifle the liquid heat of summer. "That's not what I heard at all."

For nearly a year Zosia endured his daily grumbling in the fields. Tadeusz would argue with a rock if given the chance. She tried to ignore him, but his shrill voice saturated the space around her. If he wasn't quibbling with someone, he was bragging to no one about all of the women he'd slept with. He disgusted her.

Some labor farms separated the men and women. Some farms sent men to the fields and women to their deaths. Zosia reminded herself that Tadeusz's constant drone was just an annoyance. At least his voice ringing in her ears meant she was still alive.

Alive. She was three weeks from her one-year anniversary in the fields. She'd survived. Every day of that year, every hour, her children consumed her thoughts. She hoped they'd survived, too.

Somehow, propelled by adrenaline and a little counsel from Petronela and Ramona, a woman who'd already survived

Sturmbannführer Voss's abuse, Zosia found she was not only capable but also fairly savvy at butchering chickens. Petronela gave her a simple primer: "Chop the head, let run, gather the carcass, scald, pluck, next. They're dirty animals. Better them than you. Be fast, be confident."

Ramona also supplied important advice: "Herr Voss has one weakness that any woman can play on: give him what his wife refuses. If there's trouble, drop to your knees in front of him and open your mouth just a bit."

"And then what?" Zosia recoiled, disgusted at the likely response.

Ramona shrugged. "You'll survive to kill your chickens another day."

By keeping her head down and her hatchet swinging, she'd been able to avoid that indignity. She couldn't afford complacency if she were to survive.

Leaning his shovel into the stagnant dirt, Tadeusz continued, "I've heard Germany has defeated the Americans. London is destroyed, and the British have surrendered."

"You fool. Don't believe everything the German bastards feed you," Borys didn't look up from his hoe. "Germany is fading, but they'll never admit it."

Zosia rolled her eyes. Borys was more tolerable than Tadeusz, yet in all of his optimism, Borys was just as stupid for always engaging.

Truthfully, no one knew the status of the war, and Zosia didn't care as long as her children were alive and safe. She fought to stay alive, to return to them. Meanwhile, she cultivated the sugar beets that sweetened the Nazi's tea and the corn that allowed the doomed chickens to eat better than she did.

"Just keep waiting for the cowboys to rescue you." Tadeusz clicked his tongue. He ran his fingers through his buzzed hair, a habit left over from before he'd arrived at camp with his long, slicked-back hair. Even then he was scheming, figuring out who had connections so he knew with whom to make alliances. "We'll see who is the fool."

The metallic thunder of a distant air raid shook the sky. The prisoners froze for a half second and calculated the distance in their heads. With a quick glance at each other, it was silently agreed that the bombs were a safe distance away this time. This particular blitz wouldn't send them all scrambling for their barracks with handfuls of them left in the dirt, shot for abandoning their work.

The enemy was always near. An occasional scream or cracking gunshot reminded the prisoners that the guards hovered, sometimes hidden from view. There were hourly inspections by farm administrators and the occasional terrifying visits from the Gestapo guards who kept order but also brought with them a cloud of foreboding. Bullets and billy clubs sometimes came out of nowhere.

"If we don't have hope, we have nothing," Borys said, digging his hoe into the ground. Those near him in the row grunted their agreement.

Zosia mostly blocked out their banter. Every day it was the same: Tadeusz and Borys argued endlessly about nothing. Borys was a lanky blonde from the southern edge of Poland who held an air of authority though he had none. Tadeusz was a sinewy man who had a taste for debate and would go out of his way to find it. It was a volatile combination when mixed with the backbreaking labor and debilitating monotony that flooded the fields. The two men seemed to enjoy their feuds, but to everyone else they were a unique form of torture in an already dreadful life.

In the heat of summer, someone dropped to the ground almost daily. If they weren't already dead from exhaustion or starvation, they were promptly shot by a guard to make sure. Death also lingered in the air between the granite quarries at the

Nazi camp just beyond. Rumors of what happened behind the steel gates spread like a swarm of locusts along the crop lines. In the fields death came slower, but it still stood over Zosia's shoulder and taunted her while she pushed on her shovel.

The days and months ran together, separated only by the weather, air raids, and the occasional smuggled cigarette that traveled down the rows. If they weren't swinging and pulling tools in the fields during the planting months, the prisoners were swinging and pulling tools in the granite quarries in the winter.

"What I wouldn't give for an *oranzada*," Borys said. The workers next to him murmured with thirsty lust, the hot sun beating the sweat from their pores.

"You simple man," Tadeusz said, starting his next argument. "We're men. We drink beer."

"Beer is good." Borys pounded his hoe into the ground. "But on a hot day, nothing beats *oranzada*."

Zosia didn't disagree. When she was young, it was her favorite choice when she and her girlfriends stopped at the soda fountain after school to flirt with the boys. A shiver gripped her spine. Wiktor's voice was still clear in her head, even after years without him.

"What's your name, *moja droga*?" His casual stance and warm eyes charmed her. He rubbed a zloty coin between his finger and thumb.

"My dear." Her heart fluttered. No boy—or man—had ever called her that. Not even her father. She felt her cheeks flush. He was handsome. "Zosia. Zosia Nowak."

"Miss Nowak, may I buy you a soda?"

Confused, she pointed to the orange beverage in front of her. "I already have one."

One of the other girls elbowed Zosia. "He wants your company, not to buy you a drink." She rolled her eyes, and the rest of her friends giggled.

Zosia shrank back, the heat on her face deepening, but Wiktor was kind and gentle. Maturity made him attractive. They spent the rest of the afternoon chatting. She was fifteen, and she was smitten. They were married within the year.

At first when these memories surfaced, Zosia fought them. She pushed them away as she pulled on her shovel to save her from a carelessly emotional—and possibly deadly—response. But then she realized the more memories she could save, the more human she felt. She was more than a farm tool. She was a wife, a mother, a woman. It gave her the resolve to survive, to save her children. She fixated on rescuing those distant memories, the tiny pieces of her past that balanced on the edge of her thoughts and threatened to fall, forever forgotten.

"Petra, what do you think?" Tadeusz threw the question to the large woman working next to Zosia.

Zosia looked up, remembering where she was and how she got there. The group was quiet. Petronela, still as strong as the day she was delivered to the fields, shook her head. "Don't call me that."

"You're not Petra now?"

"Only my friends call me that."

"Oh, am I not your friend?"

"Not when you're fucking around instead of working," she snapped.

Tadeusz scowled as Borys snickered, but both returned their attention to their shovels and hoes.

The team of slaves worked into the evening until it became too dark to see. When the final streaks of orange in the sky disappeared behind the coniferous forest, the whistle blew at the farmhouse and called them in to be counted.

They gathered their tools and joined the other field slaves shuffling in from the north, west, and south toward *Świński Dom*, the epithet they secretly gave the white farmhouse that held the directors' quarters and administrative offices. When they approached, the men skewed to the right and the women to the left toward the barracks.

Watery turnip soup served in dirty bowls slid into their shrunken stomachs. After a quick, cold group washing in the dark showers, the women all crawled on top of flattened, hay-stuffed mattresses and pulled moth-eaten rags over their legs. Zosia had the bunk above Petronela. She listened for her friend's soft snoring before she herself fell into a restless but exhausted sleep.

—

Early the next morning, when the rest of the group marched back to the fields they'd vacated only a few hours before, Zosia scurried to the poultry barn. The mass of chickens she encountered daily baffled her; just when she thought she'd killed most of them, a new batch reached maturity or was shipped in from a nearby farm. The slaughters became such a normal part of her day that now she barely blinked at the headless fowl. This morning, though, the door was ajar. A jolt of warning shook her.

She didn't dare slow her walk, but she carved out a quick plan to dive for the large hatchet that hung from a hook on the south wall. She put her hand on the door and pushed. She was met by Tadeusz's rear end up in the air as he tried to gather an angry chicken into his arms.

"What? Tadeusz?"

He turned quickly and dropped the chicken in a flurry of feathers. His guilty face turned into a condescending sneer. "Well hello, chicken lady."

"Are you trying to steal a chicken?" Zosia was bewildered.

"No, *nooooo* . . ." Tadeusz stood up straight and stretched his back. Zosia wondered why he wasn't in a hurry to get to the fields.

Zosia reached for her hatchet to start her work, but her hand missed. After a year of trusting the handle to fall into her fingers, now there was nothing hanging on the hook. Tadeusz watched her with an evil grin.

"I have work to do. Go on, get out of here." Zosia tried to sound tough. Tadeusz was insufferable in the fields, but she knew he was all hot air, otherwise harmless.

"See, I can't do that. I'm hungry."

"We all are, Tadeusz." Zosia grew anxious. She had a quota to reach.

"No, I don't think we all are. I don't think you are, are you?"

Zosia tried to hide the panic on her face. "I don't know what you're talking about." She looked away and immediately regretted the passive move. She should have known better than to be the one to drop focus.

Petronela, Ramona, and Zosia had been stealing chickens. They only took one per week, and were careful to not be greedy. Zosia filtered it out of what she slaughtered and handed the carcass off to Petronela. Petronela then smuggled it to Ramona, who sometimes worked in the kitchen. She prepared it quickly with minimal waste. They did this late on Sunday nights when the German guards and farm directors were tipping beers in *Świński Dom*. The three women met behind the barns after midnight to feast in secret, all while watching over their shoulders for the enemy. If they were caught, it would be certain death. They knew the alternative of surviving on only the twice-daily broth would slowly kill them anyway, so the gamble was worth it

They were careful to never reveal their secret to anyone, and they vowed to each other to choose death over confession. The only way Tadeusz could have known was if he'd somehow seen them.

Zosia stood her ground and lifted her chin. She had to sound tough. *What would Petra do?* "Fuck you, Tadeusz," she said. "Get out of here, let me do my job."

"Fuck me?" he smiled, surrendering his slippery chicken. His tone was cruel, taunting her. "Oh, yes you will."

Zosia took a step back. He got uncomfortably close. She knew Petronela would have snapped him in half by now. But, she was not Petronela.

A glint of metal caught her eye. He was holding her hatchet.

"I know your little secret, and I'm happy to tell the director about you and your friends."

"You want the chicken, take it," Zosia said, unnerved. "I'll even kill it for you. I won't say anything."

"I'll take the chicken. But I'll take something else, too."

Zosia's heart pounded. Tadeusz moved even closer, his hand reaching down toward the front of his trousers. He rubbed a bulge behind the buttons, a wicked grin stretching across his face.

"What do you want, Tadeusz?" She had to be seeing things. They were all hungry, exhausted, and mostly without hope. She couldn't understand how anyone would want sex.

Her scalp tingled. For some, sex was about power and control, things none of them had. Things some people craved. She tried to locate the door without actually moving her eyes, but realized there was nowhere to run, no one to help her. She had to either agree to Tadeusz's demands or she had to kill him right now. She let her vision fall on the hatchet, still gripped tightly in his hand.

The chicken that Tadeusz ceded meandered in front of Zosia. She considered throwing it at him, to distract him and give her a chance to run. But, Tadeusz would still accuse them of theft. Zosia, Petronela and Ramona would all die.

She shrieked as Tadeusz grabbed her arm and threw her to the ground. She held her breath and clenched her muscles, hoping it would not hurt when he entered.

But it did. It hurt.

It seemed like hours, but it could have only been minutes, maybe even seconds that she lay on the floor in a pool of Tadeusz's semen, waiting for the throbbing pain in her pelvis to subside. Tadeusz was gone. She stood and let her dress fall back over her hips while she searched for her hatchet. It was gone, too. He'd taken it with him.

Dozens of chickens clucked at her ankles, all still far too alive for the time of day. She searched the barn until she found a rusty bale hook hanging on a far wall. It was better than her bare hands. She climbed over the chicken pen to reach for it when she heard the door creak open. He was coming back for her.

She looked over her shoulder. Sturmbannführer Voss stood silhouetted in the doorway. "Why are these chickens not slaughtered?"

She couldn't hide in the pen since he'd already seen her. She knew she had to follow Ramona's advice, but she couldn't bring herself to. She sat and stared, shaking, trying to form words that could keep her alive.

"Are you fucking deaf?" He reached for his pistol.

This is it, Zosia thought to herself. *I have to do it now, or I'll die.*

She hopped to the ground and knelt in front of him. A slicing pain split through her side as his steel-toed boot contacted her rib. She fell, but pushed herself back up to her knees and tried again, opening her mouth. She squeezed her eyes shut.

His zipper crackled in her ear.

Chapter Six

One week later.

There was no wind after the storm passed. The afternoon sun eased out from behind the dark clouds to the east, casting a dawn-like, almost artificial yellow light across the patchwork landscape. Bright and blinding, the rays were accompanied by the smell of dirt, rain, and sweat. The quick, drumming downpour exposed the rotting corpses of their fellow laborers who hadn't been buried quite deep enough, adding to the stench.

Zosia readjusted her fingers and pushed on her shovel, avoiding the bleeding blisters that covered her palms. Her hands were a mass of callouses and broken skin. She could barely bend her knuckles. She leaned into the shovel to claim a scoop of mud, and wondered if her fingers would ever again be nimble enough to dance a delicate needle and thread through soft silk.

"That's a lazy way to think," Tadeusz lectured to no one in particular. His voice forced a new wad of rotten bile into Zosia's throat. Over the past week, he'd given her knowing looks and repulsive winks. Zosia didn't say a word to anyone about the rape, not even her counterparts in the theft, but she kept herself at an even greater distance from him. No matter what, he was always too close.

As time trickled away, Zosia's faith went with it. She knew someday her hell would be over, and she hoped it would be by liberation and not death. If there was ever to be an after, Zosia couldn't fathom what it would look like. She dug her shovel into the earth again, falling in time to the slopping rhythm created by the group as they dug up rocks and hoed around crops. Poland had disappeared; there was no homeland to return to. Her children floated like ghosts in her mind, and the fear they might have perished left her soul an open wound like the sores on her hands—raw, bleeding, and agonizing. If they were dead, only then would the silencing crack of a bullet crushing her skull be a welcome, comforting reprieve.

Out of the corner of her eye, Zosia saw the field supervisor approach in his Kübelwagen. The cadence of the shovels and hoes clipped along a little quicker, the sweat poured a little faster. Everyone else saw, too.

Everyone except Tadeusz. "I don't see the point in believing in fairy tales, that's all. Make your own fate. Believe the worst, that way you won't be disappointed." He went on arguing with no one as the enemy approached.

Apprehensive eyes glimpsed at each other under strings of wet hair, but no words answered him. Heads were down, muscles clenched. *Pick, slice, dig. Pick, slice, dig.* No one besides Tadeusz fell out of line with the tempo of the team.

Tadeusz turned silent when the vehicle downshifted in the mud on its way up the hill. Zosia saw that this time a Nazi guard accompanied the supervisor. Dread throbbed through the group whenever the black German military uniform with the red armband approached.

It was Sturmbannführer Voss. Zosia could see his eyes slicing her already from so far away. He jumped out of the Kübelwagen when they cleared the top of the hill. "Prisoners, is there a problem?" He marched to the line where he was met with silence.

Herr Voss was a pair of eyes in a uniform. Sharp as glass, they bore holes into anything he looked at. In a different time and place they could be lover's eyes—beautiful to fall into and drown, breathtaking to wake up to after a night of making love. They made the otherwise average man striking, even sexy.

But Voss was no lover; he was an evil monster. Zosia could still taste him as he pounded the back of her throat.

She wondered if she would ever trust a lover again. She was too tired to care.

Her thoughts distracted her, but a click next to her ear and cold metal pressed against her temple snapped her back. Her heart stopped. She would have fallen to her knees if terror hadn't kept her legs stiff. Her body quaked. *Did he already pull the trigger? Am I already dead?*

"I asked if there was a problem." Contempt dripped from his voice.

Zosia's breath caught. Her mind raced. Images of her three children, all smiling with their arms around each other, filled her head. Were they waiting for her in Heaven? *Oh, God, please watch over my children. Keep my babies safe. Take me now if it means they'll be safe.* "No," she said as calmly as she could pull together. "No *mein Herr*, no problem." Her voice shivered. She pushed the shovel into the dirt, watching the brown mud swallow the cold metal of the spade centimeter by tortuous centimeter.

"Leave her, Franz." The field supervisor left the Kübelwagen idling and ambled toward Voss, casually flicking his cigarette ashes into the dirt. "She does the chickens."

Zosia heard a chuckle of recognition bubble in Voss's throat. "Yes, she does, doesn't she?" She could hear the smile in his voice, but he didn't drop his gun. "You can find someone else to slaughter the chickens."

The field supervisor smirked. "Not like her. Leave her."

There was a pause. Voss lowered his gun to his side. Then he turned and swiftly lifted it again, aiming at Ramona. In an instant, Ramona was dead.

Zosia's eyes met with Petronela's. Rage flared in Petronela's face, but neither woman moved beyond the pull and drag of their farm tools. Zosia felt the sting of dry tears. Moments later, the prickling was replaced by a loud *thump* against her head as the metal barrel contacted her temple. A blinding pain thundered through her head.

She staggered. Voss stuffed the gun into his hip holster. Her whole body melted, but she held herself up and pushed her spade into the dirt. She wanted to cry. She wanted to vomit. She might have already shit herself. Staring at the ground through vision obscured by waves of hot tears mixed with sweat and blood from her forehead, she lifted her foot and pressed on the top of the tool. Deeper it sank, the wet mud absorbing the blade like a sword swallower at a circus.

She again looked at Petronela, who gave a slight nod and lifted her chin forward. Zosia recognized the signal: *stay strong*. She blinked twice to indicate she understood. Petronela's eyes returned to her shovel. Zosia willed her tears to stay where they were, to not fall. She was alive. She survived. *Keep working.*

"If I hear of any more theft on this farm, you will all be killed. The chickens," Herr Voss leaned in to Zosia's ear but kept yelling at the group, "are not for swine like you." He stood upright, eyeing Petronela only momentarily. "And no fucking talking. Next time I won't be so merciful."

Voss paused as if steadying his anger before he continued. "New prisoners will be joining you worthless shits. Make room for them." He waved toward *Świński Dom* where a group of people plodded toward them. Their silhouettes against the sun melted together, making them appear like a single unit. A large, multi-headed monster, captured and now punished in the fields.

They were all a part of that monster.

The supervisor walked to the Kübelwagen and pulled an armful of implements out of the back. He threw them to the ground, and the two men climbed back into the vehicle. The engine gunned and the wheels spun up sticky mud. The two men sped off down the hill.

The prisoners waited, each of them mindful of how far the vehicle was, and whether it was slowing down, stopping, or even reversing. When it got further out of sight, a collective sigh released from the group. A few workers dug a hole for Ramona.

"You've been stealing chickens?" Borys piped up first.

"Fuck you, Borys," Petronela said. "And fuck you too, Tadeusz. It should have been you with the gun to your head. You deserve it. It would be nice for us all to get a rest from your bullshit."

Tadeusz didn't look up. He was intent on his work. "Fucking deserve it?" he muttered, "I don't fucking deserve any of this."

Zosia had been holding her breath. No one else knew it was likely Tadeusz who snitched. Now Ramona was dead. Zosia knew it could have easily been her. Still shaken, she pushed her shovel into the ground with more force.

The new workers stumbled through the damp mud, chose their weapons against the earth, and fell into line with the rest of them. Zosia was thankful that a few landed between her and Tadeusz.

After several minutes, one of the new prisoners spoke. They always spoke first; newcomers wanted to understand the lay of the land, the politics of the farm, how to stay alive, and the easiest way to die if necessary. "How long have you all been here?" the man asked. The clean gold and purple P on his shirt fluttered as he pierced the dirt with his hoe.

349 days. Zosia stayed silent. So did everyone else. The conversation ceased.

Everyone kept a wary eye across the fields toward *Świński Dom* for more enemy movement. An eternity of silence followed, severed only when Borys and Tadeusz felt safe enough to start their next dispute about nothing.

"Good God," said the woman to Zosia's left, who still had recognizable color on her boots. She stood up straight and shielded her eyes from the sun, gazing toward the valley that bisected the granite quarries beyond the barns. A piercing shriek rattled the fields from a distance.

Zosia didn't hear the train whistles any more. She disciplined her ears to only hear the Kübelwagen creeping up the hill, crushing dirt and snapping twigs beneath it. But without looking, she knew a long line of cattle cars snaked through the valley below them, human arms hanging out of the tiny windows like tree limbs. She used to have to tell herself that the trains were full of only the ugliest Jews: restaurateurs who wouldn't share their trash with starving Catholics, lawyers who tricked the less fortunate, doctors who refused to help the suffering poor. No children. The children were safe. But now the slow, deep whistles of the trains no longer caught her attention. She didn't notice anymore when they slithered through the countryside, so she didn't have to make up stories about the people inside.

—

That night Zosia stared at the bare rafters that held up the roof of the barracks. "We did this, Petra," Zosia said. "It's our fault Ramona is dead."

"We all knew the risk," Petronela said. "She was a brave woman. May God rest her soul. She's comfortable now. Hell, maybe she's the lucky one of us."

"We didn't even know her," Zosia went on. "All this time, working so closely with her, sleeping in the next bunk, and we don't even know if she was married, if she had children. We are the only ones who can mourn her, and we don't know anything about her." Though Zosia, Petronela, and Ramona met weekly to eat their stolen chicken, they rarely spoke. They were terrified their voices might attract attention.

In the fields and in their bunks, Zosia avoided talking about her family. Though they were always on her mind, she never let the thoughts come out in words. Vocalizing her grief made it too real. It was likely the same for the others.

Zosia gathered her wits. *Another death. Just another death.* But this time, it was too close. Ramona was a friend, a collaborator.

Zosia should have done more to stop Tadeusz.

"Damn lice," Petronela said. The bunk shook, and in the uneasy silence of lights out, Zosia could hear the dry scraping of her friend's fingernails against her scalp. Petronela let out a tired sigh. "Tell me, Zosia," she said in an almost inaudible whisper, "do you have a husband?"

"I did." Zosia took a deep breath. She longed for a cigarette. "We were young. Too young, but it was love. I was barely sixteen when we married."

"Your father must have been furious."

Zosia shook her head, though Petronela couldn't see her. "My father was too busy emptying bottles of *Zubrówka* in the city. I don't think he ever even knew. If he did, he didn't care. My mother, though, disowned me."

She closed her eyes and was sixteen again. Her mother was on her knees with pins pursed between her lips, the hem of Brygida's dress pinched in her fingers. Brygida admired herself in the full-length mirror.

"I'm serious," Zosia said, a pout firmly on her lips.

"I'm sure you are," her mother said, her mind absent. "And in a few years you can think about marriage. But for now, don't let this boy get in the way of your studies."

"He's not a boy," Zosia said. "He's almost twenty years old."

Her mother paused and studied Zosia over her glasses, her attention caught. "Well, then he's too old for you anyway."

Brygida piped up. "I don't know what a man of twenty would see in you, Zosia. I bet you're making it up."

Zosia's vacant stomach burned from the memory. Her petty problems as a young woman were frustratingly ignorant through the filters of the farm, the war, and widowhood. Petronela's gruff voice brought her back to the stifling, stinking barracks. "Had to have been tough, my friend. You were so young. Any children?"

"Three," she said. "They are what I live for now."

"Your husband, he's dead?"

"Yes." Zosia turned onto her side. "Petra, tell me about you. What do you miss?"

"I miss the Symphony."

"You went to the symphony? In Warsaw?" Zosia had sometimes noticed advertisements in the newspaper for the Warsaw Philharmonic Orchestra, and once in a while she fantasized about having the money, time, or interest to attend a concert. It seemed so sophisticated—a reason to get dressed up, to make a new frock out of the bolt of rich green velvet she had her eye on at the market. But then, the music probably wouldn't have appealed to either her or Wiktor. She imagined they would have both fallen asleep.

Petronela seemed like the last person who would enjoy the orchestra. To Zosia, she looked to be more of the rugby type.

"No." Petronela let out her breath. "I performed with them."

Zosia was certain her eyebrows shot all the way past her graying hairline and landed somewhere on top of her head. She would have been less surprised if Petronela admitted to being a werewolf.

"*Performed?*"

"My job, back when—well, you know. Before," Petronela said bitterly. "Second chair trombone. Would have been first if I were a man. The conductor didn't believe in a woman leading a section."

Zosia always assumed Petronela was the farm laborer she claimed to be. Biting her lip in order to keep a dozen or so questions from tumbling out, she waited for her friend to speak.

After a minute, Petronela continued. "It was how I met my beloved Eliasz, my husband. I miss him even more than the Symphony. He used to sit in the front row, off to one side. One evening after a performance he asked me out for coffee." Petronela took a raspy breath. "I could have saved him. I should have done more to protect him."

Zosia heard herself in Petronela's voice. "I'm sure you did all you could," she said softly. "Is he dead?"

"I don't know. They took him early on. Eliasz is an attorney, a successful one. He'd hoped to get his files into safe storage before the Gestapo burned everything to the ground, and I was helping him box everything up. We heard a knock on the door, and I answered it. We had nothing to hide." She stopped again, steadying her breath. "I didn't realize the risk. Stupid. We should have bolted the door and shot anyone who fought his way through.

"Anyway," she said, her voice toughening further, "they pushed past me and dragged Eliasz out of the office and into the street. He fought, but he's a small man. You know, the intellectual type: slight build, bald head, little glasses, always with a thoughtful look on his face. They lifted him into the bed of the truck while three other guards held me against the wall. I would have torn those Gestapo bastards apart if they'd let go of me for one moment."

The bed shook again as Petronela rolled over. "They didn't take me. I don't know why. Hmpf," she grunted. "Maybe they were afraid of me. Fuck those cowards."

"My God, Petra. I'm so sorry."

Petronela cleared her throat. "I trust Eliasz is alive, and that trust is what keeps me alive. If he's dead, I might as well lie down in the field and let that creep Voss shoot me between the eyes."

Zosia waited. The bunk below her stayed silent, so Zosia left her friend in peace. She wrapped her arms around herself. Grief crushed her, like it had every day since Wiktor's death. *Three years without him. It feels like thirty.* She could still see his dark hair flipping in the wind, his tough jaw holding the shape of his stubbly chin, his soft, brown eyes surrounded by miles of long, thoughtful eyelashes. She couldn't resist his peace, his kindness. Neither could other women. And Wiktor, she'd learned, couldn't resist them.

"Matka," a tiny voice whispered in the darkness. Zosia was home in her own bed, far away in another place and time, warm under the wool blankets. Next to her the bed was empty. Wiktor was working late again. Or, that's what he would tell her in the morning. "Matka, I dreamt about her again."

"Who, my love?" In the darkness, she couldn't see the child, but by the tone of voice she knew it was Antoni.

"The lady. The lady in the chair."

"There's no lady, my *babisiu*."

"I know." She could almost feel him shrug in the darkness. Always so logical, even as a little boy. "I just thought you should know I dreamt about her." He waited, and Zosia knew he was embarrassed to ask to join her in bed.

She made it easy for him and flipped back her covers. "Come, my sweet. Just for a moment. Just until we know the lady is gone."

He scrambled into bed and pushed his cold feet against Zosia's legs. She didn't flinch. She wrapped her arms around him, taking in his scent of new spring grass and caterpillars. She felt his body sigh as it molded into hers.

She would give anything to feel that warmth against her

again, but all she had now was a threadbare sheet that barely kept the mosquitoes from biting.

She understood Petronela. If her children were dead, Zosia would welcome a bullet in the temple, too. The unknown was somehow keeping them alive.

Chapter Seven

May, 1945: Morning.

Zosia let the hatchet fall into the block of wood in front of her, sparing the life of the chicken whose neck she held. "What?"

Petronela wasn't making sense. She hopped from one foot to the other like the rest of the chickens in the coop, babbling nonsense with a flushed face. "Come quickly! The Americans are here!" She turned and ran out of the barn.

A stubborn fog lazed in Zosia's brain. She didn't know why the Americans would be interested in this farm, and she wasn't sure if it was worth interrupting her work.

She'd been a prisoner for twenty-one months. Nearly two years of waiting and wondering, of grueling work that nearly killed her. She had all but given up on rescue.

She struggled against her atrophied muscles to push herself up from her knees, released the chicken into the pen, and mechanically brushed her hands on the baggy men's pants cinched at her waist with a length of rope. She followed her excited friend out of the barn toward *Świński Dom*.

An official-looking man, wearing a perfectly clean and pressed uniform, stood waiting. An assortment of pins and stripes decorated his tan jacket, and a small silver medal on his lapel read *US*. His stance was casual with his hands on his hips, and he stared at the ground through dark aviator glasses while prisoners assembled around him. A less-than-official-looking interpreter accompanied him, and behind the two men was a Jeep just as battered as the field supervisor's Kübelwagen. The American lifted his head, not out of interest but duty, and watched Zosia and Petronela join the group.

His jaw chomped on a wad of bubble gum as he watched the stragglers filter in from the fields and barns. When he was satisfied the group was complete, he spoke. His voice boomed in the commanding timbre of a people who just won a war. The interpreter followed everything he said and tried to match the swagger of the American, but the Polish equivalent rolled off of his tongue with defeat veiled in fake confidence.

"I'm Captain Edward Foley, United States Army. I'm here to tell you the Allied forces have won the war with Germany."

Captain Foley paused, gnawed on his gum, and waited for a reaction. A few prisoners eyed each other in confusion, but otherwise everyone stayed still and stared at the khaki-covered man with their sunken eyes. Borys clapped softly, and it spread into a tiny splattering of awkward applause.

"That's right." The captain clapped his own hands together in an attempt to drum up some enthusiasm from the nearly dead group of prisoners. Zosia brought her hands together once in a merciful clap before letting them rest at her sides. Petronela didn't move. Captain Foley returned his hands to his hips, oblivious to the Poles' weak response.

"You are all free," the interpreter said after the captain barked his next words.

Free. Zosia was free. She could go find her children. She could finally return to them. Her chest constricted with a new wave of hope and anxieties.

"Unfortunately, your homeland is in ruins. Most of Poland is unlivable. You'll be sent to a refugee camp in Wildflecken, Germany, until permanent housing can be arranged, either back in Poland or in other areas of the world.

"We are here to help you." Captain Foley accentuated his words. "We don't anticipate your stay in Wildflecken to be more than a couple of months, at most. You will meet down over the hill at the camp gates this evening. Trains will be waiting to take you to Wildflecken."

An anxious buzz pulsed through the skittish Poles. The captain, realizing his mistake, put his hands up to reassure the group. "You are no longer prisoners. The German military has fallen, and the soldiers and guards stationed here at the farm and down at the camp have all been arrested. The entire area is under American and British control, so you have nothing to fear. You are safe. You will board the train at seventeen hundred, and depart shortly after. Bring with you only what you need.

"Any questions." The captain said as more of a statement than a query. He turned the gum over inside his mouth and gave it several hard chomps. Zosia watched his clean-shaven jaw clamp down with the arrogance of victory.

The crowd erupted into a cacophony of frenzied Polish chatter. Everyone pleaded their questions at once.

"Is there anything left in Krakow?"

"My wife was sent to Dachau. How can I find her?"

"How can you be sure the Germans won't reassemble?"

"Is Hitler dead?"

The captain put his hands up again and took a step back. "On second thought, they'll have answers for you in Wildflecken. Best if you save your questions for when you arrive there. The staff has been hand-selected by the United States government, so they are stand-up individuals." The captain raised his finger to his hat, not in a salute but more of a *good day*. "Best of luck to you all." He turned on his shiny boots and climbed into the dirty Jeep. The interpreter hopped into the passenger seat next to him. The engine growled, and the two men disappeared around the north barn in a cloud of dust and exhaust. The now-former prisoners all stood staring at each other, unsure of what to do next. After years of confinement, freedom was a mysterious idea.

Then, as if a switch was flipped, everyone scattered, aware they were no longer held to their shovels with guns against their heads. The fields were pillaged of whatever was harvestable so early in the season. In the barns, any animal that stood still long enough was butchered. A couple of women chopped wood, knowing a slaughtered pig would be worthless without a fire to cook it. A few men, led by Tadeusz, took off toward *Świński Dom* to loot whatever they could from their former captors.

Zosia returned to her chicken coop and got to work. *Chop, scald, pluck. Chop, scald, pluck.* She had always been quick, but now she'd found an even faster pace. She was on her way home, back to her children.

—

By mid-afternoon, most of the workers were assembled on the west loading platform next to the train station. The prisoners from inside the camp stayed on the east platform. The two groups scrutinized each other with wary eyes.

Zosia and the others on the west platform were gaunt and hollowed out from their years of hard labor, but the camp prisoners on the opposite side of the tracks were only spindly sticks leaned against each other. They were dressed in rags with jagged, chopped hair sprouting from their scalps. The largest parts of any of them were their eyes, which told stories of horror. Zosia realized that though they were threatened, abused, beaten and raped, the field laborers were treated relatively well by comparison.

Most of the camp survivors had some kind of limp. Rudimentary bandages and slings, darkened from dirt and blood, were tied here and there on limbs that weren't yet missing. While the farm workers rested their bones from years of exertion, Zosia noticed the camp prisoners were in continual motion, as if their lives depended on movement. Some crept and scurried, while others could only rock side to side. No matter how shattered they were, they somehow found a way to crawl along, never allowing their skeletal shadows time to cool the concrete below them.

In the fields, resting meant death, or at least a harsh beating. Zosia assumed idleness meant the same or worse inside the camp. A person in constant motion may be a more difficult target to hit. The urge to keep moving was an ingrained need for these people, like breathing. Anyone showing the slightest pause, either from virus or injury, old age or youth, was destroyed.

There were few children. A sickening sorrow pierced Zosia's long-held contempt for the Jews. They couldn't be trusted, but they also didn't deserve to have their children tortured.

The men on the platform loaded chopped wood and supplies while the women piled boxes and crates inside the cars to create makeshift walls. Two younger women and a man with a heavy limp draped a white and red cloth across the outside of one car. The flag of Poland. Zosia fought the swell that rose in her throat. She wasn't sure that red and white banner represented anything other than memories anymore.

Petronela pulled a pillaged cigarette out of her pocket and lit it. Zosia watched, hungry for a taste of the tobacco.

"I hope this isn't for nothing," Zosia said.

"What do you mean?" Petronela asked through a cloud of smoke.

Zosia nodded her chin at the happy decorators humming around the train. "Can we really trust that American captain? What if we're being led to our deaths? The rumors we've heard about the camps . . ." Zosia couldn't finish.

Petronela smiled. "Then we've all had a last gasp of joy before the cyanide fills our lungs." Petronela handed her the cigarette and crouched to lift Zosia's crate of fresh chicken carcasses. She motioned her head toward the train, urging her friend along. "Better get on board, to a new life. A better life. Promise."

Inside the boxcar, Zosia and Petronela claimed a spot against a wall between two stacks of crates. The camp survivors stayed huddled together near the other side of the car. A handful of children milled about, but they seemed to be ghosts of actual youth, old before their time. After Zosia studied the children and decided none of them were her own, she avoided them. She couldn't bear the thought that her sons and daughter could have endured these same horrors, or worse.

The train jolted alive, and a gleeful laugh wafted up from the ground. Borys was tossed into the car like a bale of hay, unconscious and reeking of booze. Tadeusz climbed in after him, followed by a few other young men. Tadeusz triumphantly held up a half-empty bottle of vodka before falling into a pile on top of Borys. The other men laughed, and one by one also passed out. Disgusted, Zosia turned her back and rested her head on an empty potato sack.

Later that night, Tadeusz and his friends awoke, loudly retching and moaning in withdrawal. Borys, though, did not. After several attempts to wake him, his body was dumped out into the countryside as easily as it had been flung into the car hours earlier. Zosia shook her head at the waste. Borys survived only long enough to die in celebration.

—

Over the next day, the former prisoners, all in different but similar states of broken, began to mix together. The gathering spot became the fire that burned in the center of the boxcar, the one that cooked Zosia's chickens, all picked clean during the first hour of their journey. When Zosia climbed down from the slow-moving train to stretch or relieve herself, she could see every boxcar had a similar fire burning. Tendrils of smoke rose from a center hole in each roof.

She also noticed the tracks were being built in front of the train, which explained the sluggish speed of their trip. They even reversed several times, further slowing their travel. In many places the tracks were destroyed or littered with trees and debris. Zosia never thought a short trip through Germany could take so long.

As the second evening set in, Zosia sat on the floor of the cattle car with her arms wrapped around her shins. She scooted closer to the fire, more to mask the stench than for warmth or light. Although there were plenty of opportunities to descend and find a spot in the woods to take care of personal business, some of the prisoners didn't. Either they were too weak, too sick, or just too tired of having to move. The rear left corner of the boxcar became the designated toilet for shit. Empty crates and beat up old suitcases fashioned a bit of privacy and odor control, but the efforts didn't work well for either.

"It's a Nazi training camp," Tadeusz said on the other side of the fire. "Most elite. Hitler himself probably visited all the time."

"I don't even see it." A toothless camp survivor named Lew wiggled his patchy mustache and studied the stolen map on his lap.

Tadeusz blew smoke out of his nose. He held his cigarette to his temple and scratched his lice-infested head. "Well no, you wouldn't, would you? If you were Hitler and you built a training camp for your best soldiers, would you put it on a map? Might as well put a big sign in front of it." He stuffed his cigarette between his teeth and dramatically spread his fingers in front of him, as if imagining the scene playing out in the air. "General Eisenhower, here it is! Bomb this place first!'" Tadeusz laughed at his own joke, and Lew ignored him, studying every millimeter of the map in the dim firelight.

"You're full of shit, Tadeusz," Zosia said. Her head hissed in loathing for him. "There's no need to scare the children."

"It's true," Petronela said quietly so only Zosia could hear. "I've heard the same. Wildflecken was a Nazi training area. Best there was."

Zosia rested her chin on her knees. She was silent. She was being fed directly into the mouth of the enemy, and she had to trust the American captain's assurances that the enemy was cleared out. That trust didn't come easy.

—

The following morning, the train slowed to an unbearable speed just faster than a stop. It pulled into Wildflecken next to a long, crescent-shaped platform. A splattering of people in a variety of uniforms and plain clothes waited on the splintered wooden decking. Zosia stood next to the open door and watched them, doubt heavy on her shoulders. She was about to find out if Captain Foley had misled them all to their deaths.

The officials on the ground pushed wooden crates up to the doorway of each car. Zosia grabbed her small bag of mostly stolen belongings and set her foot on the step. A beautiful woman wearing a sharp uniform stood by Zosia's car. She had shiny blond hair pulled up into a twist on her head and perfect makeup surrounding her eyes. She held her hand out to Zosia who skeptically took it for balance. When Zosia's feet hit the platform decking, the woman handed her a small paper package.

"What's this?" She glanced at the woman's nametag. *Violette.* The woman smiled, and with a tinkling voice said something in an exotic language that Zosia decided must be French because it sounded beautiful. Zosia took the package and stepped aside for others to exit the train. She turned the item over in her hands, squeezing it like a child trying to guess what Saint Nicholas brought her.

Up and down the platform, other former prisoners warily eyed their own parcels. Tadeusz sprinted past her, holding up his package with torn paper at one end. His mouth was full as he chewed. "Sandwiches!" he said to whomever would listen. "I love this place!"

Zosia opened her own paper package, revealing two pieces of German dark rye bread. She peeled back one slice and exposed a thin layer of canned tuna flakes. She watched Tadeusz for several minutes while he darted through the crowd and started an argument with a tall bearded man. As satisfying as it would have been to Zosia, he didn't collapse into a gruesome, convulsive death from poisoning. In fact, he had more energy than any of those who still held their sandwiches with distrust. Zosia lifted the sandwich to her lips, paused for a moment, and took a bite. She munched the dry bread and cool fish, and her defenses faded.

A look around revealed why Hitler chose this place for his training camp: there were trees everywhere, a perfect camouflage. A long, curved platform, a building that served as the station, then nothing but large, bulky trees. She couldn't even be sure that Wildflecken was a town, since she saw no roads or breaks in the forest to permit passage. If someone didn't know this little village was here, it would never be found in the dense forest. She wondered if that would also make it easily forgotten by those coordinating the relief efforts.

From somewhere on the platform a woman's voice bellowed at them without the help of an amplifier. What she said seemed important, but her stumbling fluency was largely ignored. "You will now be referred to as 'displaced persons,'" she said. "You are no longer prisoners. You are simply people who are displaced from your homes."

Displaced Person. Zosia thought about her new classification.

A more accurate description would have been *Formerly Captured, Alienated, Tortured, Almost Killed Soul Who Is Now Homeless And Has No Idea What To Do Next,* but she supposed that wouldn't have fit so neatly on their identification cards.

The woman continued to yell over the noise. "Please know we are short on some supplies, and food is, as always, precious, so please adhere to the rations you are given. Do not surrender to the black market, as participants will be punished. Above all, do not trust information purchased on the black market. The only information that is correct is what comes through our administrative offices. Respect each other and the rules we have in place, and there will be no problems."

Zosia scanned the crowd. Cigarettes and sandwiches were already exchanging between guilty hands, ears deaf to the official's warning. Her eye caught Petronela's. The hefty woman, still as strong as the day Zosia met her, lifted her sandwich in a toast. Even over the noisy commotion, Zosia heard her say, "*Na zdrowie*, my friend."

CHAPTER EIGHT

Afternoon.

The cobblestones were broken yet solid under Zosia's feet. She surveyed her new address: Blockhouse C-6. The typhus-resistant powder she'd been dusted with still clung to her sweat-stained clothes. Bent inside her sticky palm, her identification card shouted *DP* at her in large, capital letters.

Called blockhouses, they were actually former barracks—looming cinder block buildings lined up one after another, like the soldiers who used to occupy them. They were all painted uniformly, whitewashed to take advantage of the government-issued gallons left behind by the Nazis.

Hastily assembled benches were placed outside of some buildings, there to make the sterile camp seem more welcoming. Even from a distance, Zosia could see they were splintered and loose. Two little girls stood by one bench and played *serso* with a length of wire bent into a ring.

"Well, looks like a reasonable place." Petronela cracked her neck and reached into her pocket for a cigarette.

"Should be fine for a few days," Zosia said. She squinted into the sun and peered up the street. The large army truck that had delivered her, Petronela, and several other residents to their new homes sped away, a cloud of dust behind it. "Looks like a mess building over there. Do you think that's a hospital?"

Petronela grunted, struggling to light her cigarette in the wind. "Yeah, hospital." She motioned with her still-cold cigarette. "Looks like a whole row of mess buildings, unless they use those for more barracks." She turned slowly in a circle and looked around. "There, next to the Catholic church, looks like a cemetery. Stay out of there," she snorted at her own joke. "There's a school across the street from it, next to an athletic field."

"I was imagining tents and shanties," Zosia said.

"Nah." Petronela tried again with her stolen matches. "Nazi training camp, remember? Those bastards had money."

"It looks like a functioning town."

"A town with nothing but whitewashed brick buildings." Her cigarette finally lit, she inhaled sharply and passed it to Zosia. Petronela nodded toward a few people crossing the street a block down. "And we're not the first ones here."

People around them were dressed in decent civilian clothing and appeared to have places to go, or at least acquaintances to loiter with. Dresses and even hats adorned the ladies, though the clothes were dulled like the depleted tarnish of a favorite serving platter left out in the rain. Children ran in every direction, playing, as children should. Everyone still wore a battle-worn expression, but it was tinged with hope that the horrors of war were soon behind them.

The youngest DPs gave Zosia a bit of relief and hope. At least some children survived. Wherever they'd come from, whatever brutality they'd endured, someone had been kind enough to let them live.

A boy sat on a bench across from the school, swinging his legs, with a large book spread across his lap. He followed along the lines of words with his finger while he read, moving his lips to the type on the page.

Antoni. Zosia's mind went to her son. It wasn't him; this boy was younger and had a splattering of freckles across his nose and cheeks. But still, she was reminded.

She could see her children, the three of them in a happier time, gathered around the family table in their home while Zosia sliced potatoes in the kitchen.

"Who established the Commission of National Education?" Marisha flung her black hair over her shoulder as she quizzed Antoni. Antoni absently tapped the pages of the open book in front of him. Always an open book, whether he was reading or not.

"That's an easy one." Stefek jumped up and down, supporting himself on the back of Antoni's chair. "My teacher, Mrs. Babicz."

"She was alive one hundred and fifty years ago?"

"I think she might have been. She's old."

"It was King Stanislaw II August." Antoni said and turned to Stefek. "And you're lucky he did. He ended corporal punishment in schools."

"What's that?"

"It means the teachers can't beat the students." Marisha playfully whacked Stefek on the rear.

Stefek stopped jumping. "Well then," he said, "it couldn't have been Mrs. Babicz. She doesn't know about that rule."

"Oh, she beats you?" Marisha looked concerned.

"No," Stefek said. "But she did hit Artur on the back of the head yesterday when he put a frog in his mouth. The frog flew across the room and got stuck in Kamila's hair. Kamila didn't stop screaming until Mrs. Babicz cut it out with scissors."

The dusty German breeze tossed a strand of hair across Zosia's forehead. Beside her, Petronela cleared her throat and spat on the ground. "Well shit, look at that. The kids have books. This is a nice place." She folded her arms. "Wonder if I can find a trombone somewhere. My embouchure has all gone to shit. The

Nazis had military bands, right?"

Zosia ignored Petronela. Grief as sharp as pins crept in behind her eyes. Her memories of her children had broken her. She wished she'd paid more attention when she had the chance. She should have taken a break from the kitchen to sit with them and enjoy their banter. Now it was too late. She decided to avoid passing the Wildflecken schools during the day.

Petronela bent to pick up her meager belongs. "Well I'm in C-4, next door to you. You need anything, Zosia, you know where to find me." With her cigarette clamped between her teeth, she marched toward her blockhouse.

Zosia watched her go before she stepped into Blockhouse C-6 and searched for the room she was to share with three other women. There was no noise when the door to room 21 swung open, and a stark and barren sea of khaki confronted her as if she'd stumbled into the Arabian Desert. Tan army blankets hung from the ceiling all around her, clipped along makeshift clotheslines that spanned the space of the large room. Some were torn and mended with black or green thread. Others had patches sewn on here and there—small squares of gray or green covering holes beneath, in the hopes that they might endure one more season.

The wool walls fluttered from the movement of the beings within them: women, mice, cockroaches, even the ghosts of the Nazi solders who'd rested there only months earlier.

Separating the room into individual dwellings, the blankets created provisional privacy in an otherwise revealing living space. The sectioned spaces all lined a central hallway between the blankets, anchored at the end closest to the door by a cast-iron stove. As Zosia stood next to the stove and surveyed the room, the smells of stale coffee, vinegar, and mildew mingled in her nose. She bumped a metal chair that held a pile of aluminum pots and sent one clanging to the floor. Her skin tingled with the loud announcement of her arrival. The silence in the room thickened. She prowled between the blankets and hunted for an empty bed.

Peeking in to the first blanket-room, Zosia saw a handful of dresses piled onto a bed next to a wooden crutch. She wouldn't call them colorful, but they were more vibrant than anything she'd seen in years. She jumped when the woman inside spoke. "*Dzien dobry*," she said without smiling and returned her attention to the white blouse she was ironing.

"*Dzien dobry*," Zosia replied. The smell of singed rayon burned her nose. Her eye caught a purple shawl hanging over the window like a curtain, crocheted in the Polish Star pattern. The shade of purple changed halfway across the shawl, as if one skein of yarn ran out and another yarn of a lighter dye took over.

The resident in the next space looked up at Zosia with an icy, defensive stare when she parted the blankets. The woman had hair so blond it was nearly white. She sat in a wooden chair with her feet propped on her bed, a thick book resembling a bible with no cover resting on her lap. Behind her, pinned to the tan blanket with diaper pins, was a large, crinkled reproduction of the Black Madonna.

"*Przepraszam*," Zosia apologized. She turned to move on, but pictures pinned to the blanket under the holy print caught her attention. Gray images of children gazed out at Zosia from the scallop-edged paper. This woman had reminders. She could look at the photographs of her children every day and recall the tiny dimple in her son's cheek, or how the cowlick in her daughter's hair interrupted her straight bangs. Zosia pulled the blankets closed and moved on. She held images of her own children only in her memory.

Soon. I'll see them again soon.

The last blanket-room furthest from the stove was empty. Zosia stepped through the tan walls and dropped her potato sack of meager belongings onto the bed.

She had a window. She may have been far from the stove, but at least she had light. She remembered the bitter smell of coffee by the stove and figured this space was ideal, since it would be less noisy in the morning.

She realized she couldn't even remember the taste of coffee. Then she wondered how these women got coffee. Or clothing. Or coverless Bibles.

She sank onto the bed, and it creaked. The frame was rusted, but she smiled when she felt real springs in the mattress. There was even a pillow. With a sigh she kicked off her mud-caked boots and lifted her legs onto the bed. She allowed the first pillow in almost two years to cradle her head. Not long ago this same pillow supported the head of a German soldier while he dreamt of the swiftest way to kill Poles.

Mouse droppings and dead insects littered the floor. She lifted her sight to search the tan blankets. One had a patch of worn denim sewn on it. The stitching meandered and knotted. She stared, her hands itching to fix it, to right the seam.

The door opened, releasing a swooshing wind that disturbed the walls. "Wilusz?" Zosia swung her feet over the side of the bed. A twelve second rest was better than none.

Two women stood by the stove at the front of the room. Zosia recognized the blond as Violette, who had given her a sandwich on the platform. The other woman was similar in height and age to Violette, but her features were sanded and ordinary. She wore her dark hair in a stern bob that landed at her chin, and her lips were feathered with chapped skin.

As Zosia approached, the bobbed woman spoke. "I'm Lottie, and this is Violette. We have some things for you." Lottie's Polish was impeccable, though she had a slight Welsh lilt. Violette stood silently and smiled.

Lottie handed Zosia a box about the size of a small loaf of bread. "Here are your rations, outside of what you are allowed at meals. Going forward, you'll be able to pick these up every Friday morning."

"I'll get one for each day of the week?"

Lottie looked both embarrassed and amused. "No, one box per week. You'll have to conserve." She nodded to Violette. "We have some clothing we can give you." The blond dropped the giant bag she was holding and opened the top. An assortment of gray fabric burst out.

Violette squinted at Zosia and pulled out a simple gray cotton dress with a back zipper. She held it up, smiled and nodded. Zosia thanked her as she excavated more items from the bag: a pair of brown scuffed loafers, some faded black socks.

"Where did all of this come from?" Zosia squeezed the dress in her hands.

"Headquarters," Lottie said as Violette tied up her bag. "Most of it was donated. Red Cross. The United States ran a campaign to collect used clothes, I think Australia did the same. Norway sent bolts of wool. Oh, and there are rumors that the Canadians are sending coats for winter."

"Why?" Zosia wrinkled her nose. "It's June. We don't need coats." Captain Foley's promise of a couple of months in camp started to sound hollow.

Lottie gave her an odd, questioning look. "Oh, I almost forgot," she said, "they're expecting you at the main hospital, down the road and to your right, for your venereal disease exam. Should only take a few minutes, but it is required." She turned to the door, Violette on her heels.

"How can I find my children?" Zosia asked. "Can you help me?"

"You'll need to talk to Mr. Devine, the camp director," Lottie said. "He's very busy on days of new arrivals, but check with him in the morning."

The two women exited the room, leaving Zosia standing in

her rags, holding a dress that was a little less of a rag. It was clean and in one piece, so she was grateful.

She placed the dress on her bed and sat with the ration box on her lap. Lifting the lid with the large red cross on it, she shuffled through the contents: a small tin of lard and another tin of liver paste, a box of raisins, three packets of instant coffee, an envelope of sugar, a tiny box of crackers, a small piece of chocolate wrapped in dark brown paper, and a pack of German Eckstein No. 5 cigarettes. She dug through the box and flipped it over. There were no matches.

Zosia devoured the chocolate and the box of raisins. They were better than any *Wigilia* feast she'd ever eaten. As she tore into the crackers, the woman with the light blond hair peeked around a tan blanket wall. "There are showers down the hall," she said.

Zosia figured she must have an awful odor after not having had a proper bath for two years. "Did you get your dress from Lottie and Violette, too?" She admired how the muted mint-green color complimented the woman's complexion.

"Sure." Her eyes didn't meet Zosia's.

"It's nice. I suppose there's a place we can go to get more clothes if we need? Could you tell me where that is? Or even some fabric? With some thread and needles I could—"

"You'll have to ask around." The woman ducked behind the blanket and disappeared.

Zosia collected her new dress and wandered down the hall to the washroom, where she was pleasantly surprised by real soap. The lukewarm water was an even better treat, so much so that she hardly noticed the smell of backed-up sewer from the toilets.

She stood for a long time in the moldy shower and let the water run over her, washing away the evils of the past two years. Then she crouched to the floor and scrubbed her undergarments while the water bounced off of her back. She worked her fingernails into the fibers until the garments were no longer blackened from dirt and sweat and blood, but instead a grungy gray.

She dried herself and rubbed a tattered towel against her wet hair. She slipped into the gray dress, wrapped the garments in the towel, and hurried down the hallway with the towel under her arm. She walked straight out the front door. The sun was bright outside, and there was a gentle breeze, so Zosia spread her underwear on a discreet length of sidewalk. She sat back on her bare heels and waited for the sun to do its job.

A group of young men wearing United States Army uniforms passed on the street, there to remind everyone of who was in command of the camp. The soldiers seemed detached and paid her no attention as they clung together in their little group, smoking cigarettes and sizing up the young women. Now that the war was over, Zosia thought they were probably annoyed that they were still there, still cleaning up the mess.

She let herself feel the soft wind on her skin. She might have smiled. When she opened her eyes, a gasp caught in her throat, choking her. Painted on the top corner of Blockhouse C-6, partially hidden by trees, was a black swastika. Frantic, she scrambled to her feet and looked around, searching for an explanation, for an escape.

This was all a lie. She should have known not to trust them. Any of them.

At the building next door to hers, two men carried a large ladder to a similar swastika. One man climbed the ladder with a paint roller in one hand and a large tin can dangling from the crook of his arm. They flung orders at each other in an unfamiliar tongue, and the man on the ladder covered the swastika with a layer of white. The black arms of the icon could still be seen through the paint, but he descended the rungs and the two men carried the ladder to Zosia's building where the same process began again.

Zosia tried to push out of her mind the demons of the former Nazi training camp. She remembered how the partially hidden swastika fighting through its new coat of white paint was, at one time, a symbol for good luck. When she was a girl, she had a charm with the symbol on it, won at a fair when she knocked over a wooden duck. The token had never brought her luck, though. Now it was, and forever would be, an omen of bad luck—permanently ruined by the Nazis, like all of Europe.

CHAPTER NINE

July, 1945: Two months later.

"More fucking prisoners," Petronela said, turning her back to light a cigarette. "Just what this camp needs is more people." In front of them, new refugees emerged from the train.

Zosia felt like she was behind the Jewish deli all over again. She exhaled; she always held her breath while she waited for the boxcar doors to open. She imagined boisterous groups of violent Gestapo jumping out, shouting and shooting their rifles. Peacetime was difficult for Zosia to accept.

Sometimes crates of supplies were revealed on the train, and the camp police—who were really just DPs with the ambition to work—briefly looked away while the shipments were pillaged. They knew their shady routine would pay dividends later. The unemployed DPs pilfered the supplies and later would return a skim off the top to the policemen. The residents knew a little sacrificed ham or tobacco would get a DP in good favor with the police, and the police supplemented their own cache without lifting a finger.

Most often though, the boxcars were full of more liberated prisoners, more displaced people to pack into the already overcrowded camp. As it was, Wildflecken held well over fifteen thousand refugees in an area designed for a third of that. Most of these homeless wanderers were already packed into the former barracks nearly on top of each other. More refugees flowing in like water, each in a state of health and well being that ranged from below average to near-death, only intensified the misery.

Zosia kicked at the dirt with her toe, frustrated at the dusty men dressed in rags who filed off the train. At least there could have been some crates of cigarettes, maybe cans of lard. Those were decent currency in the only other way of getting supplies in fallen Germany: the black market.

She watched her scuffed loafers, traded for a few grams of tea, which were traded for her rationed chocolate. Zosia learned quickly that her roommate's mint green dress came from a gentleman in Riedenberg who collected tin which he sold as solder to the local pipe fitters. Trading in the underground economy was the best, and sometimes only, option for acquiring goods. Nothing worth buying was available though the approved lines of commerce, and currency had little value anyway.

"Welcome to Wildflecken," the female voice said over the din.

"Durzyn," Petronela said under her breath. Some of the Polish DPs had unofficially nicknamed the camp Durzyn, so they could reclaim a small part of their homeland and exist as a Polish community in the middle of Germany. The British and American officials were slow to accept it, and so was Zosia. Using a made-up name for the town would only make her harder to find, if, in fact, her children were still alive and looking for her.

"First and foremost," the woman said, "do not participate in the black market." Her warning came sooner in the welcome speech. The round woman stood on a crate and yelled into a megaphone likely acquired on the very same black market she was warning everyone to avoid.

The black market was illegal, dangerous, and corrupt,

primarily because it couldn't be governed or taxed. Anyone who passed a bootleg cigarette or block of chocolate could be removed from camp, arrested, and even killed if caught by the wrong people. But since it was the only way to trade goods in a destroyed economy, everyone in camp was some shade of criminal, even the staff. They all had to pull from their more unscrupulous sides to survive.

Zosia watched the men climb off the train, their eyes like owls in the dim cattle car. *Welcome to purgatory,* she thought. It wasn't a home for anyone. It was a staging ground, a temporary storage place for thousands of people living in the space between the worst moments of their lives and a hope for something better.

The other disappointed DPs waiting to loot with her on the platform dropped their shoulders and turned toward the road. The return to camp was always a disappointing slog with no spoils on one's back.

The new arrivals from the train sifted into the flock of thieves with their hunched-over statures. A few had arms in slings or even missing. One man had only one leg, and another man with a hat pulled down over his forehead helped him crawl off the train. Zosia stared, fascinated by the missing limb, until his friend with the hat glanced up.

Sturmbannführer Voss.

Air constricted in her chest. She met his eyes. They were the same icy blue, and though they only flashed up for a moment, they drilled into her, pulling the soul from her body and shaking it like an automobile collision.

No, it can't be. He was arrested. Wasn't he? Zosia took a step back.

"There was supposed to be flour on this train," Petronela said with a grumble. "My roommate Wanda works in the kitchen. She told me they stretch the bread flour with sawdust until—" Petronela took the cigarette out of her mouth, her attention caught by Zosia's distress. "What's wrong?"

"That man. Herr Voss. His eyes . . ."

Petronela turned. "Which man?"

"There, with the hat, helping the man with one leg."

Exhaling smoke, Petronela watched for a moment. "No, that's not him. Same eyes, though."

"How can you tell?"

"Voss was taller. Plus this guy looks a little older. Mid-thirties. Voss wasn't a day over twenty-five."

Amazed that Petronela could size up a man's height and age from so many meters away, Zosia let out her breath. "Can I have one of those?" She motioned to Petronela's cigarette as she watched the two men, mesmerized.

Petronela handed Zosia a cigarette and fidgeted from boredom. "Let's go." She hiked her skirt up onto her hips like a lumberjack pulling up his pants. Zosia pulled herself away from the haunting grip of those blue eyes, and the two women set out up the hill toward the camp.

To distract herself from visions of Voss, Zosia concentrated on the backs of her compatriots marching ahead of her toward camp. She steadied her nerves. *It wasn't him. I'm safe.* "So your roommate fell for it and went for a job? Poor, gullible girl."

"I went for a job in the kitchen, too." Petronela kicked a stone with her boot. "Wanda said she'd put in a good word for me."

Zosia nearly swallowed her cigarette. Just last week Petronela had scoffed at the camp's request that the DPs apply for work: *"Acclimating us back into civilian life? Please. Fucking Americans understaffed this place. No surprise, since they can't possibly grasp what happened here on the continent. Maybe the British, but not the Yankees. I'll be damned if I lift a finger to bail out their sorry asses."*

"What? A job, Petra? What happened? You swore you wouldn't."

Petronela glanced behind them before conspiring in Zosia's

ear. "Wanda said it's a good way to get information, especially about what and who is coming and going on the trains." She flicked her cigarette to the ground and stomped on it with her boot. "Heard about a man working in the hospital who had access to the wireless. He was able to track down his nephew's family. Eventually led to his wife and one surviving son. They're somewhere outside of Vienna. He left a few weeks ago to go find them." She shrugged. "And, well, a few zlotys here and there won't hurt."

"Aren't zlotys worthless?"

"Yeah, but information isn't."

Zosia knew her friend was thinking of her lost Eliasz and whether the employment network could help find him. She wondered if a job might get her news about her children and a way to return to them quicker. Regardless of whether they were paying in zlotys or cigarettes or a better slice of meat at lunch, Zosia would do anything for information. Besides, a job would keep her busy while she waited.

—

The hiss of static greeted Zosia when she entered room 21 of blockhouse C-6. Nearly every day her roommates returned with marvelous finds from the black market: a decorative rug next to Iwona's bed, a mantle clock sitting on Angelika's dresser. Kasia, the old woman who occupied the corner opposite of Zosia, recently acquired an intricate tapestry bag for her knitting needles and yarn. Now this morning it was a radio.

Zosia went to her bland corner of the room and pulled a clipboard and some crumpled, yellowed paper from a drawer. She sat on her bed and composed letters, but it was impossible to concentrate. Just when her ears would turn the static into white noise and push it into the back of her mind, a glimpse of a station would flicker and make Zosia jump.

Zosia looked down at the half-written letter before her. She wished she had respectable stationery. She also wished she had panties. So far she'd assembled a few outfits from the donation box outside Mr. Devine's office and a quick visit to the man in Riedenberg who collected tin, but undergarments were a challenge. A nice, stiff, supportive brassiere would be a relief, too.

She smoothed her skirt under her and pulled the pen across the paper, *"Dearest Marisha . . ."*

The static assembled into something recognizable. *"Wspomnij mnie . . ."* Angelika and Iwona cheered their success in snatching a broadcast out of the atmosphere. The song wavered through the stuffy air of room 21, and the women sang along. Even Kasia's rough voice joined from her corner. Zosia sang too—silently.

It was Wiktor's favorite song. *"Remember me . . ."* She did remember him. She could never forget her first love, her only love.

"Dance with me, *moja droga.*" She could feel Wiktor's breath on her neck, his strong hands guiding her in a waltz around the kitchen while gravy dripped down her arm from her wooden spoon. "Dance with me so you'll remember me." He gave her a dramatic dip.

She giggled and playfully swatted him away.

Swatted him away. Pushed him away. Thrown to the ground.

Tadeusz. Voss.

No. Zosia stood and paced to clear her head. She couldn't let those criminals steal her loving memories of Wiktor. As it was, the happy memories faded with time and trauma. She had to hold on to his light as long as she could.

Zosia looked down to the letter in her hand. Marisha joined them so quickly, before their first wedding anniversary. Zosia remembered nestling with the tiny child in bed, cuddled together, with Wiktor holding his arms around them both. Safe. Protected.

But not forever. *Dance with me so you'll remember me.* The request grew more urgent with his illness. Soon he stopped dancing. When he stopped moving at all, Zosia readied herself for his death. She anticipated the relief he would feel and that she would feel for him.

But there was no relief for her when that day came. When he took his last breath and Zosia stood over him, sorrow strangled her. The loneliness was overwhelming. Her children became everything to her, but they could never fill the role of her husband, her partner. A piece of her died with Wiktor. He may not have been faithful, but he was hers.

I should have done more, she thought, though she knew she'd done all she could. He'd been Catholic, and in the end that's what killed him.

Zosia wiped droplets of tears from the half-written letter in her lap. When Wiktor died, she learned that life was disposable. Hers couldn't be. She'd come too far.

I will go on. I'll find my children. I have to.

Chapter Ten

Several days.

Two men and a woman descended the stairs, passing Zosia as she climbed. The woman wept. Behind them, Mr. Devine watched from the landing. He was either very sad or very tired, or both. "Mrs. Wilusz," he said with a sigh.

"I've written some letters, Mr. Devine." Before she touched the top step, Zosia reached into the burlap potato sack she used as purse. She pulled out a handful of envelopes, all stuffed with a variety of scavenged stationery ranging from birth announcements to ivory laid paper embossed with *Dr. Heilwig Moser, Stuttgart.* Zosia drew a line through what wasn't appropriate and wrote letters to anyone she could think of. She handed the correspondence to the director. Each envelope was labeled with a name and very rudimentary address, based on memory. Sometimes it was simply, "*Large brick building across from synagogue.*"

"I can't do anything with these." Mr. Devine's tone was apologetic. "They won't go anywhere. Hold on to them for now until the mail system becomes more stable."

"There has to be more we can do to find them." Zosia

watched him for a response.

"I'm sorry," he said in perfect Polish, "I'm trying. I'll come and find you when I hear something about your family."

"Maybe you have their names spelled wrong." Zosia tried not to sound like a beggar. "Would you mind if I looked at the paperwork again?"

"The paperwork hasn't changed since yesterday."

"What have you done since then? Have you put in any calls?"

"Mrs. Wilusz," Mr. Devine said, escorting Zosia into his office. He sank into his desk chair. "I have the proper authorities working on it. But, you have to remember, there are millions of DPs across Europe and thousands in this camp alone. Everyone is searching for their family." He sighed. "I'm trying. I'm really trying."

"I appreciate that, but maybe there's more I could do? Make some calls? I could write more letters—"

"You have to trust that we're doing all we can. I made calls and wrote letters myself. I'll continue to do it until we find your children, I promise. The best thing you can do is sign up on a repatriation list. Have you done that?"

"Oh yes. Three of them."

Mr. Devine let out an exasperated chuckle. "Okay, well, good then." He stepped toward her and put his hand on her arm, seemingly as a gesture of empathy, but she knew it was more to lead her out of his office. "You don't have to keep coming here, Mrs. Wilusz. I'll find you the minute I locate any of your children, even if it's in the middle of the night."

She gave a thin smile of thanks to Mr. Devine and walked out the door. He softly closed it behind her.

More letters. If I mail enough, some have got to go through. She descended the stairs and stepped outside into the afternoon. Then she froze.

Sturmbannführer Voss leaned against a light post across the

street. He looked right at her and lit a cigarette. He paused, a slow, sexy smile spreading onto his lips. His blue eyes tore a hole right through her.

Zosia shook her head, not trusting herself. *No, it isn't him. Petra said it wasn't Voss. He was arrested.* She dropped her eyes and hurried away toward blockhouse C-6.

Crunching footsteps followed her. Her heart stumbled and flipped and her feet quickened. A large shipment truck was parked on the street and Zosia slid beside it, hiding herself from the pedestrian traffic. The footsteps got closer, louder. Stacks of heavy wool fabric piled up around her, and she tried to melt into them, camouflaging herself between the drab blues and grays.

The footsteps passed. She peeked out. An American soldier in green fatigues snapped his gum and sauntered by with his hands stuffed in his pockets.

Sweat dripped from her temples. It was absurd to think Sturmbannführer Voss was here. He was a war criminal. The man she saw had to have been the man from the train the other day. Or no one at all—just her overactive, anxious imagination. She took deep breaths until her heart steadied.

She lifted her head, straightened her back, and tripped over a stack of khaki fabric. A short man wearing a pinstriped hat with the letters "NY" on the front glanced at her and muttered something in English while he continued unloading.

That much fabric had to be destined for something greater. She stepped through the door into the building behind the truck. Another man was inside with a pencil crushed between his teeth and a clipboard gripped in his hand. He raced around in circles, counting crates and stacks and cursing to himself about the inefficiency of it all.

Zosia peered into a room off to one side and saw a goldmine of sewing machines. All brand-new, Singer 201k models. The best there was. Their shiny ebony bodies beckoned for a piece of fabric to sink their needles into.

She'd found her home.

"Sir?" She turned to the man counting the stacks of fabric. "Are you hiring seamstresses? I'd like to apply for a job."

As if just noticing Zosia in the room, the man stopped. He pulled the chewed-up pencil out of his mouth and reached up to scratch the back of his head with it, revealing a dark circle of sweat under his arm. "Ma'am, those machines are useless without needles. So is all of this blasted wool." He pushed the pencil behind his ear and bent down to recount a pile of brown fabric. "If you can find needles," he said, "I'll put you in charge of the whole damn department."

"Thank you." Grinning, she stepped past a tipped-over pile of wool in front of the door. She thought about the possible zlotys she could earn; they may be useless, but enough of them had to amount to something. Maybe she could negotiate for pounds or American dollars. Maybe she would make enough money in a couple of months to feed her children when she got home. Maybe then they would forgive her for leaving them.

A job could also bring her coveted information. It was worth the search for needles.

—

Two weeks later, the vital sewing machine needles still hadn't materialized. She met with anyone who claimed to have contacts, but when she mentioned needles they would drop their heads.

"Nope, haven't seen them anywhere."

"Seems everyone's looking for those."

"Sorry, honey. Those are so in-demand, any sewing machine needle anywhere in Germany is guarded tighter than a Prussian princess's mickey."

"I was so close," Zosia said to Petronela as they waited for another morning train to slow to a stop. They both paused when the doors were thrown open to reveal the haunted faces of more persecuted Poles. Men and women stared out into the sunlight from under their hats and babushkas. Zosia's throat closed for a second when a thin, young woman with black hair stepped down from the boxcar. When the woman lifted her head to thank Violette for the sandwich, Zosia could see she wasn't Marisha.

"You need to talk to Czeslaw Lysek." Petronela turned in disappointment. She pulled a pack of cigarettes from the pocket on her apron, assigned to her for her new job in the kitchen. "If anyone can get your needles, he can."

"I haven't heard of him." Zosia took the cigarette Petronela handed her.

"He's new here, but I guess he has connections. Met him the other day when we needed baking soda. He seemed to pull it out of thin air within the hour." Petronela's face lightened. "Hey, you probably remember him. He arrived with the group of military prisoners from Russia a few weeks ago. He was the one with the eyes—you thought he was that German bastard Voss."

Zosia's knees buckled. She didn't respond.

Petronela didn't notice Zosia's reaction. "He's a nice enough guy. Laughs a lot. Good looking. You should talk to him, he'll find your needles. He usually spends evenings with the other former resistance soldiers. They have bonfires behind Blockhouse A-12."

"I'll do it." She tried not to let her voice shake. Obviously he wasn't Voss. Petronela met him and liked him. *He can't hurt me. I won't let him hurt me.*

—

That night she peered around Blockhouse A-12. The sun was almost set, and already the fire rose to meet the darkening sky. Bootleg schnapps flowed freely, and it seemed camp officials went out of their way to ignore the revelry behind the blockhouses.

Zosia was amazed at the transformation these POWs had made since they climbed off the train only weeks before with their broken spirits and sullen expressions. But then, the Polish people had a reputation for combating their depression with joyful drunkenness. Zosia's eyes darted from one indiscriminate face to another, trying to isolate Mr. Lysek's piercing blue stare from the other sapphire eyes darkened by dusk.

"Joining the party? Ladies always welcome." A man walked up behind her with a small bottle concealed in a paper bag, his grin obviously inebriated.

"I'd like to talk to Czeslaw Lysek," she said, pressing her back against the blockhouse wall for stability.

The man nodded, as if requests for Mr. Lysek were common. "Sure thing, wait here." He approached the fire and bent down to a man with his back to Zosia. The sitting man glimpsed behind him, nodded, and stood.

It's him. Zosia's legs begged to run, but she stood firm. *No, this man is not Voss.*

"I'm Czeslaw Lysek." He ambled toward her. "Are you looking for me?"

Zosia nodded. Even in the darkness, his eyes penetrated right through her. The blueness couldn't be contained in only the word blue. She felt seasick. The shimmering water, brighter and more intense than the vast sky it reflected. This was the whole ocean in an iris. The ocean, the sky, the clouds, and even God's heaven beyond. She was drowning.

A strange feeling of desire crowded her anxiety. It elevated her already intense unease. "Mr. Lysek, I hear you can find things. Items, you know. Things that may be hard to get by using more . . . traditional means." She avoided his stare and watched the ground.

Czeslaw bent at his knees and tilted his head to get himself between Zosia and her focused gaze. When she looked up and met his eyes, he smiled. "What are you afraid of?"

"I'm not afraid." She lifted her chin assertively. She felt like a child. *He may not be Voss, but he still can't be trusted.* "Listen, I need sewing machine needles. Can you get those? I can pay in American cigarettes. I have Belgian chocolate too. Some tin cans. Whatever you want, I'll get it."

Czeslaw rubbed the stubble on his squared chin while he thought. "That's a tough order, but I may know someone. Give me a few days." He took a tiny notebook and pencil out of his shirt pocket and made some scribbles.

Zosia pushed away the weakness simmering inside her. "I'll come back."

He shook his head. "I don't know how long it will take. Could be a week, maybe more. I'll find you." He stopped and looked up at her sideways, like a shy schoolboy wanting to invite his crush to dinner. It was pure charm. She leaned her hand against the wall of Blockhouse A-12 to balance herself. "What's your name?" he asked.

"Mrs. Wilusz. Zosia."

Czeslaw smiled, winked at her, and turned to rejoin his friends. When he walked away, she felt a strange blending of relief and disappointment.

—

The next morning Zosia knelt on the sidewalk in front of Blockhouse C-6 and dipped her hands in a pail to wash a rare pair of stockings she'd found in the donation box. Crouched over her bucket of cold, soapy water, she pulled the stockings out and wrung them just as a male voice materialized beside her.

"Lovely morning, Mrs. Wilusz."

Zosia jumped and awkwardly dropped the stockings back into the bucket.

"Even lovelier now." Czeslaw smiled. He motioned

toward the pail.

Her face flushed; she knew she was defeated. She pulled the stockings out of her bucket and dropped them into a sopping pile on her towel. She squeezed out the water, feeling the dampness meet her hands as she pushed. She couldn't think of any witty comeback, and the more she searched for words, the more they evaded her. When she looked up, she was met with Czeslaw's raised eyebrows and a broad grin. "What can I do for you, Mr. Lysek?" Her cheeks burned. "I suppose I'm not allowed any dignity?"

"Not as long as you're washing your underwear on the sidewalk," Czeslaw said with a hint of teasing in his voice. "If it helps, I think no less of you. In fact, I'm happy you wash your underwear. Too many people don't. It's just not right."

Zosia couldn't help but smile. She concentrated on her towel to save herself from catching his eyes. She'd chosen the sidewalk instead of the washroom because too many ladies were readying themselves for the day, and she didn't want to defend her treasures against wandering fingers. Czeslaw didn't say any more, so they stood in awkward silence until Zosia lifted her head again. Now in the bright light of day, Zosia could see Czeslaw's youthful good looks hidden behind years of agony and tension on his face. His dark blond hair fell casually parted on the side. And those eyes. *My God, those eyes.* She shivered.

Czeslaw pulled a small brown package out of his jacket pocket and held it out. Zosia frowned. "What's this?" She timidly took the package.

"Your needles. I thought you'd want them right away."

"But we just talked last night. How did you find them so quickly?"

Czeslaw shrugged. "I know some people. Have some friends."

Zosia stared, dumbfounded, at the package in her hands.

Something wasn't right. Needles were an impossible find, yet Czeslaw had found them. "I have your cigarettes," Zosia's voice filled with doubt. "Wait here, I'll get them." Zosia ran into the building and down the hall to her room, still clutching the damp towel and the brown package. She parted the blanket walls around her bed, grabbed a small canvas bag and stuffed in fifteen packs of American cigarettes from under her mattress.

The cigarettes were a tricky find. She'd pilfered a gauzy, purple dress from the donation box, but found the zipper torn out. She'd cut the fabric of the dress into large rectangles and sold them to a few American GIs in exchange for the cigarettes. The men were happy to take what they thought were authentic French silk scarves home for their sweethearts, and Zosia had currency to exchange.

With the needles and towel still in her hand, she hurried outside with her canvas bag and handed it to Czeslaw. "A pleasure, Mrs. Wilusz." He bowed. "Let me know if there's anything else you need. Enjoy your stockings." He winked again.

"Uh, well," Zosia stopped herself, shifting the wet towel to her other arm. "I was wondering . . ." Her face burned hotter when he locked onto her eyes. He pulled his tiny notebook and a pen from his pocket and waited, the tools of his trade poised.

"Never mind. I can't possibly . . ." There was no way she could ask this stranger—who was likely as corrupt as the black market itself—to find underwear for her. That was much too delicate, too intimate.

"Mrs. Wilusz," Czeslaw said reassuringly, "There's nothing you could request that would shock me. The other day I found menstrual pads for your roommate Iwona. I understand some things seem embarrassing, but we're all in this together. I'm here to help."

Zosia considered this. She also considered how Czeslaw knew that Iwona was her roommate. *He is only a middleman,* she told herself. *I'll never see him again after this.* She hesitantly nodded toward the towel-wrapped stockings in her hand. "This kind of thing."

A comforting smile spread across his face. "Of course. Many ladies are asking for undergarments. Very common. What size?" When Zosia stammered and turned an even darker shade of scarlet, Czeslaw closed his notebook. "Never mind. I'll guess."

She didn't know if she should try to hide her body or welcome an assessment to get an accurate size. She shifted her weight. "What would it cost? For, you know . . . a full set?"

His eyes dropped to the towel that held Zosia's stockings. "Well, nylon is difficult to find. Would you be willing to trade your stockings for something more useful?"

"Here," she said as she handed him the damp towel. "All yours. I even washed them."

Czeslaw laughed. "All the better. Worth more that way." He winked at her again, which she was learning was a sort of handshake for this man.

"Thank you, Mr. Lysek."

"Call me Czeslaw. I'm shopping for your underwear. We're friends now." He smiled and turned to walk down the street.

Zosia watched him go. She squeezed the brown package in her hands with uncertainty. She was naïve for trusting him. She turned back the paper and untied the leather string on the wallet, revealing rows and rows of sparkling, steel needles.

Chapter Eleven

One week.

"Zosia," Petronela said, her mouth an impatient line, "the black market doesn't work that way. You don't just go into the center of Schlüchtern and shop the stalls."

Zosia gently massaged the bandage covering a scissor mishap on her finger. She was embarrassed that her first day back behind a sewing machine had resulted in an injury. With her seamstresses watching, she sliced through the thick army wool and right through her finger with the sharp steel blades. She finished out the day with her cheeks flushed in shame. She was determined to make it through her second day blood-free, but it was only lunchtime. "But he was so fast with the needles."

Petronela untied her kitchen apron. "Then he already had a contact. Maybe he's used up all his ladies' underwear contacts."

Zosia made a face. She regretted trusting Czeslaw with her request. Days ticked by, and so far no brassieres, no panties had materialized. Plus, after not having her monthly bleed for some time as a result of years of hard labor, it had returned; she now needed the same items that Iwona had requested of Czeslaw. That made her irritable for a number of reasons. She thought she was done with her cycle for good, and what a blessing that would have been. Besides, there was no point in bleeding. At 35, she was much too old for babies.

"Have you heard anything yet? Any news of Eliasz, you know, through your job?"

"No one knows shit." Wanda came out of nowhere and slapped her hand down hard on the table, startling Zosia. "It was all a ruse to get us in aprons."

Zosia arched her eyebrow at Petronela's roommate, who helped herself to a cramped space next to them. Physically, Wanda was the opposite of Petronela. She was a petite woman, barely a meter and a half tall with short, curly hair that furiously hugged her scalp. However, her growling personality rivaled Petronela's most surly days. "What do you mean? I thought—"

"The story about the hospital worker who found his wife and son outside of Vienna? A load of *gówno*." Wanda plopped down on the bench across from Zosia, causing the DP next to her to slosh her coffee. "A rumor, probably from Devine himself. They only wanted to get us excited about taking their puny jobs. No, the most any of us will get out of working in the kitchen or the sewing room is a handful of useless zlotys and probably a sore back."

The three women were silent. Petronela concentrated on tearing apart her stale dinner roll.

"Petra, I trusted you," Zosia said, seething. "So this means we won't be any closer to finding our families? Why the hell did I work so hard to find those damn needles when it doesn't matter anyway?"

"Sorry, Zosia."

"Oh, fuck you, Petra." As soon as it slipped out, she wished she could take it back. Truthfully, she'd been eager to hunch over a sewing machine again, but the motivation to get her there—and to get involved with a shady character like Czeslaw—felt unfair.

Her cheeks tingled from guilty frustration. Petronela and Wanda watched her, their faces twisted to identical expressions of exasperation. Zosia crumpled her month-old Polish language newspaper in her fist. "Why the hell are my children so hard to find? Why haven't any of us heard anything, from anyone?" She tossed the paper onto the table. "If they're dead, if they're alive, I need to know—"

"Zosia," Petronela broke in, "When you have no other choice, muster the spirit of courage."

Stunned at Petronela's composure, Zosia dropped her eyes. She'd told Stefek to be brave, and she'd expected Marisha to have the courage of a woman. Yet Zosia herself couldn't find the strength to get through the days. She felt shame color her cheeks. Wanda lit a cigarette and pulled the wrinkled newspaper toward her, disinterested in the exchange.

Zosia stood and walked out of the mess hall without another word.

That night she scanned a flyer explaining the repatriation process, but her mind ruminated on what Petronela had said. *Muster the spirit of courage*. As a mother, she had to be stronger than this.

She shifted a bit in bed. The pillow was knotted and lumpy under her head, but it felt right to be uncomfortable. She'd been in the camp for almost two months, and there had been no progress in finding her children or returning to Poland. Her seamstress job wouldn't gain her better information after all, but at least it might keep her mind busy. It might allow her the courage to fight through each day.

Zosia was nearly asleep when a knock shook the door to room 21. She sat up in bed. It was odd to have anyone other than Iwona's gentlemen callers knocking this late at night.

"What do you want?" Her roommate Angelika said sharply

through the cracked door. "It's late. Well, she's asleep. No, you'll have to come by later. Well that's . . ." There was a pause. "Yeah? Okay, I'll ask her. Wait here." Zosia heard the muffled footsteps of socked feet tiptoeing across the wooden floor. "Zosia?" Angelika peeked her blonde head in between the tan, fluttering walls. "Mr. Lysek is here. He says he has something for you."

"Thank you." Zosia swung her feet off the bed. She grabbed her shabby sweater, pulled it on over her thin, cotton nightgown, and glided across the floor.

"Be careful," Angelika called after her. Zosia paused for a moment, her fears confirmed. Czeslaw was dangerous. Zosia nodded and opened the door just enough to sneak through.

Czeslaw stood in the hallway. "I'm sorry to come by so late," he said, handing her a paper bag.

She opened the bag and tilted it toward the hallway light. Inside was a burgundy dress, neatly folded. It had a ruffled collar and black buttons down the front.

The bag sat heavy in her hands for a second while she considered what to do next. Czeslaw watched her with the same schoolboy look she remembered from their first meeting. She looked just past him, avoiding his eyes. "I asked only for undergarments, that's what we agreed to. I can't accept any more."

"Please." Czeslaw held up his hands. "Everything is here, plus your 'change,' if you will. You'd be surprised at what stockings will buy."

"You don't say?" She raised her eyebrow.

For the first time in talking with him, Czeslaw seemed uncomfortable. He shifted from one foot to the other. "I'm just being a friend. You know, helping you out. If you don't like something, you can trade it. Let me know."

Zosia closed the top of the bag. *Friend?* She barely knew him. She remembered Angelika's warning. "That's kind of you. Thank you, Czeslaw. I'm sure it's all fine."

He smiled and turned to walk down the hallway. She put her hand on the doorknob to the room and watched his figure disappear into the darkness.

She felt warm. Frowning, she went inside and locked the deadbolt behind her. The expanse between the blanket walls was dark except for the glow of the lamp in her space. She slinked back to her bed and sat down, huddling close to the flickering light bulb so she could study the contents of the paper sack.

Under the burgundy dress she found two lacy, once-white brassieres and five pairs of panties in varying shades of pink and beige. She ran her hand over the lace; it was a texture she hadn't felt in years. Before even putting them on her body, these items made her feel human, even feminine. She fingered the shiny black buttons on the dress. It was nice. Pretty, but not garish. She picked up the dress by the shoulders and shook out the folds. A tiny blue velvet bag fell to the floor. She picked it up, and it felt weightless in her hand. She figured it was probably some forgotten trash the previous owner stuffed in the pocket.

There were hard lumps inside the tiny bag, so she pulled open the drawstrings to dump the contents into her hand. Two delicate pink pearls tumbled out, each with a thin metal hook imbedded into it.

She stared at the tiny spheres. *Pearl earrings? What does he think, that I'm some easy camp trollop?* Her cheeks grew hot again. She considered tossing the earrings out the window. She stood to do just that, but the light hit the lustrous surfaces in a way that made the pearls shimmer in her hand. They were lovely. She couldn't throw them away.

She would return them to Czeslaw. She would make it clear to him that he was acting inappropriately and she no longer needed his services. For shame, offering such an intimate gift. She was right to not trust him.

But, maybe he didn't know they were hidden in the dress.

Maybe they'd been concealed in the pocket and he never knew. It could be innocent.

Or, maybe he was taking a liking to her. She stared at the pearls, feeling her throat go dry. Czeslaw was handsome, but dangerous. Besides, she couldn't shake the visions of Voss when she looked at him. He was no good. She needed to keep her distance.

Her face burned. She was attracted to him. Even more reason to stay away.

The pearls rolled harmlessly in her hand. She hadn't owned anything this lovely in years, not since before Wiktor died. Maybe she deserved something nice.

No. Not to be. All her energy needed to go to finding her children, to returning to them. If she let herself have feelings for Czeslaw, it would only be a distraction. She had to leave Wildflecken at the first possible opportunity. Nothing could keep her there.

Unless he can help me. Zosia's eyebrows arched. She sat on the bed again. Maybe Czeslaw was just as skilled at gathering information as he was at trading stockings and cigarettes.

"Zosia?" The soft whisper shook her out of her thoughts, and she quickly fisted her hand around the pearls. She twisted to pretend to scratch her back, hiding the earrings as if she were a schoolgirl hiding a bottle of vodka from her mother.

She gave Angelika a guilty smile. "Yes?"

"Are you all right?" Angelika's hair shone white in the soft incandescence of Zosia's lamp. With the dark shawl around her shoulders and the glowing halo surrounding her head, Angelika looked like the Black Madonna that hung from safety pins on her wall.

"Yes, thank you. All good."

"Okay then, good night."

Angelika disappeared behind the fluttering khaki wall.

"Angelika?" Zosia said. Her roommate's head returned through the blankets. "Have you found your children?"

"My children?"

"The pictures pinned on your blankets."

Angelika dropped her head. She tiptoed into Zosia's space and sat on the foot of the bed. Zosia's hand perspired around the pearls in her grip. "They're my sister's children. They're all dead."

"Oh." Zosia's throat swelled. "I'm sorry. Do you have family you're looking for?"

She shook her head. "I had a sweetheart. We were to be married a few years ago, but he disappeared one night. I haven't heard anything since." She reached over and patted Zosia's leg. "I know you're looking for your children. Iwona might know someone who can help, she has a lot of contacts. I'd trust her before that Lysek fellow. He makes me nervous."

Both women smiled a conspiratorial grin. Iwona had contacts, and she likely slept with most of them. "Thank you. Good night, Angelika." Zosia leaned over and switched off her lamp, anxious to speak to Iwona as soon as possible. She settled into her uneven pillow and squeezed the earrings, feeling the metal hooks dig in to the sweaty skin of her palm.

They probably belonged to a Jewish woman Yes, the Jews were the only ones who could afford this kind of thing before the war. Her mind wandered for a moment to the possible former owner of the earrings, and she felt sick about the fate of that person.

A doctor's wife, she justified, firming her jaw. *A wicked doctor who refused to help the poor. He would turn them away unless they were one of his own. His wife was the type who wouldn't leave the house without her mink coat. She had piles of jewels, so many that she never even thought about these earrings.*

Zosia could see the posh woman in her mind. *Yes, she would prance past a poor Catholic mother begging on the street. She would refuse to offer a single zloty. She would let the mother's children starve.*

Knots of memory cramped her stomach. She thought of Marisha as a girl, before the war changed everything—her body still padded with the plumpness of youth and sweets, her rosy cheeks dimpled as she smiled. So different from the girl Zosia left at the Warsaw train station; she was only bones wrapped in a thin skin, fragile from hunger and emotion.

Zosia defiantly pushed the hooks of the pearls into her ears, the ancient piercings still accepting them. *They're mine now,* she told the imaginary yenta in the mink coat. *That poor, starving mother now has your pearls.* She rolled over and closed her eyes. *I wonder what they're worth. Maybe back home I can trade them for a quarter of a butchered pig.*

She wondered what Iwona knew, but then her thoughts fell to Czeslaw. How was he so good at finding things when no one else could, especially after being in camp for only a few weeks? He seemed to know everyone, and everyone knew him. Angelika was right. He was not to be trusted.

CHAPTER TWELVE

The next day, lunch.

Petronela rubbed the pearl earrings against her teeth while Zosia pushed potatoes around her plate. "They're real." Petronela frowned. "I think."

Zosia nodded. A small group of DPs squeezed next to her on the bench. An elbow jabbed Zosia in the ribs as they settled in. "Should I read anything into this?" Zosia said, lowering her voice.

Petronela shrugged and handed the pink pearls back to Zosia. "Depends. Do you want all that comes with that?"

Zosia shook her head. She only wanted to go home.

"Well then, consider it a gesture of friendship. Anything else and you're probably looking for trouble."

Zosia dropped the earrings into her pocket. "Iwona might be able to find out something. I guess she has contacts."

"Iwona doesn't know any more than the rest of us. I've heard she only has a resource for Lysol, and that's why she never gets pregnant. Though I don't think Lysol actually works at preventing babies. I think some doctors looked into it."

The thought of pregnancy in this purgatory made Zosia

shiver. She was grateful she was past that point in her life. Her head spun with what and whom to believe. Clues in camp always contradicted. Maybe it was best to wait for Mr. Devine for information, since lies about the fate of her family would be worse than the worst truth out there. "I'm sorry about yesterday, Petra."

Petronela's brow knitted. "What for?"

She drew swirls in her gravy with her fork. "I got overly emotional, I guess. You know, about finding my children."

"Zosia, that's how you are, and I love you for it." Petronela stood with her plate and fork. A handful of people converged behind her, waiting for her space at the table. "I've got to get to work. We're expecting a shipment of butter this afternoon, which means we might get it by the weekend." She smirked and walked away, and a new dinner plate took her place.

"May I sit?" A masculine voice made her jump. The group of waiting diners grumbled. Zosia looked up to see Czeslaw standing across from her where Petronela was a moment ago. Before she could protest, Czeslaw climbed into the space. He bowed his head and folded his hands. After his hasty prayer, he picked up his fork. "Everything was satisfactory with the merchandise?" He tore his bread in half.

"Yes, thank you again." She was surprised at how well the brassieres fit and decided to not think about how adept Czeslaw was at guessing her size. She shifted uncomfortably on the bench, avoiding any mention of the earrings. She changed the subject. "You know, they bake sawdust into the bread," she said.

"All the more delicious for it." He grinned.

She blinked with understanding. "You know hunger, don't you?"

"I'm sure you do, too." Czeslaw took a drink of water to wash down the bread.

She nodded. Of course she was malnourished on the Nazi farm, but her mind went to the time after Wiktor died, when any food she found went straight to her children. She would sometimes exist for days without eating so they wouldn't go hungry.

"Were you in an extermination camp?" Zosia bit into her own roll.

"In a sense." Czeslaw's face went blank. "Polish Army, Tenth Infantry. My division was captured north of Warsaw. Survivors were taken to Starobelsk in the Soviet Union." Czeslaw's jaw hardened. He turned his attention to his piece of dry chicken smothered in brown gravy.

Zosia held her breath. She'd heard rumors of how the Soviet camps treated the Polish soldiers. The level of torture almost rivaled the horrors of the extermination camps. "I'm sure you have stories," she said.

"I wish they were stories."

Zosia nodded. "I'm sorry."

"Such is war." It was clear that Czeslaw was trying to lift the load that the war had dumped on him, but she could see he was buried under years of agony. He admired the piece of meat at the end of his fork. "We used to eat grass. Actually, we loved grass. Any hint of green that would dare to pop up in the prison yard was pounced on. We would wander around the fenced yard, day in and day out, searching for the tiniest spot of green. The grass was eaten down all along the outside perimeter of the fence, as far as an arm could reach. The men with the longest arms were the most likely to survive. Grass was a delicacy to us." He put the dry chicken into his mouth, savoring a full bite of meat.

"There was this one prisoner," Czeslaw continued with a bitter laugh. "We called him The Wolf. Whenever someone in the yard dropped, he would run to him and gnaw on the guy's wrists, even if he wasn't dead yet. He'd kneel down and slurp and suck. Poor dead guy would have teeth marks up and down his forearms. I think if The Wolf had a pocket knife, he would have filleted those guys before they were even cold."

They were silent for a minute. Zosia gagged on her chicken. After she'd pushed the awful visual from her head, she said, "It's quite amazing what we'll do to survive, but for what?"

"What do you mean? You have nothing to live for?"

"Well, my children, of course." She stopped. She'd said too much.

"Tell me about your children." Czeslaw shoveled in another forkful of food.

Zosia stood. "Maybe another time. I'm due back to the sewing room. My seamstresses are waiting."

"Ah, the needles. Well, I hope to see you again soon." Czeslaw winked. Zosia smiled and stepped away, leaving the man to his lunch. She noticed the chicken bones on his plate before she left. They were picked clean, not only of meat, but also of tendons, gristle, even the smaller connecting bones. She'd never seen anyone, even the most starved, clean a chicken bone so perfectly.

A shiver ran down her spine. Maybe the chicken bones reminded her of poor Mr. Wolf. Or possibly Czeslaw probed too close by asking about her children. It wasn't attraction. It couldn't be. She wouldn't let it be.

Chapter Thirteen

September, 1945.

Zosia awoke with a start and reached for the man's watch on her bedside table. The welfare director had given it to her when she started her job, with the hope she could keep the seamstresses on a schedule during the day. With bleary eyes she squinted through the cracked crystal that obscured the minute hand: seven minutes after two in the morning. She rolled over to go back to sleep when she heard chattering voices outside.

Drunks. She pulled her musty gray blanket around her. *Go to bed and sleep it off, gentlemen.*

But then, a crash. She sat up in bed, her heart racing in her chest. Kasia's light flipped on in her corner, creating a round glow against the ceiling.

Zosia slid out of bed. She parted the wall of blankets and met her elderly roommate's huge eyes. Both women stared at each other, listening.

Another crash, followed by loud cries and a gunning engine.

Kasia hobbled across the room to Zosia's space, where they pried open the window and together strained their ears for answers. A rumble outside made them jump.

"Maybe thunder, a storm coming," Zosia said. She knew it wasn't a storm.

"Maybe." Kasia's gravely voice trembled.

They both jumped again when the front door rattled open and Angelika flew into the room, her cheeks flushed from excitement, her neck slick with sweat from her sprint across camp. "Hide everything," she said, flicking off Kasia's light. "They're raiding black market merchandise and arresting everyone."

"Who is? Why?" Zosia pulled open the blanket wall so hard it fell to the ground.

"The Americans," Angelika said, sarcasm tinting her voice. "Because they're here to keep the peace and help us, remember?"

The walls danced as the women scurried. In the darkness, rugs were pulled under mattresses, clothing stuffed into drawers. Cigarettes were stashed inside pillows, fluffed to appear deceptively luxurious.

The thumping of a crutch preceded Iwona, who stumbled through the doorway on Angelika's heels, reeking of vodka. "Shit, ladies." Her face glowed in the bluish moonlight from the window. "We're losing our best traders."

"Where are they taking them?" Zosia's worry for Czeslaw surprised her. She felt fevered as she hid her few smuggled items.

No one answered. The riot outside the window drew closer, but some things couldn't be hidden. Iwona leaned on her crutch and tossed a tablecloth over the radio. Angelika and Zosia pushed the nicer furniture into Kasia's corner space, hoping the elderly woman would be the least accusable and their treasures would be safe.

Zosia removed the pearl earrings from her dresser drawer and stuffed them into the toe of her shoe.

A loud crack echoed through the forest outside. "*Psiakrew.*" Angelika cursed and stepped over Zosia's fallen blanket wall. She leaned against the window, pushing her pale hair behind both ears. "That was a gunshot."

Zosia felt vomit slink up her throat. "Why? Why do they care about who's trading?"

"Because they're not getting a cut," Angelika said. "Or because some decorated general didn't get his black market antacids. Who the hell knows?"

Outside, a handful of American GIs hurried around the corner of the neighboring blockhouse. All her anxieties crushed her at once. Zosia could see the Gestapo guard who held Antoni at the train station. She felt Tadeusz suffocating her under his weight as he pounded into her. She could hear the crack of the gun in the quarries when someone dropped from fatigue. She could feel Herr Voss's firearm against her temple, and she saw his eyes pierce her—even now—just past the steel barrel of his pistol.

"They won't take me. They won't take my things." Iwona was courageous in her intoxication. She limped into Zosia's space and crowded at the window with Zosia, Angelika and Kasia. Then she flung a brass teapot out the window and hit one of the men on the shoulder. He fell back, clutching his arm.

"Jesus, Iwona." Angelika sounded frightened and impressed all at once. "Good idea."

"I don't think . . ." Zosia spoke to no one as the women hurried to the stove to gather up all of their pots, pans, and plates. "We shouldn't provoke them—"

"Fucking pigs!" Iwona hollered. She launched a beer stein out the window. The women threw everything they could grab at the men on the street. Even Kasia proved to have decent aim. Zosia watched, scared of getting involved. In her mind, she could see each of her roommates hung for war crimes.

Residents of other floors and blockhouses followed Iwona's lead. Toasters, tin cans, pieces of rocking chairs, and even a black wig sailed through the air toward the soldiers.

To Zosia's astonishment, the men retreated, leaving behind

a trail of bartered personal goods littering the street below. The residents cheered, and Iwona and Angelika toasted with a stolen bottle of sherry.

Zosia collapsed onto her bed, exhausted, though she hadn't thrown a thing. She couldn't feel joy. They'd won the battle, but she was troubled. The victory was too easy. Either those soldiers were cowards or they would be back, angry and more determined than ever. She knew that next time, a flying teapot would not win the battle.

Chapter Fourteen

Days later.

A cloud of cigarette smoke hung in the stagnant autumn air over the seamstresses. Zosia and the other women stared at the paper flyers in their hands. The black market raid of several days prior had everyone shaken, so officials passed around propaganda to explain the dangers of unscrupulous trading and why the United States and British governments condemned it. "Law-abiding residents have nothing to fear," it said. It did little to quell nerves, since no one was completely within the law. Not even the officials who'd written the flyers.

Some women clucked about the injustice of it, but soon the chatter turned to more usual topics. Younger women discussed the handsome prospects in the bachelors' buildings, ways to avoid pregnancy, and how they could con the authorities into being chosen for immigration to Canada. The older women debated repatriation, rumors about lost children, and the tall tale about the outrageous price of lard in Poland.

Zosia kept an eye on the cracked watch wrapped around her wrist. She crumpled the flyer in her hand, unable to disregard the raids and trust the system like she was being asked to do. The system had never helped her. "Ladies," she said at half past ten, "break is over, let's get back to work."

Something between a sigh and a groan emitted from the women, but each stubbed out her cigarette, brushed off her hands and went inside to return to the overalls and coats they were making. Half would be for residents, a quarter for administrators and guards, and the rest Zosia and the other ladies would siphon out to personally trade later. Zosia took a last look around to sort her workers from the milling pedestrians and stepped up to enter the building. She didn't pay any attention to a rumbling motorcycle until it stopped nearby. A camp policeman tipped his hat, and she stiffened. Her first instinct was to block the entrance and protect her needles, but a look closer revealed Czeslaw in a smart uniform. He smiled from atop the captured Nazi BMW motorcycle.

"That's some uniform. Am I to expect there is a naked policeman somewhere in camp?" She felt strangely relieved that he was alive and well after the raid.

Czeslaw's smile grew, and he chuckled. "Camp police, here to keep the peace. Today's my first day."

"Well good, I was worried." She bit her tongue, but it was too late. Czeslaw's eyebrow arched in appreciation. "I mean, you're a policeman?"

"You can't be taken prisoner when you're the one guarding the prison." Czeslaw's grin was wicked.

Zosia frowned. In Wildflecken, there was no good or bad—only shades of existence. "Well, congratulations," she said. She noticed his hat was stitched with the words "Durzyn Police," but his brass badge said "Wildflecken Police." The camp couldn't even decide on its name. Though, through all of its contradictions, the uniform made Czeslaw even more handsome. For a moment she forgot she had a roomful of restless seamstresses and piles of waiting fabric.

Czeslaw's smile took over his face. He nodded toward the door. "And your ladies? Are they behaving? How are the needles holding up?"

"Very well. In fact, I need to get back." She put her hand on the knob. The click and hum of the Singers warbled behind the door.

"Of course." Czeslaw winked. "I'm wondering, though, if you would join me for a walk this evening? Might be nice to have some fresh air after breathing this exhaust all day." He patted the motorcycle tank.

"No, thank you. I don't think that's a good idea."

His smile flattened. He glanced over his shoulder, lowering his voice. "I have some information you should know. About the raid."

Her insides trembled. "Oh, well then, I suppose."

"I'll stop by after supper, maybe six thirty." Czeslaw turned the key on the BMW, and it snarled to life. In an instant he rode off, not giving her a chance to change her mind.

—

That evening, Zosia waited on the front step of Blockhouse C-6 wearing the burgundy dress and pearl earrings. Her palms broke into a sweat when Czeslaw walked up, now out of uniform but still just as handsome. Her attraction to him scared her. His merciless eyes shook her with a dangerous excitement. She lifted her chin. *Stay strong.*

"You look lovely." Czeslaw leaned in to kiss her cheek. She tried not to blush. "And you're enjoying the earrings. I'm glad."

She'd worn them to find out for sure if they were an intentional or accidental gift. His confirmation embarrassed her. She worried that by accepting his gift, she was condoning his advances. "How was your first day at work?" she asked, changing the subject.

"No murders or fires today, so I'll call it a success. Just found one young man stealing extra loaves of bread from Mess 1. I let him keep half of what he took, but made him return the rest and promise to not do it again." Czeslaw smiled. "I'm sure I'll see him tomorrow with twice as many loaves."

A handful of American soldiers passed on the street. They clawed at their breast pockets for their Lucky Strikes and laughed at each other's one-liners. A large group of children followed behind them. The soldiers always carried Hershey's bars in their pockets for the children, and once the Polish youth got a taste for the sweet American chocolate, the men became Pied Pipers to every youngster in camp. The children didn't care about black market raids or corruption within the ranks; they wanted candy, and would chase down Lucifer himself for it.

Zosia watched the children, her heart heavy. She wondered if Stefek would have followed them around. *Without a doubt*, she thought. At four years old he'd offered to clean their entire house just for an extra slice of cheesecake. His sweet tooth followed him as he grew. Stefek would have loved a Hershey's bar.

Czeslaw steered their walk, balancing them on the edge between the forest and the town. They idly chatted about the people in camp, the weather, the careless paintings of the Passion in the chapel.

From the hill where Wildflecken was nestled, Zosia scanned the Bavarian forest below them. A sea of green shimmered in the setting sun, flecked with the browns and yellows that signaled the approaching autumn. The valley was bathed in a fiery golden light. In town, row after row of whitewashed blockhouses and mess buildings glowed bright orange before dulling to mauve when the sun fell below the hazy Rhön Mountains in the distance. Zosia imagined winter, the world below covered in a blanket of white. She shivered. She had to believe she would be home by then, but the cold was approaching fast.

As they rounded the athletic fields, the main streets of the camp again came into focus. From a short distance Zosia could watch the crowded busyness of a camp evening. People everywhere were engaged in all sorts of activities: walking, smoking, fighting, kissing. Zosia had once heard of Times Square in New York City; she imagined that Wildflecken was a sort of backwards version of that, filled with ragged, homeless people hurrying nowhere. Vagabonds stumbling over the employed, instead of the other way around.

They paused next to a beech tree. "Here," Czeslaw said, kicking at the dirt. "Right here."

"What?" Zosia smiled. "Are you a pirate? Is there a chest of gold under the dirt?"

Czeslaw's face stayed stoic. "If you were to dig, you'd find a decorated Nazi uniform a few feet below us."

Her stomach clenched. "How do you know?"

"I put it there."

She turned her back to him to hide her fear. She couldn't fault him for killing a Nazi, but his cavalier attitude about it scared her. A decomposed soldier, leaving only his uniform behind. In whatever form it was, no matter how deserved, Czeslaw was capable of murder.

He kept kicking at the ground. Guilt drew him back, she knew it. She looked toward town to avoid Czeslaw, and she saw a man in front of Mess 2 watching them. A deeper tremble scurried up her spine. The man patted the top of his head, held up two fingers and dragged his heel through the dirt. Czeslaw pulled his earlobe. He took out his tiny notebook and made a few scratches with his pencil.

Zosia was jittery. "You said you had information?" When the sky darkened, she didn't want to be alone in the woods with a murderer and revered black marketeer. She wanted to run back to town, to the comfort of her roommates and Petronela.

Czeslaw pushed the notebook into his pocket and pulled a yellowing leaf down from the beech tree, twisting it between his finger and thumb. "It was a raid on black market items, like the officials claim, but they were looking for something specific, searching out certain nefarious traders. There's been deals on some bad things, I guess."

"What kind of bad things? What were they looking for?"

He shook his head. "It doesn't matter. They didn't find it anyway. I just wanted you to know that I'm not involved." He gave her a quick glance. "I don't want you to be scared away by what happened."

"Scared away?" She frowned to herself. He thought the raid was the reason she was cool to him. How very arrogant. If he could be presumptuous, so could she. "Tell me, Czeslaw," she said, her voice biting, "what does your wife think of your dealings here with the Germans? Or are you forever the crafty bachelor?"

Czeslaw chuckled to himself. He reached into his pocket and produced a photograph. A woman in a dark dress sat on a wicker chair, flanked by a little boy on one side and a little girl on the other.

Zosia's stomach sank at the sight of the woman, then sank further from guilt. Maybe this woman was dead, and she'd just used her as ammunition against Czeslaw. She took the picture from him and softened. "This is your family?"

"This is Henryk, my son." Even with his stern expression, the boy was a miniature version of Czeslaw. He wore short pants, lace-up boots, and a single-breasted jacket with too-short sleeves. "He is nine now. He was five when I left. Such a bright boy. He studies everything. Every little pebble, every blade of grass, every moth's wing holds wonderful secrets for him to discover. That boy, with his little mind always working . . . he'll be a doctor someday, or a scientist. Something important.

"Janina is my daughter, she's six," Czeslaw said, and Zosia

looked at the little girl with the bobbed hair and tentative grin. "She was a baby when I left, barely two years old, but she's my darling *dziewczynka.* I remember her starting to walk. Every time she fell down, she would giggle and pull herself up again. She refused to cry. She had no fear." Czeslaw fell peaceful, and Zosia stole a glance to see him stare lovingly at the picture. "She is my light."

Zosia could feel the love brimming in Czeslaw for his children, and it melted her. She thought no more about the dead Nazi; after all, Czeslaw was a soldier, his job was to kill Nazis. She Instinctively reached over to take his hand but stopped before their fingers met. He grabbed her hand anyway and held it with a gentle squeeze. It was large and strong and felt warm against the coolness of the forest air. Zosia let go. Her heart pounded in her ears.

Zosia studied the woman in the picture. Her hands resting in her lap, the woman sat on the chair with stiff discomfort. Her expression was one of both emptiness and resilience. Zosia searched for a kinship with this other *matka*—another woman raising children alone without their father somewhere in Poland—but instead she could only feel sourness toward her. Shame overwhelmed her.

She turned the photograph over in her hand. Sloppy handwriting spelled out, *"1943. Franciszka with Janina, 4 and Henryk, 7. Much love, Pawel."*

Zosia waited for an explanation of Franciszka, but none followed. She asked instead about the photograph itself. "You said Janina was two when you left, but in this picture she is four. How did you get this?"

"My brother. He sent it to me."

Zosia stopped walking, hope erupting in her heart. "You've been in touch with your family? How? Do you have a source?"

He shook his head. "I have some friends, but in this case I got lucky. It came to me earlier this summer, when I was still at the DP camp in Bamberg. One day a relief worker brought me the envelope. It was addressed to *Czeslaw Lysek, Polish Army*. That's it."

She hoped the desperation didn't show in her voice. He was much better networked than she was. "How? How did it find you?" Her voice dropped to a whisper. "Please, I need to know. Did you write letters? I have a pile of letters I've written—"

"And that Devine fellow told you not to send them, right? They have one like him in every camp—an overworked director whose job is to link up thousands of desperate mothers and husbands and brothers with each other." Czeslaw sighed. "Unfortunately, he's right. Anything sent through the post now is just floating around out there, lost in the German mountains. Mail is not a priority where it isn't completely broken." He looked at her. "If I know Pawel, he sent this the day it was taken, more than two years ago. It ambled around the continent for years before it came to me."

Czeslaw looked out through the trees toward the Bavarian horizon, now a dark shadow against the waning orange and purple sky. "I cried when I received it. Until then, I didn't know if Henryk and Janina were alive. I hoped, but of course, we never know. Now, I can hold them here in my hand." He motioned toward the photograph that still rested between Zosia's fingers. "They are alive, and they are waiting for me."

Zosia's hand shook when she returned the photograph to him. They strolled in silence while Zosia wondered if there was a letter out there waiting for her too—a letter that would arrive one day after months or years bouncing around a devastated postal system.

Curiosity overtook Zosia. She had to know about the mysterious woman in the photograph. "Tell me about their mother."

"Franciszka is my wife." Czeslaw's voice was flat and

emotionless and was followed only by their feet crunching on the damp leaves and twigs.

"I'm sure you miss her very much."

He didn't answer. After a few minutes, Czeslaw cleared his throat. "It's your turn. Tell me about your family. Where is your husband?"

Zosia felt Czeslaw's hand against her back, leading her through the tangle of tree roots and fallen branches. She didn't wriggle away. She missed the feeling of a strong arm around her. She was also becoming more and more certain that he could help her. She put aside her distrust. "Dead."

"Oh, I'm sorry. Germans?"

She shook her head. "Jews."

"The Jews killed your husband?"

"They didn't save him," Zosia said with a sigh "Wiktor died of tuberculosis several years ago, shortly after the occupation started. When he fell sick, I ran to every doctor in town and begged for help. I offered all of our money, and money we didn't have, to every one of them. They all refused to see him. All of the doctors in my town were Jewish, and by then they were only helping other Jews. They wouldn't even give me medicine to take to him. They didn't want to waste it. One even said to me, 'I'm sorry he's not Jewish, then I could help.'" Zosia shook her head. "I know they felt anxious by the occupation. We all did. I know they felt they needed to huddle together, to protect their own. They could have helped him, but they didn't. They let my husband suffer.

"After he passed, we had nothing. I tried to take food from the trash behind the Jewish restaurants in town to feed my children, but the Jews would chase me away. I wasn't a thief." Her voice was resolute. "I was only trying to feed my children."

"Of course you were," Czeslaw said, agreeing with the proper amount of anger and compassion. "I'm so sorry."

Zosia nodded. "A couple of years after Wiktor died, we found my son Antoni had contracted the disease."

"Oh my God, your son." Czeslaw said and made the sign of the cross. "Please tell me he survived."

"I don't know. He was sick when I left. The Gestapo tried to take him, but I found him and took his place on the train."

Czeslaw stopped walking and turned to Zosia, a mixture of shock and fascination on his face. "You volunteered yourself in place of your ill son? You're a brave woman."

She didn't feel brave, but she did feel hope for the first time in a long time. The tiny voice inside her questioning Czeslaw's intentions fell mute. "I'm trying to find them. Marisha is my daughter. She was seventeen when I left, nineteen now. Antoni is my middle son, he's fourteen. Stefek is the youngest at eleven. I left them all alone. I don't know if they are dead or alive. I have to find them. I have to." She looked up at Czeslaw. "Do you know of anyone? Maybe your contacts? Is there anyone that can help?" She was aware of the hysteria in her voice, but she couldn't stop it. Her body trembled.

Sturdy arms wrapped gently around her. She melted into them, giving up the last of her resistance. He was a married man, but it didn't mean he couldn't be a friend. For the first time in many years, she felt safe and protected.

"There is someone," he said.

Chapter Fifteen

October, 1945.

The air was sharp in Zosia's lungs as she pulled the smoke through her cigarette and ran back to Blockhouse C-6 from Blockhouse C-2, where the toilets were not broken. She pulled her fur-lined hat—one Czeslaw had found for her in exchange for a dozen spools of silk thread—down over her ears and trotted across the cobblestones.

Autumn had already given up its fight. It was cold, and she shivered against the evening wind. She never expected to still be in Wildflecken when the days shortened and the air thinned out. She wondered if Stefek and Antoni were getting to bed early enough for school, if Marisha was helping them with their arithmetic. She wondered if there were any schools left. She wondered if they were still alive.

The shrill call of a gray partridge came from around the corner of her building, startling her. *The signal.* She surveyed the empty street and followed the sound, darting around the whitewashed cinder block wall.

In the moonlit darkness, she only recognized Violette because the woman couldn't help but glow. Her blond hair fell in soft waves around her shoulders, and she wore a man's coat that looked feminine by the sultry way it draped around her. A cigarette between her cherry lips smoldered in the same way her steamy amber eyes did.

During the day, Violette was a starched symbol of Western rescue and recovery efforts, smiling her welcome and handing out sandwiches to the bruised and brittle as they descended from the trains. But by night, Violette was Mata Hari.

Violette peered at Zosia. "Wilusz?"

Zosia nodded. "Mr. Lysek said I should speak to you."

Violette shook her head and held up her hand. "*Non, non.*"

Puzzled, Zosia opened her mouth to speak, but nothing came out. Did she misunderstand Czeslaw?

The blonde motioned into the darkness with her cigarette. "*Attendez.* Wait."

Zosia leaned against the wall. She stubbed out her own cigarette, and Violette took a sexy puff on hers. The two women who didn't share a language stood and waited. For what, Zosia wasn't sure. Answers? Arrest? Death? Zosia trembled from nerves and cold.

Both women swung their heads toward a quick pattern of jogging footsteps. Out of breath, Lottie joined the women against the white wall. She whispered something to Violette, who nodded. Then Lottie turned to Zosia. "I'm only here to translate. I'm not a part of this. Do you understand?"

"Yes." Zosia knew information was just as illegal and potentially dangerous as the wristwatches and citrus fruits that changed hands in town.

There was a dead lull. Violette and Lottie waited for Zosia to speak first, their stares burning holes into her skin.

"Czeslaw Lysek says you may be able to help me find my children." Zosia kept eye contact with Violette as Lottie translated Polish to French for them.

"Tell me who they are and where they might be." Lottie turned to Zosia and spoke for Violette.

Zosia recounted details of her children. Violette didn't take any notes. Her only movement was her eyes flitting back and forth from Lottie to Zosia.

When Zosia was finished, she waited. Violette narrowed her eyes and spoke. Her voice sounded like delicate fingers brushing upper register piano keys, though her words were firm and straightforward.

Lottie tried to keep up while Violette tinkled and plinked. "I may be able to help you. I have connections that I can't disclose. I've been able to find people, but I'll warn you, it is not always good news. I do not censor what I learn, and I get the information to you through official means if I can. My contacts are truthful, but it is up to you whether or not you choose to trust them. Or me, for that matter. But, before I am able to make requests from my sources, I will need payment."

Violette, Zosia, and Lottie all fell quiet. Zosia naïvely hadn't thought of payment. She floundered, "I have some American cigarettes. I can also get a few spools of thread."

Lottie dropped her shoulders. "That's not going to work." She didn't bother to consult with Violette. "She requires cash. You have to understand, what she is doing is dangerous." Violette watched their exchange with an expression of feigned interest. "I know Violette, and thread isn't enough."

"It's silk thread . . ."

"Do you have cash?"

"I have Zlotys."

Lottie paused. "How much?"

Zosia did a quick calculation in her head of what she'd earned as head seamstress. "Maybe two hundred."

Lottie rambled something to Violette, who vehemently shook her head. "*Non, non, ce n'est pas. Non. Zloty, non. Dollars*

Américains." Upset, Violette's voice turned from a tinkle into a rattle as she spoke in her native tongue.

"Zlotys are worthless," Lottie translated the obvious to Zosia. "Violette only accepts American dollars. Any European currency is too unstable."

Zosia didn't dare admit she didn't have what they needed. "What else can I do? Please, I need help." Zosia would open her own veins if necessary.

Lottie rattled off a few quick words to Violette, who pursed her lips and continued to shake her head. "I'm sorry," Lottie said to Zosia. "If you get cash, then we can talk, but Violette will not barter simple countryside goods for this information."

Violette uttered a terse "*bonsoir*" and disappeared around the corner of the building with Lottie fast on her heels.

Zosia dragged herself back to room 21. She briefly considered robbing one of the American GIs but thought better of it. She doubted any of them carried much cash, anyway. Goods were king in Wildflecken to everyone except the French double agent.

Iwona and Angelika sat at a small table, playing cards and sipping *nalewka* when Zosia entered the room. She shuffled past them and disappeared into the blanket walls where she fell to her bed.

"Zosia, join us for a hand?" Angelika asked from across the room. When Zosia didn't answer, Iwona appeared where Zosia's blankets parted. She seemed mostly sober, which was out of character. Iwona leaned on her crutch and folded her arms, waiting.

It was difficult for Zosia to pretend to sleep when Iwona stood a meter away staring at her. Zosia sat up and flicked on her light. "Where can I find American dollars, Iwona?"

The color drained from her roommate's face. "You've been to see the Partridge."

"I don't—"

"Be careful, Zosia," Iwona said. "The black market is one thing, but there's a lot more danger out there, and you never know who's involved."

Zosia stared at her roommate. Though her legs were weak and the crutch kept her upright, her arms and shoulders flexed with strength. "You know things, don't you?"

"I don't know anything."

"I've heard you might. That you have contacts."

"Oh, Jesus, Iwona. Tell her." Angelika's impatient voice carried through the blankets.

Iwona scowled. There were no secrets when your lives were separated by only tan wool. She limped over and sat on Zosia's bed. "I might be able to help you. But it's not safe." She lowered her voice further. "Not even Angelika really knows. She thinks I'm trading Listerine and spermicides."

"Can you help me?"

"I was able to track down my uncle. He's not well, but he's alive. We've exchanged letters. I don't want anyone to know, because my sources are sensitive." She leaned back and stretched her weak leg. "If I help you, will you help me?"

"Of course. Anything."

Iwona nodded. "I'll see what I can do. But no promises." She stood. "And please, Zosia, stay away from the Partridge. And stay away from whoever sent you to her. Nothing but bad news there."

Zosia knew she'd told Czeslaw too much. She flicked off her light and rolled over. Iwona returned to her cards. "Pair of kings," Zosia heard her say through the blankets.

—

The next morning, Czeslaw found Zosia in Mess 2 and helped himself to a seat across from her. In a voice barely above a whisper, Zosia sliced through the rumble of the breakfast crowd to explain what happened with Violette.

"She wouldn't help?" He folded his arms and let out his breath in a slow, whistling sigh. "That's too bad. I didn't expect that. American dollars are hard to find." He ran his fingers through his hair. "I suppose that's why she wants them. Word has gotten out that she has sources." Czeslaw leaned forward and reached for Zosia's fingers. "I'm sorry."

Zosia didn't take his hand. "It's fine. It's better to not be involved. Wouldn't want to be arrested in the next raid, anyway. I'll wait for Mr. Devine." She could feel tears burning inside her, but she didn't let them fall.

"I wish there was more I could do," Czeslaw said, his brow wrinkled in concern. "I don't trust anyone else who offers intelligence on the black market. You can't believe most of the whispers. Clothing, cameras, stockings, cigarettes—those things I can see and feel. If I request a camera, I get a camera. I can blow off the dust, check to make sure it works. Information, though . . ." He shook his head. "Words can too easily be lies."

"I understand." Zosia picked at her thumb to keep her tears in check. "I just hope Mr. Devine can find them. In the meantime, I'll write more letters. If I write enough, one will get through. Someone knows something." She didn't tell him about Iwona. It wasn't his business. Iwona said Czeslaw wasn't to be trusted, and Czeslaw said the same about Iwona.

Somehow, Zosia had to find her children herself, and not be killed in the process.

"Mr. Lysek," Petronela said as she walked up to them. She slapped Zosia on the shoulder in a good-natured *hello*. "A couple of requests?"

"Of course, Mrs. Kloc." He pulled out his tiny notebook.

"Some of the same. Pork lard for sure, and we need a new sharpening stone. Also, a challenge, I'm afraid. Vanilla extract."

"Oh, that's excellent news." Czeslaw's smile widened.

"Nothing bad can ever come from vanilla."

Petronela rolled her eyes and wiped her hands on her apron. "Just wait. The cook will find a way to ruin it." She turned to Zosia and crinkled her brow in concern. "My friend, what's the matter?"

Zosia took a breath, but when her eyes fell to Czeslaw's, he shook his head. Dealings with the Partridge had to be kept in the strictest confidence. "It's nothing new. Just trying to muster my spirit of courage." Zosia smiled, repeating Petronela's wise words.

"Of course." She squeezed Zosia's shoulders with her arm, crushing her. "Soon. We have to believe we'll hear soon." She nodded to Czeslaw and returned to the kitchen.

When Petronela was out of earshot, Czeslaw looked up and met Zosia's eyes. "I'll take your letters into town to mail for you," he said. "I only hope they get somewhere and don't sit in a bag in Frankfurt forever."

She smiled in gratitude. She knew it was probably futile, but she had to keep trying. Any one day spent idle could be the one opportunity missed. She couldn't accept the notion that her children were lost forever. Somewhere, there was an answer.

CHAPTER SIXTEEN

December, 1945.

The residents of Wildflecken bustled to stay ahead of the massive snowdrifts and blinding ice storms that were expected with winter upon them. The sewing machines clattered well into the evening most nights to keep up with the need for warm garments. Zosia usually fell into bed already asleep, exhausted from work, rumors, and worry, her fingers stiff from sewing and writing unread letters.

"Petra?" Zosia's boots crunched along the road as they followed the whistle of the incoming train. "Has there been no news about Eliasz?"

"Nothing."

"Have you spoken to Czeslaw at all?"

Petronela clumped along, her voice surrounded by puffs of white steam against the frigid air. "No."

"Why not?"

"People aren't packages of butter."

"So, you'll wait for official word from Mr. Devine?"

Petronela sniffled against the cold. "That's the only way we know for sure."

"Iwona said she found her uncle."

"Iwona's full of shit."

Zosia stopped and turned to her. "Why do you say that?"

"Zosia," Petronela said with a sigh, "Iwona told you to stay away from Czeslaw, didn't she?" Zosia nodded. "Figures. She's been trying to get Czeslaw into bed since he arrived here."

"Jesus." Zosia's stomach sank with a mix of envy and relief. "Well, she has nothing to worry about with me. If she wants Czeslaw, I'm not going to stand in her way."

"Just be careful, Zosia. Rumors are that Iwona spreads false information like she spreads crabs."

Rumors about rumors. Zosia's head spun. Though waiting for Mr. Devine was tortuous, maybe Petronela was right. Besides, Petronela was the only person in camp that Zosia knew she could trust.

—

Christmas approached, and with it came a bittersweet melancholy among the residents of camp. No one was where they wanted to be, but they were still alive. They were cold, lonely, and uncomfortable, but for the most part, they weren't being beaten or overly starved. They'd lived to witness another celebration of the birth of Jesus. Who knew where they would all be next year and whether they could expect better or worse.

"Mrs. Bankowski." It was a frosty morning only days before Christmas. Zosia greeted her seamstresses as they shook off their babushkas and kicked the packed snow off of their boots. "Miss Tkacz, Mrs. Jurczyk. Oh, Mr. Devine!" Her stomach vaulted into her throat at the sight of the director and the stack of papers and folders under his arm.

"Good morning, Mrs. Wilusz, may I have a moment?"

Zosia broke into a sweat in the cold room. Her children were found. She followed Mr. Devine into the hall and stood, shaking. Sitting on the bottom step of the stairs, he arranged the files on his lap and shuffled through them. When he located Zosia's folder, he licked his thumb and flipped through the papers in slow motion. Zosia lowered herself onto a stool. Her throat closed as if a noose squeezed around her neck. She was frozen, her huge eyes intent the director.

"The UNRRA has taken over the camp," he said. "That's the United Nations Relief and Rehabilitation Administration. We were hoping this would happen, because it would organize all of the camps under one . . ." He looked up at Zosia, who was lightheaded from holding her breath. He softened his voice. "All this means to you right now is that some information opened up. Your family appeared in the files Violette handed me this morning."

Zosia was shocked. Violette came through after all, even though Zosia couldn't pay. A surge of gratitude nearly knocked her over.

"The short of it is," he said, "I have good news and unfortunately bad news." He pulled a paper out of the stack and tilted his head back to study it through the bottom part of his bifocals. "The good news is that Marisha Wilusz married Maxim Hirsch. We found a marriage license for them dated earlier this year." He paused and studied the paper. "February second, 1945."

Before I was even released. Even though Zosia had encouraged Marisha to marry Maxim, she recoiled at the thought of her daughter being saddled with unhappiness for the rest of her life. She blamed herself for every minute of Marisha's sadness. *Dear God, help that beautiful girl find peace and strength.*

"Are you all right, Mrs. Wilusz?"

Pulling her tear-heavy eyes up to meet his, she remembered this was supposed to be the good news. She smiled in a way that she hoped looked sincere. "Yes, of course. Does it say where they are? Are they still in Minsk Mazowiecki?"

Mr. Devine searched his papers. "It doesn't say. Many

of these lists come from Germany, but a few have come from Poland, too. Sometimes even Czechoslovakia and Hungary. This one isn't specific."

Zosia nodded. Her thoughts went to Antoni and Stefek. There was bad news coming. She prepared herself for a statement of death. "And the bad news?"

Mr. Devine counted down several sheets of paper in his stack until he found the one he was looking for. "Antoni Wilusz is listed as deceased, Mrs. Wilusz. The date of his death was September eighth, 1943. He died of tuberculosis and is buried in the cemetery in Minsk Mazowiecki."

Next to his father. Zosia had braced herself for this news, but it still took her breath away. Dead for more than two years, since shortly after she took his place as a prisoner. She rubbed her hands together and rocked on her stool. *Antoni. My sweet boy.*

She tried to give Mr. Devine a brave smile, but instead she sobbed loudly, spitting saliva all over her lap. Her tears stung behind her eyes until they overflowed.

It wasn't supposed to be this way. Marisha, Antoni, and Stefek were supposed to have had the childhood that Zosia didn't. A present father. A loving mother. Siblings who were allies—loyal and supportive. And alive.

The director watched her. "I'm sorry." She nodded and pulled herself upright again on her seat. He handed over his handkerchief; she blew her nose into it and passed it back. He patted her knee. "You keep that, Mrs. Wilusz."

She gripped the handkerchief in her fist. *Antoni is with his father,* she reminded herself. Taking a deep breath, she tried to regain composure. *Wiktor can watch after him. Maybe they would go fishing, like they used to.* She wasn't sure if there was fishing in Heaven, but if there actually was a Heaven, there had to be. She took another deep breath. Then another. Antoni had been painfully sick. That was all over now. She felt a hesitant peace.

She watched the man in front of her stuff papers into his file folders. "Thank you for your hard work, Mr. Devine." Her voice trembled. "What did you find about Stefek?"

Mr. Devine's stare was empty. He stopped with his papers and looked blankly at Zosia. "Stefek?"

"My youngest son, Stefek. He would be eleven. No, now he'd be twelve. He just had a birthday." She felt anxious again. How could he have forgotten when she stopped in his office almost every day? How could Violette forget her youngest son?

"Of course, Stefek." Mr. Devine made a feeble attempt to page through his paperwork one more time. "We've found no record of him yet. There's no trace of a death certificate, which is good news. Of course, if it was a death camp, there wouldn't be." Mr. Devine stopped short and cleared his throat when Zosia gasped. He softened his voice. "Mrs. Wilusz, since we found your other children, I'm sure it was an oversight. I'll look into it. Chances are good that Stefek is fine."

"When can I return? When will they open Poland up to its citizens?"

"Repatriation will begin in early February." He pulled a yellow piece of paper from the stack. "I don't have an exact date for you, but soon, for certain. March at the latest. Unless we're snowed in here, that will certainly delay—"

"Make sure I'm on the first train," Zosia said. "Make sure I'm in the first car of the first train going back."

"Of course, Mrs. Wilusz."

Zosia wondered if he told all of the desperate mothers in camp the same thing. She thanked Mr. Devine again and returned to the sewing room.

She couldn't think. Her thread knotted and broke. Her mind filled with a lonely headstone heralding her son's name and two dates, the second of which she never wanted to see. When she tried to not think about her poor boy's death, her thoughts turned to her still-missing son and her sad, abused daughter. She imagined Marisha's wedding portrait: Maxim standing proudly in his uniform flanked by his new wife, who was thin and sad with the haunted stare of a woman anticipating a lifetime of beatings. All the while she would be thinking, *my mother told me to do this.*

After two hours of poor sewing through watery vision, she stood. "Ladies, get to a finishing point quickly, then go and enjoy Christmas." Everyone gasped in shock, not noticing the quaver in her voice. "I'll see you next Thursday after the Feast of St. Stephen." She watched the women close up their machines and toss covers over them, throwing scissors and pincushions into drawers to be searched for after the holiday.

After the last woman clicked the door shut behind her, Zosia let her head fall forward into her hands. She wept in a way she hadn't let herself for years. The answers she now had, that she'd wanted so desperately, only made her soul ache. It was no consolation that her one son was now forever safe in the arms of God. It was a God she knew was fickle and often cruel. Anger lurked behind her sadness, but God didn't care about anger. She learned that lesson when Wiktor died. God just went about killing children and husbands and letting evil live.

After allowing herself a few minutes to cry, she wiped her nose, threw the cover over her own Singer, and grabbed her coat. She would wait until next week to deal with the fallout from the stacks of untouched fabric.

She walked to room 21 in Blockhouse C-6 and climbed into bed without taking off her clothes. She pulled the covers up over her head and forgot about supper.

She hadn't been there to hold Antoni's hand while his life slipped away, or to hold Marisha's flowers as she promised forever to a monster, or to hold Stefek when he trembled in fear from the raids and incoming bombs.

Zosia closed her eyes. She wanted to sleep forever.

CHAPTER SEVENTEEN

Christmas Eve.

The screech of furniture scraping across the wood floor woke Zosia. The room was lit from the morning sun, and happy chatter contrasted with bursts of grunts and heaves.

After spending the weekend in bed, she pulled herself upright and peeked out through her blanket walls. A little round table was set up in the small center space between the blankets. Angelika struggled a small spruce tree into a clamp on the table while Iwona leaned on her crutch and watched, the cigarette between her fingers ashing on the floor. Behind them, Lottie and two other uniformed women pushed a bed into the room.

"What's going on?" Zosia motioned to the furniture-moving officials.

"New roommate." Iwona rolled her eyes.

"Here? Where?" Zosia's eyebrows shot up.

Angelika shrugged, her pale blonde hair tied in a messy bun. "Packing us in tighter. Soon we'll be two or three to a bed."

"That's not so bad, depending on who." Iwona grinned from her crutch.

Zosia dressed and, in an effort to occupy her mind and

avoid her grief, helped her roommates trim the tree. She bent straw into stars and angels as the other women seesawed between merrily adding traded treasures to the branches and cursing the officials who rearranged furniture around them. Angelika and Iwona ricocheted between cheerful and annoyed, silver tinsel and red bulbs.

In the German-occupied fields and quarries, she'd hardly known one day from the next, and Christmas was no exception. Sometimes a dry "*Wesolych Swiat*" would pass down the lines, but it was quickly forgotten. Now, taking in the spindly little tree, she had no desire to celebrate. Christmas was about God and children, and she had neither. The holiday incited only sorrow, with the knowledge that her son would never sing another carol or eat another *kolaczki*.

Christmas. Antoni's favorite. The boughs of the tree reminded Zosia of another Christmas, years earlier. Antoni was there, but still inside Zosia's womb so not yet with them.

"Well, isn't that lovely." Brygida's voice dripped with sarcasm. As plain as if it were yesterday, Zosia could see her sister in front of the snowy window, her stylish green day dress festive against the red bows and gold garland. Brygida lit a cigarette and motioned toward Zosia's flat stomach. Soon it would bulge with her second child. "And what makes you deserve another?"

"What do you mean?"

"Bronek's job is better than Wiktor's. We can afford a child, yet we have none. But you . . ." She trailed off and shrugged. "I guess if you think you can support another, fine. It certainly isn't fair, though."

"I'm sure children will come—"

"Yes, I'm sure." Brygida cut her off. "I'll just sit and wait in my empty house and listen to the silence in the meantime."

Silence sounded beautiful to Zosia, but she held her tongue. Brygida would know soon enough when she also became pregnant. Zosia hoped it would be soon so her sister would finally outgrow her bitterness toward her.

"Auntie, will you have a baby, too?" Marisha was curled into the safety of Zosia's arm, her little hand gripping a rag doll.

"Oh, *dziewczynka*, I think God wants your *matka* to have the babies instead of me, though she hardly deserves them." Brygida turned her sharp eyes back to Zosia. "How you can let your child carry around that toy is beyond me. She's not an infant anymore, Zosia. For shame. Will she have that doll witness her wedding?"

Later when Bronek's job relocated them to London, Zosia was relieved. She no longer had to endure Brygida's resentment.

But even now, years and miles away from their home, Brygida still haunted her. On Zosia's bedside table inside room 21 there were several letters started, "*Dear Brygida . . .*" But Brygida had never been "dear." Brygida was also probably the last person who would waste ink on a reply, but Zosia had to try. Even if her sister was vicious, she would share information if she had it; if nothing else, she would use it to hurt Zosia.

It was Christmas, and Zosia was no longer a prisoner, yet she was still unable to leave Wildflecken. She should have been home by now. She'd been promised only a couple of months in camp. It had been almost eight.

After the tree was decorated, the women invited Zosia to join them for lunch, but she declined. She climbed back into her bed, which was now situated in a smaller space between the blankets. Her repatriation flyer had fallen to the floor. *Help Rebuild Our Homeland of Poland*, it requested.

I'm trying.

Anxious voices entered the quiet room. Bags and belongings thumped to the floor, and a new, foul smell hovered in the air. Though now new arrivals were no longer coming in from the concentration camps, refugees were being still shuffled around Europe as DP camps opened, closed, and restructured. Rumors reported that some DP camps weren't much better than the prisons they replaced. "Olga, here's your bed, love." Zosia heard Lottie's comforting lilt.

"Ryszard, oh *Ryszaaaaard,*" a woman's voice wailed between mournful sobs. Zosia rolled over in her bed and stared at the denim patch on her blanket wall.

—

Afternoon was a whirl of excitement as Christmas Eve roared to life. Zosia's roommates returned from lunch and, together with a few of their friends from down the hall, fretted over large pots and platters of smuggled food and stolen rations. The women haggled with each other over who would wear the shoes that Iwona swore had once been worn by a duchess. They argued whether a bracelet was genuine ivory or painted plastic.

Kasia rocked in her chair and watched the activity while she finished knitting little gifts for the children. Iwona poked her head into Zosia's space and begged her to get up and fix the hem on her too-small party dress. The clinking of tiny bottles of bootleg schnapps accompanied the chatter throughout the day until evening, when the bells atop the Catholic chapel rang out six o'clock. They signaled a special dinner before the early "Midnight" Mass, to be held at half past seven so worshippers could attend parties afterwards. Even Kasia went out to the festivities, anxious to see the children's reactions to her mittens and hats.

Zosia stayed in her bed. She had no desire to celebrate, even after Petronela came over and tried to eject her from her room.

"Leave me, Petra," Zosia said into her lumpy pillow. "Antoni is gone. I need to grieve."

"I'll give you time," Petronela said, "but not too much."

The distorted music and gaiety from the evening celebrations flowed all over the little settlement of broken refugees. The cheer echoed from beyond her window, but it only served to deepen Zosia's emptiness. The community needed an opportunity for joy, and now that there was one, Zosia wanted no part of it.

She stood and gathered her shabby robe, probably donated from an American housewife who'd heard of the plight of the refugees on the radio and had assembled a bag of discarded clothes to help the cause. She went down the hall to the washroom for a warm shower. With everyone else out at Christmas parties, she knew she would have time alone and a better chance for hot water.

The water poured over her for several minutes. She waited for it to wash away the pain and ugliness inside her. It didn't. After she toweled off and wrapped herself in the robe, she padded down the hall to her room but stopped when she came around the corner. A uniformed man was knocking at her door.

"Zosia, are you in there?" It was Czeslaw.

She ducked behind the corner. She couldn't let him see her like this, practically naked. He was a married man, and Zosia wasn't going to be a mistress. There were plenty of single men around if she wanted that sort of thing.

"Zosia, it's Christmas Eve, and you shouldn't be alone," Czeslaw said to no one through the door. He waited, and Zosia held her breath around the corner. After a few moments, he rested his hat onto his head and turned to leave.

She watched him retreat down the hall, and with him, her hopes of finding Marisha and Stefek. Maybe Czeslaw could still help her, even if Iwona, Violette, and Mr. Devine all failed. He'd been in contact with his family. He could find her family, too.

"Please stay." She stepped from around the corner.

He stopped and looked behind him, a paper bag gripped in his hand. "I was worried when Angelika and Iwona said you were staying in by yourself tonight." Czeslaw and Zosia approached each other in the dim hallway, and Czeslaw gave her a half-hug with his free arm. "People don't stay in by themselves on Christmas Eve unless something is wrong."

Zosia nodded, swallowing tears. "Yes, something is wrong. Come in." She pushed open the door to room 21. Czeslaw placed his bag on the table next to the little Christmas tree while Zosia disappeared behind her curtain of blankets to change. She wrapped a convenient dress around her and ran her fingers through her damp hair. She pulled the top drawer of her bedside table open to reveal the pearl earrings, which she hooked through the slits in her earlobes. *Why not? It's Christmas.* The dress clung to her damp body. She parted the walls.

Czeslaw had moved the Christmas tree to the floor and dragged Kasia's rocking chair to the center of the room for Zosia to sit. She settled into the chair, and Czeslaw pulled an old silver canteen out of the bag. "I have something for you." He unscrewed the lid. Steam escaped from the flask, and a balanced aroma of vinegar and vegetables wafted out. She took a deep sniff.

"Borscht?"

"It isn't Christmas Eve without it." Czeslaw pulled a couple of bowls out of his bag and poured the soup.

"As long as you don't ruin it with the Jews' sour cream, I'm sure it's delicious."

Czeslaw's expression cringed. He poured the liquid into a small bowl. "Strained clear, no cream in sight." He handed her the bowl and a spoon. He produced a small loaf of rye bread. "No sawdust, either." His face softened and he winked at Zosia.

She smiled, grateful for the food.

"*Ryszaaaaard* . . ." A voice whimpered from the other side of the room.

Czeslaw frowned, and Zosia shrugged. "Newcomer. Lost her husband."

"My God." Czeslaw made the sign of the cross.

"Oh, no," Zosia said, taking a sip of the deep red broth. "He didn't die, he left her for a young Latvian woman." Zosia closed her eyes and enjoyed the pleasure of good food for the first time in years.

"So, what's bothering you?" Czeslaw perched on a stool from Iwona's space.

"They found two of my children. Antoni is dead."

"Ah, Zosia, I'm so sorry." Czeslaw bowed his head for a moment in prayer. He then leaned over to wrap his arms around her. "He's free now. No one can hurt him. He's with his father."

She nodded. "Marisha married her German boyfriend. I told her that was best, and he would keep her alive, but he's—" She stopped, ashamed to even admit it. "He treated her poorly. He beat her, and I still told her to stay with him. What kind of mother am I?"

"Sometimes every option is a losing one, and we can only choose the least wretched," Czeslaw said. "At least she is alive."

Zosia chewed her bread, deep in thought. After several minutes she spoke. "I'm so grateful to Violette for helping me, even though I couldn't pay her."

"You deserve to know what happened to your family. I felt terrible that I couldn't do more to help." He stirred his soup. "Those feelings of not knowing, wondering, hoping—they're crippling. When I heard from Pawel, my heart burst from the fear and worry leaving me. I know my children are alive and safe. You deserve that relief, too. You've been through too much. We all have."

Zosia's eyes misted. "Mr. Devine didn't have any information about Stefek though. I don't know if Violette forgot, or if there was a miscommunication."

"The Partridge isn't one to forget. I doubt that's it."

"Forget?" Zosia snorted. "How can anyone forget a child? He's out there somewhere. Or he's . . ." Zosia couldn't finish.

"It's hell, isn't it? The not knowing." Czeslaw reached into his bag and pulled out a small glass bottle of clear liquid. He gave her a gentle smile. "Would this help?"

She didn't like to use schnapps to calm her nerves, but after learning of her child's death she felt she deserved a small sip. "Only a little," she said.

Out of the large bag came two crystal shot glasses, each cut into a beautiful, multi-faceted flower pattern. He set them on the table, and Zosia's mouth dropped open. "Oh, my goodness."

"You like?" He smiled and pulled the cork out of the bottle.

"They're beautiful. I haven't seen Polish crystal since . . . well, you know." She reached out and gingerly touched one, letting her fingertips brush over the bevels.

Czeslaw filled the glasses. He passed one to her and lifted his. "To finding peace in answers and hope in those answers we don't yet have." They clinked their glasses and each took a sip. The liquid tingled Zosia's throat as it drained down. It made her feel warm, and if she dared think it, comforted.

"What about your family? Have you heard anything more?" Zosia dipped her spoon back into the borscht, stirring up the vegetables that had settled at the bottom of the bowl.

Czeslaw shook his head.

"My Ryszaaard . . ." Zosia and Czeslaw sat still and tried to ignore the anguish from the corner of the room.

"Listen, there's something you should know," Czeslaw said, but then stopped. Zosia held her breath. It was the raid, she was certain. He was the one they were after all along. Or it was about the Nazi soldier he'd killed. Why was he telling her this, whatever it was? Why now? Vulnerability clutched her. She regretted inviting him in.

"My wife," he said, and Zosia looked up, confused. "My marriage, it isn't what you think. I mean, it's hardly a marriage. It's for the children only. I have no love left for Franciszka. I did at one time, of course, but things changed."

Zosia watched pain overtake his face. She didn't know how to respond to a confession she didn't expect. "What changed?" she asked in a barely audible whisper.

Czeslaw leaned over to refill both of their glasses with schnapps. Then he turned the small glass between his fingers, swirling the liquid inside. "I don't know." He gazed at nothing. "Bitterness, maybe? Maybe I expected too much from her. Maybe she expected something from me that I couldn't give her. We were fine until Janina was born. That was a turning point. Franciszka was a good mother to Henryk. Then that beautiful baby girl came into my life. Our lives." Czeslaw stared at the ground, lost in his memories. "I was overwhelmed with love for her. Franciszka was a good mother to her too, but Janina would struggle out of her mother's arms and reach for me, always. She would cry unless I held her and rocked her before bed. I don't know, maybe it hurt my wife. Mothers are supposed to do those kinds of things, I guess.

"After that, Franciszka turned on me. She would throw shoes at me and yell for no reason. She accused me of sneaking around in town with other women, which of course was not true. I didn't know what I did wrong."

Zosia stayed quiet. Jealousy revealed itself in heartbreaking ways. She swallowed her drink.

"After that, I stayed away from her. We stopped talking. When I left to join the army, there was no love between us. I know she'll take good care of the children, but I don't crave her company anymore. My children, absolutely. I live for them. Janina kept me alive all those dark years in Russia. And Henryk, what a bright boy. I can't wait to see him again. But not Franciszka." He straightened his slumped shoulders. "But I will see her again. She's my wife, and I made a promise. Maybe things have changed. I don't know." He was quiet.

Zosia didn't nod or utter a sound. She concentrated on the

sparkling reflections in the bevels of her glass. Marriage was never easy, even when two people were in love. Marriage had to be agonizing when a divide goes up between husband and wife. She tried not to think of Marisha and her new husband.

Czeslaw stopped talking and drank the schnapps to avoid the discomfort. Zosia stirred her soup, not wanting to eat. She didn't understand why he told her this. It didn't matter, anyway. Like he said, he'd made a promise, and he would return to his family. Zosia was not a part of that.

The commotion outside the window assembled into something recognizable. Zosia heard the gentle verses of "*Bóg sie rodzi*" floating from a nearby blockhouse. Though the Poles were some of the most depressed people in Europe, given an opportunity to celebrate, they did so with gusto.

She met Czeslaw's eye, and the two of them smiled at the joyousness of their countrymen. They rushed to the window next to Zosia's bed. Czeslaw pulled open the double-hung pane, revealing clear voices penetrating the frozen sky.

As he dropped his hand from the window, his fingers brushed her hip. She felt a spark of heat surge through her body, and her mind scrambled. Her body felt weak, and so did her resistances. She let her eyes fall to slits. Czeslaw's deep voice behind her sang softly: "*Cóz masz, niebo, nat ziemiany? Bog porzucil szcescie twoje.*" Comforted, she sang along to the carol, moving her lips but barely making a sound.

Her body let go of the constant weight it had carried for so long. She felt her shoulders relax and she leaned back into the solidness of Czeslaw behind her. His hands rested on her hips, and her skin tingled where his grip met her body. The strength of his fingers gently cupping her sides felt right. She didn't fight it. *We are friends. Friends can hold each other. Friends can comfort each other. It's Christmas Eve. We can be family to each other, since our families are so far away.*

The warm smell of schnapps and borscht mingled with the soothing scent of a strong man. It felt good to be held.

His arms tightened around her waist, and still she didn't fight it. Somewhere deep inside her mind, there was a tiny voice reminding her over and over, like a staticky phonograph stuck on a scratch, that he was a married man. But the longer it played, the easier it was to ignore and forget.

She stiffened when she felt his breath on her neck.

Tadeusz.

Voss.

The last time a man's hands had been on her body, two men raped her within minutes of each other. Her throat started to close, and she wiggled out of his grip.

Czeslaw's hands relaxed, and his breath on her neck steadied. "I won't hurt you," he said softly in her ear. "We've all been tortured, but we deserve comfort and joy. We can't let them take that from us." His arms gently embraced her. "If you want me to go, I will."

She relaxed. The voices outside crescendoed into the next more exuberant and more drunken Christmas carol. Czeslaw's lips fell against her shoulder. The soft sensation shook her, tempting feelings she hardly recognized. His mouth carried up the side of her neck and tickled her behind the pink pearl at her ear. Desire overwhelmed despair.

A voice deep in her head, muffled from schnapps, reminded her that he was married, but the buzz in her head pushed it back.

It had been so long. *Maybe only this once. This isn't real anyway. Wildflecken isn't real.*

She melted into Czeslaw's arms. His fingers ran up her side, and she turned to him and pressed her lips against his, wrapping her arms around him.

It felt so safe and so right that she forgot how wrong it was. She felt her body betray her better judgment, but she didn't stop it. He nudged the dress off of her shoulders, letting it drop to the ground. She didn't feel vulnerable. She felt safe. She felt alive.

As their bodies moved together as one, finally, something felt right.

Chapter Eighteen

New Year's Day, 1946: 12:03 a.m.

"Szczesliwego Nowego Roku!" Iwona hugged Zosia and kissed her cheek. The clock had just struck midnight; it was 1946. The camp administrators threw the party, hoping for a truce over the recent raid—or misunderstanding, as they called it—and a respite from the drunken misbehavior that overtook Wildflecken at Christmas. Officials carried large trays of treats and mingled with the residents. The Poles couldn't resist the siren song of free food and legal drink.

"Let me walk you home." Zosia held Iwona up, her crutch failing at its job.

"No." Iwona shook her head violently. "I'm fine. Fine! I'm going home with that handsome man there." She tipped her glass toward a tall man eating a donut by the door.

Zosia frowned. "Does he know that?"

Iwona hung on Zosia's shoulder. "You're my best friend. Do you know that? The best." Her words held a sleepy slur.

"Come with me, honey." Angelika took Iwona's arm. "That man is married."

"Doesn't ever stop them," Iwona said.

Zosia turned her head to hide her shame. She was a horrible woman for making love to a married man. Wiktor would be disappointed.

Wiktor. He had been her only lover. A dark dread washed over her as she remembered another man assaulting the back of her throat. *No.* Voss was a monster. So was Tadeusz. She'd only ever had one lover. But now, she'd had two.

Zosia moved to follow her roommates out into the cold when a hand clamped on her shoulder. "A happy New Year to you." Petronela handed Zosia a plate of cabbage pierogi and hugged her with her free arm.

"Same to you, my friend." Zosia folded into Petronela's armpit. "But I already ate."

"Then eat more." Petronela stuffed a pierogi into her mouth. Angelika and Iwona had dragged Zosia out for the New Year's Eve festivities. Zosia resisted until her roommates recruited Petronela to help.

Zosia took a bite of the warm dumpling. It was a bittersweet taste; it was home, but home was just out of reach. She searched the crowd, as she'd done since she'd arrived.

Petronela followed Zosia's wandering gaze. "He's not here."

"I don't know who you mean."

"Oh. Okay." Petronela winked at Zosia. Zosia surveyed the dancers, the drinkers; she couldn't help but search for Czeslaw, even though he'd been her biggest mistake. Petronela was the only soul she'd confided in about it.

When Zosia awoke Christmas morning, her only bedmate had been a note written on a small piece of lined paper: *Thank you for a beautiful evening.* She turned it over in her hand to reveal an old note to himself: *Two bags sugar, fifty cigarettes. Looking for beef, pork.*

Though her bed was empty, she hadn't been alone. Snoring women surrounded her behind walls of blankets, each sleeping off a hangover before they were due at Christmas Day mass. She was relieved Czeslaw was gone. It was a mistake, and she regretted it. Marriage was to be respected at all costs. She'd learned that with Wiktor; especially after finding lipstick stains on his shirt.

Violette carried a large food tray, her blond hair in a neat braided bun and her bright smile charming the Poles around her into choosing a cookie.

"Petra, excuse me." Zosia set the plate down on a nearby table and closed in on Violette.

"Szczesliwego Nowego Roku!" Violette beamed, the practiced phrase sounding wooden on her foreign tongue. She met Zosia's eyes and showed no special recognition. "Please, take a treat."

"Many thanks for all that you do." Zosia held Violette's eyes, taking her time in reaching for a cookie. "You know," she said quickly, knowing she had Violette's attention for only a moment, "my sister lives in England, and they have a song they sing this time of year about a partridge."

Violette's eyebrow arched. "Yes, I'm familiar," she said with hesitation in broken Polish. "In France it is a lone partridge, but I believe the English have the bird sitting in a pear tree." She laughed her tinkling laugh. "Although, I think in this part of the world, it would do better under a giant sycamore."

"That's right," Zosia said, playing along. "I wonder though, would the partridge stay there all night?"

"Oh, *non, non*." Violette watched Zosia carefully. "I believe they fly before daybreak. Five-thirty is when I hear the partridge."

"Of course." Zosia took a small nibble of her cookie.

Violette moved on to the next partygoer. "Take a treat! Enjoy!"

—

At five-thirty, before the sun rose over the Rhön Mountains, Zosia stood under the giant sycamore tree behind Mess 3. Violette floated in, followed by a yawning Lottie.

"Thank you for the information about my children." Zosia reached out to Violette's arm, but the woman shrank away. "I'm so grateful, especially since I couldn't pay."

Violette's expression twisted into confusion. She turned to Lottie for understanding. "Zosia," Lottie jumped in, "Mr. Lysek brought your payment. He delivered it shortly after we met." She frowned. "He said you'd sent him. Was that a mistake?"

"No, of course not." Inside her parka, Zosia felt hot. She tried to keep her words level as the blood in her body rushed to her head. *Stefek, ask about Stefek,* the voice inside her screamed, but her tongue felt like a brick.

"You want something more?" Violette trilled with a thick French accent, "You have more dollars?"

Zosia shook her head, unable to speak.

"Do not waste my time." Violette and Lottie rushed off, each in different directions.

Zosia leaned against the sycamore trunk and felt nausea roll through her. Her eyes burned. She stared at the ice pooled at the tree's base. Czeslaw had paid Violette.

She had to leave Wildflecken as soon as possible.

Chapter Nineteen

February, 1946.

Zosia removed her watch and handed it to Ludka. "It may not look like much, but it does work." She smiled and touched the girl on the arm. She was the best candidate to take over for Zosia—always the first to arrive each morning, often volunteering to help count thread spools and folds of wool, and yet she still always finished her pile of coats on time. "I'm happy you're taking over. You'll do well."

"Thank you for recommending me for the job, Mrs. Wilusz."

"You deserve it." Zosia would miss the hum of the Singers, but soon she would be back at her own clunky but comfortable sewing machine.

If it was still there. If *anything* was still there. She'd heard gruesome rumors about the shambles that was Poland: entire city blocks leveled in Warsaw, the streets lined with rubble. Zosia had to believe Minsk Mazowiecki survived. Otherwise, she was returning to an empty hole in the earth that had swallowed everything she cherished.

Ludka hugged Zosia. "Good luck, Mrs. Wilusz. Be happy at home in Poland."

Zosia didn't show her nerves. She picked up her coat and stepped out into the frosty afternoon.

Petronela stood waiting outside. "What time is the train tomorrow?" Her nose was red against the harsh February air. Winter was stubborn in the Bavarian hills.

"I don't know." Zosia shrugged. "Do we ever know?"

"I thought since you were a passenger, you might have inside information." Petronela pulled the collar of her coat up toward her ears. They both turned in the direction of the UNRRA office for a final check-in with Mr. Devine.

Zosia had packed her belongings, passed her job along to the most qualified seamstress, and prepared to say her final goodbyes to a few friends that evening before leaving the next day. She was ready to go home.

She would forego Czeslaw's goodbye. They hadn't spoken since their night together. A few times he'd caught her eye in the mess building, smiling shyly and raising his eyebrows as if asking to join her. She always dropped her gaze and shook her head. He left her alone.

She wasn't able to forgive herself. She was ashamed and embarrassed that the evening had gotten out of control. She didn't want the reputation of being a harlot. If Czeslaw had any sense of honor, he would be ashamed, too. Marriage was a covenant, and he broke that. They both had. It was best that he stayed away.

Still, her fantasies drifted.

Zosia's legs wobbled on the stairs up to Mr. Devine's office, to the point where Petronela rested her hand on Zosia's back to steady her. At the landing, Zosia threw open the director's door without knocking.

"Oh, Mrs. Wilusz." It was the usual, startled response she got every day. "And Mrs. Kloc." Mr. Devine ducked his head and shuffled through some papers on his desk. "Mrs. Wilusz, I'm sorry, but there's nothing new today. But Mrs. Kloc, I have something for you." He handed her an envelope. "It came this morning."

"Thank you." Petronela took it and squeezed it in her fist. She turned to leave without another word.

Zosia followed, lightheaded. She took the stairs slowly to avoid a tumble and caught up with Petronela on the street.

Petronela was still, staring at the paper in her hand.

"What is it? Petra? Tell me."

"They found Eliasz."

Blackness oozed into the sides of Zosia's vision. "Where is he? Is he safe?"

A stout silence fell between them until the towering woman spoke simply: "His remains were identified at Auschwitz."

"Oh Petra." Still woozy, Zosia reached up to hug her friend. "I'm so sorry."

Petronela was too tough to show her grief. "I expected it. But, you know, we all still try to hope." She felt stiff in Zosia's arms, barely returning the embrace.

They stood, Zosia wanting to comfort her friend while Petronela silently had none of it. Zosia turned the news around and around in her head until everything was spinning. "Petra, how do they know it was him? How can they be certain?"

Petra studied the envelope with dry eyes. "Auschwitz," she said softly, ignoring Zosia. "Well, that's it, then." Beneath Petronela's solid façade, Zosia saw her crumble.

Zosia widened her stance to offset her dizziness. *Maybe something I ate or not enough sleep* . . . "I'm sorry, Petra. It's a sad day. I hope this news will give you closure, an ending. We can believe he's found comfort and light."

Petronela put her hand on Zosia's arm. "I'm going to miss you, Zosia. You're a good woman."

Zosia took in a quick breath. Her knees buckled. "Petra . . ." Everything went black, and she felt her body fall.

—

When she opened her eyes, Petronela was still in front of her, but they were no longer outside. "Doctor, she's awake." Petronela watched Zosia with worry knitting her forehead. "Zosia, how do you feel?"

"What happened?"

"You fainted. I brought you to the hospital."

"You carried me?"

"You're not that heavy."

Zosia grimaced. "Petra, I'm fine. I need a glass of water, not a doctor." Doctors in camp didn't have time to treat a simple fainting spell. They were overworked, irritable, and frustrated at the lack of resources. She'd heard only patients on the verge of death were triaged into a bed. Though their intentions were mostly good, they were as bad as the Jewish doctors in Minsk Mazowiecki. She pulled the covers away and swung her legs over the side of the bed. When she did, her head swam with vertigo.

"Lay down. The doctor wanted to talk to you when you woke up." Petronela pressed Zosia's shoulder.

"I feel better. I have too much to do before tomorrow."

"Mrs. Wilusz." A man in a coat that used to be white approached Zosia's bed. He gave Petronela a pleading look, as if asking permission. Zosia got the idea that Petronela had strong-armed her into a bed. "Glad you're awake. Mrs. Kloc, would you mind giving us a moment."

Petronela stood. "I'll be back soon."

The doctor sat on the edge of the bed. "I'm Dr. Krupka."

"Are you a Jew?"

Dr. Krupka gave her a curious look. "No."

"Okay, then." Zosia relaxed.

The doctor shook his head, as if to clear it. "I'd like to keep you here for a few days. Your iron levels are low, and in your condition you need to be careful."

"I can't stay here. I'm going home tomorrow." She froze, processing what she'd heard. "Wait a minute. What is my condition?" Her fingertips went numb. *I'm dying. That's the only way they'd keep me here.*

"You're borderline anemic."

"Oh. That's all?"

The doctor sat his clipboard on the tiny table next to the bed. "Mrs. Wilusz, you're pregnant. I would estimate a couple of months. You need to take care of yourself, for your child's sake."

She stared, her eyes glazed over. "That's not possible," she said, although she knew it was. "No, I can't . . ."

The doctor gave a bored sigh. "You're not the first mother to argue my diagnosis, but I guarantee you, you are with child." He picked up his clipboard, adjusted his glasses on his nose, and stood. "I'd expect you to be due in September, around the middle of the month. Maybe later. For now, you should stay here until we can get your red blood cell count up. Then upon discharge I'll send some vitamins with you, if I can find some."

Zosia's mind went in every direction, and her stomach heaved. *He's wrong. This is a dream. This isn't real. I'm not pregnant. It has to be a dream.*

Wake up. Please, wake up now.

A few minutes later, Petronela roosted on the edge of the bed where Dr. Krupka had been sitting. Zosia divulged what she still didn't want to believe. Petronela exhaled deeply, blowing a stray strand of brown hair off her forehead.

"Well Zosia, you have some options."

Zosia nodded. She couldn't think about her options. She only willed herself to wake up from her nightmare. "Okay."

"You could sneak out of here and still make your train tomorrow."

"Yes, I'll do that."

"But," Petronela said in a tone that made Zosia flinch, "you would put yourself and your baby in harm's way. You've been on these cross-country treks, and you've seen the pregnant women in the cars. It isn't easy on them. Hell, one woman on my train from Warsaw miscarried right in front of everyone. She bled so much she couldn't even sit up. The baby was dead of course, about the size of a small rat. Someone in the car threw it out the door. The woman was hysterical for the rest of the trip, barely conscious. She had to be dragged out when we stopped. Ended up with the butt of a rifle to her chin. They took her into the camp. I'm pretty sure she didn't survive long, but who knows."

"Are you trying to scare me?" Zosia raised her eyebrows.

"Maybe," Petronela said, "because I don't think that's what you should do. But, it is an option. You just need to understand what you're getting into."

"You said there are other options?"

Petronela lowered her voice. "You could have it . . . you know. Taken care of."

The thought had entered her mind, but she couldn't do it. Especially now, after Antoni's death, she would have to be unbearably desperate to purposely end a pregnancy. She didn't yet know if she was that desperate. She'd only known about this baby for about seventeen minutes.

"What else?" Zosia asked flatly.

Petronela stared at a spot of nothing on the wall. "You could talk to Czeslaw. You said he doesn't love his wife, so maybe he'll leave her."

Zosia gave a dry laugh. She could tell by Petronela's dim tone that she didn't believe it was a valid choice any more than Zosia did. "Okay, Petra. That's a great idea. What else? Should I believe he's a long lost prince, and he'll make me the queen of his kingdom?"

"I think he deserves to know about this baby."

"Why?"

Petronela turned to look at her, glaring with a mother's disdain. "Why do you want to hurt him?"

Zosia searched for the words, but nothing came. She didn't want to hurt him; in fact, quite the opposite. In the depths of her heart, she yearned for him. But it was impossible. She couldn't do to another woman what had once been done to her. She knew the pain of infidelity. The fact that he'd paid Violette complicated matters even more. Zosia felt indebted to him. She couldn't afford that, not when her children were waiting.

"It's not the right thing, Petra." She chose her words carefully. "He'll return to his family. He's made that clear. I don't want to confuse things."

"I'd say he had a part in confusing things," Petronela said with a huff. "But it's your business."

They were quiet for a minute, sitting in awkward disagreement with each other. "Any other options?" Zosia asked.

"I'll have to keep thinking." Petronela glowered at her friend. "You know, Czeslaw is a good man."

"He's a married man."

"Who doesn't love his wife."

Zosia sighed. "It doesn't matter how he feels about his wife. The fact is he made a promise to her, and he loves his children. That settles it."

Petronela leaned forward and brushed the hair off of Zosia's forehead like a mother would. It was an oddly feminine gesture from such a masculine woman. She smiled. "But now one of his children is inside of you. Doesn't that count for something?"

Zosia was silent. She should have never let Czeslaw in that night. Somewhere out there, his wife was raising his two children and waiting for her husband to return home, while Zosia was making love to him. She disgusted herself.

"Tell me this." Petronela sat up straight. She meant business.

"Do you love him?"

Zosia felt her face flush. "No, of course not."

"Really?"

Frustrated, Zosia sat up and reached for her coat. "Petra, it doesn't matter. I slept with a man who isn't mine, and now I'm pregnant with his child. I'm living in a strange place with my children either dead or scattered God knows where. My homeland is devastated, and any money I have is worthless. I have very few options." She stood, shrugged the coat over her shoulders, and tied the belt around her, giving an extra tug to get her point across. Then she sat again, her legs feeling like overcooked pierogi.

Sheepishly, she remembered her friend's grief. "I'm sorry." She softened and reached for her hand. "And I'm so sorry about Eliasz."

"Life is precious," Petronela said, her brazen eyes glinting with uncharacteristic tears.

"I'm leaving tomorrow."

"I won't let you."

"You can't control me, Petra." Zosia set her chin. "Nothing can keep me from my children."

"Your newest child could die."

"We don't know that."

"Yes we do." Petronela's voice cracked. "And you could die, too."

Zosia stared at Petronela. Then she forced a smile. "Okay, Petra. I'll stay." She would be on that train tomorrow. Somehow, she would have to get past her friend.

She hardly slept on the thin hospital cot, but when she did, her dreams filled her with grief. She was in a car, her father was driving. He sang Christmas carols. She sat next to him, a dark veil obscuring her vision. She held a baby.

"Stop, Papa."

Her father only laughed and pushed on the gas pedal.

"No, please, stop." The baby in her arms squirmed as the car sped. She knew the crash would come, but she couldn't hold the baby tight enough. He was too wiggly, too slippery. He felt like he was coated in petroleum jelly. Vernix. He was only just born. Her pelvis ached. Was this her baby?

She could see the lamppost ahead. The car headed straight for it. "Papa, stop! Stop now! Please!" Her tongue twisted. The words she tried to form only came as mumbles.

The sound of wrenching metal and breaking glass distracted her from the baby.

He was gone. She searched for him through the broken windshield. In the dim glow of the headlights, there was nothing but a skinny, headless chicken strutting away between the lines of sugar beets. Tadeusz, still sweaty from the work in the fields, picked it up by its feet and stuffed it into his coat. He looked back at Zosia through the broken windshield and gave her an evil grin.

—

The next morning, Zosia stood by the bed and buttoned her coat. Petronela and Dr. Krupka both watched. "I wish you would stay in the hospital for another day or two, Mrs. Wilusz." The doctor tapped his pen on his clipboard.

"Thank you for your concern, but I'm fine. Someone else can use my bed. I'll go back to my blockhouse and rest."

"Mrs. Wilusz, you need to take care of yourself." He pushed his glasses up his nose. "I would encourage you to delay repatriation until after the baby is born."

She tied her babushka under her chin. "Yes, Doctor."

Dr. Krupka gave Petronela a look. Petronela shrugged. The doctor sighed and handed the clipboard to Zosia, who quickly signed it. Petronela cleared her throat. "I'll keep an eye on her, Doctor."

"I appreciate that, Mrs. Kloc." He held his clipboard out to the side, motioning for the women to pass. They walked through the temporary hospital and stepped outside into the chilly air. In the distance, she heard the whistle of the train winding its way through the Bavarian hills. Since coming to Wildflecken, she'd let the trains tease her ears again. Now they sometimes carried opportunities—pork, cigarettes, a way home—instead of only suffering.

It was her train. Petronela kept her hand on Zosia's back while they walked, to make sure she didn't slip on the ice or make a run for the platform. Zosia's plan was to grab her suitcase and steal away to the station after Petronela reported for her job in the kitchen.

Zosia sensed Petronela's emptiness. "Petra, I wish there was something I could do to ease your pain about Eliasz."

"You have enough troubles of your own, Zosia. Don't worry about me." Petronela lifted her chin. *Stay strong.*

As they turned the corner toward Blockhouse C-6, Zosia stopped. A motorcycle sat next to the front door. Petronela's firm hand guided her along.

"Petra, wait. Why is he here? How did he know? Did you—"

"Of course not," Petronela said. "He's probably here to say goodbye, since he thought you were leaving."

Zosia dragged her feet forward, combating Petronela's strong stride next to her. Czeslaw sat on the concrete step by the door. He stood when he noticed them coming.

"Mrs. Kloc, Mrs. Wilusz." He touched his police hat, not removing it in the cold air.

The three of them shuffled for a minute on the delicate edge of discomfort before Petronela patted Zosia on the arm. "I spoke to Iwona and Angelika. They're going to watch over you. I'll stop by later to check in. Mr. Lysek, good to see you." Petronela walked away.

Zosia watched Petronela go until it felt odd that she was still watching her. She dropped her gaze to the ground.

"It probably seems like I've been avoiding you," Czeslaw said. "But I haven't been. Not on purpose."

She nodded, not knowing what to say. She had, in fact, been purposely avoiding him.

"I just . . ." Czeslaw stopped and readjusted his hat on his head. "Well, I wanted to say goodbye, I heard you were going back to Warsaw today."

When she didn't answer, Czeslaw continued. "You have to understand, Zosia," he said, digging the toe of his boot into the slushy snow on the ground, "I felt something with you. Something that, well, scared me." He shuffled his feet. Zosia caught his eye and fell into the blueness of them. She couldn't tear herself away.

"What do you mean?" she asked, her voice stumbling.

Czeslaw took an unsure step toward her, reaching for her hand. She tried to step back but her feet were rooted to the ground. His fingers interlaced hers, and she didn't feel the coldness in the air anymore. "It's been years since I've made love to a woman, and I've never felt the way I did with you. It frightened me, because I know she's waiting, but . . ." His words hung between them like he wanted to continue, but he didn't.

They stood motionless for a moment. Zosia knew she couldn't tell him the truth now. He was already conflicted about his feelings, but he had to return to his family. It was the right thing to do. In less than an hour she would be boarding her train. She wouldn't be his burden.

"Why are you telling me this?" Zosia asked when the silence became too thick.

He gently wrapped his arm around her waist. Her cheeks burned. "I needed to say goodbye. I needed to tell you, I love you."

Tears welled, but she sucked in her breath and stopped them. For a moment, a flash of life with this man flickered in her mind. He was holding her, dancing with her, loving her and her child. Her children. His children. All of them, together as one happy family.

Zosia shook her head. This wasn't a fairy tale. She lifted her chin. *Stay strong.* She stepped back.

"Well, the train is at the station," Czeslaw said, regaining his composure. "You don't want to be late."

She nodded.

"Promise me," Czeslaw said, "you'll send word when you're safe in Warsaw."

"I'm going home to Minsk Mazowiecki."

Czeslaw's face clouded. "Zosia, no, please." Czeslaw held her hand in his firm grip. She tried to keep herself from melting into the snow. "Nothing is left in Minsk Mazowiecki. Nothing. I've heard it's flattened, burned. Your home is gone, Zosia. It's not safe."

Zosia stared at him. "Gone?" *My God. Marisha, Stefek . . . where are you?*

"Warsaw is in bad enough condition, but the satellite towns are devastated. Tell me you'll only go as far as Warsaw. Please, I need to know you'll be safe." Czeslaw pulled her closer to him. She didn't fight it, but his lips, only centimeters from hers, made her body ache.

"No." She pulled away. "I'm not your concern, Czeslaw. You're a married man. You have a family waiting for you." Her vision got bleary. "I know you paid Violette, and I'm grateful. But what we did was a mistake and I regret it. For your own good, stay away." She turned and walked into the blockhouse, closing the door behind her. She leaned against it and slid down until she was on the floor. She sat alone and wept.

There was no point in returning to a home that didn't exist.

When she opened her eyes, Iwona was crouched next to her, her crutch leaning against the wall. She reached out and brushed a stray strand of hair off Zosia's frozen cheek.

"Zosia, I think I can help you."

CHAPTER TWENTY

One month later.

"You have the candy?" Zosia shook her head. *No, not right.* "I'm here for the candy." She frowned and dug the toe of her boot into the still-frozen ground. She brought her cigarette to her lips and inhaled sharply, listening for the rustle of an approaching trader. The bag of letters hung heavy in her hand—she took every opportunity she could to inundate the potential postal routes. One day they had to open up.

"Hand over the candy." She stuck her chin out to the moonlit emptiness of the forest. It was absurd. Though it was penicillin, Iwona instructed her to call it candy. "If you call it penicillin or medicine, you may be in trouble. Everything is in code." It made Zosia sound like a child, asking for candy out in the woods. She practiced, looking for the right words. "Please, can I have the candy?"

Her back shivered. Her youngest boy's voice rang in her head. "Matka, please? More candy?" Stefek had learned his manners only by asking for sweets. Zosia watched her shoe pick at the frosty mud. For a while, Zosia called Stefek her *mała rodzynka*—her little raisin—because he loved sweets so much.

She'd forgotten about that.

Lost in her memories, another voice from long ago filled her head. "For you, *moja droga*." It was Wiktor. She could see him standing in front of her at her family's front step. He held a bag of *krówki* caramels in one hand, and two yellow lilies in the other; one for her, and one for her mother. Her mother ignored the gesture and left the lily on the kitchen table to shrivel. Zosia, though, felt her heart soar out of her chest. She placed the lily in a glass of water and hid the bag of *krówki* in a drawer so Brygida wouldn't steal it. Each time she ate a caramel from the bag, Zosia was reminded of Wiktor's sweet smell, and soon, the sweetness of his lips on hers.

"Mrs. Ptak," a deep voice inquired from behind her in the forest, shaking her out of her daydreams.

Zosia turned and stood face to face with a man she knew. "Oh my God. Tadeusz." She brought her hand to her mouth, the cigarette dangling between her fingers. She hadn't seen him at all in Wildflecken and figured he must have run off somewhere, possibly pulled into a renegade gang of former prisoners who'd found camp life too stifling. She imagined him haunting the surrounding forest, robbing anyone with a town pass.

A prickly feeling ran across the back of her neck. She could feel his fingers squeezing her arm, see the mass of feathers flying as he threw her to the ground in the chicken coop. "*Fuck me? Oh, yes you will.*"

Her knees wobbled. She glanced toward town and wondered if she could outrun him. It was possible. Her pregnancy made her feel weak, but she didn't yet feel the overwhelming heaviness that she knew would soon come.

"I thought your name was Zosia Wilusz."

"It is." Though she tried to stop it, her voice trembled. "I mean, I'm here for a friend. What are you doing here?"

Tadeusz peered into the sack. "Some friend," he said with a

sneer. He pushed the bag up under his arm and reached inside his jacket to pull out a cigarette and a fancy brass lighter. "So how are you? You look healthy. I mean, it's hard to gain weight on a rationed diet, but somehow you have."

Though her pregnancy was still early, she'd been careful to keep her coat tight around her body. Nevertheless, her emaciated physique showed every little change. "Give me the drugs," she said, hardening her voice. "I mean, the candy. Just give me the bag." Her mind flashed to the poultry barn, where trying to emulate Petronela's toughness hadn't saved her against Tadeusz. Now, with her growing belly throwing her off-balance, she was even more of a caricature.

His mouth pulled into a wicked grin, and he stared at her midsection. "Oh sweet Jesus. You *are* a whore, aren't you?"

She shoved a handful of zlotys at him, dropping the letters onto the wet ground. She left them, since they had the same chance of getting delivered there in the mud as they would in the postal boxes in town. But she could not leave this package, it was too important. "Tadeusz, give me that bag."

He paused, a cigarette thoughtfully waiting on the edge of his lips. "No." His face fell from a grin into something expressionless. "I can't give you this."

She seethed at the thought of the deal failing, especially at the hands of Tadeusz. It was a means to opening up information that might be in Berlin. *"I can get to it,"* Iwona had said, *"but my sources need penicillin, and that's why we need the exchange. It's only fair."*

"Fuck you, Tadeusz." Zosia dropped her cigarette butt and ground it into the dirt with her foot. "Hand it over." She squared her chin. The only thing he could do to hurt her was to deny her the package. She would do anything to make this deal go through.

He watched her as if trying to figure out what to do. His face was surprisingly thoughtful, which gave Zosia pause; it didn't suit him. He reluctantly held the bag out to her. "You shouldn't get involved in this, Zosia."

"You mind your own business." She snatched the package and stuffed it under her arm. She turned and hurried away from him.

Trembling from anger and panic, she reached into her pocket for her cigarettes. She ripped the pack open, revealing emptiness. Gone. The packs under her mattress were gone, too. Now without a job, she had little cash to trade and had to depend on the weekly rations and a few simple black market exchanges to sustain her habit. The waiting list for seamstress jobs was as long as the lists to leave Germany. Ludka had tried to pull some strings for her, but there were previous negotiations and bribes well ahead of Zosia.

The sun set, and darkness fell around her as she entered the center of town. A group of boys gathered around a bench and watched an older fellow expertly roll cigarettes under a streetlight, their anxious breaths making clouds in the cold air. Several drunken men stumbled on the cobblestones and whistled at a young woman who hurried by. Zosia nodded hello to a few familiar faces, each passing with a determination to get to their destinations quickly in the chilly twilight.

Zosia's ears were turned back like a cat's listening for Tadeusz's footfalls. She kept a wary eye glancing behind her, searching for threatening shadows that mimicked Tadeusz's shape. She nearly jumped out of her skin when a pair of strong hands grabbed her shoulders.

"Zosia? Where are you going?" Petronela's voice huffed at her.

"Home," Zosia said, relieved to be safe in her friend's arms.

"Were you out trading?" Petronela poked at Zosia's package. "What is this? Cigarettes?"

Caught off guard, Zosia stammered, "I wasn't . . . I don't—"

"Zosia!" Iwona's silhouette waved to her from the doorway of blockhouse C-6 across the street.

A mix of disappointment and frustration crossed Petronela's face. Her voice lowered. "You're not working with Iwona, are you?" Her whisper was hot against Zosia's cheek.

"No, of course not." Zosia looked past Petronela. Petronela crossed her burly arms and waited. "She said she could help me," Zosia said, conceding. "She has a source in Berlin."

"Zosia," Petronela said, visibly disappointed. "There's no source, believe me."

Zosia's face flushed. "Petra, I do believe you. You're the only one I really trust. But I have to follow any lead. I can't just keep waiting."

Petronela pulled her face into a frown. "Just be careful, especially in your condition." She leaned in close again. "Does she know about Czeslaw?"

"No."

"Good. Keep it that way. I don't trust her."

"I'll see you at lunch tomorrow." Zosia patted Petronela's arm. She turned toward Iwona but watched her friend out of the corner of her eye. She seemed to amble aimlessly.

News of Eliasz's death had shaken Petronela more than Zosia anticipated. Her towering friend had toppled in the past month. Zosia acutely understood the devastation of losing a husband, but even she didn't know how to rescue Petronela. Petronela could only save herself. As was true with them all.

CHAPTER TWENTY-ONE

July, 1946.

Marisha,
My dearest daughter, I love you and am desperate to return to you and Stefek. If this letter finds you, please get in touch. I'm at the displaced persons camp in Wildflecken, Germany. Some have started calling it Durzyn. I'm trying to return to Poland but have come across delays and problems. I know Antoni died, and my heart breaks. Please find me.
All my love, Matka

The stack of letters on her dented metal desk wouldn't go anywhere. There was no information to be found anywhere. Zosia was still trapped in Wildflecken, still blind to the whereabouts of her surviving children.

After missing her repatriation train, she learned that waiting lists to return home were long and lethargic. She still checked in daily with Mr. Devine, who was as tired and sweaty as ever, but he never had new information on Stefek or Marisha. He seemed annoyed that she had gone and gotten herself pregnant, missing her window to leave and be one less refugee hassling him for answers.

She would have set out and walked back to Poland alone if she could have, but she could barely make it to the mess buildings across camp. Pregnancy was difficult for an old woman of 36.

Also, the thought of what she would find upon her return frightened her.

Zosia had received nothing but excuses from Iwona. She'd gone on several more of Iwona's "candy" adventures, though Zosia always first confirmed that Tadeusz wouldn't be on the other end. However, her efforts only resulted in more requests. Petronela merely grunted at Zosia's frustration and withdrew further into her grief for Eliasz.

And Zosia continued to avoid Czeslaw. After several failed attempts, he'd given up trying to speak to her. When the summer warmth set in and Zosia was forced to shed her coat, she caught him once in Mess 1 looking at her belly with an expression of shock and sadness. She could no longer hide her growing baby, but it was best for her to stay away. His wife waited for him at home.

Though it was early evening and the sun was only starting to stretch shadows outside, Zosia left her fountain pen to roll off the desk into the cobwebs on the floor and crawled into bed, exhausted. Her rickety bed, once perfectly adequate, now felt like a bag of rocks. Even with her winter coat stuffed between her legs and a rolled up army blanket under her belly, sleep was fitful. She dreaded the two months she would have to suffer through before the child was born.

She never did well with pregnancy. Antoni had been especially difficult. She didn't sleep more than an hour a night for the last half of his gestation, and, of course, once he was born she barely slept at all, much to Brygida's delight.

Her boy, now deep underground, would never be seen again.

Her heart broke.

Pregnancy sharpened her senses. Each time she heard the crunch of footsteps outside her window, she wished they belonged to Czeslaw. She stared at her tan blanket wall. It swayed with the air from Angelika's fan, left on for the women's comfort even though Angelika had gone to Gersfeld for the evening. The moth holes in Zosia's blanket wall marked her time like a prisoner's slashes on a jail cell wall. She wished for her solid little home in Minsk Mazowiecki. She wondered if she would ever see it again.

The sound of pounding outside her window, like a hammer drumming a board of wood, startled her. She pulled herself out of bed and searched the sidewalk below. Next door, outside of Blockhouse C-4, Petronela stood punching a bench, splintering the wood with her fist. A few people watched in a half-circle. One woman reached out to console her, but Petronela pushed the woman, causing her to stumble. Everyone scattered, shaking their heads as they walked away.

Zosia threw on a loose maternity dress and padded outside into the shade of evening. "Petra?" Zosia approached carefully. "Petra, stop. Please. I'm here. Stop."

"Go away, Zosia."

Zosia waddled up behind Petronela, her gait awkward from her bulging belly. Petronela stopped pounding the bench and leaned on it with her arms, catching her breath. Zosia sat and took Petronela's hand. Petronela winced, a bloody knot the size of a golf ball throbbing red on her middle knuckle.

"Petra, what's happening?" Zosia asked. Petronela stayed silent, the only sound between them was her labored panting. "Please, sit with me."

"No, Zosia."

"What's going on?"

Petronela brought her bloodshot eyes up to meet Zosia's. She didn't speak.

"What can I do, Petra? I want to help you."

"You can't do anything. He's gone, Zosia." After a moment, Petronela sat wearily next to Zosia on what was left of the shattered bench. "No one can do a damn thing."

"I know." There was nothing she could say. No one could bring Antoni back. No one could bring Wiktor back. Death was excruciating to the survivors. She patted her friend's hand gently, just like she patted Marisha's hand several years ago when she hadn't been chosen to sing in the choir.

Zosia thought about Wiktor's death. There had been no hand-patting then. Zosia, Marisha, Antoni and Stefek wrapped their arms around each other and wept openly. Zosia knew Petronela would have none of that.

"Zosia, I just can't . . ." She stopped, her voice hanging with the weight of grief.

"You can, Petra. You have to." Zosia stood, worried that the broken bench would collapse under their combined weight. "Please, join me in a walk."

Petronela let out a deep sigh but stood. She and Zosia walked in silence down the street, Zosia hoping the evening breeze would lift the cloud that her friend endured. They walked until Zosia realized they were in front of the church.

"Petra, this kind of thing has never really helped me, but maybe it will help you. Will you come in?" Zosia motioned to the chapel doors.

Petronela shook her head. "No, I just need to sleep it off. I'll see you tomorrow."

"Just join me for a minute, we—"

"Zosia, leave me alone. I said I'm fine." Petronela turned and retreated up the street without another word.

Everyone said they were fine, though no one really was.

The bells on the tower beside her rang the hour: nine o'clock. As a child, the priests always preached of a Church that was a haven, a place of safety. Maybe the thick, holy walls could protect her. Maybe she could find some much-needed guidance. God didn't save Wiktor or Antoni, but maybe she was praying wrong. Maybe she didn't pray hard enough. Maybe God could send her answers about her children in Poland, the child inside her, the man she loved but would never admit to loving.

Nothing but useless fairy tales behind that door, Zosia told herself. She turned to follow Petronela back to the single women's blockhouses when she recognized derisive eyes watching her a block away.

Tadeusz.

The heavy door of the chapel creaked when she pulled it open, revealing the dim sanctuary within. It used to be a small training gymnasium, but now it was decorated with poorly-painted holy pictures. At one end stood an altar, cobbled together with mismatched wood. A large painting of the Madonna hung above it on the wall. Father Terlecki flittered around, lighting candles and brushing dust off the altar. A few indiscriminate heads bowed here and there in the pews. Zosia made the sign of the cross upon entering and slipped into a pew without genuflecting. Folding her hands in her lap, she stayed sitting; kneeling was too difficult. The door creaked a few more times as believers came and went. Each time she swung her head around, but each time it wasn't Tadeusz.

Our Father, she started, silently reciting all of the prayers she knew by heart twice. She then rested to collect her thoughts. *Dear God . . .* She felt foolish for making up her own prayer, so she kept it simple: *Wherever my children are, give them strength and love. Let them know their* matka *loves them, and I won't rest until I find them again.*

Please let Antoni find peace and comfort. And Eliasz, too—for Petronela's sake. Help Petronela through this difficult time.

Lord, I know I don't deserve anything for myself, but please forgive me for being so weak with Czeslaw. Help him to find happiness at home. Watch over his children.

She dropped her hand to her belly. *God, please, let this child be strong and healthy.* She paused for a minute and decided short was best. *Amen.*

After she was satisfied with her prayers, Zosia let her eyes wander over the altar and the paintings on the walls. The low lights and smells of burning wax comforted her.

A distressed, masculine sob broke the impossible stillness in the church. It came from a dark figure on the far side of the sanctuary. He'd been there when she came in. Now the shadow bobbed, heaving from silent tears.

Please, give that person peace. Whatever his pain, Lord, help him to find strength. The prayer sped through her mind automatically.

The crumpling of paper was as loud as a jet engine in the soundless room. The man stood and walked out. She could tell by his gait that it was Czeslaw.

Zosia held her breath and watched him from the corner of her eye. The door slammed shut behind him. The sanctuary again sat in an electrified stillness.

Goose bumps formed on her arms. She slowly got to her feet, hoping to not be seen by the remaining worshippers in the church. She tiptoed across the room to the pew where Czeslaw had been sitting. Crumpled paper and a torn envelope lay on the floor.

She sat and leaned over her enlarged belly to pick up the envelope. It was addressed simply: *Czeslaw Lysek, Polish Army, Eastern Front.* The envelope had a postmark on it, and she squinted in the darkness to make it out. It was faded and dirty and appeared to have spent years stuck to the bottom of a soldier's boot.

October 28, 1944. Nearly two years ago. It came from Warsaw.

She again bent to her side and this time picked up the paper. Careful to not crinkle it and alert others of her snooping, she unfolded the creases.

> *Dear Czeslaw,*
> *I'm writing this with a heavy heart. Franciszka, Henryk, and Janina are dead. A hand grenade detonated inside your house, killing them instantly. We think the children found the grenade outside and, not knowing what it was, they brought it inside to play with it. You can take comfort in knowing there was no pain. We buried them in the family plot next to Uncle Bernard.*
> *Czeslaw, wherever this finds you, if you're thinking of returning to Poland, don't. There's nothing left. Make a life for yourself somewhere else.*
> *Godspeed, my brother. I hope to see you again someday.*
>
> *Pawel*

Small circles of water dotted the page, expanding outward into the paper as they fell from Zosia's cheeks. His beautiful children, who'd kept him alive all those years in prison, were dead.

Czeslaw's wife was also dead and had been for some time. She'd died before Zosia even met Czeslaw. Zosia's stomach leapt.

She dropped her head into her hands. *God, forgive me for my selfish thoughts. Please let those two innocent children and their mother find rest in Your Kingdom.* Zosia still didn't know if God was listening, but if her prayers would allow those children peace, she'd send up a thousand.

"You deserve to know what happened to your family." She remembered what Czeslaw said to her. *"I know my children are*

alive and safe. You deserve that relief, too."

He needed to know about her baby. Their baby. If she told him, it could be a tiny bit of light in a life that had now turned even darker.

But telling him now, after she'd learned his wife was dead, would only make her an opportunist.

She knew she had to wait for him to come to her.

The letter rested like an anvil in her hands. She dropped it to the floor, crossed herself again, and hurried toward the door.

CHAPTER TWENTY-TWO

Weeks. August.

Kasia was ill. The old lady thrashed in her stinking sheets while Angelika stood vigil, a constant cigarette poised at her lips and a glass of stale water waiting in her hand for when Kasia begged. Zosia, Iwona, Angelika and Olga exchanged anxious glances; they'd become fond of the little old lady and her knitting. Olga also had an intense fear of living in a room where death visited. They hoped for Kasia to recover, but knew it was unlikely. The hospital had already refused her, for their lack of beds and her lack of youth.

Two more women dealt from a different DP camp had been placed in room 21, squeezing them all closer together. Being strangers, the new residents waited quietly on their rickety beds for Kasia to die so her space and belongings could be consumed.

Grief and suffering held Wildflecken together like mortar, and diseases were the tiny rocks and stones that dotted the paste. As more people came into the camp and more bricks of people piled up, the mortar became thicker, stickier, more riddled with stones. The longer they all stayed in the camp, the less pliable their outcomes became. When illness swept through the camp, the very old and very young were the first to perish. Bricks crushed by more bricks piled on top.

As she neared the end of her pregnancy, Zosia found the smells of sweat and infection in the room unbearable. She spent evenings sitting alone on a bench outside of blockhouse C-6 to avoid the nausea and heartache. When her belly quivered with early contractions, she took deep, cleansing breaths of forest air to calm them.

On the fourth night of Kasia's fever, Zosia fiddled with a chewed pencil and tapped her fingers on the unfinished letter beside her on the bench. *"Czeslaw, I know about your family,"* it started, "*and I'm so sorry.*" It was not likely to get any further, since words written on surrogate stationary did nothing but fail her. Twilight had settled, anyway.

She stared into the deepening darkness. Someone had started a bonfire; she could smell the burning timbers in the air. She scowled at the waste of wood that could have been used to build more housing. With two new roommates and a new baby on the way, space was becoming tighter and tighter. She hoped for word soon from Mr. Devine, word that would finally send her home to Marisha and Stefek.

Angelika sprang from the blockhouse door, troubled. "Zosia, what is this?" She held an unmarked pill bottle in her hand.

Zosia studied it, bewildered. She recognized it as one she'd received from Tadeusz. It should have gone to Iwona's contact in Berlin. "It's medicine. Penicillin."

"I don't think so. I don't recognize it." Angelika dumped a few large, white tablets into her palm. "I worked in a field hospital for a short time during the war. This doesn't look like penicillin." She sat on the bench next to Zosia, who hastily gathered her letter and stuffed it in her pocket. "This makes me nervous. I'd give her some, but I'm not sure . . ."

Zosia met Angelika's anxious eyes. "Kasia's getting worse,

isn't she?" Angelika nodded. Zosia let out a long breath. "We need to get a doctor. Or find Iwona."

"The doctors won't help, we've tried. They say she's too old."

"Aaaangelikaaaa!" Olga threw open a window upstairs. "Come quickly, we need your help."

"Zosia . . ." Angelika's eyes were glassy in the moonlight.

"Do you know where Iwona is?"

Angelika looked around. "Something is burning. If the men are all drinking around a bonfire tonight, it's a good bet Iwona is there."

"I'll go." Zosia pulled herself to her feet and took the bottle from Angelika.

"Zosia, you shouldn't go alone, not in your condition."

"I'll only be a minute." Zosia patted Angelika's arm. "Go, take care of Kasia."

Zosia tottered down the street, each step coming down with the weight of a thousand army trucks. She inched toward the smell of burning wood, the bottle of pills tight in her grip. She knew there was a good chance Czeslaw would be at the gathering, but she had to ignore her own feelings to help Kasia. She had to find Iwona.

Something wasn't right. The fire was too large. Even from blocks away she could see the sky lit up orange from the blaze. She approached, and the voices rose with the embers. But instead of the hooting and singing that usually accompanied the fires, the chatter was more subdued, careful.

She turned a corner and saw flames curling out of the windows of a wooden building just a little larger than a double outhouse. The roof had been reduced to nothing more than charred scaffolding that crackled before collapsing into the blinding orange fire. Circling the building, onlookers made no movement to stop the inferno. Most tipped back bottles wrapped in paper while they watched.

Awestruck, Zosia stopped fast when she saw the blaze. Like a moth, she was drawn to it, and soon her feet brought her to join the crowd. "My God, what happened?"

"Burning a distillery," a man next to her said. He raised his flask to his lips.

"Why? Why does no one stop it?"

"Set on purpose. Police business. Devine is trying to slow the production of alcohol. We made sure the equipment was moved before we set the fire, though. Vodka will be brewing again by Sunday. The police sure know how to put on a show."

Czeslaw was police.

Zosia raised her eyes. Across the fire, Czeslaw's met hers. He stared, oblivious to the female arms wrapped around his waist. Iwona's arms. She leaned intimately into his solid body and cuddled him.

Sick at the sight of the burning building and her roommate's affections, Zosia wanted to run but didn't. She had to talk to Iwona; Kasia needed her. She moved slowly around the perimeter of the fire until she was behind Iwona and Czeslaw. She felt stupidly awkward with her huge belly. Her heart pounded in her chest. She tapped Iwona on the shoulder.

"Zosia!" Her smile was thick with alcohol. Zosia could see Czeslaw's shoulders tighten. He didn't turn toward her. Iwona threw her arm around Zosia in an embrace. "Join the party!"

"Kasia needs our help. Is this penicillin?" Zosia held out the bottle.

Iwona sobered. She barely glanced at the bottle before turning her attention back to the fire. Her arms slinked back around Czeslaw. "I don't know what you're talking about. I've never seen that before."

Zosia was taken aback. She watched Iwona, confused at her denial. "But Iwona, this is your—"

"Come, my love." Iwona sweetly looked up into Czeslaw's

stoic face. "I'm tired."

My love. Zosia's stomach churned at the thought of Iwona with Czeslaw. *I let him go. This is his decision. I had my chance.* Sadness brimmed in her, but she put it aside for Kasia's sake. "Iwona, please." She wiggled her way in front of the couple and held the bottle out to Iwona. "Tell me what this is."

Czeslaw snatched the bottle out of her hand, making Zosia jump. "What in the hell are you doing with this?"

"I . . . she . . ." Zosia stammered. Iwona watched through wary eyes.

"Tadeusz," Czeslaw said with a snarl. Zosia felt the presence of a man approach behind her. She didn't want to know it was Tadeusz, and she didn't want to know he was Czeslaw's friend. Zosia took a step away, but Czeslaw grabbed her wrist. Holding Iwona's hand, he led both women away from the crowd into the trees. Zosia staggered along.

Once they were removed, Czeslaw reached down and extracted a knife from his sock. He flipped it open. Iwona shrank back. Zosia's stomach flipped at the glint of the blade. Her mind went to the Nazi he'd buried in the forest. Czeslaw was dangerous. She wrapped her arms protectively around her belly as strong hands held her from behind. Bile burned her throat knowing it was Tadeusz.

Czeslaw used the knife to scrape a tiny bit off of one of the pills. He put it to his tongue to taste it. "Shit." He handed the bottle to Tadeusz, spitting the bitter powder onto the ground. "Take it to the chief, I'll be along in a minute." Tadeusz let go of Zosia and trotted away without a word.

"Czeslaw," Zosia said, "I need that. Kasia needs that."

"It won't help Kasia." Czeslaw flipped his knife shut. "It's illegal."

"Isn't this all illegal?" Zosia was baffled.

"This is worse."

Iwona's eyes were round in the sparkling light of the fire. "Zosia, what have you done?" She leaned in toward Czeslaw. He stayed aloof, not reacting to her and concentrating his frustration at Zosia.

"But, this was yours." Zosia looked from Czeslaw to Iwona. "I got it for you."

"I don't know what you're talking about," Iwona said. "I only ever traded aspirin and a little penicillin, never Benzedrine."

"Czeslaw?" Zosia could only speak his name as a whimper. She saw him reach for a pair of handcuffs. "No, you don't understand, it was Tadeusz." Zosia trembled and hurried through an explanation. "He gave it to me. Iwona sent me. She told me it was penicillin—"

Czeslaw pulled Iwona's arm behind her back, making Zosia jump. "How did you know it was Benzedrine?" he asked hotly into her ear.

Iwona's eye's narrowed. She fought against Czeslaw, but he held her tight.

An explosion cracked from the fire behind them, and they all jumped. "We forgot the bottles under the sink basin!" someone in the crowd shouted. "Run!" The bystanders whooped and fled as the fire raged and more forgotten bottles of vodka burst in the heat.

Iwona wiggled out of Czeslaw's distracted grip. She ran into the woods with no trace of a limp. She easily absorbed into the mob.

"Fucking Christ—" Czeslaw ran after her.

Zosia stood alone in the woods, her body weak and her mind clouded with confusion. Even at a distance, she could feel the heat of the fire against her face. She watched it, hypnotized by the uncontained beauty of the flames against the night.

Kasia needed her, but there was nothing she could do. Iwona was gone, and so was the penicillin, or whatever it was. Zosia was rooted to the ground, unable to think.

Men brought buckets of water, and soon the building was engulfed in steam and smoke. People left a few at a time as the fire quenched, leaving the smoldering embers to be dealt with in the morning.

A hand rested on Zosia's arm, and she recoiled. "Zosia?" a soft voice asked. "Zosia, are you okay? Did you find Iwona?"

In the moonlight, Angelika looked like a fairy with her pale hair surrounding her face. Zosia shook her head. "Angelika, I'm sorry. I think Iwona's gone."

"Zosia!" another voice cut through the trees. "You have no idea the danger you were in." Czeslaw's forehead glinted with sweat as he stepped out of the shadows.

Angelika cringed. "Mr. Lysek? Zosia, what's going on?"

"I don't know," Zosia searched her pocket for a cigarette. Her fingers brushed the letter she'd been writing Czeslaw. "Czeslaw, that was penicillin. I don't understand."

"Iwona lied to you. If that was penicillin, she'd be the most popular trader in Germany." Czeslaw angrily ran his fingers through his hair. "We've been following her for months, watching for her to make a mistake so we could arrest her. Now we have confirmation and she's gone, I lost her."

"Arrest her?" Angelika looked back and forth between Czeslaw and Zosia. "Why?"

"Running illegal drugs. And you were helping her." He looked at Zosia.

"Zosia?" Angelika's voice squeaked.

"No, not Iwona." Zosia violently shook her head. Iwona was her friend. "Czeslaw, I got those drugs from that little shit Tadeusz. He's the criminal."

"Tadeusz works for us."

Stunned, Zosia took a step back.

"Who's Tadeusz?" Angelika looked from Czeslaw to Zosia.

"Leave us, Angelika." Czeslaw's voice was tight.

"I'm not going to leave you alone, Zosia."

"It's fine, Angelika," Zosia said, not taking her eyes off Czeslaw. "I'll be along in a minute. Meet me at the street. We'll walk home together." Angelika shifted her weight apprehensively, then she retreated through the trees.

"Czeslaw, this was all a mistake. I didn't know—"

"Zosia," Czeslaw cut her off, his own frustration growing, "Tadeusz and I were undercover. We were trying to catch Iwona, but this was nothing but a fucking failure. A waste of time." He angrily kicked at the dirt. "Just like when you picked up the package from Tadeusz. He was livid when he told me. I didn't believe him." Czeslaw snorted a bitter laugh. "Do you remember the raid last fall, when Iwona wounded an official by throwing a teapot?"

Zosia nodded.

"They were looking for drug traders. Tadeusz and I have been trying to prove she was a source of the Benzedrine since then." His eyes drilled into hers. "She sent you to do her trading when she figured out we were on to her."

Zosia couldn't speak. Her head spun trying to keep it straight. Her roommate, Iwona, was a criminal who'd even lied about her limp.

"I suppose she promised you information about your family?" Czeslaw asked.

Zosia stared at the ground.

"Why did you go to her? Why didn't you come to me?" Zosia looked up to see his face melt with emotion. "Even after you learned of my wife's death, and my children's."

He knew. Tadeusz must have followed her into the church after all. He'd seen her read Czeslaw's letter and reported back to Czeslaw.

She turned her head to hide her own tears. "You can't help

me, Czeslaw. Nobody can help me." Zosia knew no one could find her children except her. It was a mother's job. She had to return to Poland.

"Is that my baby?" His defeated voice crushed her.

Tell him. Tell him now. The words didn't come. Zosia choked on her own breath. "I'm so sorry, Czeslaw." She closed her eyes and waited. All that followed was painful silence, broken by the crunching of Czeslaw's boots as he walked away.

"It's yours," she whispered after him. "Of course it's yours."

Chapter Twenty-Three

Two weeks.

Kasia died, and Iwona never returned. Angelika, Zosia, and Olga watched Kasia's body be carried from their room, their arms wrapped around each other. A handkerchief passed between them. Olga was the most distraught, since she now had to live in a space haunted by the Reaper.

They couldn't hide the old woman's death, so Kasia's bed was filled with another new arrival before the end of the day. The women concealed Iwona's absence, though, by absorbing her space and disassembling her bed. To keep up the appearance of Iwona's residence, Zosia and Angelika shared her weekly rations with the newcomers, but Olga refused. She felt the lard and raisins were cursed, too.

August was waning when Kasia was laid to rest in the Wildflecken cemetery. After the service, Petronela approached Zosia, a cup of pale, weak coffee in her hand. "Come, sit with me."

Zosia nodded. She followed her friend to a bench out of earshot of the cemetery and eased herself onto it. "I never knew Kasia was a nun," Zosia said. "She never mentioned it. I feel bad that I didn't know more about her. Just like Ramona. We'd shared months of stolen chickens before that bastard Voss killed her, and we never knew her."

"People are allowed their secrets, I suppose. It doesn't make us any less of a friend if we aren't in on them." Petronela took a drink of her coffee. "Though, I suppose I'd prefer my friends' secrets weren't criminal in nature. Any word from Iwona?"

Zosia shook her head. "Nothing. Did you know she didn't even have a limp?"

"You're lucky you weren't hurt." Petronela scratched her knee. "Iwona's secrets could have killed you."

Secrets. Zosia was good at those, especially where they concerned Czeslaw. "We're all criminals, I guess." Zosia lit a cigarette. "You know about Czeslaw, about his family?"

Zosia could feel Petronela nod. "Heard bits here and there."

"Another thing I've spoiled." Zosia fingered her spent match.

"He's hurting, Zosia." Petronela heaved a massive sigh. She watched a group of boys kick a ball down the cobblestone street. "He just learned his entire family, including his beloved *dziewczynka,* was violently killed. What did you expect? He's grieving, and he's angry at the world."

Zosia rubbed her belly. It was as hard as stone. "We're all grieving." She heard a childish whine in her voice, and it disgusted her. "Everyone in *Europe* is grieving."

Petronela leaned forward and put her hand over Zosia's. "When we're at our lowest, we tend to hurt those we love most. It's hard to understand another person's motives when we're so wrapped in our own despair." She paused. "I know he loves you."

Zosia knew, too, but she looked up. "How do you know that?"

"He told me."

The baby fluttered inside her. "Well, it doesn't matter. There's no future for us."

"Why not, Zosia? There's nothing stopping you now, except your own inability to trust him. And yourself."

Zosia stared at the ground. She wanted to allow herself to love him, to let him love her, but there was too much in the way. In Wildflecken, a lifetime of hurt could overwhelm any single moment. A displaced persons camp was no place for comfort and happiness.

Wanda approached from Mess 3 in the distance and Zosia pulled herself to her feet. She wasn't in the mood for Wanda's abrasiveness, and she also hadn't fully forgiven her for seducing them into jobs with the hopes of better information. "I need to return to Poland, right away."

"Zosia, you should rest."

"No, I've made enough trouble. My children need me. I'm going to check when the next train to Warsaw is scheduled, and I will be on it, even if I have to stow away." She took an unstable step, not considering how that was impossible in her condition.

"You don't know if they're still there."

"It's a place to start. I have to go somewhere, do something."

Petronela laid a firm hand on Zosia's shoulder. "I'm not going to tell you again. Sit down."

"Don't argue with her, Zosia." Wanda ambled up. Zosia shot her a look and sat. Wanda tapped Petronela on the arm. "Shift change, Petra."

"I'll talk to you at lunchtime, Zosia. Stay off your feet." Petronela walked away in the direction of the mess buildings, and Wanda took her seat next to Zosia.

"So, you're going back to Poland soon?" Wanda asked.

"Soon as I can."

"You going with Czeslaw?"

Zosia eyed the woman. "How do you know he's involved?"

Wanda shrugged. "Gossip spreads like gonorrhea around here, Zosia. You know that."

Zosia glared at the ground. "I'm not going anywhere with Czeslaw."

"Well," Wanda leaned back on the bench. She stuffed a cigarette into her mouth. "If you don't want him involved, you better go as soon as possible."

"I know," Zosia said.

"I mean, really soon." Wanda nodded toward Zosia's belly.

Zosia eyed the little woman. "Why?"

Wanda waved out her match. "Heard some ugly stuff. I guess fathers have some say over the baby once it's born. Happened to an old friend of mine in Schauenstein. Her baby's father kept threatening to take the infant back to Latvia, and I guess he could have done just that, legally. She had to stick around and pretend to be a family, but she made life hell for him until he got sick of her. He finally signed some paperwork giving up rights to the child, and she practically ran back to Lodz." She inhaled her cigarette. "Big pain in the ass, though. Could have ended badly."

Zosia trembled. She felt heavier than usual. "I better go lay down," she said to Wanda and pulled herself upright.

"You sure you're okay?"

"Yes." Zosia took a careful step, pretending to have no trouble in the world walking across the street.

Instead of going to her blockhouse, Zosia walked to Mr. Devine's office and climbed the stairs slowly, resting against the railing after every few steps. When she arrived at the director's door she leaned on the doorknob and entered without knocking.

"No, that can't be. You don't understand." A woman with black, unkempt hair stood in the office, her hands clenched to her chest and her cheeks wet. Both she and Mr. Devine looked up when Zosia stumbled in.

"Mrs. Wilusz, are you all right?" Mr. Devine hurried around his desk.

Zosia leaned against the back of a chair and held her breath.

"Mrs. Urbanowicz, I'll do whatever I can to help you." He held the door for the woman, who retreated after throwing a disdainful look toward Zosia. Then the director helped Zosia to sit, fanning her with a filing folder. "Just rest for a minute."

She nodded and let out a long exhale. "I have to return to Poland. Now."

"I know. I'm working on it, Mrs. Wilusz." He returned to shuffling his papers.

"You don't understand. I have to go. Now. I can't wait until tomorrow."

Mr. Devine gasped. "Mrs. Wilusz?"

She bent her chin to her chest and squeezed her eyes shut. A puddle of water appeared under her chair. "Mr. Devine," she said, "please go get Mrs. Kloc. She's working in Mess 3."

"Let me take you to the maternity hospital." He helped her stand and opened the door. "One step at a time." They hobbled down the stairs. "There's a Jeep parked behind the building, I'll go get it. It will only take a minute. Wait here."

"No."

"Less than a minute. You can count the seconds—"

"Stop. No!" Zosia's fear of cars felt amplified with the baby ready to fall out of her. She thought of her brother, Oskar. "Please, no Jeep," she said. "Walk. Just walk."

"But the hospital is on the other side of town, maybe a kilometer."

"I can do it." Zosia gritted her teeth.

Mr. Devine didn't argue, but he did call to a young boy on the sidewalk and offered him a few coins to run ahead and warn the nurses they were coming. Zosia figured if the boy had any brains, he would disappear and use the money to buy candy or tobacco.

After a laborious walk across camp, they reached the hospital where two nurses trotted out to meet them with a lopsided, broken wheelchair. Zosia gratefully rested into it and leaned in the direction the chair was bent. She silently thanked the boy for his honesty.

Within a few minutes Mr. Devine had fetched Petronela, who began barking orders—most of which were ignored—at the flurry of doctors and nurses. Zosia was light-headed and thirsty, but she couldn't get her thoughts across to anyone. She heard Petronela shout for painkillers, but a nurse answered there were none. Someone brought Zosia water, which she sipped and promptly vomited.

All she could do was thrash about and moan until she felt sudden pressure on her wrists and a sharp pain in her leg.

The room stopped. The pain stopped. Everything was dark and still. She could feel her eyelids hover between open and closed.

In the dense bog of her mind, she heard their song. *Wspomnij mnie . . .*

Remember me . . .

Where was Wiktor?

"Zosia, your husband is here."

No he's not. People surrounded her. They felt familiar yet she couldn't place any of the faces. Wiktor was nowhere. *Where is Wiktor?*

". . . Zosia . . ."

He was at the door. It wasn't Wiktor. All she saw was his eyes, and Wiktor had brown eyes. These were blue. *Czeslaw. Yes. No . . .*

Baby Stefek cried. *No, not Stefek. Stefek is a big boy. Whose baby is that?*

The man came closer. The scorching eyes burned a hole into her like the blue flame of a stove burner. She couldn't turn away. It wasn't Czeslaw. It was Voss. He had a gun pointed at her. The light reflected off of the shiny metal and blinded her. Her eyes hurt. She struggled to keep them open, squinting into the glare.

She was on her feet, yet she couldn't move. He kept coming. She tried to take a step but fell to the ground. Voss was holding a baby. Her baby. *He has my baby.*

". . . Zosia . . ."

Someone held her down. She couldn't get away. Was it Tadeusz? She tried to crawl. She tried to stand up. She couldn't see. She searched for some crack of light to prove she was still alive.

That was when she knew her eyes were open.

A slow squeak kept time next to Zosia's bed. She couldn't make out the shadowy figure in the rocking chair. Was it Death sitting next to her, waiting? And where was the baby? Was there even a baby at all?

She worked her jaw to speak, but her mouth stumbled over her dry tongue. She licked her lips and whispered, "Who's there?"

"Zosia, it's me." Petronela sat up in the chair.

Zosia pushed herself upright. "Help me, Petra. Czeslaw took the baby."

"Your baby is right here, Zosia. It's a boy." Petronela stood and flicked on the lamp next to the bed, causing Zosia to wince in the brightness. She bent to show Zosia the bundle of blankets. "He's healthy, just over two and a half kilos. Lots of dark hair." She slid the infant into Zosia's welcoming arms.

It had been a long time since she held her own baby. Zosia clung to the warmth and peace of the child as she studied him.

"I don't remember what happened."

"You got the Dämmerschlaf," a voice spat from a nearby bed, "while the rest of us had to suffer."

"Don't pay any attention, Zosia. They're jealous." Petronela leaned forward. "A friend pulled some strings." She patted Zosia's arm. "You lost a lot of blood, but you're fine. You need to rest."

"Petra, I don't remember this being so hard with my other children."

"You weren't an old lady then." Petronela grinned. She paused for a second. When she spoke again, her voice was soft. "It was a difficult birth, Zosia. You should know, the doctor said it's not possible for you to have any more children."

Zosia nodded; she didn't plan to. She studied her son for a minute before looking up pleadingly at her friend. "You have to help me. I have to escape."

"Escape?"

Zosia's mind was still foggy, and every coherent thought took effort. "He's going to take my baby."

"Who's going to take your baby?" Petronela appeared genuinely concerned. She looked around the vast room filled with beds, bins, and trays and loudly cleared her throat. A few people who were sleeping in nearby beds twitched and rolled over.

Zosia tried to slide out of the bed with her baby but Petronela held her down. Panic simmered inside her. "He's going to take him. Petra, I have to take the baby back to Poland right away."

"Zosia, who? Who's going to take him? Czeslaw?"

"Yes!"

"I don't think so . . ." Another exaggerated cough.

"Yes." Zosia's eyes were full. She held her newborn son tight against her. "He's going to—"

"I'm not going to take your baby, Zosia." A male voice halted her. Czeslaw appeared from the shadows, his face haggard.

"Where the hell were you?" Petronela seethed.

Czeslaw lifted a small, chipped cup. "Coffee. Had to make it."

"Fucking hell."

"Czeslaw?" Zosia gasped.

"He's been here all night," Petronela said. "Since he brought the injection."

Zosia shivered.

He gave a meek smile. "Is it okay that I'm here?"

Zosia nodded, and Petronela slipped away, her footsteps squeaking against the tiles. The door clicked closed behind her.

Czeslaw knelt next to the bed, reaching his finger out to touch the baby's hand. "Does he have a name?"

"I think, Jerzy."

"It's a good name. Strong." Czeslaw's peaceful face was damp.

"Czeslaw, listen," Zosia said. "I'm sorry—"

"No, I'm sorry. I've been so angry since . . ." He stopped. His fingers absently massaged Jerzy's foot. "I shouldn't have taken it out on you."

They were quiet for a moment before she took Czeslaw's hand. "I'm so sorry about your family, Czeslaw. I wanted to come to you, but it didn't feel right."

He wept and rested his head against Zosia's chest. Zosia wrapped her free arm around his shoulders. "All this time, I thought they were well," he said. "It was all a lie."

Zosia held him and held her newborn son. Both were helpless in her arms.

After several minutes, Czeslaw lifted his head. "Zosia," he said, his voice rough, "you're my life now. You and Jerzy."

"You hardly know me."

He dropped his head and pressed his lips against her hand. "That doesn't have to be." He slid onto the rocking chair behind him. "The past is done. Those people we loved, they're gone. Franciszka, Henryk, Janina, Antoni, Wiktor . . . We can keep them in our memories. We can still love them and grieve them, but we can't live for them anymore." He motioned to baby Jerzy sleeping in Zosia's arms, "He is what's important now."

"Yes, Jerzy." Zosia stroked the infant's cheek, "And Stefek and Marisha, too."

"And I'll help you find them Zosia." Czeslaw's weary face was drawn, possibly from a night or even weeks without sleep. "I promise. You can trust me."

Zosia didn't respond.

"Marry me."

Her lips quivered. She tried to move them to speak, but there was no sound.

"Don't answer. You had a rough night. You need to rest. Think about it." He turned his body, readying to stand but stopped. "This boy needs me. I need him, and I need you." His voice cracked. "Jerzy needs us both."

CHAPTER TWENTY-FOUR

October, 1946.

A shriek punctured the chilly room. Barely awake, Zosia rolled over and peered at her son in the dim light of early morning. Jerzy slept peacefully next to her in the hammock she'd fashioned out of a bed sheet. She listened again, but this time only heard the harsh creaking of bedsprings and moaning from behind the tan blanket walls.

"Oh, *Kryssssztoffff*. . ." Zosia folded her pillow over her head to block out the euphoria. Olga had clearly gotten over Ryszard.

Jerzy turned his head and stretched his arms. He grunted, scrunched his face into a grimace, and wailed. Groggy, Zosia jumped to her feet. She grabbed his rinsed glass bottle and reached for a can of condensed milk. There wasn't one. She'd used the last can in the middle of the night.

Jerzy's cries became more insistent. She searched under the small dresser and behind her chair, in case a can had rolled out of sight.

Angelika appeared between the blankets with drowsy eyes and sleep wrinkles across her cheek. "Only a few more days," Zosia said apologetically.

Her roommate nodded and handed a *Nestlé's* can through the blankets. "Here." Zosia gave her a quizzical look, and Angelika shrugged. "I use it in my coffee." She disappeared behind the sea of khaki and said, "Olga, for God's sake, have some dignity and keep your voice down."

"Sorry," a sheepish voice answered.

Zosia assembled Jerzy's bottle with the milk, a little water, and a few drops of Karo syrup, just like the nurses had advised. She scooped him up, slid the nipple into his mouth, and settled into her rigid seat, her shoulders swaying side to side to make up for the lack of a rocking chair.

He looks like Antoni when he was born. Antoni had a mess of black hair, too. The memory pulled on Zosia's soul.

When Jerzy finished eating, Zosia changed his diaper, slipped a fresh nightgown over his head, and wrapped him in a ragged quilt. She settled him into an old mail cart she kept stored by the stove. It had been waiting for disassembly into firewood behind the administrative building, so she took it as a wagon for Jerzy. One wheel was bent, which gave it a bad wobble.

She pulled on a thick sweater and pushed the cart out into the hallway where she almost collided with a new, pale yellow baby carriage. It had a shiny steel frame and large wheels. Inside there was a dark green knit blanket and a small scrap of paper:

Zosia, this will be more comfortable for Jerzy.
Czeslaw

She inspected the carriage, admiring the tiny white embroidered leaves on the sides. There was no squeak when she pushed it back and forth, and the canopy glided easily up and down. She smiled and placed Jerzy inside, tucking the green blanket around him. The feel of the knit tickled her fingers, and she longed to feed that fat fabric through a sewing machine, to make a warm bunting. She left the mail cart in the hallway; she knew some children would find it and convert it into an army tank or fire truck.

Hoping Petronela could smuggle a few cans of condensed milk for her, Zosia pushed Jerzy toward the mess buildings. The intense cold of fall had settled over the camp. Her bones ached as she thought about how winter would furiously swallow Wildflecken, cutting the town off from the rest of Germany for days or possibly even weeks at a time.

Repatriation wouldn't happen until spring, at least. Crumbled infrastructure and bad weather would keep her from her children for yet another Christmas. Sad and angry at the thought of another winter full of uncertainty in Germany, Zosia stomped ahead, staring at tire tracks in the autumn mud.

There had to be a way, and she had to trust Czeslaw to find it. She would ride all the way back to Minsk Mazowiecki on the back of Czeslaw's motorcycle with Jerzy strapped to her chest if she had to.

As if summoned by her thoughts, a motorcycle's rumble approached. Out of respect for the baby's brand-new ears, Czeslaw stopped several meters away and cut the engine. He climbed off the motorcycle and approached Zosia, a smitten grin on his face.

"How's Jerzy? And how's Matka?"

"We're both fine." Zosia felt comfort when Czeslaw approached. Once she'd released her distrust she felt safe and protected. "Thank you for the carriage."

"Should work well for you. For us." Czeslaw patted its canopy with pride. They both turned and walked together, moving in an unspoken way that suggested they'd been married for years.

Their wedding was planned for Friday, the eleventh of October. Three days away.

"It's getting so cold." Zosia took a breath of frosty air. "I find myself already wishing for spring. I hope we're back in Poland before Easter." The pause between them felt anxious, so Zosia continued. "We haven't talked much about repatriation. I know it's difficult to think about returning to Poland. It breaks my heart that your children aren't there waiting for you. But I assure you, when we find Marisha and Stefek, we'll all be happy. All of us, together." Czeslaw's silence agitated Zosia further. "Do you think there is anything you can do to get us home sooner? Devine says it won't happen until spring, but it's only October. Maybe we can still get back to Poland before Chris—"

"I'm going to help you find your children, Zosia. I swear to you, we'll find them."

"I know." The uneasiness in Czeslaw's voice made her squirm. She felt too warm under her coat.

They were quiet for several minutes before Czeslaw spoke again. "Zosia, I'm not going back to Poland."

If you're thinking of returning to Poland, don't. There's nothing left. Make a life for yourself somewhere else. Her mind was too thick from poor sleep to place the words. Where did they come from? She stopped walking and stood, staring ahead.

Pawel's letter.

The last few weeks of plans and dreams in Zosia's head now felt like a cruel trick.

"But I'm going to find Stefek and Marisha," Czeslaw said. "We'll make sure Marisha is safe, then we'll bring Stefek with us."

She met his pleading eyes. "With us? Where?"

Czeslaw pulled a folded brochure out of his pocket as if he'd been waiting for the right moment to show Zosia. "I've been reading about Australia." He unfolded the paper and there, in brightly colored ink that Zosia thought only the Nazis had access to for their propaganda, were large blue letters shouting "*AUSTRALIA! LAND OF TOMORROW!*" in Polish.

"Is that a kangaroo?" Zosia studied what looked like an oversized rat under the headline. She'd seen these flyers around, encouraging Poles south of the equator to the strange, backward lands Down Under.

"They're taking families, and I've heard wonderful things. They have homes already built, waiting for people to move in."

"I'm not going to Austr—"

"See?" Czeslaw opened the pamphlet, and it burst with color. A small drawing in the bottom corner showed a generic red barn situated within hilly green pastures under a solid blue sky. "We can live on a nice farm. I've been researching which crops are grown there, and I think—"

"You're a farmer?"

Czeslaw gave her a perplexed look. "Yes. What did you think?"

She didn't answer. She'd thought of Czeslaw as many things: policeman, trafficker, soldier, prisoner, father, lover, and possible husband. She'd thought a lot about his family before the war, but not about his occupation.

"The weather is nice, always warm," he went on. "Wouldn't that be wonderful?" He pointed to another illustration, this one was a happy couple with a young boy, not unlike their own fledgling family. The woman was drawn with blonde hair, and she wore a yellow bathing suit. The man sported green swimming briefs and sunglasses, and held a large, striped beach ball. The boy sat on the ground building a sand castle. All three laughed with joy. The pamphlet tried awfully hard to express how happy everyone was in Australia.

But was this blonde woman also missing a son, lost and possibly dead half across the world? Did she have a daughter married to a monster and another son already in the ground? She wouldn't be so carefree on the beach if that were the case. "We have to return to Poland. It's the only way we can find my children."

"Zosia, I can't return."

"I know Poland is a mess now, but it will get better, I know it. I'm sure it also must be very hard with the memories of your children. But—"

"No." Czeslaw's voice was ragged. He kept his gaze on the happy beachgoers in the pamphlet. "I was a member of the *Armia Krajowa*. I supported the Underground State. With the communists in power, the best I can hope for if I return to Poland is prison. More likely, I'd be hunted down and killed."

A burning spear of anguish punctured Zosia's chest. She couldn't survive another dead husband. "I don't understand, I thought the Allies won the war."

"Poland didn't win anything."

"But, what about your family? You said you were going to return to them."

"No." He shook his head. "I never said I would return to them. I was hoping to get them out."

The hope that Zosia held in her heart, that kept her moving from one minute to the next, seeped out of her, betraying her. "If you want to settle somewhere besides Poland, why not England? Or France? Somewhere closer."

"Because those places are destroyed too, and it will take years to recover. I don't want to rebuild my country while I'm also rebuilding my life."

There was a pause as they both stared at the primitive little pictures. "I can't abandon my children, Czeslaw. You know that."

"Zosia, trust me, please." He took her hand. "We can have a good life in Australia, I'm sure of it. We can be a family. I promise to take care of you. You, Jerzy, and, God willing, Stefek. We'll find him. And we'll help Marisha too."

"I'm sorry, Czeslaw." She pulled her hand away and took a step forward toward Mess 3. She didn't respond when Czeslaw called after her. She quickened her pace, pushing Jerzy along in his carriage. She would push him all the way home to Poland if necessary.

CHAPTER TWENTY-FIVE

Afternoon.

"So that's it, then? That's why you won't marry him?" Petronela asked after patiently listening to Zosia's review of the situation. She sat behind a line of condensed milk cans and held a napping Jerzy in her thick arms. The disparity of the sturdy, muscular woman holding the tiny, delicate child seemed bizarre to Zosia.

"Can you blame me?" Zosia chewed her sawdust bread. She stared at a small, engraved sign on the wall past Petronela that said "Wildflecken Mess 2," but covering the word "Wildflecken" was a piece of tan tape with the word "Durzyn" written on it in black ink.

Petronela didn't answer. She kept her eyes on Jerzy, pretending to be distracted by the child. She rocked back and forth, bumping into the DPs on either side of her.

Zosia swirled her fork in the pools of grease floating in her gravy, making loops of brown on her plate. Over the months, her slices of meat gradually became smaller as more DPs crowded an already stretched-thin camp. "You think I'm making a mistake?"

"Yes." Petronela looked up. "He's handing you a great opportunity. You know, Zosia, I love you, but I think you're a fool."

Zosia stopped chewing. "A fool to search for my children? There's no other choice. Don't you want to return home?"

Petronela's face was stony and pale; her grief continued to consume her. Time wasn't as healing as anyone would have liked. Her demeanor was concerning to Zosia but not uncommon. Every person in Wildflecken was infected with a wide, deep chasm of lost loves and missing lives. "No. I won't return," Petronela said. "Not ever. Even if I had someone waiting there." Her voice was subdued and strangely mismatched with her imposing physical presence. "Do you remember Lew? He was on our train when we left the farm."

Zosia recalled his patchy moustache. "I remember him. I still see him around camp now and then."

Petronela shook her head. "You don't *still* see him. You see him *again*. He went back to Poland on the first train, the one you were scheduled to take."

Zosia crumpled her nose in confusion. "But I swear I saw him the other day."

"Yes." Petronela picked up a piece of bread with her free hand and took a bite. "He came back." After she swallowed, she went on. "I talked to him, and he said Poland is miserable. Everything is in ruins. Warsaw is crumbled. Anyone left in the city just wanders around in shock, shitting in the streets, looting whatever is left to take. Everyone is starving. They're eating dogs and rats to survive. Bodies were left to rot in strange places, so when he was out scavenging for food, he would sometimes trip over a human skull. Warsaw is forever haunted. All of Poland is.

"Lew battled his way through the German forests at night to return here. *Here*," she said, waving her bread in the air. "To this halfway point to hell. He risked his life and walked—*walked*—back from Warsaw because this is better.

"And the worst part is," Petronela said, wiping crumbs off her lip, "once you repatriate, you can't return. He's living here illegally. If Devine or anyone else from the UNRRA discovers him, he'll be arrested and sent back to Warsaw. There is nothing in Poland. In fact, Poland has less than nothing."

"Poland has Stefek and Marisha." She paused, remembering what had happened to Czeslaw's family. "I think. I hope. And Antoni—"

"Antoni is gone, Zosia."

Zosia stopped short.

Petronela sighed. "I know you need to find your children, but the authorities in Poland—if you can call them that—will be less helpful than the authorities here. I think you might have better luck working with the immigration offices in Australia. They didn't just survive a devastating war, so they're hungry for excitement."

Lew's story made Zosia anxious. Home was becoming even further away.

Petronela's eyes became uncharacteristically wistful. "You don't know how lucky you are to have this opportunity, Zosia. Go with Czeslaw."

"So where will you go, if not to Poland?" Zosia asked.

"I don't know." Petronela's face was pained with melancholy.

"Why don't you go to Australia?"

"They won't have me. Australia is only accepting families, which I don't have."

Zosia rested her hand on Petronela's. Petronela had no one in the world besides a few vagabond friends in this camp. Zosia understood her loneliness.

After loading Jerzy into the carriage, Zosia returned to Blockhouse C-6 under the weak autumn sun. A chilly wind punched through the holes in her sweater. That yellow bathing suit in Australia was looking more attractive.

If she went with Czeslaw and kept their family together, Jerzy would have a chance at a better life. But she would be forever plagued, knowing she'd left her son and daughter behind.

She had little time to decide with her wedding only days away. It consumed her, leaving her sleepless in those moments when Jerzy was peaceful.

By Thursday morning, she was worked into a fit that rivaled the ferocious wind whipping leaves outside her window. Czeslaw had approached her several times to reason with her, even going as far as tossing stones at her window like a schoolboy, but Zosia pushed him away. "I need time," she told him.

"Zosia, we don't have time. The wedding—"

"Just please, let me be."

Jerzy must have felt her strain, because he spent most of Thursday morning fussy. Her roommates left to escape the racket, and Zosia spent hours walking her son around the room. With each step, she turned her choices over in her mind.

There was a tap at the door. Zosia switched her howling son to her other shoulder and answered it. Father Terlecki's white collar stood firm and judged her from behind the furry lapels of his coat. "Father?" She was dumbfounded and a little annoyed at the unannounced visit while Jerzy was so distraught. She pulled the door open and said in a monotone voice, "What a pleasant surprise. Please, come in."

"Mrs. Wilusz, good morning." His voice was equally flat as he stepped through the door. Neither were happy he was there. "Oh, someone is quite upset, isn't he?"

Her knees and back burned from bouncing the child. She offered a half smile. "He's usually a happy baby."

"Well, maybe he feels the Kingdom of God slipping away." The priest looked at Zosia intently, getting right to the point. "You do intend to baptize this child?"

Zosia flushed a deep red. "Yes, of course, Father. It slipped my mind, I'm sorry." She was sweating, from both the exercise and the interrogation. She shifted Jerzy a little, who calmed to a whimper.

"We discussed Petronela being his Godmother, but . . ." Zosia trailed off. The priest would not understand *too busy.*

"We must never forget our commitment to our faith." Father Terlecki smiled reassuringly. He pulled out a small notebook similar to Czeslaw's booklet of trades. "Let's plan on it directly after the marriage ceremony." His pencil scribbled across the page before he looked up and gave Zosia a smug smile. "Two flies with one swat and all that."

Zosia wasn't sure how she felt about her child and her marriage being compared to insects, but she figured maybe, as a man of the cloth, he didn't quite understand the saying.

They never understood. All her life she'd been taught to confess her sins to men like Father Terlecki—men who were jealous of her discretions, who punished her with guilt and shame.

But were they right? Would Zosia have a clearer soul and a more straightforward path if she confessed her hesitations to this man?

"I also needed to discuss with you the—Mrs. Wilusz?"

Zosia caught herself staring at the floor, not hearing the priest. She returned her attention to his grave face. "I'm sorry, Father."

Father Terlecki crooked his head. "You're troubled by something?"

Zosia nodded, wiping at her eyes.

"Tell me." He softened. "It's not Mr. Lysek? Are you having doubts about the marriage?"

"He wants us to move to Australia," she admitted.

"That's wonderful. I've heard good things." Father Terlecki stroked his bearded chin. "I don't see the problem."

"The problem is, I have a son and daughter lost somewhere in Poland. Well, I think they're in Poland. I'm trying to find them. My son is only twelve. I can't leave Europe without him."

He nodded. "Ah, I see." He thought for a moment. "You know, Mr. Lysek is a good man. Loyal, faithful." Zosia cringed inwardly; she knew too well of Czeslaw's infidelity. "I trust him. He comes to Mass every Sunday and always sits in the same place. What does he say about your lost children?"

Zosia wondered if Father Terlecki knew she only made it to church about once a month, if that. "He said he would help me find them, that he would stop at nothing. And when we do, we can bring Stefek with us." Zosia slowed her bouncing to a gentle sway, since Jerzy had fallen asleep.

"Well then, that sounds like a reasonable solution, don't you think?" The priest rested his hand on Jerzy's back, watching it rise and fall as the boy slept. "This little one seems to think so."

Zosia turned her head toward the window.

"So what is your real apprehension?"

"What if he can't find them?"

"Has he tried?"

Zosia couldn't say anything about Violette or Czeslaw's dealings in the black market, so she shook her head.

"Then I suggest you give him a chance."

"Australia is so far away."

"It doesn't matter where you are if God is with you."

Zosia nearly rolled her eyes at the priest's dogmatism.

"In the eyes of God," he continued, "you are already married to Mr. Lysek. You need to do what's best for this little boy. Your son and daughter in Poland will forgive you. Their faith will persevere. This child, though, needs you. Give him a chance."

"I can't leave my children, Father. I just can't."

The priest patted Zosia's arm. "He says he'll help you, right?" Zosia nodded. "Do you think he would be as willing to help you if you called off the wedding only the day before?"

Zosia's breath caught in her chest. "But he . . ."

"Mrs. Wilusz," Father Terlecki said, his eyebrow arched, "if anyone can find your children, it is Mr. Lysek. Did you know he was the one who found our chalice and consecration bells? That was no easy task."

It appeared that Czeslaw's black market dealings had the Church's blessing. Zosia knew there was no arguing with Father Terlecki, so she forced a smile and moved a half a step toward the door to encourage him to leave. He didn't.

"I would think," he went on, "that a man would be more likely to help a woman if that woman was his wife. Otherwise, aren't you just some other woman?"

"I'm the mother of his child."

Father Terlecki's patience was growing thin. "Which, like I said, makes you already married in every way that matters."

Jerzy sighed on Zosia's shoulder. The man was right about one thing: her infant son deserved a chance at a better life. Zosia cursed a world, and a God, that made her choose between her children. She forced a smile. "You're right, Father. There's no problem. We'll see you tomorrow morning."

"Well, that brings me to the reason for my call. Just a small detail." He pulled out his little notebook again. "Do you have a death certificate for your husband?"

A bolt of panic grounded her. "I had one, but of course it's not here."

"That's fine. I just need his name and the date and location of his death." Zosia rattled off the information, and Father Terlecki flipped his notebook shut. "Good. My secretary will type this up." He smiled from under his knit hat. "May the peace of the Lord be with you."

"And also with you," she echoed automatically. She didn't know priests had secretaries, especially ones willing to write up a death certificate on the spot. She moved to close the door, but it caught on the toe of Father Terlecki's boot.

"Oh, one more thing." He peered at her through the crack.

"Mrs. Kloc will not be able to serve as godmother to your son."

"What?" She threw the door open wide, startling Jerzy again.

"You'll have to talk to her about it. I'll leave that between you folks. I'm happy to serve in her place." His smile felt patronizing to Zosia. "She's fine as your marriage witness, though. Have a nice day." He walked down the hall before Zosia could regain her wits.

She stood gaping at the empty hallway. After several minutes she closed the door and laid Jerzy into his hammock, tucking his swaddling around him. She kissed her fingers and touched his cheek with them. She pulled a few blank papers and some envelopes out of the top drawer of her bedside table. First things first: time was running out on Stefek and Marisha. She dug through her desk for a fountain pen and started writing.

Chapter Twenty-Six

One hour later.

Zosia fumed next to Petronela's bed in Blockhouse C-4 next door. Her coat hung open. She held Jerzy in one arm and squeezed a pile of letters under her other arm. She balanced a cigarette between her fingers, a centimeter of ash hanging from the end of it. On the other side of Petronela's tan blanket wall, someone sang loudly and off-key, increasing Zosia's irritation. "Why not? Tell me."

"I just can't, Zosia." Petronela sounded tired. She sat on her bed, a book held together with too much tape resting next to her. Between the rips and folds on the cover Zosia could read its title: *The Motion Demon*. "I have this thing about baptisms. I'm no good at that kind of thing. 'Spiritual advisor' and all that. No way. I'll be there to watch, but I can't be his godmother."

"But Petra, why? You said you would."

"I never said that. I told you I would witness your marriage, but to find someone else for Jerzy."

"But you love him," Zosia said. "Don't you?"

"I do. I love that boy."

Zosia squared her shoulders for the standoff. "You have to."

"No, I don't. Zosia, I can't be his godmother. Just stop asking. I'll be his honorary aunt. I'll be his best old lady friend. But I won't be his godmother. Now please," she said, reaching for a pen on her bedside table, "what time do you need me tomorrow?"

"Well, if you're not—"

"For Christ's sake, Zosia, don't be a child about this. I'm still your matron of honor. Now, what time?"

Zosia squinted her eyes at her friend. Petronela was unyielding, and Zosia still had work to do before her wedding. "The ceremony is at half past nine. Father Terlecki said to be there fifteen minutes before. Meet me in my blockhouse at, oh . . ."

"Eight thirty. I'll be there at eight thirty." Petronela made notes on her hand in ink.

"Fine." Zosia glared at Petronela for one last moment before surrendering.

—

It was well past dark when Zosia tacked the last bits of delicate trim onto a tiny, white cotton gown for Jerzy. For several evenings the previous week Zosia had snuck into the sewing room and pieced together enough scraps of fabric to make a simple wedding dress for herself. Now with only hours to go, she had to finish her outfit and also cobble together a tiny baptismal gown for Jerzy. In the dim light from the incandescent bulb above, she finished with aching eyes and fingers.

Barely able to keep her eyes open, she flung the cover over the sewing machine, gathered up her belongings, and hurried out into the darkness.

Jerzy was sleeping when she returned for her final night in Blockhouse C-6. Angelika dozed in the chair next to his hammock. Zosia gently shook her shoulder to send her to bed, then she climbed into her own bed. She hoped it would be a restful night and that Jerzy would sleep through until morning.

She blinked her eyes shut.

"You're late, Zosia. Come on. Get up."

Zosia sat up in bed with a snort. Her heart raced. She tried to get her bearings while she scanned the room, her head thick with sleep. "What time is it?"

Petronela stood over her, Jerzy crying in her arms. "Eight forty-five. You have to get up." Zosia scrambled out of bed and reached for Jerzy, but Petronela shook her head. "I'll feed him, you don't have time. Get dressed."

Zosia knew better than to argue when Petronela's voice carried that particular tone. When Zosia handed over a can of condensed milk, she noticed Petronela's notes on the inside of her thumb: *9:15 church – 8:30 meet Z.*

Zosia pulled her dress from the hanger and let it fall over her shoulders and hips. It wasn't beautiful, but it would do. It was a dull, beige rayon, stitched together from leftover fabric used to line winter coats. Zosia gave it a full, calf-length skirt, butterfly sleeves and a tucked detail along the bodice. A series of glass buttons ran down the front of the dress. She'd come across them in the bottom of a button bag over a year earlier when she was still managing the seamstresses. She'd hoped to trade them for hair dye.

A scratched mirror helped her outline her lips with a shade of lipstick that wasn't quite right. She reached for her hairbrush and dragged it through her hair, silently scolding the gray at her temples. Glancing down at the glass buttons, she wondered if she'd made the right decision in not trading them.

There was one detail left—Czeslaw's pearl earrings. She pushed them through the slits in her ears. For the first time, it felt appropriate to wear them.

She turned to look at Petronela. "He's fine," Petronela answered before Zosia even asked the question. "Eating like a champ. Don't worry about us." Petronela propped Jerzy onto her shoulder and patted his back. "You're beautiful."

Zosia scowled. "I'm still mad at you."

"Fine." Petronela wore a dignified, deep blue velvet suit trimmed with black edging. It looked to Zosia like something that was at one time worn by a sensible female member of the British Parliament. An ivory silk blouse peeked out from under the jacket, and beige stockings covered her legs and hung at her knees. Petronela looked strikingly, and uncharacteristically, feminine and sophisticated.

Zosia tried not to smile. "Petra, you're beautiful too."

Petronela grunted her displeasure.

"You're so good with him." Zosia nodded to her son. "Even if you won't be his godmother, it makes me happy to know you'll always be in his life."

Petronela's smile was forced, and Zosia remembered they would soon be leaving her to go to Australia. Zosia stopped talking. She dressed Jerzy in his gown and bonnet, and the two women tucked the baby into his carriage and set out toward the chapel.

Czeslaw waited outside the front door in a new suit, smoking a cigarette and digging his toe into the dying October grass.

"I'm so sorry we're late." Zosia hurried her pace across the brown lawn.

"I thought you were going to leave me at the altar." He flicked his cigarette to the ground and caught her in an embrace. She felt safe. "Zosia," he whispered into her hair. She let herself melt into his arms. "I may have found Stefek."

She looked up into his hopeful eyes. "What?"

"I'm trying to get a picture to confirm, but we found someone matching Stefek's description."

Zosia covered her gasp with both hands. "Are you sure?"

"No." Czeslaw's eyes were fluid with compassion. "But it's a lead. When we get a picture we can be certain. But I have to tell you, I have my doubts."

"Why?"

"It doesn't quite fit. I'm worried he might be older than Stefek, but we'll see. A friend of a friend was digging around in a small town in northern Germany, and somehow a photograph turned up. I'm trying to get ahold of that picture."

She clasped her hands together to keep them from shaking.

Petronela stepped forward and put her hand on Zosia's shoulder. "We should go in." She gently guided Zosia, and said quietly, "Don't get your hopes up, Zosia. Be realistic. Be strong."

Zosia nodded and lifted her chin. She knew there were probably hundreds of young men wandering Europe between the ages of ten and sixteen who went by the name Stefek. But maybe this was her Stefek.

Father Terlecki stood in front of the altar lighting candles. When he heard the creak of the door, he turned and held out his hands to welcome the small group.

Czeslaw took Zosia's hand, and the couple approached the altar, followed by Petronela pushing Jerzy's carriage. The priest immediately began the marriage ceremony, anxious to get everyone in good standing with God so he could get on with his Friday afternoon prayer meetings.

As Zosia stood in front of Czeslaw and promised her life to him, she was reminded of how similar this wedding was to her first: alone with only her groom, a priest, and a friend to witness. Yet, everything was different. She and Czeslaw had survived atrocities they might never be able to reconcile. But here they were together, hanging their hopes on each other to find a slice of happiness in the decay.

Father Terlecki started the baptism as soon as he'd pronounced the couple man and wife. Czeslaw held the baby while the priest poured droplets of water across his forehead, declaring him now saved and loved by God. In less than thirty minutes, they were in proper standing in the opinion of the Church. Zosia lifted Jerzy to rest on her shoulder, and they all retreated to the entrance of the chapel.

"Oh, wait!" Czeslaw patted his jacket pocket. "Father, please—do you mind?" He handed Father Terlecki a small Foth Derby camera.

Zosia tilted Jerzy up to show his face to the camera while Czeslaw and Petronela fell in on either side. They all smiled, and the priest snapped the picture. Then Petronela pulled Zosia into a tight embrace. When she pulled away, Petronela, still as intimidating a presence as the day Zosia met her, had the slight sparkle of a tear in her eye. "I have something for Jerzy." She reached into her small pocketbook and handed Zosia a miniature gray box.

"Oh, Petra." Zosia opened the box. A miniature triangle pendant lay nestled on the velvet. It was attached to a delicate silver chain.

"I know a boy probably won't wear something like this as jewelry, but maybe he can keep it in his pocket, to know he's loved and watched over. Triangles are a symbol of strength, you know. A three-legged table will never wobble."

Zosia's irritation with Petronela softened. She couldn't help but feel the sting of tears behind her eyes. "It's beautiful. Thank you." Zosia wiped her nose on her handkerchief.

"Mrs. Kloc, thank you for doing this today. It means the world to us." Czeslaw slid up next to Zosia and slinked his arm around her waist. She dropped the small box into her pocket.

"Of course. Congratulations to all of you." Petronela turned and left the church.

Father Terlecki, who had been curiously studying the mechanics of the camera, approached the couple with a winning smile. "God bless the three of you, and may God watch over you on your journey." He made the sign of the cross and held his hand out for Czeslaw to shake while Zosia bent to put a drowsy Jerzy into his carriage.

It wasn't even lunchtime yet, and Zosia had a new husband, a saved newborn son, and a possible lead on her missing son. She smiled to herself as Czeslaw wrapped her coat around her, cocooning her in the warm wool layers, and leaned in to kiss her neck.

She couldn't help but think of Wiktor. Then, she'd been young and impulsive. Now she was neither, yet somehow, even at 36, Czeslaw made her feel youthful again. She returned his kiss, keeping it light and respectful within the walls of the chapel.

Czeslaw grinned, giving Zosia the mischievous look that melted her when they first met. "No one is looking." He nuzzled her ear, and she playfully pushed him away. "We better get going." He straightened himself. "I have something for you, a wedding present." He handed her a key. "Your new home. For now, anyway. We have a room in the former sergeants' quarters along the east side of camp, near the main road. The rooms aren't big, but they're private." He stuffed his hands into his pockets. "I promise you, Zosia, one day we'll have a house. I'll build it with my own bare hands if I need to."

"I believe you." Zosia smiled. They walked out of the church arm in arm, pushing Jerzy in front of them.

They weren't three steps outside the door when a whir of movement startled her. A man sprinted up past Zosia and stopped in front of Czeslaw.

It was Tadeusz. Her stomach seized.

"I have the picture. Here." Tadeusz handed Czeslaw a crumpled, dark photograph. Czeslaw passed it to Zosia.

Confusion and hope weakened her knees. Her mouth fell open when she looked at it, but not because it was her son. The photograph was of a young man, maybe fourteen, with spiky blond hair and an angry scowl slicing across his face. He had a crooked front tooth and a small mole beneath his left eye that looked like a tick.

She stared at the picture in shock. She knew this boy.

"Is it Stefek? Zosia?" Czeslaw watched her while Tadeusz stared off into the distance, not acknowledging her in any way.

The photograph shook in her hand. "It's not Stefek, Czeslaw." She looked up at her husband. "It's Maxim."

"Your daughter's husband?"

Zosia nodded. "It was taken several years ago when he was a boy, but I'd recognize him anywhere. It's him." She watched Czeslaw's confused eyes. "What does this mean? Is Stefek with Maxim and Marisha? Are they in Germany?" Her voice rose with every word until it became a flustered screech.

"I don't know." Czeslaw turned to Tadeusz. "What do you know about this?"

"Nothing, sir. I'm only delivering the photograph. This is what he gave me."

"You have to go back to your contact, wherever you got this." Czeslaw was firm. "Find out what it means."

"I can't. He's dead."

"Shit." Czeslaw pulled a cigarette out of his pocket and lit it. "How?"

"Shot himself."

Czeslaw nodded as if that made sense. Zosia sucked in a deep breath, horrified at the suicide and frustrated that the photograph only created more questions. Still not able to look at Tadeusz, she turned to Czeslaw and searched his face.

Czeslaw put his arm around her. "Happens more than you think. There are more suicides after wars end than during. Pretty common."

Zosia wondered what it said about the world when suicide had become a "common" solution.

"Tad, thank you for your help. If you learn anything else, let us know right away."

Tadeusz sneered at Zosia and walked away. "Czeslaw," Zosia said, her voice heavy with contempt, "Tadeusz can't be trusted."

"Why not?"

Zosia held her tongue; Tadeusz might be able to provide answers about her family. She couldn't tell Czeslaw the truth and sever that connection. She had to pretend to trust the man who'd attacked her. "Never mind." She pressed a smile onto her lips.

"I'm sorry it wasn't Stefek, Zosia, but I think we have a good lead. We just need to find someone else who knew Tadeusz's contact." Czeslaw didn't sound at all certain.

"I know." She wouldn't let Tadeusz and his lack of answers ruin her wedding day. "We'll find Stefek. This has given me a little faith. At least Maxim is family. Sort of." She touched her husband's cheek. "Let's go home."

CHAPTER TWENTY-SEVEN

Saturday morning.

It was early and Jerzy had not yet cried, but Zosia stared at the strange gray walls anyway, unable to fall back to sleep. She wasn't sure if the gray was painted on, or if it was a trick of the diffused light that seeped through the brown curtains over the window.

She reached her arm over in the bed and found only cool, rumpled sheets. Shocked that Czeslaw wasn't there to wake with her on their first morning together, she sat up in bed and searched the unfamiliar surroundings.

"I'm here, Zosia," Czeslaw said from the corner of the room next to Jerzy's new crib. His outline swayed in a heavy rocking chair. When her vision adjusted, she caught the shine of the bottle Czeslaw held for Jerzy. The baby was comfortable in his father's arms.

"Why are you feeding Jerzy?"

"Because he was hungry," Czeslaw said without pause.

She watched him for a minute, impressed. "How do you know how?"

Czeslaw chuckled. "I'm the eldest of five children, and I had babies of my own."

"Of course, I didn't mean . . ." Zosia wasn't used to seeing a man care so tenderly for an infant. "You could have woken me. That's usually women's work."

"I wanted you to sleep." His voice faltered. He moved Jerzy to his shoulder and wiped at his eyes.

"Czeslaw?"

He pulled in a shaky breath. "He reminds me so much of Henryk."

Zosia slipped out of bed and perched on the arm of the rocking chair. She wrapped her arms around him.

"I should have been there, I could have saved them." His voice was heavy with grief. "I would have known it was a grenade, and I could have gotten rid of it before they pulled the pin. What kind of father am I? I should have been the one blown to bits."

Zosia stayed silent, knowing there was nothing she could say that would heal his pain. She wiped his damp cheeks with the cotton sleeve of her nightgown. Czeslaw looked at her in the dim light. "I will never let anything bad happen to Jerzy. I promise you."

"I know," Zosia said.

As the sunlight strengthened through the window behind her, she took in her new home. A simple, wooden wardrobe was shoved into the corner next to the bed. Against the opposite wall sat a small stove, countertop, and a washbasin darkened with mineral stains. A card table and two chairs were situated behind the door that opened from the public hallway. It was the most basic of kitchens, but Zosia was excited to be able to make her coffee without having to bear the morning gossip of other women.

"Jerzy's asleep." Czeslaw stood. "Join me." Together, they settled the infant into his crib before descending onto the bed. He pulled the blanket over them to ward off the chill of the room and let his fingers dance across her skin, not dropping his eyes from hers. She allowed herself to be drawn in.

Later that morning the sun streamed into the room as they held each other tightly, desperate to find comfort after years of despair. "All of this," Czeslaw mused, "you, Jerzy, the warmth of this bed . . . It's a blessing to find this happiness. Such a sliver of beauty in a world that's been so very ugly." Though the war was long over, darkness still hovered over every aspect of life. Everyone had lost someone, and everyone lived with the incalculable weight of grief on their backs.

Petronela came to mind. "I forgot to show you." Zosia scooted toward the wardrobe. "Petra gave me something for Jerzy." She reached into the pocket of her coat and fished out the small box. She handed it to Czeslaw.

He opened it and touched the pendant with his thumb. "Beautiful. A triangle is strong. Fits Jerzy." He studied it, turning it over with his fingers. "My beloved Petronela, I'll love you forever. Yours, Eliasz."

Zosia leaned over and squinted at the pendant. The engraved words on the back were tiny but visible. "Czeslaw? This has to mean the world to Petra. Why . . .?"

Czeslaw's lips were pursed, his forehead creased with a frown. "We'll stop in to check on her this morning, invite her to join us for breakfast. I'm sure everything is fine."

—

With Jerzy dozing in his carriage, they walked to Petronela's building at a determined pace. They nodded to other DPs racing across the cobblestones for either an early bowl of oatmeal or a late crawl into bed after a night of vodka.

"You and Jerzy wait here," Zosia told Czeslaw. "I'll just be a minute." She stepped through the front door of Petronela's blockhouse with false confidence, her insides in knots.

Women milled about in the hallways, heading to the

washrooms and brewing their coffee. Zosia made her way to the room Petronela shared with five other roommates. She turned the knob and peeked in.

The blanket walls swayed with activity. A hacking cough echoed from one sectioned space, followed by the unforgettable smell of alcohol-tinged vomit. Zosia found Petronela's blue velvet suit casually draped over the back of a chair in her blanket-room. The bed was made. Petronela was not there.

"Has anyone seen Petra this morning?" Zosia called out.

Two or three negative grunts rose from between the blankets. Zosia returned to the hallway. A few more women stumbled past, some still dressed in their refugee-style finery from the evening before. "Have you seen Petronela? Mrs. Kloc? Has anyone seen her this morning?" Confused frowns and shaken heads were her only answers.

Zosia moved down the hallway toward the washrooms. When she turned the corner, she was nearly knocked over by a wave of women rushing toward her. Some were half dressed, others were wrapped only in thin, tattered towels. One sobbing woman raced past, soaking wet and naked, her arms wrapped across her breasts with soap bubbles sliding down her wet skin. Zosia's face burned, and she tried to swallow her panic. She pushed against the flow of people.

A deepening sense of dread settled in her throat. "Petra? Petronela?" She walked along on her toes, searching above the hurrying heads for her friend and cursing the commotion.

"Zosia?" The voice was familiar but too high and feminine to be Petronela's. Lottie moved toward her on the lead end of a long wooden plank that doubled as a stretcher. A doctor whom Zosia didn't recognize followed on the other end. Two other women in nurse uniforms helped carry the load in the middle.

"Lottie? Where's Petronela? What's going on?" Zosia stared at the blanket-covered mound on the plank. It was the size of

Petronela. A sob caught in Zosia's throat. "Is that—?"

"I'm sorry, Zosia." Lottie kept moving, pushed along by the doctor and nurses.

"What happened? Wait—" Zosia grabbed Lottie's arm. "Is this Petronela? Are you going to the hospital? Is she okay? What's going on?"

Lottie shook her head, and Zosia fell into step with her. "We found Petronela in a broken shower stall." Lottie panted from carrying the heavy weight. "She hung herself. I'm sorry."

"No, it can't be." Zosia's legs hurried to keep up. The officials carried the body toward the front door, and Zosia put her hand on the cold, lifeless lump. "Oh God, Petra." Her eyes stung. "I could have helped you."

"I don't think there was anything you could have done." Lottie's voice was compassionate despite her labored breathing. "This isn't your fault."

"Ma'am, please move aside," the doctor said sternly.

"Bloody hell, Ludwik," Lottie said. "She was a friend." She turned to Zosia and stopped, further annoying the doctor. "You take your time, love. You were all she had." The doctor spewed a few Polish curses under his breath. Zosia moved to lift the sheet covering Petronela's face, but Lottie stopped her. "Wait, Zosia. You might not want to look, dear. It's, well . . . hard to see."

Zosia closed her eyes to stop the flood of tears. She reached under the blanket and touched Petronela's stiff hand, wrapping her fingers around it and pulling it gently out from under the blanket. The skin had a grayish hue, and though it was smeared and faded, she could still read the scribble next to her thumb: *9:15 church – 8:30 meet Z.*

"Please, Petra." Zosia squeezed her friend's hand. She brought her lips to the cold skin and kissed Petronela's thumb. *My dearest friend, may you be at peace now. I hope you and Eliasz find each other and live in happiness throughout eternity. May God save your soul.* Zosia made a sign of the cross over Petronela's body because she didn't know what else to do.

Lottie and the others carried Petronela through the door and out into the cold. They marched past Czeslaw, who held Jerzy tight against his chest. He watched the death procession with an aura of unsurprised defeat. Zosia followed them out the door and fell to her knees. Czeslaw knelt beside her and pulled her close with his free arm. She sobbed for a long time. She cried for Petronela. She cried for Antoni. She cried for Marisha and Stefek, Henryk and Janina. She cried for Wiktor and for Poland and for the rest of Europe. Her nose ran, and her head ached. Her eyes and cheeks stung from the tears freezing in the chilled mountain air.

Czeslaw held her with one arm and Jerzy with the other. He kissed her hair and whispered calming words into her ear. With her face pressed against Czeslaw's chest, Zosia opened her eyes and was met by her newborn son's gaze.

Arm in arm, they shuffled back to their room. Zosia placed Jerzy on the bed and climbed in next to him, wrapping her arms protectively around the infant. Czeslaw kicked off his boots and climbed in behind her, resting his hand on her hip. He nuzzled his lips behind her ear and held her.

First her husband, then her son. Now her confidant. Before that, her mother, her sister, her father—not dead, but still gone. A lifetime of heartbreak pushed on her, wringing the tears from her eyes and the life from her soul. She shook with grief, gasping for air as Czeslaw held her. So heavy was her grief, when Jerzy woke and cried for his bottle, Zosia couldn't pull herself to her feet to take care of him. Czeslaw fed him, changed him, and rocked him back to sleep. Zosia continued to weep, her body wracked with painful sobs that left her muscles weak and aching.

Czeslaw rejoined her in bed. He lifted her to sitting, and she fell into his shoulder. "Zosia, here." He rolled a red and blue pill into her hand. The colorful bullet stuck to her sweaty skin, but she felt no curiosity about what it was. It was heavy against her palm. "Take it. It will help you sleep."

Zosia didn't question him. She swallowed the pill and chased it with water from a glass foggy with fingerprints next to the bed. Then she fell into her pillow with Czeslaw behind her. The couple stayed there, wrapped together in a strange bed in a cold, foreign part of the world, for the rest of Saturday.

CHAPTER TWENTY-EIGHT

Two days later.

On the morning of Petronela's burial, Zosia stared at the ceiling above her bed for a long time while it was still dark out, unsure if she'd slept or not. Over and over, she debated what she might have said or done to save her friend. A warm arm wrapped around her.

"Are you all right?" Czeslaw's voice was hoarse from sleep.

She cleared her throat and coughed out, "Yes." She climbed out from under the blankets, unable to stay still any longer. She sat on the chair next to Jerzy's crib while the boy slept, unaware of the misery surrounding him. *Good. May he always be blind to the pain.* She leaned forward, elbows on her knees, and rubbed her eyes violently with the heels of her hands. She brought herself to her feet and reached for the dress she'd chosen for the service, which hung on the outside of the wardrobe. In one motion, Zosia pulled it off of the hanger and sat on the bed, almost on top of Czeslaw. Her energy for the day was spent.

Her mind raced. She pulled her legs up onto the bed, crumpling the dress against her chest. "Please, give me another pill. I only want to sleep forever."

"No, *moja kochana*."

"Why?"

"That was my last one."

"Can you get more?"

Czeslaw stroked her hair. "Zosia, Dr. Krupka gave those sedatives to me a few months ago, to help me sleep after I got word of my family in Poland. He said to be very careful with them. Too many could be dangerous, and they were also difficult to come by."

"Dr. Krupka?" She turned to him.

"Of course." Czeslaw wrinkled his brow. "Where did you think I got them?"

Zosia only stared at him, her mind not working. Her look gave her away.

"Zosia, I got those pills legally. I don't trade any kind of drugs. It's too dangerous." His eyes glossed with hurt. "I thought, after Iwona, you knew that."

"What about my injection when Jerzy was born?"

"I sent word to a doctor friend in Bad Bruckenau. He drove it in himself and gave it to Dr. Krupka, who administered it."

She felt her shame spill onto her cheeks in a hot flush. She still didn't trust him, even now as her husband. "Czeslaw, I'm sorry. I feel so afraid of everything."

He pulled her close. "I know. We all do."

Czeslaw rose, dressed, and made coffee. Zosia lethargically pulled herself from the bed. After trying to drink a sip from her trembling coffee cup, she slipped her dress over her head. She wrapped Jerzy in two blankets, and the new family set out for Mess 2. Because Petronela had taken her own life, her remains were not welcome in the church.

Despite this, Father Terlecki had generously offered to officiate the funeral and stood welcoming mourners at the door. Another man wearing a kippah stood with him. Zosia eyed him with contempt, but she and Czeslaw nodded soberly to both men as they entered. They found their seats in the middle set of chairs, which were set up like makeshift pews.

Zosia settled Jerzy into a little nest of blankets on the chair next to her. She leaned in to her husband. "Who is that Jewish man with Father Terlecki?"

Czeslaw stayed quiet. He motioned to the priest at the front of the room. "I think he's going to start the service."

"Friends, good morning. May the peace of God be with you," Father Terlecki said. The mourners murmured their replies. "Before we begin, please welcome Rabbi Solomon Wexler from Fulda. He's recently ordained, and he's agreed to join us today to honor Mrs. Kloc's faith."

Zosia frowned. Jerzy wiggled in his nest, so she rested her hand on his chest. "What does he mean, her faith?" she quietly asked Czeslaw.

Czeslaw glanced at her, apprehension furrowing his face. "Petronela was Jewish." He gently put his arm around her shoulders and gave her a light squeeze.

"No she wasn't."

"Yes, Zosia, she was."

"No." Zosia's whisper grew hot in the hushed room. She shrugged off her husband's arm. "Czeslaw, this is no time for jokes."

"She hid her faith to survive the Nazis."

"No. Stop lying. Stop it." Her voice was sharp against the quiet of the congregation. A few people turned to look. Father Terlecki started a prayer with one eye trained on her. "She never wore a star, only the purple P, like the rest of us."

"This wasn't the time to tell you, Zosia. I didn't know they'd bring in Rabbi Wexler. I'm sorry you had to find out this way."

"Find out? No. She wouldn't lie to me." She stood without thinking. Her shrill voice echoed through the silence of Mess 2, and the priest stopped talking. "It's not possible. We had no secrets. She would have told me if she was a Jew."

"Shhh—" someone nearby scolded.

"Oh, go to hell," she said. Jerzy started to cry.

"Mrs. Lysek, please. Sit down." Father Terlecki glared at Zosia.

"Zosia, please." Czeslaw tugged on her arm. She sat hard on the chair and fumed. "She knew how you felt about Jews. She didn't want to hurt you."

She picked up Jerzy to comfort him. While she rocked, her mind raced. "No. You're wrong. This is all wrong." She stood again, her baby on her shoulder. "This is all a mistake."

"Zosia—"

"Mrs. Lysek, I'm going to have to ask you to leave." Father Terlecki's voice was matter-of-fact.

"You're kicking me out?" Zosia's head buzzed. Jerzy cried with more urgency. "You're all wrong. Maybe you have the wrong person. Did you check? Maybe it isn't Petronela, and she's still alive." Her trembling was uncontrollable. "She wouldn't kill herself. She wouldn't do this. This is all—"

"Zosia." Czeslaw stood and eased Jerzy from her arms as she wailed with grief. "Zosia, it's okay. Come with me, please." Zosia's hands clutched at her face while she sobbed. She allowed herself to be led away by her husband.

Ten minutes later on a cold bench outside, Czeslaw stroked Zosia's hair while she pressed his soaked handkerchief against her eyes. Jerzy was finally calm, bundled in blankets in the crook of Zosia's arm. "Why, Czeslaw? Why did she kill herself?"

"I don't know, my love. Her grief was too much to bear, I suppose."

She nodded. "How did you know she was a Jew?"

"She told me."

She nodded again. Her husband and her best friend had trusted one other enough to share their deepest secrets, yet Zosia was left oblivious. "Petronela was my dearest friend, Czeslaw. What kind of person must I be if she felt she couldn't tell me she was Jewish?"

Czeslaw patted her knee. "I'm sure she forgives you."

"I was wrong. I have to make it up to her." Shame filled Zosia. Her long-held prejudice had forced a wedge between them that she never even knew existed.

Petronela had been her conscience, her compass. She was everything Zosia wished to be. And she was Jewish—the one label that Zosia could never overlook. Through it all, Petronela never showed bitterness. She knew of Zosia's contempt for her people, yet never judged her for it. Neither had Czeslaw. Somehow, these people still loved her and were able to find forgiveness despite Zosia's faults.

Czeslaw put his arm around Zosia, and she melted into him. Her heart was sick with guilt and grief. She wondered if she'd taught her children the same intolerance after Wiktor died.

She stroked Jerzy's foot. She would not make the same mistake again. Jerzy would know to love the Jews as brothers and sisters. Petronela would live on through this young boy.

CHAPTER TWENTY-NINE

January, 1947.

"THE AMERICANS HAVE LIED TO US!"

Zosia's hand shook as she read the flyer, created by the uneasy and untrusting Poles in camp. They accused the Americans of being as corrupt as the Nazis. "*Do not attend the mandatory screenings,*" the flyer demanded, "*It is all a lie! You will be returned to Poland against your will, to a life of poverty and hardship! Repatriation means death!*"

She hugged her baby and thought of Captain Foley's words when the Nazi farm was liberated. Of course he'd lied.

"Zosia, I'm telling you, this doesn't concern us." Czeslaw paced back and forth in the small room. "They can't repatriate us when we've already committed to Australia."

"Then why does it say the screenings are required for every DP?"

Czeslaw took the paper out of Zosia's hands and scanned the page as he brought a cup of cold coffee to his lips but didn't drink. "It doesn't—I don't know. The papers Devine passed around earlier this week didn't say that." He dug through their small trashcan until he found the flyer balled up toward the bottom under that morning's coffee grounds. "See? Well, wait.

This doesn't really say anything."

Czeslaw held the contradicting flyers—one official from the camp administrators, the other unofficial from their fellow DPs. The official paper said she and Czeslaw were due at Mess 1 on Friday to be "screened." It claimed the screenings were nothing more than a census to determine nationalities and vaguely mentioned that no one would be forced to repatriate.

Now it was Friday, the day they were due to be screened, and they'd received this new flyer circulated by their own enterprising people, warning them to not attend.

"They can't make us repatriate, can they?" Zosia bounced Jerzy, searching for his mouth with the nipple of his bottle.

"Of course not."

Just a week earlier, Zosia would have been more divided on forced repatriation, when they'd celebrated yet another New Year trapped in a snowed-in camp of transients. Her children might still be waiting for her in Poland, but to return would put her husband in great danger. No answer was the right one.

Since then, however, she'd received a letter from Brygida, dirty from travel across a war-battered continent. Czeslaw had torn the letter into pieces and grumbled, "What a charming bitch you have for a sister," but Zosia had memorized the words anyway:

> *Zosia,*
> *You asked about Stefek, and I feel compelled to tell you he is safe, living in Germany with Marisha and her husband. She adopted him as something of a son. I wouldn't bother getting in touch with them, since they will not forgive you for leaving them. As for your new bastard child, I only hope you will be a better mother to him than you were to your existing children.*
>
> *Brygida*

She finally knew that Stefek was safe with Marisha, but she still felt a profound emptiness. Her sister's hateful words overshadowed her relief; the challenge to Zosia's love as a mother hit especially hard. Though Brygida's cruelty was nothing new.

The letter had confirmed that there was nothing left for Zosia in Poland. However, knowing her children were in Germany didn't bring them any nearer, nor did it make them any easier to find.

"I'm going to get this straightened out." Czeslaw folded the flyer and stuffed it into his coat pocket. "Don't worry. Stay here with Jerzy, I'll be back soon."

"Czeslaw, wait." Zosia's heart thumped. Jerzy wiggled in her arms. "Please, don't go near the mess buildings. What if you're taken away?"

Czeslaw chuckled. "They can't force a screening on me."

Zosia wondered if the Jews had thought the same thing early in their persecution. "Just stay here, let this pass."

"I can't." Czeslaw's eyes were sad. "I can't stand by and wait. If there's any injustice happening, I can't just watch from a distance."

"But—"

"Zosia," Czeslaw said, wrapping his arms around her, "did I ever tell you why I joined the army in Poland?" She shook her head, and he led her to a chair to sit.

"Early on, the Gestapo came through Warsaw and assigned each Jew their star. Around the same time they distributed the purple P to Christian Poles in the city. I'm sure you got one, too."

Zosia thought about the gold and purple diamond that Antoni had stuffed into her hand at the train station. She hadn't realized the Poles in Warsaw had worn them for years. She wondered how Minsk Mazowiecki escaped that branding.

"Well, my friends and I were sick of it. We didn't want to wear them. It was our country, and the Germans were pushing in.

If anything, *they* should be the ones marked. So one day, I went with a buddy of mine, Marcin, to the store to buy cigarettes. I was getting milk for Janina, too. We didn't wear the P on our clothing. We were tough guys, you know? We'd show them." Czeslaw snorted. "When we were in the store, a couple of S.S. agents came in. They asked us why we were not wearing our labels."

Czeslaw took a deep breath. "I told them I forgot. I hung my head. Fucking coward. They beat me anyway. I couldn't see for a week from my swollen eyes. But Marcin spoke up. He said what we'd planned. He said it was bullshit that we had to wear them. I think his words were, 'You can eat your fucking Ps.' Well, they beat him too, and took him away. They left me, the coward who was practically shitting his pants, but they took my friend.

"I never saw him again. I was ashamed. He was my best friend. We had a plan, but I didn't have the courage to follow through. He did. I had to make it up to him. So I joined the army hoping to rescue him." Czeslaw clenched his jaw. "Of course, I never did. But I hope he got out alive, wherever he was."

"But Czeslaw," Zosia said, "if there was any debt to be paid to your friend, you've surely already paid it. You spent years imprisoned."

"It's not about that debt anymore." He shook his head. "Marcin was someone's son. I can't let my own son grow up in a world where he's punished for his courage. I can't stand by and let something happen that might compromise that. I will always fight for the brave." He kissed her on the forehead. "I'll be back for supper."

Zosia stared out the frosty window into the white nothing of a Bavarian winter as Czeslaw marched away across the snow-packed street. The glass in front of her fogged from her shallow breath.

As the day drew on, she watched more and more people

stumble over snow banks and slip on the ice on their way toward the mess building. At first she thought they'd succumbed to the screenings, but they seemed angry, agitated. Then she noticed the red and white armbands.

Militia. Violence.

Riots.

This time, Iwona wasn't here to throw teapots.

Her eyes fell to her innocent baby. She'd had enough revolution. She only wanted her husband to come home for supper. She wanted her family together. She wanted a life where she could enjoy true peace. These were all things that seemed impossibly far away.

Zosia sat in the rocking chair and held her child. With nothing else to do, she waited. Though her stomach grumbled and her lips burned from thirst, she barely noticed over her chafed nerves. Her fingertips drummed the chair like the needle of a Singer.

As the late afternoon sun waned a group of women stumbled over the snow banks below her window. She recognized Angelika, Olga, and Wanda in the group when Olga stopped to light a cigarette. Zosia drew on her coat and lifted a sleeping Jerzy out of his crib, silently apologizing for the chaos of his life. She carefully snuggled him inside of her coat and buttoned it around him. Finding comfort in her friends, she decided go out and find her husband. Before she left she surveyed their room for a weapon: a glass baby bottle, their only bedside lamp, Czeslaw's shoe. She chose her sword by picking up her heavy clothes iron. She gripped it so tightly her knuckles turned white.

Once outside, she could feel the electricity of trouble crackling in the air. "Angelika," Zosia called after her former roommate.

"Zosia, thank God you're all right." Angelika caught Zosia in a hug. "Where's Jerzy?" Zosia motioned to the inside of her coat. Angelika nodded. "And Czeslaw?"

"He went to Mess 1. He said he was going to help get things sorted out."

The three women exchanged glances, and a few other women in the group raised their eyebrows.

"Why? What's going on?"

"All of the men and a lot of women went to do the same," Olga said.

"Guess it's a hell of a brawl." Wanda rubbed her belly. She looked almost giddy, her coat stretched tight across her midsection.

Angelika eyed Wanda. "You really should be more careful in your condition."

"Mind your damn business, Angelika," Wanda snapped.

"Zosia, I hear they're going to force us back to Poland," Olga said, ignoring Wanda as she puffed on her cigarette.

"They can't do that," Zosia said. "Czeslaw said they can't do that."

"Your husband doesn't run the place, Zosia," Wanda said with a snarl.

Zosia shivered. They couldn't see Mess 1 from where they stood, but Zosia could hear the commotion from across camp. Every shout and shattered window startled her. The distant rumble of discord shook her like an air raid. Mess 1 was being bombed, but by sticks and fists instead of missiles. She squeezed the iron tighter in her fist.

A green Volvo drew up next to the crowd of women. "Who needs a ride?" the female driver yelled across the passenger seat.

"Barbara, where did you get this?" someone asked.

"Doesn't matter, I'll take as many as I can fit."

"Let's go." Wanda waddled closer. Olga followed. Many of the women hung back, including Zosia. Zosia wasn't even sure if the driver was heading toward trouble or away from it. Either way, she would not go there by car. She'd rather walk barefoot across sharp, frozen gravel, especially with Jerzy inside her coat. She could never forget the vision of her baby brother as he was ejected through the windshield so long ago.

A few brave souls piled into the car, and it rumbled away, leaving a scowling Wanda behind in the darkening twilight with Olga, Angelika, Zosia and several other women.

"We should go *hoooommme*," Olga said uneasily. No one moved.

"Who is that?" Angelika squinted down the street in the direction the car disappeared. In the distance a woman hurried toward them. Zosia could see she was an official; the skirt of her blue wool suit hung below her warm coat. One woman from the group turned and ran away. Angelika linked her fingers through Zosia's and squeezed.

"That's Violette," Wanda said. "Zosia, she's probably after you since you're married to her paramour."

"What?" A knife shot through Zosia's stomach. She nearly dropped her iron.

"I see them around all the time, bent over their little notes and paperwork. All very secretive." Wanda smiled.

Zosia watched Violette approach. It was true. She'd come home a couple of times to find Czeslaw and Violette alone in the flat, huddled over the card table with papers and secrets passing between them.

Zosia had preferred denial to scrutiny about infidelity. It was less exhausting.

Violette walked straight up to Zosia. Her nose was red from the cold, and she had a slight gash on her forehead, mottled red from clotted blood. Her face was framed by the furry edge of her coat's hood. Looking soberly at Zosia through a cloud of cigarette smoke, she flipped down her hood. Zosia had never seen her in such disarray. Her hair was drawn back into a messy bun with strands dangling loose around her face and neck, and her lips were pale and cracked.

The entire group of women circled them and held their collective breath.

"*Dzien dobry*, Mrs. Lysek." She spoke loudly and clearly. Her Polish had improved, but her deliberate way of speaking felt like an eternity to Zosia. "Your husband has been arrested."

Chapter Thirty

Moments.

Zosia dropped her iron into the snow. As the words registered and her body gave way, Jerzy whimpered and cried within her coat. She dropped to her knees before Violette, her eyes pleading what her voice failed to say.

"Oh God, Zosia," Angelika wrapped an arm around her shoulders and helped her back up. Wanda stayed still, watching with interest.

"Please, may we go in?" Violette glanced over her shoulder. "We can discuss."

Zosia nodded, and the two women went inside the flat in silence. Once there, Zosia mechanically placed Jerzy in his crib while Violette hurried to the window, ignoring the distraught baby next to it. Her eyes darted around the darkness outside, and she snapped the curtains shut. "The door, it's closed? Tightly?"

"What do I . . . How—" Zosia stuttered.

"Here is your assignment in Australia," she said, stumbling over her Polish. She handed Zosia a pink sheet of paper. "But if anyone asks, it didn't come from me."

Zosia took the paper but paid it no attention. "But Czeslaw . . ."

"He's fine. We have to keep him overnight, but he'll return home in the morning."

"He's not arrested?"

"Of course not," Violette said. "He works for us." Zosia didn't know which "us" she was referring to. "We needed to make an example, and he volunteered. That was why I put on such a show of it outside. He sends his love and apologies and asked me to share that with you," she nodded at the paper in Zosia's hands.

"The screenings . . ."

"There will be no more screenings. It was a mistake. The Americans assumed they could push around the DPs. Tonight they learned otherwise. Don't worry; soon you will be in Brisbane, and this will all be over." Violette again peeked out the window between the curtains. "I must go. Do not speak of this to anyone."

Still not sure of which side Violette was on, Zosia thanked her. As Violette hurried out into the night, Zosia was troubled by what lingered behind: French perfume. It was the same scent that Zosia had noticed on Wiktor's collar so many years ago.

Nothing was over.

—

She didn't remember falling asleep, but dreams filled her head. A hand grenade rested on a table. Antoni studied it carefully, jotting notes in his book. Stefek ran in, anxious to play. He picked up the grenade and tossed it from one hand to the other. Marisha sat, wilted, on a chair, a black veil obscuring her face. She didn't move, but spoke to Stefek in a low voice. *"I'm your* matka *now. You have no one else."*

Stefek giggled and pulled the pin.

Zosia woke to a gentle hand on her shoulder and dim morning light silhouetting the curtains that Violette had closed so vigorously the night before. "Oh, Czeslaw!" She sat up, and threw her arms around him. Relief pulsed through her. "Thank God, I was so worried."

Czeslaw wrapped his arms around her, consoling her. "I'm sorry I left you alone. Did Violette come by?"

Zosia pulled back, suspicious. She stood and pulled on a housecoat. "Yes."

"Good. She's a good woman, we can trust her."

Zosia was quiet while she fought the jealousy that raged in her stomach. "What happened?"

Czeslaw ran his hands over his face. "It was a mess, Zosia. It started peacefully enough, but it turned into a riot. No one wants to be forced back to Poland, and people are scared. I bumped into Violette and volunteered to be arrested as an example, to try to calm the crowd." He shook his head. "Everyone in camp is on edge far more than I realized. Our time here is running out. If the US troops don't shut us down first, the camp will implode on its own."

Zosia didn't care anymore. She didn't care about the camp or about Mr. Devine and his idle excuses. She didn't care if the DPs were all let loose into the German forest to fend for themselves. They might have a better chance of moving forward that way.

"How was jail?" Her face was rigid.

"Not as bad as you'd think. I had dinner and a cigarette, then I went to sleep. Couple of other drunks locked up, that's it."

She pushed the thoughts of Czeslaw and Violette tangled together all night in Violette's bed from her mind.

"We got our assignment." Zosia nodded toward the pink paper on the table.

"Ah, our sponsor. We're on our way. We leave this summer for Brisbane." He took the paper in his hands and admired it like an oil painting. "This is the best news yet."

"The best news would be from Marisha and Stefek," Zosia snapped.

He looked up. "We'll find them."

Any decent mother would have already found her children, or died trying. Instead, Zosia sat rotting in a fetid refugee camp, biding her time uselessly, waiting for someone else to save her children. While Czeslaw happily scanned their emigration assignment, Zosia sat on the bed and stared at Jerzy, watching him watch her.

"Brygida is right," she said.

"Zosia?" Czeslaw laid the paper back down onto the table.

She stared straight ahead. "It's true. All of it. I don't deserve to be a mother."

"Your sister is full of *gówno*." Czeslaw approached, his face worried. "What have you been doing to yourself all night?"

Zosia had mixed a strong cocktail of jealousy, regret, and grief, and chased it with cigarettes. Her eyes were dry as she ground her teeth, still staring straight ahead. "They are in Germany. Maybe we can find them now. That picture of Maxim . . ." She trailed off.

Czeslaw scratched his chin. "I can get Tadeusz to look into it further. Maybe you should speak to him yourself? Give him a better description."

"No." Her stomach heaved at the thought.

He furrowed his brow. "Why not?"

Zosia bit her tongue. "I trust you to take care of it. It makes me anxious."

Czeslaw put one hand on either side of Zosia's face. He kissed her. "I understand. We'll find them. Somehow. I don't know why it's so difficult, but we'll find them. Someday we'll be happy. I promise."

Happy. Zosia had to be happy, for her baby. Jerzy deserved that. She lifted him out of his crib and nuzzled his cheek. He was the one child she could still hold. "Are you ready to be an Australian boy, my Jerzy? Will you run with the kangaroos and chase koala bears?" She wrapped her arms around him and rested her chin on the top of his head.

Australia was a world—and a lifetime—away. Once settled, Jerzy would never remember anything about this life, but without Marisha and Stefek, Zosia would never forget.

Chapter Thirty-One

June, 1947.

Two years she'd been in Wildflecken. Two years previous she was held as a slave on a Nazi farm. Two years before that, a starving widow. She wondered if she would ever find two years of peace and happiness.

The mess building was less crowded than usual, either because more and more DPs were finding permanent homes or, more likely, because Zosia was eating a late lunch. The open space was a welcome relief; it seemed that in the weeks since the summer air had rolled into Wildflecken, all Zosia did was sweat. Next to her Jerzy sat in his carriage and occupied himself with tearing apart an English language newspaper.

An Australian ladies' magazine, dated three years earlier, sat on the table in front of her. A stack of similar magazines waited near her elbow. Foreign words heralded from the top of the page, and though Zosia didn't understand them, Lottie had introduced them to her as *Australian Home Journal*.

When Zosia opened the magazine, tissue paper patterns fell into her lap from within the pages. She turned back to the cover where three elegant women wore stylish, colorful dresses.

Between the women were the words, "*These patterns enclosed.*" She looked at the patterns in her hands, which matched the pictures. She understood and smiled.

Maybe someday she'd be back behind a sewing machine. She'd have to keep these patterns, just in case. Zosia chewed her lip. She wondered if she would ever fill out a dress again, the way a woman should.

She turned the page and was greeted by ads for toothbrushes, silver polish, laxatives and Lucky Strike cigarettes. Full-color pictures helped her decipher what was what, and she slowly figured out some of the English words in the magazine. She knew what Ex-Lax and Brylcreem did. She knew "soap" made you clean, and a "toaster" browned your bread. She decoded the word for "red" by matching an advertisement for lipstick to an article about the Australian Red Cross, and learned the words "luxury" and "comfort" by comparing ads for cars, Rolex watches, and airlines.

Zosia was proud of herself until she got to the ad for Vegemite. It appeared edible, but she couldn't make out what it was: meat in a jar? A mixture of mashed vegetables? Jam? She felt her stomach heave. While she thumbed through the magazine, she encountered a few more pages showing the mysterious substance, proving this was a staple in the Australian diet. One ad even showed a mother giving it to a child about Jerzy's age, with the text saying something about how it was "great for baby." Baby seemed happy.

In his carriage, Jerzy slobbered all over a teething biscuit and scanned the room intently. "How about that, Jerzy? Would you like some Vegemite on your biscuit?"

"Weeyoweeyoweeyo," Jerzy babbled and threw his biscuit on the floor.

"Ah well. I'm sure we'll love it."

The table shook when a tray slammed down across from

her. "Zosia." Wanda slid onto the bench. The limp curls in her short hair suggested she was trying to gain another day out of yesterday's hairstyle. A tiny baby was wrapped against her body in a sling, its bald head situated just below Wanda's chin.

"Hello, Wanda. How are—"

"Long time, no see." Wanda tore into her sawdust bread.

"Yes. Congratulations. Beautiful baby." When Wanda didn't respond, Zosia continued. "I miss Petra so much, I'm sure you do, too."

"A good woman," Wanda said. "May she rest." She motioned with her chin toward Zosia's magazine. "Australia. Is that where you're headed?"

"Yes."

"Nice that the IRO took over operations around here. Things are moving again. God damned standstill under the UNRRA."

"Sorry? IRO?"

"Anyway, you're a lucky woman," Wanda continued. "I hear Australia is lovely, if you survive the passage."

"What do you mean?" Zosia stared at a recipe for a meat pie on the page in front of her. She swallowed to choke back vomit.

"A friend of mine went with her family to Australia last fall. She had a little boy. Cute fellow." Wanda swallowed her coffee. "Well, she wrote me a letter. She's settled now and likes Brisbane, but she said the passage was gruesome. Worst two weeks of her life, and she said that included her time in Stutthof."

The picture of meat pie didn't help Zosia's stomach. She instead inspected a scratch in the Formica tabletop and prayed for her insides to settle. "What was so bad about it?"

"It was fine until they crossed the equator. Too hot. Everyone got sick. Too many people on the ship, and no one could get air. Then people started dying. I guess it was the food. Contaminated, you know." Wanda held up a slice of meat on her fork. "No refrigeration. Anyway, a few children were vomiting, but soon everyone had diarrhea. Everyone. Most people had it coming out both ends, if you know what I mean."

"Diarrhea killed them?"

"Sure." Wanda shrugged and chewed her lunch, indifferent to the horror she was describing. "The water was contaminated too. Someone shits in the water and it's all over." Wanda gave a sickly, satisfied laugh. "People were dehydrated, and there was nothing anyone could do. The worst were the babies, she said. Half of the children on board died, and the youngest were first to go, of course. So the crew, whoever was left, piled up the bodies in the lower decks. The smell of rotting flesh wafted through the whole ship, making everyone even sicker. The cruel cycle started all over again." She absently patted her baby's back.

"Good Lord." Zosia didn't know what else to say.

"Like she said, worse than Stutthof. Honestly, I'll take my chances with England or Norway."

Sweat strangled Zosia. She fought the urge to vomit all over the stack of *Australian Home Journals*. "Well, thanks for the warning, Wanda. You take care, now." Wanda gave a distracted wave, and Zosia stood and dumped her magazines into the carriage with Jerzy.

Once outside the mess building, she bent and vomited into a shrub.

Chapter Thirty-Two

Two days pass.

In his stifling hot office with Jerzy balanced on her hip, Zosia faced off with Mr. Devine. Though it was early, the director looked haggard, like he'd already put in a long day and only wanted to put his feet up and listen to Glenn Miller on his radio.

"Mrs. Lysek, you have to understand, there's a waiting list for Australia forty meters long." Mr. Devine always seemed tired when dealing with Zosia, but today he was more so, probably because Zosia had just announced the Lyseks were reconsidering their emigration. "If you don't take this sponsor, the rest are spoken for ten times over. There won't be another chance."

"There has to be another option," she said. "Mr. Lysek can do any kind of work, not just farming. He can build houses, work in a factory . . ."

"That's not the issue, Mrs. Lysek." Mr. Devine put his elbows on the desk in front of him and leaned forward to rub his face. "We get pressure daily from headquarters to move the DPs out, but there's nowhere to put them. Anyone who wanted to go back to Poland has already gone, and Canada, Australia, France and the United Kingdom are close to their quotas already. America's president is trying to convince his Congress to accept refugees, but the process is slow and stubborn. There are no guarantees." Mr. Devine shuffled papers on his desk. "Are you sure you don't want to repatriate?"

Zosia shook her head. "Can we stay in Germany? My children are here somewhere."

"No. Absolutely not," Mr. Devine said. "Wildflecken—or Durzyn, whichever you prefer, I suppose—is slowly dying." He glanced at Zosia. "The relief effort has limited funding, and when the money is gone, the camp will shut down. Germany is not equipped to absorb any of the DPs still left in Europe. They just lost a war, and recovery here will be slow and painful. It's still a dangerous place. Anyone living in Wildflecken when it closes may very well be sent back to Poland, like it or not."

"I've heard rumors of that, Mr. Devine." Zosia was careful to not give up too much information. "But I've been told there would be no more screenings."

"Screenings, no." He leaned back and ran his fingers through his greasy hair. "But once the camp closes, there's nothing more we can do. The compassion of the International Refugee Organization has an expiration date. When that passes, things will go sour."

Zosia understood. This was likely their only chance at a new life. Not enough countries were willing to welcome the forgotten residue of war: the surviving prisoners, the former victims, the floating refugees. That left most of the residents of Wildflecken and other camps across Europe homeless, exhausted, and without a plan. Mr. Devine was one of the unlucky souls held responsible for returning those vagabonds to a society that didn't want them.

Wildflecken was like an abandoned spider web, holding tight to the naïve and apathetic with its sticky strings until a good wind came and blew it out from under them all. Zosia couldn't let Jerzy grow up in such a transient community, with a cloud of unknowing hanging over his head.

But she couldn't let him die on a ship in the ocean, either.

"Mrs. Lysek, Are you sure you've talked this over with Mr. Lysek? He has been nothing but thrilled about this opportunity."

"Of course," Zosia lied, her forehead creasing at the director's lack of faith. "Mr. Lysek and I most certainly agree on this."

In truth, Czeslaw was gone on a trading trip and wasn't expected back for another day or so. In the time since she'd talked to Wanda, Zosia had tortured herself over and over. Alone, she tossed and turned all night and contemplated and vomited all day.

She was pregnant.

This time she knew before seeing Dr. Krupka, but she'd gone anyway to be certain. The doctor was quick to write her off: "Nausea is likely due to nerves, Mrs. Lysek. Have you tried schnapps to settle your stomach?"

"I've also missed a cycle. Or two."

"Well then, you're probably pregnant."

She cocked her head, giving him an accusatory look. "After Jerzy was born, you said that wasn't possible."

"I did? Well, maybe you got into that bad batch of chicken last week? Several people came in sick after that."

She shook her head. "Shouldn't you give me some kind of test or something?"

"Do you need a test?"

"No," Zosia answered. She knew. "We're supposed to be leaving for Australia soon, possibly in a month or so."

"That might work well. The trip overseas will be an opportunity to flush this from your system."

"I'm sorry, flush?" A horrified tremor shook her.

"Doctor, her chart." A nurse appeared at Dr. Krupka's elbow. He took the clipboard and flipped through the pages.

"Mrs. Lysek, it says here that your son was a difficult birth," he said. "And a few weeks early. Your body isn't in any shape for this. You're underweight, and at 37 you're much too old for pregnancy. There's a high risk of premature birth, and the baby may not survive anyway. Best to miscarry, the sooner the better."

May not survive. Zosia shivered. She was already defensive of her newest child, still yet to be born. "Is there any way to save this baby?"

"Don't travel," the doctor said without a pause.

It was the answer Zosia had hoped to hear, though she knew forfeiting their new home would put the family in a precarious position. But she couldn't risk Jerzy's life by crossing the equator, and she couldn't take any chances with the baby growing inside her. She'd gone straight from the hospital to Mr. Devine's office. She couldn't leave Europe and risk sacrificing her growing baby, her young son, and her missing children all at once. She had to cancel before Czeslaw could stop her.

With a defeated drop of his shoulders, the director picked up the phone receiver and dialed a few numbers. "Director Hodgkins, this is Benjamin Devine, Wildflecken DP Camp. I have a family scheduled for Australia next month that needs to be cancelled. Yes, that's right." He spoke in a combination of German, Polish, and English. Zosia strained her ears to make out the important information with her very limited grasp of anything other than Polish. "Yes, sir, Lysek. Czeslaw, Zosia, and infant son Jerzy. Cancel all three. *Anulować*." He accentuated the word in Polish, meeting Zosia's eye. "Thank you, Director." There was a pause while Mr. Devine tapped a pencil on his desk." Yes, I understand. Wait, *three hundred*? We can't . . . We don't have room." His voice was drawn. Eventually, he sighed in defeat. "Okay. Yes, fine, we'll expect them in the morning."

He put down the phone and considered the nomad across from him. "Mrs. Lysek, I hope you know what you're doing. I don't want to see you stuck out here in the woods with no help when we're closed down."

Zosia lifted her chin. "What about Marisha and Stefek? Is there any news?"

He gave another frustrated sigh. "No. After the IRO took over administration of the camps, we thought information would come easier, but that's not been the case." He shook his head sadly. "Germany is a massive haystack, and your children are but two of millions of needles."

CHAPTER THIRTY-THREE

The next day.

"Zosia, you can't believe everything you hear at lunch." Czeslaw washed his hands at their tiny sink while Zosia repeated Wanda's chilling story to him. He'd just gotten home and she'd immediately given him a kiss, a beer, and a sermon.

"We can't go, Czeslaw. I can't do it. Can you imagine? Jerzy could die in transit. We all could. I won't take that chance." She swallowed the lump that collected in her throat.

"I'm sure Wanda exaggerated a bit." Czeslaw wiped his hands on a small towel and draped it over the edge of the sink. He ran his fingers through his hair, using the moisture left on them to tame his cowlick, which had gone awry in the summer wind. "Besides, I'd think the crew of the ship would have learned some lessons, if that story has any truth to it. I'm certain the authorities will make sure it doesn't happen again." He put his hands gently on Zosia's shoulders and held her in front of him. "Trust me, we'll be fine. We'll arrive in Australia fit and healthy and ready to fight the kangaroos." He jumped, ducked, and shadowboxed an imaginary marsupial.

"Czeslaw, we can't—"

"We are going," he said, his voice resolute. "There are no other choices."

Zosia was quiet.

"My goodness. Look at this boy," Czeslaw said, dismissing the discussion by motioning to Jerzy, who was toddling along while holding himself upright against the bed. "He'll be walking any day. It's so good to watch him grow." Czeslaw kissed Zosia on the forehead.

She paused. "I'm pregnant."

His expression was one of calm confusion. Zosia waited for the reality to sink in. "Zosia," he said, his eyes growing misty. "Are you certain?"

She nodded. Her husband's face flushed, and a broad smile spread across his features as he absorbed the news.

"This is wonderful, Zosia! How perfect. The baby will be born in Brisbane, a natural citizen of our new home."

"No." Zosia said, stopping him. He had to know the truth. She took a deep breath and prepared herself for the fallout. "Czeslaw, I already talked to Mr. Devine. I cancelled our journey. Australia is not an option."

His smile turned wooden, caught in the unsure space between excitement and utter devastation. His scarlet cheeks drained to white. He tried to speak, his lips forming shapes that looked like words, but no sound spilled out. Zosia was the bearer of both the best and worst news possible. She watched through the veil of her own personal anguish while Czeslaw tore himself in two.

"You cancelled . . ." Sound had finally rejoined the words in his mouth. "You cancelled without speaking to me? You just . . . cancelled?"

"Please, sit." She led him to the rocking chair, and he moved surprisingly easily. It was as if he had no control over the muscles in his body. His expressionless face hung limp on his head. She brought him his beer from the countertop. "Let me explain." She perched on the bed across from him.

As she talked, Czeslaw answered only with a flicker of his eye or a twitch of his nose. She knew he was angry, but he was also so overjoyed by the news of a baby that he just sat in a conflicted, ear-splitting silence and stared at his sweating bottle of beer.

After she'd told him every detail of the past several days, Czeslaw looked up at her, the rage in his eyes slicing through her. "Zosia," he said, his voice low yet forceful. "You should have spoken to me first. You should never have made this decision without me. You and I are strong. We could have made this trip. Jerzy, too." Zosia started to speak, but Czeslaw held up his hand to stop her. "Wait, let me finish." Zosia closed her mouth.

He stood and sat next to Zosia on the bed. She couldn't look at him. "This child worries me," he said. When Zosia frowned, he continued. "Jerzy has the warrior in him. I see it all the time. You and I both have it, that's how we've survived this long. I know Jerzy would have survived the trip. But this baby . . ." He put his hand on Zosia's belly. "This baby could be a poet, to balance to the warrior. We both have the poet in us, too—peaceful and loving, but easily hurt." He gave her a weak smile. "I have a feeling we are expecting a poet."

"I threw it all away, didn't I? I ruined everything." Zosia shivered. "What have I done?"

"You did what you do."

"What do you mean?" She twisted her face in confusion.

Czeslaw sighed. "Zosia, you are the love of my life, but you live in a constant state of mistrust and regret. You are so afraid of making wrong decisions, of trusting yourself, that it controls you." He looked down at his hands. "But that said, I don't think either of us could bear it if something bad were to happen to this baby—or to Jerzy—that we might have prevented."

Stunned, Zosia stared at her husband, his understanding of her filling her lungs, her head, her heart. "So you're not angry with me?"

"I'm angry as hell. But Zosia, I love you. We'll get through this."

CHAPTER THIRTY-FOUR

October, 1947.

Zosia stood on the crescent platform, waiting for the evening train to roll into the Wildflecken station. She wasn't looking for any specific items, but anything above and beyond their weekly rations would be a welcomed treat—or, at least an asset for Czeslaw to barter. Above her, a Wildflecken sign was painted over with big, white letters spelling "Durzyn." The Poles kept trying to make the town theirs.

A cigarette wiggled between her fingers as she eyed the other looters and waited for the train to grind to a halt. Her hand protectively went to her rounded belly. She wondered if the tiny baby inside her would slow her down. She wished for Petronela to be standing next to her, spouting some sarcastic comment to lighten the mood while she sucked on her own cigarette. The sound of train whistles carried on the cool air of fall would always remind Zosia of Petronela.

The doors slid open and piles of people spilled out of the boxcars. *Shit. More people. More of the displaced.* Zosia dropped her cigarette onto the wooden planks and crushed it with her worn boot.

Displaced. Unsettled.

Even now, years after the war, Europe was still packed with involuntary drifters. Some were forcibly moved from place to place by the strained relief efforts so camps could close and governments could see progress, but others moved around on their own accord, searching for family, friends, or even just people who shared their beliefs and backgrounds. These vagabonds hunted for a permanence that never came. The residents of Wildflecken were considered some of the lucky ones. While they hung curtains and planted cucumbers, people at other camps never dared unpack their meager suitcases.

Camps for the homeless continued to close in waves, consolidating DPs into fewer and fewer spaces and crushing people together like sardines in a tin can. People kept coming in to Wildflecken, but the movement out was slow and labored. There were now nearly twenty thousand squatters in the tiny Bavarian village, with more arriving daily. Space was at a premium, along with food, water, and even air. Wildflecken was becoming one of the last surviving camps, swelling with the human debris of the other camps around it. Eventually, Wildflecken would collapse under its own weight too.

Zosia stepped aside to avoid the crowded confusion. Some new arrivals spread blankets on the platform after an announcement was made that they would have to spend the night at the station. Housing had not yet been arranged.

She wrapped herself in her knit shawl and was reaching for another cigarette when she heard a desperate voice rise above the mob. "Please, have you seen her?" A small, bald man with round wire glasses pleaded with anyone he encountered. He held a picture in front of him. No one paid him any attention, since the officials were too busy barking orders and handing out sandwiches, and most everyone else was a new arrival. Only a few bounty hunters around the perimeter of the platform, including

Zosia, could be of any help, and they'd grown numb to the newcomers' endless pleas long ago.

"This is my wife. I heard she might be here. Petronela. Her name is Petronela Kloc."

Zosia nearly swallowed her cigarette. She pulled it away from her lips and coughed, choking.

His eyes landed on her. "Please!" He ran toward her, and she gaped at him. He was exactly as Petronela described Eliasz, and Zosia marveled at how such a slight man could have survived Auschwitz. He was an intellectual. A poet to balance Petronela's warrior, as Czeslaw would say. They were usually the first killed. Eliasz must have been more warrior than he appeared.

He handed the sepia-toned photograph to her, but Zosia couldn't look at it. Instead she stared into his hollow face. Fearful hope filled his eyes. She noticed a small triangle on a string around his neck. It was similar to the one Petronela had given Jerzy, but upside down.

Her eyes were drawn to the man's extended hand. She saw the black identification number tattooed on his forearm under the sleeve of his ragged coat. She took the folded picture and held it in front of her face, hoping to hide the emotion it caused. Nestled between the worn fold lines was Petronela. She stood proudly in a white blouse and long dark skirt, holding a trombone and staring with an expression that dared you to cross her. Her image swirled in Zosia's vision.

"*Oy vey*, you know her?" His voice was shallow, as if his very existence hung on Zosia's answer.

Zosia could only nod.

"She's not well? Is she dead? Please, tell me."

"I'm sorry," Zosia said, fighting the swelling in her throat. "I'm so sorry."

Eliasz's face paled further. His lip quivered.

"She was my best friend." Zosia drew in a trembling breath.

"She's dead."

The small man fell forward and sobbed into her shoulder. They held one another, strangers mourning the woman they both loved so much.

Eliasz drew away from Zosia. "How? Did she suffer?"

She couldn't bear to tell him that it had been the grief of losing her husband—now standing in front of Zosia very much alive—that drove Petra to take her own life. She handed the picture back to him, shook her head, and said simply, "She was ready."

He nodded and wiped his eyes with grubby fingers. He looked around, lost. Zosia understood, figuring his only motivation for trekking from place to place was now gone.

Zosia's eyes again fell to the triangle at his neck. She pulled Jerzy's pendant out of her pocket, and Eliasz gasped. He untied his own pendant, and they held the triangles out to each other. They linked together perfectly, creating a Star of David. There had been a time when that symbol meant nothing to Zosia. Now, however, it represented the woman who believed in her and encouraged her, the friend who helped her survive all those years. It represented hope, and courage.

"It's beautiful." She fingered the linked star, her heart lodged in her throat. "How were you able to keep it at Auschwitz?"

"I hid it in a crack in the wall of my barracks. Same with the picture."

Zosia turned the pendant over: *Love to my dearest Eliasz, Petronela.* Zosia knew the risk he'd taken by keeping the pendant. Had it been found, they would have killed him. She thought about Petronela, late at night, picking slivers off of the wooden bunk rails. Had she been hollowing out a spot to hide her treasures? Zosia wondered how many other keepsakes might be hidden around Europe, secreted in cracks and crevices, under loose floorboards, and behind bubbled wallpaper.

"Mr. Kloc, you need to meet with the officials to get your identification card and your housing assignment. I know there are only a few beds available, so you have to be quick or else you'll be sleeping on the platform." Zosia put her hand on Eliasz's arm and pointed toward a row of tables assembled at one end of the platform. "Go and check in there, tell them who you are and where you came from. Tell them you know Czeslaw Lysek, my husband. It might help you get a better bed, maybe an extra pack of cigarettes. Good luck. My name is Zosia. Come and find us if you need help."

The broken little man nodded, looking like an abandoned child. Zosia knew he needed to be watched. Everyone in Wildflecken was living on the edge of suicide, but Eliasz was especially vulnerable. He drifted toward the registration area when a surge of blood rushed to Zosia's head.

"Wait, Mr. Kloc." Zosia reached out and touched the man's arm. She knew he would hear about his wife's death by the end of the day, and rumors fueled by the tedium of camp life would probably have twisted the story into something even more painful than the horrific truth. "I need to tell you about Petronela."

He turned, his face a contorted mask of anguish as if he knew Zosia's words before she spoke them.

She squeezed her eyes shut and willed herself to exhale the words she didn't want to speak. "You should hear it from me, since anything else could be nonsense." She opened her eyes and looked just past him to shield herself from his pain. "Petronela got word that you were dead and she killed herself, Mr. Kloc. She loved you. She loved you so much, she couldn't stand to not be with you."

His eyes lost focus, but his face stayed stoic. When the words made contact with his mind, his body sagged like a limp sail in a sudden calm. He bent at the waist as if to vomit. Zosia reached for him, fearful he was about to collapse, but he kept his feet. He stayed bent in half and frozen for several seconds before pulling himself upright. He nodded at Zosia.

She took his hand. "You're needed, Eliasz. You need to go on, for her. You know she would want that."

He cleared his throat enough to speak. "Thank you for telling me. I appreciate the truth." He turned and dissolved into the crowd of people.

Zosia walked home, one hand resting on her growing baby. There was so much death around her, yet in the least likely of places, life grew inside her. Like a tiny sapling pushing its way up through the rubble of war, life forges on against the odds, even while everything else around it shrivels and dies.

She hurried back to the little room in the former officers' quarters where she'd given the fourteen-year-old girl next door a bottle of red nail polish to watch Jerzy for an hour.

As she came down the hall, she heard Czeslaw singing to Jerzy. "*Wlazl kotek na płotek i mruga, ładna to piosenka niedługa.*" Zosia recognized the lullaby. Her mother had sung it to her when she was a baby and again to Brygida when she came along. After Oskar was killed she stopped singing altogether.

Zosia smiled. This was one time she was thankful for the thin walls. The close quarters allowed for very limited interactions between married couples. Disputes were argued in whispers, and sex was restrained since no one wanted to be the subject of camp gossip. She never complained. She knew the only reason they had a private room at all was because of Czeslaw's connections. Many couples and families shared blanket-walled rooms, offering no privacy whatsoever.

She was relieved Czeslaw was home early; she had to talk to him about Eliasz. They needed to find a way to help the man. She opened the door to find her husband holding their son in the rocking chair. Jerzy's head rested on Czeslaw's shoulder, his eyelids drooping as the rhyming song about a kitten on a fence lulled him. Czeslaw was still in his police uniform, his hat sitting on the small table next to him.

Zosia's body warmed, starting deep within and radiating outward. Maybe the peaceful heat was coming from the new baby. Their little poet heard the lullaby and knew everything was right. *"Nie długa nie krótka lecz w sam raz . . ."* Zosia imagined Antoni was there, reading a book at Czeslaw's feet. Behind them, Marisha hunched over the stove, making tea while Stefek sat at the card table and fashioned a ridiculous fishing lure out of feathers.

As the door clicked shut, Jerzy turned his head and smiled at his *matka*. Czeslaw didn't look up. *"Dzien dobry."* She bent to kiss Jerzy's head and waited for Czeslaw to turn his lips upwards toward her, but he didn't. "Czeslaw, I have to talk to you about—" She noted the set of his jaw and stopped. "What's wrong?"

"I've learned something unpleasant."

"About what?"

"You."

Zosia's face burned. She raced through her mind, trying to think of what ghosts Czeslaw might have dug up. Her forehead prickled. "What did you hear?" As soon as she said it, she realized: Tadeusz. Why he'd chosen now to slander her, she didn't know.

Czeslaw stood and walked Jerzy to his crib. The boy snuggled into his blanket, already asleep. Then Czeslaw turned to her, his glare icy. "I hear you were quite popular as a prisoner." His voice dripped with disgust.

"What did he tell you? What did that little *gówno* Tadeusz say?"

"That during your time at the Nazi farm you were quite popular with the men. You had sex with anyone who would have you. Tadeusz said you even approached him, seduced him." Czeslaw took a deep breath. "And that you're still doing it now."

Zosia fumed, her insides twisting. "And you *believed* him?"

"He's my associate. We've worked together closely for a long time."

"And I'm your wife."

"He's never lied to me."

Zosia reeled as Czeslaw glared at the floor, a mixture of confusion, guilt, and anger on his face. "Czeslaw . . ." She couldn't continue.

"I didn't want to believe—"

"Then don't." She marched across the kitchen. She brushed some crumbs off of the counter into her hand before angrily tossing them on the floor anyway.

"Why would Tadeusz lie to me?"

Zosia kept her back to Czeslaw. If she told him the truth, she might lose the only lead she had on her family's whereabouts. But she had to believe Czeslaw would do the right thing for her. If she wanted him to trust her, she had to trust him. "He raped me." The words sliced through the air between them.

There was silence. Every hair on Zosia's arms stood on end. She was afraid to turn to her husband. She heard him lower himself into a chair at the card table. When he spoke, his voice was heated. "Tell me."

She faced him. She sat at the table and told him everything. She talked about Tadeusz, about the stolen chickens, about Sturmbannführer Voss, even about how she'd once mistaken Czeslaw for Voss because of their eyes. She told him every detail and watched his face swerve from rage to concern and back again.

When there was nothing left to tell, she collapsed her head into her hands. No tears fell, but exhaustion took over. The baby inside her fluttered.

Czeslaw stood and flipped on his uniform cap. He moved toward the door, not saying a word.

"Wait, Czeslaw?" Zosia lifted her head.

He stopped and looked at her for a moment, then knelt

beside her and collected her into his arms. They embraced for several minutes before Czeslaw kissed her. "I need to take care of something. I'll return in a day or two." His voice was soft, but his eyes flared dangerously.

"I have to tell you, Czeslaw," Zosia said, reaching out and squeezing his hand, "Eliasz is alive. He was on today's train, passing around Petra's picture, looking for her." Her eyes filled. "She died for nothing."

"My God," Czeslaw said. His strong hands held hers.

"We have to watch over Eliasz. He could . . ." She couldn't bring herself to say it.

"I understand." Czeslaw's voice was calm. "And I'll take care of it. You stay here. Rest. Don't worry about anything. I'll be back soon."

Zosia watched him go. She didn't know what he would do. A strange worry that Czeslaw would kill Tadeusz shook her. She thought of the Nazi buried somewhere out in the forest. He'd killed before.

She went to Jerzy's crib. She stood over him for the longest time, watching his chest rise and fall in sleep. So gentle, innocent. Her hand rested on the other being inside of her. So pure.

Yet here she stood, wondering if their father was capable of killing again, and wondering if she was bothered by that wonder.

Outside the window, golden leaves swirled in the autumn wind. She saw Czeslaw sitting on his motorcycle. He hadn't started it yet. He rubbed the key between his fingers, occupying his hands while appearing deep in thought. He looked up at someone who was disguised in the shadows. Zosia craned her neck, but the angle didn't allow her to see. Czeslaw inserted the key and kick-started the motorcycle. Exhaust billowed from the tailpipe.

A woman walked away from him, hands in the pockets of her trench coat and blond hair trailing behind her. *Violette.* Had she been waiting outside for Czeslaw?

Zosia stood for an eternity and watched the bustle of a Wildflecken evening without actually seeing anything. An overwhelming loneliness engulfed her.

When will Czeslaw return?

Will *he return?*

CHAPTER THIRTY-FIVE

Three days.

An exaggerated farce played out between Zosia and her young son for the next few days. She didn't want the boy to know she was distressed, since he napped better when he was calm. Yet in her quiet moments, Zosia was a wreck.

Jerzy stacked tin cans at her feet with Rafal, another little boy who was a few months older. Lottie pointed to Zosia, waiting.

"My name is Zosia," she answered in English.

"That's correct." She swung her arm toward the woman sitting to Zosia's left. "And you?"

"My name is Nadia."

"Yes."

As Lottie's attention moved to the others in the room, Zosia leaned over to her neighbor. "Do you have an assignment?"

Nadia shook her head.

"I don't know why we're bothering with this." Zosia blew a strand of hair off of her forehead. Since abandoning Australia, no new opportunities had opened for the Lyseks. It seemed pointless to Zosia to learn English so prematurely. "Wouldn't it make better sense to learn the language of the country we're going to?"

"We're hoping America opens up," Nadia said. "Besides, it's good to know a second language. It might as well be English." Lottie held up another flash card for Zosia.

"The soup is hot." Zosia rubbed her swollen belly. The drawing of steaming soup on the card made her hungry.

"Choop!" Jerzy shouted.

Lottie laughed, as did a few of the other English students. "Ah, see? This is good for the children too. They repeat everything at this age." Lottie moved on to someone else.

With attention off her, Zosia again leaned in to Nadia. "Is America even an option?"

Nadia shook her head, not moving her eyes from Lottie. "I don't know, not yet. My husband says there's talk, but isn't everything talk?"

"Thank you, students," Lottie said slowly in English. "I will see you next week."

After she tugged on her coat, Zosia approached Lottie. She kept her voice low. "Lottie, has Violette said anything to you about Czeslaw?"

Keeping her smile bright but knowing, Lottie laughed. "Oh, you know, we don't work closely anymore," she said. "And do you know why?"

Zosia shook her head.

Lottie tapped the stack of flash cards. "She's learned other languages."

"Oh." Zosia was disappointed. Clearly Lottie wasn't in a position to give up Violette's secrets, whether as a black marketeer or a mistress. "What are the chances America will open up to refugees?"

"You need to talk to Mr. Devine about that. From what I know the chances are small, but things change daily." Lottie zipped her bag. "Have a nice evening, Mrs. Lysek. And try to talk Mr. Lysek into joining us for class."

If he ever comes back. Czeslaw had refused the English tutoring. He claimed he learned all he needed about foreign languages while dealing with his accomplices in neighboring towns. "Friendly smiles and handshakes speak louder than simple sentences," he'd said. Zosia knew it was really because the classes would interfere with his appointments to trade Chesterfields for Kielbasa.

The trek across camp took longer now because Jerzy was no longer satisfied to ride in his carriage and instead wanted to practice his unsure steps. The boy toddled along the cobblestones and pointed at each broken streetlight and bench as they passed. Zosia waddled next to him. Walking became easier for the boy while it became harder for his mother.

The suspicious feelings Zosia had toward her husband troubled her. She didn't want to know what type of revenge he'd sought against Tadeusz. She just wanted him home.

Time moved slowly. She read books, sang songs, and tapped on bowls with spoons to keep Jerzy entertained. She pulled crumpled up beginnings to letters out of the trash bin for the boy to bat around.

> *Marisha,*
> *I miss you so much, you and Stefek both. And Antoni. And your father too. I miss our home. I miss*

There were no words left. She'd done everything in her power to find them, but none of it had been any use. Marisha and Stefek were nothing more than ghosts and memories.

While Jerzy played, she couldn't help but ruminate over her husband's whereabouts. She wished for a sewing machine to distract her, but knew she wouldn't be able to sew a straight line anyway with her insides all tied up in knots. Her mind created melodramas more easily than it did reasonable thoughts. In her head, Czeslaw had killed Tadeusz and run away with Violette. Or, he'd lost a duel with Tadeusz, and his body was rotting somewhere in a Bavarian stream, being picked apart by vultures.

Thoughts of a second widowhood entered her mind. To prepare herself, she collected her memories of the days and weeks after Wiktor died. How had she gotten through?

My children. She hated putting that kind of responsibility on Jerzy. Zosia would have to do it alone this time.

By the time she climbed into bed on the third night alone, she was calmly hysterical. She listened for the slow breathing and sleepy sighs that signaled Jerzy had fallen asleep, then she stared at the wall beside the bed and fought tears.

Late that night Zosia felt warmth slip into bed behind her. Czeslaw wrapped his arms around her. Her tension eased.

"What happened?" she asked. "Where did you go?"

"Nothing for you to worry about."

In a bleary fog, she turned her head to him. "Did you kill Tadeusz?"

Czeslaw chuckled. "No. Go back to sleep."

She didn't know she *had* slept. Exhaustion must have won the battle against her unease. She tried to coax herself back to slumber, but it was a struggle to keep her mind still. After a few minutes, she heard the gentle buzz of Czeslaw's snore. She knew that whatever he had or had not done to Tadeusz, his conscience was clear enough for him to sleep peacefully. She let herself be comforted.

Chapter Thirty-Six

December, 1947.

The winter of 1947 rolled into Wildflecken and flattened it like a newly paved autobahn. It seemed as though the thick forest was thinning, allowing in winter winds that whipped and punished the little refugee town on the hill. Extreme cold and towering piles of snow worked to disable the army trucks, keeping them parked by the access road.

Every winter Zosia promised herself it would be her last in Wildflecken. Every time it had been a promise broken. This was her third winter in the camp. After years of waiting and disappointment, she could no longer imagine anything else.

Czeslaw was often gone for longer periods, stranded by storms. Whenever he was away, Zosia wondered if that would be the time he wouldn't return.

Law enforcement had strengthened since the IRO had taken over, and black market commerce was always in their crosshairs. Offenders were punished severely when caught. Of course, Czeslaw was part of the police force too; the lines between good and bad were blurred in post-war Germany. His colleague one day could be his captor the next.

Czeslaw always came home exhausted, whether he was out arresting criminals or making deals with them. Zosia couldn't help but wonder if a lovely French woman was the source of his fatigue.

As new DPs piled into the camp and crowded the existing residents, everyone became more restless. Crime spiked. The miserable winters had once kept the thieves and other assailants at bay, but with everyone stacked on top of each other, even the bitter cold didn't stop the frustrated and bored from becoming crooks and villains. Czeslaw and his team tried to keep the peace, sometimes resorting to bargaining and blackmail. Wildflecken was a cruel, cycling swirl of blizzard winds and corruption.

Zosia never asked what Czeslaw did to Tadeusz. If she didn't know for sure, she could believe he wasn't a savage. Yet there was still a Nazi buried deep in the woods, thanks to Czeslaw. Tadeusz could be buried there next to him.

This division within her kept her distant from her husband. As much as the Nazi and Tadeusz might have deserved their fates, she was still married to a murderer.

While Jerzy napped one December afternoon, Zosia sipped her coffee at the card table while Czeslaw paged through a German newspaper.

"Eliasz is a funny man," Zosia said over her coffee. "That story he told last night about Petra and the kitten? My goodness."

"I chuckle every time I think of it." Czeslaw smiled over the newsprint. "I'm happy he joins us for dinner so often. He's a good man, I like spending time with him."

"Me too." Zosia watched the tendrils of steam rise from her cup. She and Czeslaw took Eliasz into their care whenever possible. He joined them for meals several times a week, and often Zosia would find Eliasz and Czeslaw either chatting on the sidewalk outside or huddled over the couple's card table with a bottle of vodka between them.

She preferred him to Violette.

As Czeslaw went back to his paper, Zosia searched across the table for words she recognized. There weren't many. Czeslaw stopped at an article with a large headline containing the word *Amerika*. She craned her neck over her large belly to read. Czeslaw noticed her effort and translated for her. "They're still trying to get the United States to accept refugees."

"Who is?"

"Everyone." He tapped his finger on the paper. "Devine said they're sending requests weekly to the Immigration Department in the US, but they always go ignored." He shook his head thoughtfully. "Their government is getting a lot of pressure, but there are no guarantees, of course. America will do what America will do, and that's that."

Zosia chewed her lip in thought. "Czeslaw, if they don't accept refugees, if it doesn't become an option . . ."

He reached across the table and squeezed her hand. "We'll figure it out."

"Can't we stay in Germany until we find Marisha and Stefek?"

"I'm working on it. We'll find them, I promise." He leaned back and stretched. "But for now, my boy has the right idea. Join me for a nap?"

Zosia hesitated. Though she was tired, she had too much to do. The thought of spending the day lolling in bed with Czeslaw should have been enticing, but it only annoyed her. She climbed into bed with him anyway and soon heard his purring snore.

She couldn't relax. Her mind was restless, and so was the baby inside her. Zosia counted each day she stayed safely pregnant as a blessing, especially after Dr. Krupka's warnings. But now, nearing the end of her term, she felt a bit of relief over each contraction.

Her fifth child. Her eldest was now almost twenty-two. She hadn't seen Marisha for nearly five years. Her children felt like a far away idea she'd once had, lost to time and distance.

Aside from the troubling thoughts and jittery baby, Zosia couldn't stand the smell of Czeslaw's socks. The stink was enough to induce labor. The more she tried to ignore the stench, the more she gagged. The rotten alley behind the Jewish deli had nothing on Czeslaw's feet. She stood and gently removed the socks from Czeslaw, who only flinched a little and smacked his lips. She collected Jerzy's diapers, Czeslaw's pants and whatever else needed to be washed, and she set out for the Laundromat.

Outside, the wind stirred white snow into a blinding sky before settling it back onto the white streets. The brightness hurt her eyes, even though the sun was nowhere to be seen. *Wherever we end up*, Zosia thought, *I hope with everything in me that the winters are not as severe as they are here in Bavaria.* Their crossing to Australia was supposed to have happened months ago. If all had gone as planned, they would be in their new home by now, arranging unfamiliar dishes in fresh cabinets and stacking folded shirts in bedroom drawers. They would be preparing for their first foreign Christmas. She couldn't help but think how it was now summer in Australia. Zosia mourned the lost yellow bathing suits and sand castles. She had to believe that by cancelling their voyage, she'd done the best thing for her young family. But, she was skeptical.

She lugged her laundry bag across camp and fell into line behind a woman giving her clothing a final wring. Zosia dumped out her bag and sorted through pockets—a habit she'd begun after finding two British pound notes in Czeslaw's pants pockets the previous spring.

A small, folded piece of notebook paper emerged from the breast pocket of one of Czeslaw's favorite shirts. She held her breath while she unfolded it, expecting a feminine hand professing love for the handsome Pole with the striking blue eyes.

Instead she was met by the most unique handwriting she'd

ever seen. The swoops and flips were almost artistic, yet it still retained a masculine form:

Czeslaw,
I thought about it, and I'll do it. Thank you.
Eliasz

She read the note two or three times, and worry pushed up further into her throat. *Do what?* She slid the note into her own pocket and filled the washing machine with hot water from the copper. Her maternal feelings toward Eliasz didn't surprise her; she'd felt protected by his wife, and now Zosia was the protector. She owed it to Petronela's memory.

The longer she watched the washing machine agitator slay the demons that infested Czeslaw's socks, the more she wondered about Eliasz. *He's too delicate,* she thought. *Whatever it is that Czeslaw wants of him, he shouldn't get involved.*

Her stomach pitched. *Had Czeslaw recruited Eliasz to help seek revenge on Tadeusz?*

—

When Zosia returned home with clean but damp laundry, Czeslaw was sitting on the edge of the bed watching Jerzy play. He eyed her sadly when she walked in. "You left."

"I couldn't sleep, so I did the laundry." She pulled out the drying line that Czeslaw had installed in the kitchen.

He patted the bed next to him, and Zosia came and sat. "*Moja kochana*, what's wrong? You've been distant, and you seem uncomfortable."

"I'm pregnant. I *am* uncomfortable." Zosia said with more venom than she'd intended.

"That's not what I mean." He looked at his hands. "What's going on? Are you angry with me?"

Zosia locked eyes with him and out of nowhere, cried. Big, childish tears fell from her cheeks, leaving great round splotches on her dress. For weeks she'd wrestled with what Czeslaw might have done to Tadeusz. She had to know.

"What is it?" Czeslaw wrapped his arms around her.

"Did you kill Tadeusz?" She asked between sobs, avoiding a volume that would alert the neighbors.

"What? No. I told you that."

"Did you have Eliasz kill him?"

"Of course not. Nobody killed Tadeusz. Why would you think that?"

She sniffled and stared at the wall. "You've killed before."

"I have?"

"The Nazi you buried in the forest."

Czeslaw's smile grew and he broke into a chuckle. "Oh, my love," he said, "I never buried a Nazi. I told you it was a Nazi uniform."

"Yes, a soldier." Zosia's face grew hotter as humiliation and anger joined the overwhelming sorrow and confusion in her heart.

He shook his head. "No, Zosia. A *uniform*. Clothing. In fact, I used it to get our revenge on Tadeusz." He put his arm around Zosia and squeezed. "I've never killed anyone, even as a soldier. My squad was captured too quickly."

She sniffled, and he handed over his handkerchief. She felt like a fool. She took a deep breath and wiped her face. "Okay." After a few more breaths, her voice calmed. "Why did you bury a uniform? And what does that have to do with Tadeusz?"

Czeslaw paused and picked at his fingernail. "You know how this was an old Nazi training camp?"

Zosia nodded.

"When I first moved into the blockhouse, there was a line of lockers along the back of the room where I was assigned. I was anxious. I'd been freed from the Soviets, but their shadows followed me. I couldn't relax or sleep; not many of the men in my building could. I inspected every corner, ran my hand along every wall. I went through every locker. I found a box in the bottom of one of them with an old Nazi uniform inside. I took it. I didn't know if the 'peace' was going to last. I thought I might need the uniform for protection. A disguise, or maybe I could use it for blackmail or even to trade for something. That was when I buried it out in the forest, in a place where I could find it again if I ever needed it."

Czeslaw lit a cigarette, handed it to Zosia, and lit another for himself. "When you told me what Tadeusz did to you, I was livid. I'll admit, I thought about killing him. I wanted to. But I knew that would only create more problems. I didn't want to be sent to prison and leave you, Jerzy, and this little one all alone." He rested his hand on Zosia's belly.

"So I dug up the uniform," he said. "Then I went into Münnerstadt with it stuffed in the bottom of my bag. I hunted around for a day or so and found Tadeusz in a bar, drinking dopplebocks and eyeing the waitresses.

"I sat with him, laughed at his jokes, slapped him on the back. I stroked his ego. I bought him strong drinks and got him drunk. In fact, I got him so drunk I had to carry him out. I lugged him around the corner into an alley and dumped him onto the ground where he smiled at me, pissed himself, and passed out.

"I pulled off his clothes and dressed him in the uniform. Then I left him there to sleep on a pile of stinking boxes. I went to the police station a few blocks away and told them an escaped Nazi officer had been disrupting the peace and was out behind the pub."

Zosia didn't smile, but Czeslaw's caper amused her.

"I hid around the corner and watched the police pick him up. He vomited all over the front of the uniform. What a fucking *dupek*."

"So he's gone? What will happen to him?" Zosia watched

Jerzy reach for a block that slid under his crib on the floor.

"Yes. Gone. He'll probably be tried for war crimes. He never carried identification on him. Thought it was bad luck. So he has no way of proving who he is, or isn't. He won't be back here, though, even if he is found innocent. His pride is delicate. If he's released, he knows his story will be all over town. He'll be too humiliated."

"What if he comes after you?"

Czeslaw smiled and patted Zosia's knee. "He won't. He knows better. And besides, if he does return, he won't last a day. I made sure everyone in town knows that he was a Nazi collaborator."

"Was he?" Zosia asked.

Czeslaw winked.

"What about that picture of Maxim? Tadeusz had a connection."

"Tadeusz was only ever a means to an end," he said. "We're no further ahead or behind with him gone."

Zosia finally smiled. "You're a clever man, Czeslaw." She wiped her eyes one more time before handing the handkerchief back. "But what does Eliasz have to do with this?"

Czeslaw looked genuinely confused. "Nothing."

She took the note out of her pocket and handed it to him.

"Ah." Czeslaw smiled. He stood and went to the wardrobe. On the bottom shelf he moved a few boxes to the side and pulled out a ledger. He handed it to Zosia, and she flipped through the smudged, yellowed pages. Blue ink covered them in Eliasz's unique handwriting. She read some of the entries.

Three pairs denim overalls with steel buckles.
Four bottles condensed milk.
One Mercury 35 mm camera.
Forty sewing machine needles.

Zosia stared at that entry. It was dated around the time when she and Czeslaw first met. She tapped the line of text. "This is me."

Czeslaw nodded.

"You had him transpose all of your transactions?"

"I was amazed he could read my notes." He smiled. "Lousy chicken scratchings."

"You gave him a purpose."

Czeslaw paused for a moment. "He came to me for a gun," he said. "Instead, I gave him a job."

"You saved his life." Zosia smoothed her hand over the inked page as if it were a collection of memories in a photo album. She was holding a full record of Czeslaw's involvement in the black market.

Frightened yet fascinated, she turned a few more pages. She read one entry in detail from the top.

> *Wenzel Bauer, Farmer. Between 11-noon, outside the deli in Bischofsheim an der Rhön. Likes brisket sandwiches and black coffee. Wife Gretel. Likes red lipstick, cast iron pans. Son Dierk, 10. Plays football. Daughter Ava, 6. Wants livestock feed, crop seed, fertilizer. Often has butter to trade, trinkets, some baby items.*
> *June 10, 1946: 4 kilo coffee beans for 10 kilo butter*
> *July 27, 1946: 1 kilo barley seeds and 1 football for 4 liters corn oil*
> *September 24, 1946: 2 kilo chicken feed for baby carriage*

"This is Jerzy's carriage," she acknowledged. The detail Czeslaw put into his notes in the ledger proved he'd been more than a simple farmer before the war; he was a smart businessman.

While the dangers of the black market still scared Zosia, she felt some relief knowing how conscientious Czeslaw was.

Czeslaw turned a few more pages. "Here's where things start to change."

"Change?" As she read through the entries copied by Eliasz, Zosia noticed an interesting detail. Many of the notes mentioned items, and not much was surprising. However, here and there, she noted the word *fakty*.

Facts. Information.

Her scalp tingled. Czeslaw always made clear that he didn't like to deal in easily falsified information. She turned the pages, and *fakty* showed up more and more. He'd broken his own personal rules and bartered on the black market for information, trading canned hams for headlines. Family names and locations became more of a constant, rather than cigarettes and cooking oil. Though it appeared he'd been helping many families locate lost loved ones, a number of entries had a star next to them. They all concerned "Z."

> *Discussed Z.* fakty *with Adam Urbanek, Bad Brückenau. No help.*
> *Discussed Z.* fakty *with Fryderyk Nitka, Riedenberg, No help.*
> *Sent Z. to the Partridge. Paid $80 American.*
> *Partridge found two children. Sent* fakty *through director.*
> *1: Married, whereabouts unknown. 2: Deceased. 3: Unknown*
> *Partridge unwilling to work further on Z. Problems with contacts in Munich.*

Czeslaw had worked tirelessly to find Zosia's children for years, even while grieving his own family, and even when he was angry with Zosia.

She flipped to the last several pages. The very last entry before the sheets went blank was from only a few days before.

> *December 15, 1947: Foth Derby camera for expedited passage to America. Waiting to hear from Partridge.*

She looked up at Czeslaw. "America? When?"

"I'm trying," he said quietly, not lifting his eyes from the ledger.

She closed the book. "Czeslaw, there's one more thing." Most else had been explained, but she needed to know everything. "What is going on between you and Violette?" Her voice was hoarse as she spoke.

"Oh, Zosia." Disappointment creased the corners of Czeslaw's eyes. "You need to trust me."

"I've seen you with her, huddled over paperwork, whispering back and forth. I'm not angry, I just need to know."

Czeslaw stood and pulled another thin notebook out of the wardrobe. This one was mostly empty, except for a few pages filled with Czeslaw's own messy handwriting. He flipped to one page in particular. "I didn't have Eliasz copy everything."

A name jumped out at Zosia: *Kloc.*

> *E. Kloc coming from Eschwege. Trying to reroute to Seedorf.*

"You knew he was alive?"

Czeslaw rubbed his hands over his face and head. "It was fairly recent. Late summer, early fall. Violette found him, and she was horrified. Even more so when she learned he was coming here." Czeslaw rested his head into his hands, his hair rumpled from the rubbing. "She came to me, and together we worked to try to get him reassigned. We both knew it would destroy him to come to the same camp where his wife had taken her life." Czeslaw held Zosia's eyes. "We knew it would hurt you, too. I thought it would be better if you didn't know." He sighed a heavy breath. "He showed up early. We were still working on getting him sent elsewhere when all of a sudden, he was here, and you'd already spoken with him."

She nodded, keeping her eyes on the book in her lap. She should have been angry that Czeslaw had kept information from her, but she wasn't. She understood.

She was finished with lies and mistrust. She leaned into Czeslaw.

The bed felt damp and warm under her.

Chapter Thirty-Seven

The next morning.

The baby girl struggled to open her eyes. Zosia peeked into them. "Good morning, Janina."

Czeslaw sat next to her, tears streaming down his face. "This is a beautiful way to honor my *dziewczynka* Janina, gone too soon."

"I know how much she meant to you and how much this little girl means to you. It feels right."

"Thank you," Czeslaw pulled Zosia and Janina into a strong hug. He held them for a long time.

"Mrs. Lysek," Dr. Krupka pulled back the curtain, "you have visitors." They broke their embrace. Eliasz held Jerzy's hand as he toddled along, his dark hair messy from sleep. Jerzy hugged a ragged stuffed puppy in his free arm. "Someone wants to meet his new sister." Eliasz smiled. He let Jerzy lead the way, and the little boy rushed to Zosia's side.

He peered at the baby, and Zosia patted his head to try to tame the cowlick that flopped to and fro. Jerzy looked up at Zosia with an expression of awe. He held up the puppy for everyone to see.

"Is that for Janina?" Czeslaw smiled with pride at his family. The little boy laid the puppy on the baby's chest and put his fingers in his mouth. He looked up to his father for approval. "Good boy, Jerzy." Czeslaw kissed his head.

Eliasz watched from a distance, then he turned to leave.

"Eliasz, wait," Zosia called.

He stopped and smiled shyly at her. "Oh, please. I want you to have your moment with your family."

"You are family." Her eyes met Czeslaw's. He seemed to know what she was thinking, and he nodded his approval. "We want you to be Janina's godfather. Would you do that for us?"

Behind Eliasz's glasses, an emotional shine gilded his eyes. "I'm moved, Mrs. Lysek, but it's not allowed. The Catholic Church—"

Zosia shook her head. "I don't care what the Catholic Church allows. There has to be a way around it. These are trying times, and we need to make exceptions. Father Terlecki should understand that."

Czeslaw nodded. "Father is a reasonable man, but this is a pretty big rule to break. I'll talk to him and see what we can do."

A week later, Eliasz joined the family as an "Exceptional Personal Witness" to Janina. Zosia and Czeslaw were proud of the designation they'd created. Father Terlecki agreed to be the official godfather to Janina, but under their unique circumstances, he would surrender any non-Christian nurturing to Eliasz. They made the same arrangement for Jerzy, too. Although it would not be formally recognized by either of their faiths, Eliasz was now an honorary member of the Lysek family.

CHAPTER THIRTY-EIGHT

July, 1948.

Zosia was tired. This time, Jerzy was the one crying. At first, he was excited to help with the baby and cheerfully brought Zosia blankets and bottles from across the room. But as the months and monotony drew on and the novelty of being a brother wore off, Jerzy became bored and irritable. Such was the way of life in Wildflecken.

Outside, the camp blazed orange with the summer sunrise. Inside, Jerzy's cheeks blazed red with anger. Zosia had paced most of the night with Janina to keep her peaceful. The baby girl *had* been sleeping well, but recently changed her mind. Now Zosia often greeted the mornings with her shoulders wet with Janina's spit up and her cheeks wet with her own tears of exhaustion. Czeslaw offered to walk Janina before he left for his shift, but Zosia refused. This was her place. She was the *matka*.

Now, the girl curled her fingers around the bottle of condensed milk and Karo syrup and cuddled into Zosia's arms. But Zosia made one mistake: "Jerzy, my *misiu*, please bring me that blanket from the table." The question hung in the air for several moments until Jerzy shrieked in jealous frustration, bewildering his mother. He threw his picture book under the bed, and Zosia made a mental note that it was there, knowing he would cry later when he couldn't find it. She watched the liquid in Janina's bottle lower and counted the seconds until she could take her children outside for fresh air.

The morning was already warming when they tumbled out the door of their building. Janina slept in her carriage, and Jerzy, distracted by the change in environment, ran ahead and searched for dandelions. With her children finally happy, Zosia took in the subtle acceptance of permanence around the camp.

Wildflecken was only ever intended to be a stopping off point in a grander journey, yet it was clear many DPs had given up hope that the next step would come. Small squares of lawn had been converted into garden plots with cucumbers and beets pushing up through the dirt. Nicer curtains framed some windows, and a few were even complete with lace sheers under them. Flowerpots decorated entrances, and freshly shaken rugs were placed in front of doors. The passage of time had allowed for the settled nuisances of peeling paint and creeping weeds. The blandness of the camp evolved into a town as its inhabitants relinquished their hopes for the future. A known purgatory became a better option than a vague hope in nothing.

At the height of summer, the mountains and forests did little to keep the air fresh. It was as if the musty odor from the sweat-ridden Nazi uniforms that once hung in the lockers of the blockhouses had seeped outdoors, enveloping the residents in a stale air. They were all wrapped in the stinking exhale of war.

As always, tomatoes were planted and harvested, vodka was distilled and consumed. Rations were hoarded and cigarettes traded. Chocolate melted in the pockets of the American GIs, but the children ate it anyway. Now Jerzy was one of those who chased the soldiers down the street.

She couldn't blame the American Captain Foley anymore.

He hadn't canceled their passage to Australia. She had.

"Zosia!" Czeslaw appeared out of nowhere and pulled Zosia into an improvised polka on the street, sweat trickling down his temple beneath his police cap. "It's done! Look!" Czeslaw handed her a newspaper. On the front page were a lot of big English words. Under the headline was a picture of a man wearing a business suit and thick glasses. He sat at a desk with a pen in his hand.

"What is this? I can't read any of it."

"It's an American paper." Czeslaw pointed to the picture. "This is President Truman. He signed the bill! America is accepting immigrants!"

Zosia squinted at the paper, reluctant to believe anything that would signal good news. "Are you sure? He could be signing anything."

Flustered, Czeslaw slumped his shoulders. "My friend Reimund in Gersfeld can read English. He said the story confirmed it."

"Reimund?" Her eyebrow arched.

Czeslaw folded the paper, stuffed it under his arm, and grabbed Zosia's hand. "Come on." They marched across camp, Jerzy struggling to keep up with his impatient father and skeptical mother. They left the stroller parked on the street in front of the administration building, and the family climbed the stairs with Janina on Zosia's hip.

Czeslaw opened the director's door without knocking. "Mr. Devine."

The director jumped. "Oh, Mr. Lysek." He answered Czeslaw with the same surprised, nervous greeting with which he always greeted Zosia.

Czeslaw dropped the newspaper on the desk. "What does this say?"

Mr. Devine didn't have to look. "Yes, you are the ninth or tenth family to ask about it this morning. It says, 'Truman Signs

Displaced Persons Bill; European Refugees Will Be Brought Stateside.'" He took off his glasses. "The United States will allow some immigrants in, but it won't be easy. Each family needs a sponsor, and sponsors will be hard to find."

"Why?" Zosia frowned. "I thought Americans wanted to help."

"By sending money or old clothes, not by taking strangers into their homes." He rubbed his eyes, then put his glasses back on. "Americans are jittery, and foreigners frighten them. Just because the president signed a bill doesn't mean you'll be welcomed with opened arms."

"So America wants to forget us, pretend we're not here," Zosia said with disdain.

"Now Mrs. Lysek," Mr. Devine said in his usual, tired way. He led her to a chair by the desk. "I know you're frustrated, but don't be so quick to judge. There will be sponsors, we'll just have to be nimble enough to find one that is a good fit for your family."

Zosia sat with Janina wiggling on her lap. Jerzy stood obediently next to the big mahogany desk and eyed a painting of a Lancaster bomber on the wall.

"Please remember," Czeslaw said, "I'm willing to help in any way."

The director nodded. "I know I can count on you, Mr. Lysek, but I wouldn't expect anything to happen until autumn at the earliest. It will take several months to work through the logistics." He walked toward the door and opened it, signaling it was time for them to leave.

With Janina perched in her arms, Zosia stood, took Jerzy's hand, and led him to the door. Czeslaw followed, but Mr. Devine stopped him. "Thank you for your help yesterday. We'll miss you when you leave." The men shook hands. Zosia didn't know if Czeslaw's help was as a law officer or lawbreaker. She supposed they were one and the same.

Chapter Thirty-Nine

A month.

"Zosia, join us!" Nadia waved.

"Look, Jerzy. There's your friend from English class. Go play." Zosia pointed to Rafal, who was chasing a ball on the field with the pack of children. Jerzy gleefully took off toward his friends, full of giggles and flushed cheeks. Zosia switched Janina to her other hip and approached the rotting picnic table where the mothers gathered.

Zosia had stumbled upon this group of women who met almost daily next to the athletic field to gossip, smoke cigarettes, and let their little ones run. Zosia adjusted their morning routine so Jerzy could stretch his legs, and she could chat with other adults.

Nadia kissed Zosia's cheek. "When will we see you again in English class?"

Zosia motioned to Janina. "When she's in school?"

"Aww, what a sweet baby *dziewczynka*," Ela clucked, beaming at Janina who grimaced in return.

Zosia bounced Janina gently. "When she's sleeping." She gave the knowing smile of motherhood, and the women all returned a sympathetic nod.

"Fussy baby?" Sabina lit her cigarette. "Danika was like that too. Poor little cherub. And poor *matka*. Have you tried brandy in her bottle?"

"Not yet."

"You didn't burn her first diaper, did you?" Wanda scoffed, her young daughter digging in the dirt at her feet. "She wouldn't be having trouble in her tummy if you'd burned it properly."

The other women rolled their eyes. "Oh, Wanda." Sabina's smile was pure evil. "You can stuff that diaper—"

"We got our assignment!" Ela said, her excitement diplomatically diffusing a potential squabble. "Milwaukee, Wisconsin."

"Oh, Ela, that's wonderful," Nadia cheered with blatant envy.

Wanda snorted. "Beer," she said. "You'll be brewing beer."

Everyone ignored Wanda while they applauded with a happy veneer, but underneath, each woman seethed, especially Zosia. "I'm hoping we'll be matched with a sponsor soon too." Zosia tried to keep her voice buoyant. "Czeslaw's been working closely with Mr. Devine. When do you leave?"

"Rafal! Rafal, my prince, don't pull Kasienka's hair. No, no, Rafal." Nadia ran off toward the children. Wanda huffed and sucked at her cigarette.

Ela turned to Zosia. "Soon. Two weeks. By the way, how is Mr. Lysek?"

"He's well," she said, trying to keep her eyebrow from arching. "How do you know him?"

"My husband worked for the hospital for a while, kept track of inventory. When he first started there were no scalpels. None. How can a hospital not have scalpels? Anyway, Mr. Lysek found some. Traded a *Myszka Miki* watch for a case of them. Can you believe it? Since then he's found other things for us, too. He found a crib for Kamil."

Zosia nodded, and Nadia rejoined the mothers. "Is there a

cough going around?" Several of them shrugged.

"There's always something going around," Wanda said with her usual grumble.

"Rafal has been having little coughing fits." Nadia frowned. "Ah well, you're probably right, Wanda. Nothing new. Again, congratulations, Ela."

The group of women broke apart as one child had skinned his knee, and another mother had to meet her husband for lunch. Zosia followed the routine of retrieving a flushed, excited child from the field, then praying all the way home for her family's own American sponsor.

—

Zosia, Jerzy, and Janina maneuvered the cobblestone streets of Wildflecken almost every day to visit the children and their chatty mothers. It was a nice reprieve for Zosia. When summer turned into fall, however, it seemed Zosia was mistiming her walks. The field was often empty when they approached, and Jerzy would become mopey again.

"I don't know, my *misiu*," Zosia consoled one morning as she watched Janina pull herself up to standing at an empty bench by the field. She knelt down to button Jerzy's sweater against the cool October wind. "Maybe the chilly weather chased them inside. Or maybe they're all at school. We can check back later this afternoon."

"No!" Jerzy ran off.

"Jerzy! Come to Matka!" Zosia scooped up Janina, deposited her into the carriage, and ran after him though the pitted brown grass. The baby girl screeched in terror while the wheels bumped over rocks and marmot holes.

The boy came to the edge of the athletic field next to Blockhouse B-5 and stopped in his tracks. Several people dressed in black stood huddled around a tiny coffin at the cemetery across the street. Zosia recognized Nadia. Her hands were pressed against the top of the coffin, and her husband stroked the gray babushka that wrapped her hair.

The coffin was half-sized.

"Oh, my God." Zosia snatched Jerzy up into her arms and carried him toward home, pushing Janina and stumbling against the weight and wrestle of the growing boy.

"What they doing, Matka?" He wriggled in her grip.

She didn't want to tell Jerzy that his little playmate was dead, so she simply said, "They're remembering someone who isn't here anymore."

"Where they go?"

"They went home." It was the best Zosia could come up with.

"Like we go Amarka?"

"Kind of like that." It was nothing like that, but she was desperate to end the questions. There was still no word on a sponsor for them, but that fact didn't stop Czeslaw from brimming with excitement and describing America to Jerzy as his new home. Zosia, however, was jaded. She couldn't find any confidence or comfort in their future until her feet were on American soil, with Stefek's hand in hers and Marisha's voice in her ear. Until America was a sure thing, she was uncomfortable with the possible lies Jerzy was led to believe.

They rounded the corner toward their building and saw Czeslaw parking his motorcycle. "I just came from Devine's office," Czeslaw beamed. "He found us a sponsor in America. We're going, and we have a date: November fifth. It's really happening!"

Less than three weeks away. "That's great." She fell into his embrace.

"What's wrong?"

With cold tears hanging in her eyes, she turned to Jerzy. "Go find me a pretty brown rock, Jerzy. Find the biggest one." She motioned to a small pile of gravel. When the boy was out of earshot, she told Czeslaw about the funeral.

"Yes." Czeslaw dropped his head. "There have been a lot of those lately. It's a shame. We've been sending some of our policemen to help dig the graves, just to keep up."

"It was one of Jerzy's little playmates. I didn't know how to explain that to him."

"His playmate?" Czeslaw's voice rose.

Zosia's heart skipped. "Yes. Why?"

"Zosia." Czeslaw's voice dropped to a whisper. "Pertussis is spreading through the camp, and it is extremely contagious. Children are dying."

Zosia had never heard of pertussis, but she was terrified. "What is that?"

"Whooping cough."

She looked down at her son. Jerzy was carefully inspecting the multicolored flecks in a small chunk of granite. He coughed. Czeslaw and Zosia looked at each other in horror.

"No, no, no." Zosia scooped the young boy up in her arms. "No, he's fine." She carried him inside. Czeslaw followed with Janina.

Cough. Jerzy's little body shook.

He had been coughing recently. She knew the truth, but didn't want to accept it. *Jerzy hasn't been in school with the sick children, only outside where the illness could dissipate. He's fine.* Jerzy rested his head on Zosia's shoulder.

Cough.

Zosia stopped and looked behind her. That cough didn't come from Jerzy.

"She's fine. A little tickle in her throat." Czeslaw's voice was a whisper.

Zosia and her husband locked eyes for a long moment. They hurried down the hall to their tiny room, a cloak of dread descending upon them.

Chapter Forty

Two weeks later.

"It's best to keep the boy inside and give him hot tea with honey, Mrs. Lysek," Dr. Krupka said, giving Zosia an exasperated look. "Just like I've been telling you."

Tea would not keep her child out of the grave. "Is there nothing else we can do?"

Dr. Krupka shrugged. "I told you yesterday, we had a little penicillin, but it's long gone now. Just about every child is affected in some way. You're not the only one hoping for a miracle. We can't do much else but let it run its course."

"You mean, let the children die."

He took a deep breath, and let it out. "I'd guess that Mr. Lysek has a better chance of finding penicillin than I do at this point."

Zosia cringed. Czeslaw had recanted his vow to not trade drugs and had already made his rounds through every nearby town, searching for antibiotics. "He's tried." Czeslaw hadn't really slept since Jerzy fell ill, and neither had Zosia. She desperately wished that all of Iwona's "penicillin" actually existed.

"Well, then, there's little else we can do. You don't have to keep coming back."

Zosia brought Jerzy to the hospital every day since he'd become sick. She didn't care how much she annoyed Dr. Krupka, she would not allow her child to die.

It was agonizing for Zosia to watch her normally healthy and happy boy tortured by such misery. His coughing fits could last nearly ten minutes, and he often vomited during and after his spells. Zosia stayed up nights, sitting next to Jerzy's little cot and rocking Janina in her arms, wishing she could breathe for the boy herself. She watched every breath he took and waited anxiously for the next.

Czeslaw was dozing in the rocking chair when Zosia and Jerzy returned from the hospital. Janina was asleep in Czeslaw's arms. Zosia shook him gently.

He twitched awake.

"How is she?"

"Fine." Czeslaw cleared his throat. "She seems fine. I think she's okay."

Zosia pursed her lips and led Jerzy to his bed to rest. "Czeslaw, next week . . . I mean, what if—"

"It'll be fine." Czeslaw settled Janina into her crib. "Don't worry. It's all arranged. All we have to do is be at the train station on time. The rest will fall into place."

Zosia recognized the look of uncertainty in Czeslaw's eyes, but she didn't question him. She wanted to believe that their passage to America would be easy, so she did.

The date of their departure loomed, but Zosia put all of her energy into her babies and did nothing to prepare. She knew very little about their new country, aside from what she'd seen years before in the cheap matinees back home. She knew New York City was a bustling metropolis, and Los Angeles had sunshine and palm trees. Aside from that, America was big and free. And overwhelming.

Czeslaw told her they were going to a place called North Dakota. It was an agricultural area, which was a perfect fit for Czeslaw's farming background. That's all she knew about their prospective home. It would have to be enough.

Cramped in a camp that had become a village, where if one person fell sick everyone languished, the thought of wide-open spaces gave Zosia apprehensive comfort. But vast spaces also meant it could be a long journey to find a doctor or buy food and supplies. She would have to learn to drive a car. She shook her head to clear that thought. Czeslaw could do the driving.

One thing she tentatively let herself look forward to was the day she could go to a store and buy something she needed, rather than waiting for the local barter system to spew the item out of its spin. She would not miss the volatility of the black market and the constant competition for goods.

"I'll go out and bring back some sandwiches from Mess 2." Czeslaw stood and stretched, glancing out the window at the long evening shadows. "Tomorrow I'll get a lift into Fulda. I heard there's a retired doctor there who has a surplus of penicillin left from the war." He stuffed his hands in his pockets and shook his head. "It's a lead. Probably not true, but it's something."

"Czeslaw, do you know where Iwona went? Maybe she—"

"Zosia . . ." Czeslaw's voice was tired, but his eyes understood. They grasped at every slim hope and outrageous idea that passed through either of their heads. Their eyes searched each other's. They both knew Iwona had only peddled lies. "I'll ask around."

—

That night, Zosia sat by Jerzy's bed and prayed that the retired doctor in Fulda was eccentric enough to have stockpiled ample medicine to treat every child in Wildflecken. If not, she hoped there would be at least one dose hidden there, and that dose would save her son.

With her eyes half open and sleep tugging mercilessly on her, Zosia felt Janina become still in her arms—more so than just a restful sleep. A dead still. Zosia's eyes bolted open. She rested her hand on Janina's chest and waited for the up and down motion of a deep breath. It didn't come.

"Janina." She gently wobbled the baby. She patted her cheek. "Janina?" There was no response. "Czeslaw," she whispered loudly, hoping to not wake Jerzy who was finally asleep after a fitful evening.

In an instant her husband was there. Trembling, she handed the child to him.

Czeslaw held Janina upright and patted her back. Even in the darkness, Zosia could see that her lips were gray and her face held a limp, lifeless expression. "Janina. Janina, wake up. Janina." His whispers rose with panic.

It may have only been seconds, but to Zosia, a lifetime passed before Janina finally took a deep, difficult breath. She coughed several times and let it out, her eyes fluttering on the brink of either sleep or death. Janina continued to wheeze as Czeslaw returned her. Zosia cuddled her baby close, locking eyes with her husband. Without exchanging any words, they both understood: she was stricken, too. Czeslaw climbed back into bed and stared at the wall to wait for daylight.

Janina's illness was even more terrifying to Zosia than Jerzy's. Jerzy could cough himself to death, but a baby as young as Janina could just stop breathing with no warning. Zosia rocked Janina, counting every breath and not taking her own until she felt the baby's chest rise and fall. *Give me their illness,* Zosia prayed to a fickle God until the sun came over the distant hills. *Give them my health, and give me their illness. Let them survive this journey.*

I'll be damned if either of these children die. I will lie down and die next to them.

CHAPTER FORTY-ONE

The next week: November 5, 1948.

It was cold on the open platform of the Wildflecken train station. When Zosia had arrived there more than three years prior, trees had surrounded the station and threatened to swallow it whole. Now the woods retreated as if the station had a disease the forest feared. The trees were all destroyed, chopped down for buildings or fences or firewood. She supposed it finally signaled the full transformation from Wildflecken, "the wild spot," to Durzyn, which took its name from a tiny village in a wide-open, agricultural area of Poland.

Zosia held Janina tightly wrapped in a blanket to keep the chill off. Despite all of Zosia's prayers and tears, her daughter's health had worsened. Janina had bouts of apnea; sometimes her face turned red or even blue from lack of air. Zosia hadn't let her baby out of her sight for a moment since she'd become sick. All she could do for her daughter was to hold her, rock her, and pray harder to a God she'd never really trusted.

Jerzy stood next to Czeslaw on the platform, holding his father's hand and crying between coughs. The boy was weak, but at least he'd been able to occasionally sleep. That was more than could be said for Zosia, but she didn't complain. She would never sleep again if it meant her children would survive. Even at their healthiest, the journey would be a challenge. Zosia was leading her delicate children into the mouth of a dragon.

The train rumbled into the station and lined up next to the crescent-shaped platform. Father Terlecki mingled amongst the crowd, offering blessings and farewells. He shook Czeslaw's hand and laid his fingers on the children's foreheads. Zosia wondered if his prayers traded at a higher currency than the ones she'd offered up.

Zosia never suggested cancelling the trip and never considered trying to talk Czeslaw out of it. She knew they were out of options. They were to get on this train with the help of the IRO or be returned to the wasteland of Poland to die, unwanted and unhelped. They no longer had the luxury of choosing safety over emigration. This was their last chance.

The priest stepped away to bless other vagabonds and the family took a timid step toward the train. They were nearly to the line of cars when an out-of-breath voice broke through the racket of the crowd.

"Czeslaw, Zosia, wait!" Eliasz reached out and grabbed Czeslaw's shoulder. "This came for you." He handed Czeslaw an envelope. "From Violette, in the director's office."

"Oh, thank God," Czeslaw said. He tore open the envelope and scanned the letter. A pained smile spread across his face for the first time in weeks. "Zosia, I found Marisha and Stefek."

She lifted a hand to her mouth, which had fallen open in shock. The despair she'd felt over her younger children's illness was now complicated by a cruel, distorted hope. After all these years, she couldn't bear to believe. She certainly couldn't speak.

Czeslaw pulled Zosia into his arms. "They're to meet us in Bremerhaven." He stroked Zosia's hair while she wept over the baby in her arms. "We've found them, my love."

Her body was limp. When Czeslaw released her, she fell into Eliasz's embrace, too. That hug, a simple touch, would have to communicate all that she couldn't say. The pertussis, the imminent voyage, the promise of the impossible reunion with her children . . . She was overwhelmed.

"Take care of yourself, Eliasz." Czeslaw shook his hand, then wrapped his arms around the small man. "We'll miss you, my friend."

"Thank you both." Eliasz's voice trembled. "I'll be managing the camp supply inventory for Mr. Devine, starting Tuesday. Czeslaw, I wouldn't have gotten that job without you. And Zosia," Eliasz said and took her hands in his, "you welcomed me into your family. You made me want to live again."

Eliasz knelt to hug Jerzy. He kissed Janina's forehead before stepping out of the way of the crowds. Zosia and Czeslaw watched him for a moment, then turned toward their future.

The train whistle blew and drowned out Jerzy's pitiful cough. Janina fell into a fit of hacking and gagging too—the illness exacerbated by the train's exhaust. Zosia bounced her, rocked her, comforted her, but Janina still fought for air. She patted the baby's back and murmured in her ear, "Stay with me, *dziewczynka.* Matka is here." She couldn't hear her own voice over the constant hum that rang through her ears, an echo from her years of standing next to the trains. This one, she would not see roll away.

The family settled onto the floor in the far rear corner of their car. Zosia held Janina tight and tried to ease the baby's pain. Jerzy coughed until he vomited and leaned on Zosia, exhausted. Czeslaw sat firm and straight against the wall, his eyes sharp as he watched for anything that might either be dangerous or helpful.

As the train rocked in its forward motion, Jerzy's body calmed. His breath became steady, and he fell asleep against his mother's shoulder. Janina coughed through her tears, her tiny body quaking with each gasp. Zosia stayed still to avoid waking her son. She sang to Janina in a hushed tone, hoping the baby girl would hear through her fits. "*A-a-a, kotki dwa . . .*"

The early winter sky darkened above the setting sun as they accelerated through the woods. Janina's struggling coughs became further apart, until at last she was still with sleep. Zosia kept her hand on the baby's chest and waited for each rise and fall of breath, thanking God each time she felt it.

"Is it true?" Zosia asked Czeslaw. "Did you really find my daughter and son?"

Czeslaw nodded slowly. She'd never seen him so crushed by fatigue. "Violette has an associate who was in touch with Maxim. He agreed to meet us."

"Do you know who Violette's associate is?" An image of Tadeusz flashed in her head.

"Yes." Czeslaw was quiet for a moment, as if contemplating his words. Then he rolled his head against the wall to look at his wife. "He's a former Nazi agent. Franz Voss."

She stopped breathing.

Her stomach rolled.

When she finally forced a breath, the air felt hot as it vibrated her chest.

Czeslaw's face was expressionless. He stared out ahead into nothing. He said no more, and neither did Zosia. The rumbling noise of the train filled her head, stuffing her ears and thoughts with a conflicted, sticky cotton.

She didn't want to understand anymore. She didn't care who brought the information, as long as it came. She was surrounded by shades of gray, the distinction between good and evil blurred and jagged at best.

She could never forgive Voss. But if he could connect her to Marisha and Stefek, even unwittingly, she would accept it. She no longer had the energy to fear him. Zosia leaned into the solidness of Czeslaw's trunk and closed her eyes.

—

When Zosia next opened her eyes, she was greeted to a vision of the sunlit countryside rushing past through the partially open doors of the boxcar. The trees and mountains of Bavaria were behind them, replaced by the rolling farms and countryside of central Germany. It was morning.

Janina gazed up at Zosia, her clear, hazel eyes blinking softly. Her face was pink, and her breath kept a healthy rhythm. Jerzy adjusted his body, his head now in her lap. His eyelids flickered as he dozed. Zosia watched in disbelief as Janina's chubby cheeks lifted, pulling her mouth into a smile. She was the picture of a healthy baby.

This can't be real. Did I die? Is this heaven? She looked at Czeslaw, whose red eyes told of another sleepless night. He smiled. They survived.

"She stopped coughing," Czeslaw's voice was rough. "I made sure she was okay. You both slept. Jerzy, too. You all needed it. I think the worst is past."

Zosia marveled at her daughter's recovery. Even Jerzy had mostly stopped coughing. Zosia wondered if the stagnation and restlessness of Wildflecken had somehow been poisoning them—not just their minds, but also their bodies.

Throughout the boxcar, a splattering of vagrants huddled together and apart, each headed toward what they hoped was something better. Some played cards, some sat and stared at nothing. Children spoke in tiny voices, singing little songs and telling important stories while mothers and fathers prayed they were making the right decision. A small fire smoldered in the center of the car, like always.

The train rolled to a stop outside a farming village to take on water and fuel. Zosia led her children to the door to replace the illness in their lungs with fresh, cool air.

"I'll be right back." Czeslaw jumped down from the car.

"Where are you going?" Zosia's throat tightened.

"To find food. Stay here."

"Please, don't go. We don't know how long we'll be stopped. We have some bread, we'll be okay."

"I can't eat any more of that sawdust shit," Czeslaw said from the ground. "I'll only be a minute." He disappeared into a field of tall weeds and old corn.

Zosia waited, her legs dangling off the edge of the car. She gave Janina a bottle and Jerzy some bread. She changed Janina's diaper and washed the used one in a bucket of melted snow. She kept one eye on the fields for any sign of Czeslaw. The brush swayed as other passengers pushed their way through the overgrown crops in their return to the train, but Czeslaw didn't come.

When the whistle blew to signal they were ready to move on, Zosia's unease turned to alarm. She couldn't leave Czeslaw, but she also couldn't abandon the train with her two young children in tow. She would have to find a way to go on without him. Her heart, which she didn't think could break any further after so many years of grief, again found new cracks.

The mighty train lurched and started a very slow creep forward. Zosia had to make a decision. In her panic, she readied herself to grab Janina and Jerzy and jump to the ground. That was when she spotted Czeslaw, running from between the decaying corn with something wiggling and squawking under his coat. He heaved himself onto the train with one arm, keeping the other wrapped tightly around his bounty.

"What on earth?" Zosia helped him to his feet. "Czeslaw, I was worried sick."

"Zosia, when are you going to trust me?" Czeslaw smiled and proudly displayed the angry rooster he had stuffed inside his coat. "Eggs! Eggs for everyone!"

Zosia frowned. "You know that's a rooster, right?"

Czeslaw's face fell as he glared at the livid bird. "Shit," he said. "I was in a hurry, I just grabbed. I thought they were all hens." He continued swearing to himself, missing when he kicked at the bird. It shrieked back.

"Give me your pocket knife." Zosia passed Janina to her husband to hold.

"Why?" he asked, collecting the baby into his arms. He hitched her onto one hip, dug into his opposite pocket, and handed over the blade.

Zosia grabbed the rooster and had it dressed for cooking in minutes. She threaded the bird's carcass onto a stick to serve as a spit to hang above the fire. Then she wiped her hands on a rag.

Czeslaw wrapped his free arm around her waist and squeezed. "You amaze me. I love you so much."

The passengers in the car feasted on the chicken while Zosia observed her children. Jerzy sat near the fire and held Janina, who stared at the flickering flames and waved her arms excitedly. They listened to an old Polish woman tell stories of their homeland.

They were healthy and happy.

CHAPTER FORTY-TWO

The following day.

As the train lurched through Bremerhaven toward the station, Zosia's nerves pulled into tighter and tighter knots. Would Marisha and Stefek forgive her? Would she even recognize them?

Zosia and Czeslaw gathered their meager belongings, and stepped onto the platform with their children. Throngs of people pushed this way and that with their scabbed luggage and broken-down carts. Jerzy hugged his mother's leg. It took considerable effort just to stay together and not become separated. "Where are they? How will we find them?" Zosia scanned the mob for Marisha's dark hair.

"The dock. I was told to meet them at the dock." Uncertainty laced his voice. "Still, keep an eye out."

They followed the mass of travelers trudging along the roads for about two kilometers until they came to the harbor. Large military carrier ships, repurposed for shuffling civilians, stood anchored and waiting. Czeslaw reached under his coat and pulled the crossing tickets from his chest pocket. "*USAT General J. H. McRae*, dock six. Departs at four o'clock this afternoon. All passengers on board by half past two." He glanced at his watch.

"Ten minutes after one. We have time."

They pushed along. Zosia scanned every face and compared every woman and young man to her memories of the strangers Marisha and Stefek had since become. The sea of people only parted for a honking car or a trolley of baggage. The ropes lining the edge of the dock kept the waves of refugees lapping against them from spilling into the ocean.

Czeslaw stopped next to a gangway and pointed up to the sign above it. *PASSENGERS ONLY. LAUNCH 6-B.* "Here. This is it." His eyes darted everywhere, searching the crowd. "Do you see them?"

Jerzy stuffed his face into Czeslaw's leg and cried about the stink of idling vehicles, dead fish, and unwashed travelers. Zosia spun around with Janina on her hip. "Marisha!" She yelled their names with all the voice she had left. "Stefek!"

Antoni? Antoni? Please, my son . . . She could never forget that day so long ago.

"Let's just wait, Zosia. Maybe we're early."

She nodded, but her feet wouldn't let her linger. She held Janina and wandered in a small circle.

An hour passed. Zosia's stomach lodged in her throat. Jerzy whined with hunger. Janina dozed on Zosia's shoulder. Czeslaw read back through his tiny notebook again and again, searching for any details he may have missed.

Time slipped by. An official paced the platform, warning travelers to board now or be left behind.

"Wilusz."

Zosia recognized the whining, condescending tone of the voice. "Maxim!" She lunged to throw her arms around her son-in-law but stopped short. His expression was anything but welcoming. "Where's—?"

"Where's Marisha? That little whore you call a daughter?" His lips flattened into a sneer. He lit a cigarette.

Rage burned inside Zosia, but her voice was icy. "Where is she?"

Czeslaw put his arm protectively around Zosia's shoulders. "Mr. Hirsch, I'm Czeslaw Lysek. I believe you know Franz—"

"I don't care, Mr. Lysek. Franz Voss is a war criminal, and I'll never admit to knowing him." He returned his contemptuous gaze to Zosia. "You, however . . ." He cracked a cruel smile.

"Please, Maxim, don't do this." Zosia kept her voice calm, and she hugged Jerzy and Janina close to her. Her children gave her strength, cleansing the fury from her blood and restoring her patience. "Where's Marisha?"

"Your guess is as good as mine. She ran away with that little idiot brother of hers."

"She left you?"

"Fucking hell," Maxim said. "No, of course not. I kicked her out. I couldn't have that kind of woman calling herself my wife. At least the boy was good for a decent cover. Living as Stefek Wilusz has kept me out of the courts." His smile was evil.

Zosia's cheeks scorched. *The picture.* "When? Where did they go?" She couldn't tell if it was relief, anger, or a brand new set of anxieties churning within her.

"I told you, I don't know where she is. Are you stupid?"

"Mr. Hirsch," Czeslaw said, his voice stern, "I'll not tolerate you speaking to my wife that way." He took a slow, stabilizing breath. "If you had no intention of reuniting Marisha and Stefek with their mother, why did you come to meet us?"

Maxim took a step toward Zosia. Czeslaw took a step toward Maxim. Zosia wrapped her arms tighter around her children.

"You owe me money for what your daughter did to me," Maxim said.

"I owe you nothing, Maxim."

"You owe me for the food I brought your family while you were starving."

"I never asked you for food. You brought it yourself. You had decency at one time."

"He's worthless, Zosia. Let's go." Czeslaw pressed his hand against Zosia's back.

"I'm not done with you." Maxim grabbed Czeslaw's arm. Czeslaw drew back and swung a powerful right hook, striking Maxim under the eye.

Jerzy shrieked in fear, and Zosia pulled him out of the way. Two port guards hurried in to break up the scuffle. One secured Czeslaw's arms behind him. The other stomped his boot down hard on Czeslaw's foot, his own worn boots providing no protection from the crushing blow. Czeslaw howled and fell to his knees. Jerzy hid his face in Zosia's leg and sobbed.

"Czeslaw, my God!" Zosia screamed.

"Please, we mean no harm, officer," Czeslaw said, panting, his face contorted as he doubled over his foot.

"Sir, he's a policeman. One of your own." Zosia shuffled her children in her arms. She reached into her husband's coat and pulled a handful of notes and paperwork from his pocket. "See?" She thrust his police identification toward the guard.

"Wildflecken Police," Czeslaw said, struggling to stand. "We have tickets for this ship. We're only trying to board."

"Go then." The guard tapped Czeslaw's shoulder with his billy club. Then he pointed it at Maxim. "You, be on your way."

"Can you walk?" Zosia asked. Czeslaw nodded, and Zosia helped him to balance on his good foot.

"You're as bad as that *pizda* Marisha," Maxim called after Zosia as they limped up the gangplank. "I hope your ship sinks." Zosia saw him retreat into the crowd.

Her only chance at finding her daughter and son was gone.

Once they reached the ship and Czeslaw presented the family's tickets, he pulled them all into a tight embrace, burying his face in Zosia's gray-peppered hair.

"Czeslaw, your foot."

"It's fine. I'll be fine." He leaned into the ship's railing. "Zosia, we can still find your children. I promise. America has people who can help. Once we're there, we'll find them. I promise you."

Zosia stared out toward the port. It took her a moment of clear thinking to grasp what her daughter had done: she left her husband. It was a relief to Zosia, but if Marisha was on the run from Maxim, she had likely changed her name, and Stefek's too. A search for either Marisha Wilusz or Marisha Hirsch would, therefore, come up empty.

Zosia had also changed her name when she married Czeslaw. If Marisha had tried to find her, she would have encountered the same problem.

And now Zosia was leaving the continent. She and her daughter would be like two archers, shooting arrows across a vast ocean at invisible targets.

It was too late.

CHAPTER FORTY-THREE

Thirty minutes.

With Janina snug against her chest, Zosia followed Czeslaw in turning sideways to fit through a rounded doorway. The hallways were tiny, and she could feel them narrowing further as they descended deeper into the bowels of the ship. Every so often, the line of people would encounter these rounded portals; it reminded Zosia that parts of the ship could be sealed off with ten-centimeter-thick doors in case the vessel took on water. Her scalp prickled when she thought about being on the wrong side of one of those doors.

An American GI in green fatigues stood several meters ahead of them, motioning each approaching family into a room.

The echo of hundreds of refugees chattering and shouting in Polish, Latvian, Ukrainian, and a gaggle of other languages filled Zosia's head. Janina was quiet but anxious, her fists white as she clung to the collar of Zosia's coat. Jerzy's eyes snapped around, taking in the people, the noise, and the newness.

Next in line, Czeslaw and Zosia stepped up to the soldier. Before he could speak, a deafening alarm pierced the hallway and red lights flashed along the ceiling. Zosia nearly climbed out of her skin, and Janina and Jerzy both wailed. Other children and several adults around them screamed and cried. The masses of people crammed between the tight walls peered around in terror, searching for evacuation routes past the piles of bodies and baggage.

The alarm rang for three heart-stopping seconds before it ceased, followed moments later by a gruff English voice barking a few staticky words over an intercom. The crowd remained panicked until an educated soul with enough understanding of English further up the line deciphered the message and passed it down the hallway: "Drill only, no danger. As you were."

Czeslaw met his wife's eye. His expression begged the same question that filled Zosia's head: *Is this really safe?*

It was their turn to be inserted into a room. Czeslaw hopped along on his good foot, a suitcase balanced in one hand and the other against the doorframe. They stepped into the tiny chamber. Czeslaw hit his head on the top bunk and cursed in Polish as he tumbled onto the bottom bed.

Zosia first noticed the lack of a window. Sweating in her winter coat, she tried to distract herself with Jerzy and Janina's needs. "Where will the children sleep?" she asked the soldier in broken English. He muttered something she didn't understand in his foreign tongue and moved on to the next family.

Czeslaw squeezed Zosia's hand and rubbed his forehead. "It's fine, don't worry. I'll find something for Janina. Jerzy can sleep with you on the bottom bunk. It's only for a few days."

Zosia poked around their new space. Miniscule wasn't a word small enough for it. Designed as sleeping quarters for two active-duty sailors, the room was equipped only with the necessities of rest and war. Beside the steel bunk bed was a desk and chair that were a step above child-size. Next to the wall-mounted radiator and electric fan there were two skinny lockers. She opened one, and a bright-orange life jacket crept out toward her. She closed the door and opened the other one. Two gas masks stared back.

No matter how diligently she searched, there still was no daylight. She sat next to the folded sheets and drab flannel blankets resting in a pile on the bed. Czeslaw stood, agitated. He tried to pace on his uninjured foot, but the space only allowed him to turn his body back and forth. "I'll go find something for Janina."

"Now? But Czeslaw, your foot."

"Zosia, it's fine. Trust me."

"You'll only be fighting crowds."

"We'll be fighting crowds the whole time we're here. Besides, if there's anything we need that isn't on board, there's a chance we could still get it while we're docked." Zosia knew it was an excuse to leave the tiny room. She didn't argue.

While Czeslaw explored and pillaged, Zosia made up the beds. After tucking in the sheets, she sat on the bottom bunk and held Janina on her lap. The baby wiggled and fought, too excited, tired, or both to be held. Jerzy hopped around next to Zosia, babbling a made-up story about the ship that Zosia could only half understand.

In all of her time as a prisoner and a DP, she'd always had access to outside light. Sometimes it was unwanted, like on the farm when the cracks in the walls of the barracks welcomed the cold winter wind, but it was available. She'd always taken for granted the ability to know day from night, to see the sun, rain, wind, and snow. The naked light bulb hanging from the ceiling above them was their sun now.

She closed her eyes, not to sleep but to collect her breath. She didn't know what time it was or even how long Czeslaw had been gone, but at least she knew he was on the ship. If they started moving, he would move with them. No matter how skilled a negotiator he was, no one would allow him to go ashore so close to departure. She had to believe that, even if a small part of her wondered if he'd limped to the dock to find better spoils or possibly to find Maxim and finish the job.

The ship was only barely starting to rock when Czeslaw returned and triumphantly held up a large steel basin. "For Janina to sleep in!" He placed it in the corner of the room, lined it with an additional blanket he'd stuffed under his arm, and stood up straight, wincing. Zosia settled Janina into it and rocked the makeshift bassinet. She pulled her knees up underneath her, wiggled her little bottom, and stuffed her thumb into her smiling mouth.

With their dwelling as comfortable as they could make it, the family climbed the stairs to the main deck and watched Europe drift away from them. Zosia bid farewell to the pain and the suffering but also to the only beauty and happiness she'd ever known—*home.*

Zosia said goodbye to her eldest daughter and son.

The ship advanced through the mouth of the Weser River, past an offshore, red lighthouse topped with a green turret, and into the icy North Sea. The November wind pushed up massive waves that battered the ship. Czeslaw held Janina, and Zosia squeezed the railing so tightly she thought the steel might snap under her grip. Her stomach jumped. *Nerves,* she thought. *Maybe hunger.*

But instead of eating that night, she spent dinner in the communal bathroom with her head hovering over a toilet. By the sounds around her, she wasn't alone.

—

The further they moved away from land, the rougher the sea became. Sometimes it seemed like the bow of the ship lifted almost vertically out of the water and crashed down onto the harsh waves below. The constant pitching motion of the ship in the winter storms wreaked havoc with Zosia. She couldn't eat;

even a sip of water caused her to gag and vomit. She couldn't sleep, either, since the cyclones inside her and outside the windowless walls wouldn't let her rest. Hour after hour she spent moaning, curled in a ball on her bed with a bedpan gripped in one hand.

Czeslaw kept the children with him, to give Zosia peace to rest. Often he would bring Janina to their dark room to nap in her basin. He would softly sing songs to her in Polish as she drifted off. The singing also comforted Zosia. Between delirious bouts of restless sleep and dry heaves, Zosia dreamed of her little girl retaining the language of her homeland.

When he wasn't on an adventure with his father, Jerzy busied himself by playing in the hallways with other boys from nearby rooms. Zosia worried his pertussis would flare again, but she was so weakened she couldn't even ask him to rest. *He's healthy. He's fine,* she repeated in her head to calm herself. *Let me be the one who's sick.*

Through a haze of darkness one evening she heard Czeslaw's voice. "I think I found a way to help you." Her husband stood over her, shaking her arm to rouse her. Past Czeslaw's shoulder was a man in a white coat, illuminated by the light from the hallway. As soon as she gained wakefulness, her stomach rolled again.

"Mrs. Lysek, I'm Doctor Youngerman." The doctor spoke in English, but slowly enough so she could understand him. He flicked on the overhead light and she saw he had blond, curly hair and a port-wine stain birthmark on his neck, just grazing his chin and cheek. "I'm going to give you a shot to help your nausea."

After years of rumors about the Nazis, Zosia was suspicious of injections, but she would offer up her bowels for removal with a rusty spoon if it would help her seasickness. She nodded her approval. The doctor tapped the syringe, pulled Zosia's skirt aside, and stuck the needle into her hip while Czeslaw squeezed her hand. After a few minutes, she propped herself up onto her elbow and gave a feeble smile.

"How do you feel?" the doctor asked.

She was so weak from lack of food and water that she could hardly hold herself up, but she was grateful the sickness passed. "Better. Hungry."

"Excellent." Dr. Youngerman turned to Czeslaw and handed him a sheet of paper. "My bill. You can pay before you disembark in New York."

Czeslaw took the paper, folded it, and placed it in the breast pocket of his shirt. He thanked the doctor, who then disappeared through the door.

"How much did that cost?" Zosia had spent all of the money she'd made as a seamstress on supplies for her babies and information on her older children, and Czeslaw rarely dealt in cash.

"Don't you worry." Czeslaw sat next to her, stroking her hair. "Let's get you something to eat."

Zosia wobbled but managed to stand. She ran a comb through her mangled hair and emerged from the room with her family. They climbed the stairs to the dining room, and she surveyed the ship. It was obviously a former military ship, but civilians attempted comforts where they could. A room once used to practice drills was now a dance hall, and the mess deck had been rechristened as the "Dining Room." Carpeted runners further softened the hard edges of the old war machine.

Through the porthole in the Dining Room, the inky horizon swayed violently against the winter sky. It nearly flipped all the way over. Zosia decided not to look out any more portholes. She ate dry toast and drank tea.

After dinner, Zosia saw that Czeslaw's limp lingered. "Czeslaw, your foot. It's still—"

"Nothing to worry about," he dismissed with a wink.

"Already feeling better."

For several hours, Zosia felt well. But when the injection wore off, the nausea returned—along with most of what she had eaten. She spent the rest of the trip in bed, bargaining with God to let it be over.

Zosia ruminated on her children's health and Czeslaw's injury, as only a mother and wife could. *He's just always moving,* she thought, passing into the fog of sleep. *If he could sit and rest, he'll heal.*

He will. We will all *heal.*

Chapter Forty-Four

November 14, 1948: Nine days after departure.

"Matka! Matka wake up! We here! Amarka! Amarka!" Jerzy patted Zosia's cheek and she opened her eyes. The door to their stateroom was open. Jerzy must have been up early to play in the hall.

"Oh, I don't know." She tried to sit up in the tiny bottom bunk. The ship had settled into a softer rocking motion, so her stomach had settled, too.

The bed above her creaked and Czeslaw's socked feet swung in front of her face. One was swollen larger than the other. He jumped to the floor on his good foot and held his hand out to Jerzy. "Let's go see!" Czeslaw was as excited as his son.

Zosia's head was dizzy but her curiosity was sparked. She imagined a sunlit glow of freedom radiating from the tall New York buildings. Though weakened from lack of food and water, she put on her coat. Janina was asleep in her basin so Zosia wrapped her in a blanket and lifted her gently. "What about our things?"

"We'll come back. We're only going to see what America looks like." Czeslaw's grin consumed him.

They fought their way through the stimulated crowds until they emerged onto the deck above. The air was sharp from cold. Zosia kept a tight hold of Czeslaw's hand while the family squeezed into a spot against the railing.

"I see! Amarka!" Jerzy pointed to the horizon. Zosia couldn't see anything at first, but as they watched, a silver edge of jagged skyline winked with morning sunlight and rose from the ocean like a serrated knife slicing upward through a cube of blue ice.

Jerzy held onto the railing and bounced in delight. Janina cuddled into Zosia's shoulder, her tiny sighs warming Zosia's ear. Czeslaw gazed to the west, mesmerized.

The city became more distinct as the ship advanced on New York Harbor. Watching her new country approach, Zosia's previously sloppy stomach now tied itself up in knots. She could see the giant green lady standing in the middle of the water, holding her lantern high. *"Welcome, let me light your way . . ."*

Zosia wondered if America would truly welcome them. She wondered if she would miss Poland.

Always.

Czeslaw smiled and pointed with his son. Zosia envied her husband's innate confidence and optimism as they began their new life. Czeslaw was fractured too; he'd also left everything he'd ever known. At least Zosia could still cling to a tenuous hope of someday finding her lost children, but Czeslaw's were gone forever. She wished she could grasp how he was able to find brightness in the darkest of moments.

Zosia turned a waking Janina so the baby could see the harbor ahead. "Look, *dziewczynka*! Our new home." She lifted her voice, adding joy. "You will be happy here. I promise."

The *General J.H. McRae* slid into the harbor, and the family returned to their room to gather their belongings. After a rushed breakfast—for Zosia, only a cracker and tea—they joined the long lines of immigrants ready to descend on New York. Inspectors, officials, and hordes of people were all that stood between Zosia's family and the promise of a new life. She squeezed Czeslaw's hand while they waited in line. He squeezed back. He occasionally leaned on her to rest his battered foot, and she leaned on him to rest her weakened body.

Shuffling forward, the family reached the gangways of the ship, then solid ground, then the immigration building. Zosia's back ached from the hours of taking slow steps with an irritable baby on her hip.

The cavernous building was raw and brilliant, much like she imagined America itself. The massive, arched ceiling enveloped them, scooping them all inside like giant cupped hands corralling hundreds of ants beneath. Dust danced in the cold sunlight pouring through the rows of high windows. Red and white striped, blue cornered American flags soared in brackets along each wall, above lines of soldiers who stood at attention below them.

The smells of a thousand strangers mingled with wetness and mildew, creating an odor that piled high in the room on top of the baggage and unease. No one was comfortable; the newcomers were confused, the staff stressed. Guards kept one sharp eye on possible hoodlums, the other on their supervisors to see if they could sneak a cigarette. Apprehension was as thick as the smell. The continual buzz of an unused public address speaker added to the tensity of the room.

At the front of a line that seemed to never end, fellow passengers stuck out their tongues for inspectors who peered into their mouths and pulled up their eyelids. Zosia shivered. The children might carry lingering evidence of their pertussis, which could detain them. They'd come too far to be sent back now.

After an eternity of standing and waiting, they stepped up to the inspector who barked out one word: "Nationality?"

"Polska," Czeslaw said.

The man shifted his weight and paged through the paperwork on his clipboard, searching for the proper sheet. He spoke in barely recognizable Polish. "Name?"

"Czeslaw Lysek. This is my wife, Zosia. Son, Jerzy, and daughter, Janina."

Without looking up, the inspector made notes on his sheet and queried a dozen other questions, including how much money they had and the name and address of their sponsor in America. Then the inspector put down his clipboard and adjusted the reflector on his forehead. "Open mouth, please."

Czeslaw turned to Zosia. "You go first," he said and gently steered her toward the man. She stumbled forward, her feet unsure. Her dehydration, paired with the crushing crowds, slicked her face with sweat and made her knees weaker than jelly.

The inspector studied her mouth, her ears, and under her eyelids. He ran his hands down her arms and across her stomach, poking and prodding at random places. Zosia teetered as she stood. Czeslaw watched with concern.

"You've been sick," the inspector said.

"Seasick. I feel better now."

"You're very thin. Weak."

"I'm fine." Zosia lifted her chin.

The inspector put a quick mark on Zosia's coat. He did a similar, albeit miniature inspection on Jerzy. The boy's eyes were huge from fear, but he didn't cry. Then the inspector scanned over Janina without touching her.

The inspector moved on to Czeslaw. He squeezed his swollen foot before reaching up to mark an L on Czeslaw's collar with a piece of chalk. "Step forward and wait in that room." He handed Czeslaw a card and waved toward a doorway.

The family congregated a few steps out of earshot. "What does this mean?" Zosia pointed to the L on her husband's coat.

"I don't know." Czeslaw pulled out the collar so he could see the mark. "Maybe it's for our last name?"

Zosia glanced at her own mark. It was a P. She remembered the purple P she wore as a prisoner. "So, you are marked for our name, and I'm marked for where we come from?" Not convinced, Zosia peered into the room to which they'd been sent. Rows of men and women sat in recycled church pews with handfuls of children leaning against them. Everyone looked pale, sad, and tired.

And still. Everyone in the main immigration area moved, even if slowly. But not these people. They all sat motionless while they waited. Zosia had learned long ago that movement meant survival. She glanced up, and the word "Holding" was painted above the door in black, stenciled letters. "I don't like this."

"I'm sure it's fine," Czeslaw said.

"No, it's not," Zosia leaned in close, conspiring with her husband. "No one else has these marks. It means something, and it can't be good." She took him by the hand and led him and their children around a pillar for cover. "Take off your coat, turn it inside out." Zosia glanced over her shoulder. "Quickly. I'm not going to sit and wait in that stuffy little room. We have to keep moving."

Czeslaw frowned, but did as she said. "I'm sure it means nothing."

"I'm not." Zosia tore away patches of lining from the inside-out coat before she helped Czeslaw back into it. She smoothed out the reversed lapels. "That's better."

"What about you?" Czeslaw motioned toward the P on her coat.

Zosia switched Janina to her other arm and draped her blanket over her shoulder to conceal her own mark. Czeslaw nodded at the successful cover. "I've been watching," Zosia said, "and everyone else moved over there after inspection." She pointed to a spontaneous photography studio set up in a corner with bright lights, a small stool, and a simple ivory paper background hanging from clamps on two tall tripods. "Let's go."

The family fell into line. After the lights flashed for Zosia, she placed Janina on the stool. The photographer gave Janina a light blue plastic rattle. Janina studied the strange toy, surprised at the wonderful noise it made when she shook it. Czeslaw stood near the photographer and waved his hands to get Janina's attention. "Bookabookabooka!" he sang. Janina looked up and the lights flashed. The process was repeated for Czeslaw and Jerzy, and the photographer motioned all of them toward another table.

As they moved along, Zosia wondered if they would ever see those photographs. They were priceless. She would give nearly anything for photographs of Marisha, Stefek and Antoni. Especially Antoni. She longed for something to hold, to help her remember.

Czeslaw handed the small card to a man at the table dressed in green army fatigues. "It says here you're lame," the man said, studying the card.

Zosia recognized the word lame from Lottie's lessons, and she knew what it meant. "The L on your coat," Zosia translated for Czeslaw. "Your limp. He thinks you're lame."

"Of course I'm not lame," Czeslaw said with a laugh, assuming the man was joking. He shook his head. "No. No lame."

"Walk from here to that wall over there," the man said, finally looking up.

Zosia spoke to Czeslaw in Polish. "Walk over there with no limp. Do not limp, no matter what."

Czeslaw walked easily to the other wall with a spring in his step. Upon his return to the table, he did a little jig to prove his point. Zosia recognized the agony in Czeslaw's face but laughed along to support his show.

The man at the table crossed out the word *lame* on the card and handed it to Czeslaw. "You and your children are cleared for passage. Your wife will stay behind."

Stay behind.

To Zosia, everything around her slowed down. The official's words caught in the thickened air, smothering her in a tourniquet of heat. She couldn't find her hands, her face, her body. She didn't trust her basic English skills so she only choked out, "What?"

"You're marked as having a physical illness, and clearly you're not well. You'll need to stay here in New York until you regain your health. We'll put you in a hospital for a few days."

"Stay? No!" Zosia's voice boiled, and so did the blood in her body.

"Ma'am—"

"*Polska!*" Zosia wasn't willing to gamble with English. She couldn't possibly have heard what she thought she had.

The man at the table whistled and waved to another man in a striped shirt and a dark blue cardigan sweater. "Yes, Donnie?" The cardiganed man sidestepped stacks of paperwork on the floor and squeezed behind people in folding chairs.

Donnie gestured toward the Lyseks and repeated the problem. The man nodded, then spoke. "I'm Abraham Ripley, an interpreter," he said in Polish. Donnie impatiently tapped his pen against the Masonite table. "You've been very sick," Abraham continued, "so we need to admit you to a hospital here in New York for a few days for monitoring. Your husband and children can go on to your destination, and you will follow when you are well."

Zosia's eyes glossed over. "Czeslaw?" The sound barely fell from her lips. Her body shivered with a sweat-drenched chill.

"No," Czeslaw's voice was unflinching. "No. We stay together."

Abraham shook his head. "We can't house you and your children while she's admitted, and we can't allow her to travel since she might be contagious. It will only be temporary."

"We won't be separated," Zosia whispered.

Czeslaw's voice was tough. "She's not contagious."

"This is our procedure."

"You're a good man, Mr. Ripley, I can tell." Czeslaw's voice changed from angry to genial, startling Zosia. "I know you will help us." She watched her husband reach out to shake the official's hand.

Abraham looked equally confused, but he took Czeslaw's hand, obliging. Zosia saw the folded American bills transfer from her husband's hand to the interpreter's before he slipped them into his pocket. "Mr. Lysek," Abraham said slowly, looking up at Czeslaw, "I can have you arrested for bribing an official. Now please, take your children and come with me. Donnie, show Mrs. Lysek where she can either wait for her transport to the hospital or wait to be deported."

A large woman in a stern military uniform tore Janina from Zosia's arms. The sob that escaped Zosia's throat held more heartbreak and agony than any she'd uttered in her life. She reached her arms out to her daughter, who screamed and fought against the strange woman. Donnie grabbed Zosia's arms and pulled them behind her back, holding them as if she was a criminal.

A stream of Polish obscenities poured from Czeslaw's lips while Janina and Jerzy wailed for their mother. Fighting, Czeslaw was led away with the children and their bags. His face was flushed with defeat and anger. She thought she heard him shout, "I'll fix this," but she wasn't sure in the noise of the room. Zosia's heart pulled out of her chest as her children disappeared into the crowd, their howls melting into the discord of the large space.

CHAPTER FORTY-FIVE

Moments.

The room marked *"Holding"* was stale and soundless, though now the air was stirred by Zosia's uncontrollable trembling. She sank her thin body onto a repurposed pew and pulled her oversized winter coat tight around her. She covered her face with her hands to keep her emotions contained. Static, gray-skinned people sat like crumpled mannequins around her, each holding the posture of one who has given up.

I'll catch up. I'm sure after a day or two, I'll catch up. I'll see them again. She froze with when she remembered Czeslaw had the name and address of their sponsor in his coat pocket. Zosia had no information on how to find them. *He'll find me. He has to.* She had to put all of her trust in her husband.

The interpreter's words echoed over and over in her mind: "*I can have you arrested.*"

Czeslaw and her children could be on their way to jail. She leaned over and took small swallows of air to keep from vomiting or fainting.

A handkerchief flittered in front of Zosia's face. She forced herself to sit up straight. "*Dziękuję,*" she sniffled and took it. She wiped her eyes and blew her nose.

She glanced at the man who gave it to her. His coat was grimy and he had an unruly beard. He watched her with a squint. "What did they get you for?" he asked in Polish before coughing into his sleeve.

She didn't answer. She stared straight ahead, wishing for her husband to return with her children, waiting to wake up from this nightmare.

"Guess I've got the damn pneumonia," the man said. "Probably getting sent back. Waste of time crossing the ocean after all."

"Sent back?" Zosia snapped her head toward him. She squeezed the handkerchief in her hand and dropped it on the floor. She'd wiped his pneumonia all over her face.

He exploded into a fit of raspy laughter that ended in a choking cough. "Sent back. It's where most of us are headed. Unless you got money?" He waited for her response with bait in his eyes.

Zosia turned and stared at the wall across the room. The man tried to make small talk, but she didn't hear any more. Instead, a silent scream filled her ears. He eventually nodded off to sleep on the bench.

Minutes, hours, days, years passed—Zosia didn't know. She didn't move except to sniffle. A nurse in a white uniform brought her a paper cup of water, which Zosia held but didn't drink. Nobody left the room, but a few more drab individuals were ushered in. A uniformed man stood guard at the door.

Her despair blistered into fury.

They took my babies away.

Her neck burned under her coat. A familiar anxiety washed over her. *Czeslaw took my babies. He said he wouldn't. He promised. Now he's gone.*

She imagined Czeslaw boarding the train with her children,

sitting next to a pretty American woman who resembled Greta Garbo. They'd talk and laugh. The woman would cuddle Janina . . .

No.

"You can't do this to me," she shouted at no one, slicing the hush with her feral scream. The haunted, empty faces of the ill and undetermined lifted to gawk at her. "You can't take my babies. I've had enough of this!" She stood and threw the cup of water at the floor. It felt good.

"Ma'am . . ." The guard took a step forward. She saw only the wavy movement of a gray uniform. The stifling heat of the room shimmered in her peripheral vision. Rejected transients watched her in stupefied awe.

"Do you hear me? I'm not sitting here any longer. Take me to my family. Now!"

Donnie ran in from the other room. Zosia made a dash for the door, but he grabbed her arm. "Mrs. Lysek, calm down. You need to sit."

"Don't touch me," she tugged away. Though her body was frail from dehydration and hunger, she reeled with a burst of rage while her mind blinked in and out, short circuiting in an exhausted fog. "You won't take my children from me."

Abraham Ripley blocked the door, and several other people circled her as if she were a dangerous tiger escaped from the zoo. It wasn't far from the truth—her cubs had been stolen from her. All of them. More staff entered the room and rushed to Zosia's side. She lashed at them, kicking and shrieking in a combination of Polish and English, damning everyone from God to the government to Hitler himself. She heard the echo of her voice bouncing off the walls, and it sounded foreign, bizarre. She tried to breathe, but her chest was tight. She fought to take in air.

A man with curly blond hair wearing a white coat rushed in. She braced her stance and readied for a fight, certain the doctor would try to wrestle her into a straightjacket. She glared at the man. He would have to kill her first. He said something in English that Zosia didn't understand and held his hands out in front of him to calm her. Then she noticed the port-wine stain on his neck.

She knew this doctor.

His face twisted into a frustrated grimace. "Who is in charge here? Who put her in here?" Donnie and Abraham both muttered something unintelligible. "You goddamn morons. This woman isn't infectious, she was seasick. Jesus Christ you two. Do you want to fill up the hospitals with people like her? We're already overcrowded. Ripley, you should know better."

"Our orders . . ." Abraham said sheepishly. Donnie crept toward the door.

"She's late. She's coming with me." Dr. Youngerman hurried her out of the room.

Suspicion gripped Zosia as she ran with him, her body sticky with panicked sweat beneath her coat. "Doctor—"

"Do you understand me?" Dr. Youngerman asked in English. She nodded. "Good. Your husband is waiting for you, but there's very little time. The ferry won't be delayed." He pointed down a hallway. "Run. Run as fast as you can."

"Why are you helping me?" Zosia was leery, her mind racing to translate his words.

"Because your husband was the only one on the ship who paid for my services. He paid in American dollars. Now go. Run!"

When Zosia fell into Czeslaw's embrace on the ferry bench with Jerzy by her side and Janina in her arms, they were all in tears. "I thought I'd lost you, then I saw the doctor. Thank God I recognized him." Czeslaw buried his face in her hair.

"Thank God you paid him," she said, laughing through her tears.

"We're going home." Czeslaw looked into her eyes. "We made it."

CHAPTER FORTY-SIX

Evening.

Non-transferable ticket. Good for one passage
Grand Central Terminal, New York to LaSalle Street Station, Chicago
On Delaware Lackawanna & Western, Phoebe Snow
LaSalle Street Station, Chicago to Minot, No. Dak.
On Great Northern Railway, Empire Builder
Lysek: Chester, Sophie, George
2 ½ Full fare passage
Class: Pullman Cars. Subject to all tariff regulations.

After a noisy ride across the cold harbor, a rush through the streets of Manhattan on commuter buses because Zosia refused to ride in a cab, and a confusing walk through the largest train station in the world, Zosia, Czeslaw, Jerzy, and Janina, now known as Sophie, Chester, George, and Unknown Baby Girl, boarded a train and were ushered to a compartment that was, for once, not a cattle car.

Zosia settled into her seat with Janina cuddled up against her chest. She didn't care that Janina was overlooked on the ticket, as long as she knew the girl was safe in her arms. She let herself delight in the comfortable cushion. She wasn't livestock this time. Next to her, Jerzy leaned against Czeslaw with heavy eyes and listened to his father tell stories and fairy tales. The big city rolled away into darkness outside the window.

For two days Zosia sat in her velveteen seat and watched America blur past. Chicago was thick and dirty when they sliced through the sea of briefcase- and fedora-clad commuters, the filthy train windows giving everything a brown haze. Low, gray clouds cloaked the city, and the dampness and heavy overcoats outside the window made Zosia shiver. It was the last city Zosia recognized on the map, and where they changed trains. They climbed off the *Phoebe Snow*, sat for a few hours on benches in the station's mammoth waiting area, and climbed aboard the *Empire Builder* to head further west.

The train pushed through the snowy hills and barren trees of Minnesota. Zosia tucked Janina's wool blanket tighter around the little girl and pulled her close, letting the child's breath warm her. The snow swirled outside the window, whipping in the wind split by the train. As they approached North Dakota, the weather deteriorated further.

Zosia changed diapers and sang songs. They ate their lunch and dinner, but the view outside the window remained an endless sea of white until it was swallowed by nightfall. The landscape flattened, and the trees disappeared, but the weather persisted.

Though only nine in the evening, it had been dark for hours when the *Empire Builder* pulled into the city of Minot. The town glowed orange against the thick clouds from streetlights reflecting off of the blank snow.

"All passengers for Minot prepare to exit the train," the steward at the front of the car announced. Attendants walked through the car, waking the deep sleepers and checking for forgotten luggage.

Czeslaw stared straight ahead. Zosia touched his shoulder. "Are you ready?"

"Of course." His tone was terse.

She dropped her gaze to her son, whose expression matched her own angst. She smiled for his sake. Zosia wondered if Jerzy would retain any memories of Wildflecken. She knew Janina would only ever know America, but deep in the back of Jerzy's mind he might remember. Zosia hoped they would be good memories of chasing balls in grassy fields and eating chocolate finagled from the pockets of their protectors.

The Lysek family collected their belongings and each other, and stepped off the train onto the snow-packed cement platform with the other travelers. Hugs and handshakes met some, while others headed in the direction of the parking lot, their heads down against the wind and their hands stuffed deep in their coat pockets.

Czeslaw and Zosia stood alone with their children next to the huffing train. Jerzy hid his face in Zosia's coat. "Now what?" Zosia looked at Czeslaw, whose eyes were framed by rogue snowflakes landing on his lashes.

"Shit," he said. There was no one waiting for them, and the other travelers had all disappeared. A small brick station stood between them and the parking lot, so they stomped through the snow toward it. Czeslaw slowed and fell behind, his limp worsening. Zosia looked back, concerned. "I'm fine," he bit off into the wind.

Once inside, Czeslaw hopped to the ticket counter and communicated with the counter agent via gestures and grunts. "Klinkner," he said. The elderly agent squinted his sleepy eyes. He scratched the scruffy growth on his chin, a product of a forgotten shave or possibly a double shift at the counter due to the snowstorm.

"I don't know what that is." The agent yawned, studying the

map on the counter in front of him. "Klinkner? Is that a town?"

Zosia reached into Czeslaw's pocket and pulled out their sponsorship paperwork. She pointed to the sentence describing their final destination. "Klinkner. *Farma* Klinkner. Lansford, North Dakota."

The agent took the paper and held it up to the light. A pair of glasses hung from a ragged string around his neck, which he lifted to his nose. "You're looking for the Klinkner farm, outside of Lansford." He said. Zosia nodded. "That's going to be a tall order for a taxi, but you can try. I think Frank's out there in his Chevy." The agent waved toward the window.

Czeslaw squinted at him, unable to translate. "Chevy?"

"Taxi. Taxi." The agent rolled his eyes. He pointed out the window to the small cab parked at the curb with exhaust billowing from its tailpipe. "Take taxi. Drive." He put his hands up as if gripping a steering wheel. "*Rrrrnn rrnnn.*"

Zosia swallowed the sinking feeling in her stomach. At least she understood. "Frank," she said to her husband. "A man named Frank. He can help us. He can drive us to the farm."

Czeslaw arched his eyebrow at Zosia. He knew her fears, but didn't say anything.

The family trudged out into the darkness and snow, huddled together to create shelter for the little ones. They peeked inside the driver's window where a man with a moustache and bulky coat slept with his mouth wide open. Czeslaw knocked on the glass, and the man jumped so violently he hit his head on the car's headliner.

"God dammit Jesus Christ!" Czeslaw and Zosia both easily understood that part as the driver rolled down his window. The heater hummed at full blast inside the car, and the warm air spilled out against their faces. Jerzy pushed up onto his toes to get closer to the window and the heat. "What? Whaddya want?"

"Lansford? *Farma* Klinkner?" Zosia stuffed the sheet of paper into the man's face. "You take us?"

"I don't go that far, lady. Especially in this weather." He started to roll up his window, but then noticed Janina held tight in Zosia's arms. "Crimony, you've got a baby out here? In a blizzard?" Zosia followed the driver's gaze to her child. Janina watched the man expectantly, shivering in the cold. "Ah shit, you're one of those refugee families, ain'tcha? Heard about you. Bad news over there in Europe. My brother was there. Air Force. Bombed the hell outa Berlin and that Hitler bastard. He's back now. Blind in one eye."

Zosia understood *Berlin* and *Hitler*. "Lansford? You take us to Lansford?" She struggled to find the words in English.

He sighed a long, grumbling sigh. "I can't take you to Lansford, but I'll take you as far as I can. Maybe the Parker Hotel. You can grab a room for the night, get someone to take you the rest of the way in the morning. My fare to the Parker is forty-five cents."

Zosia translated what she could for Czeslaw. "We need forty-five cents for the fare," she said in Polish. "How much do we have?"

"None."

"None?"

Czeslaw shook his head. Zosia sensed his irritation from the journey and the pain and a litany of other things. "Abraham Ripley pocketed the last of it in New York."

Zosia's cheeks burned against the bitter wind. She reached up to her ears and pulled the pearl earrings out of her lobes. She handed them through the window to Frank and watched him, shrouded in hope.

Frank stared at the little pink balls nestled in his palm. "Ah shit, lady. Don't give away the family heirlooms. I'll take you to the Parker. Call it my civic duty." He handed the earrings back. "Get in," he motioned behind him with his thumb. Frank watched the rearview mirror while they piled into the back seat. "Makes up for not going over there myself," he said under his breath. "We're even now, Uncle Sam."

Zosia hadn't ridden in a passenger car since Marisha had driven her to Warsaw to find Antoni. She felt sick climbing in. She stared out the windshield and could see nothing but a whirl of snowflakes. Her throat constricted. She pulled herself down in the seat and cuddled Jerzy and Janina close to her. *Soon we'll have some kind of bed to lay our heads on.*

Soon we'll be safe.

She rested her cheek against Jerzy's warm head and distracted herself from the car sliding through the icy streets. She would have to start calling her son by the name given to him when they passed through New York: *George*. In fact, they should all embrace their new American names, although *Chester* was difficult for Zosia to say. And poor Janina was skipped over—they hadn't given her an American name.

Janina fussed from hunger and exhaustion. Jerzy's stomach rumbled, too. Zosia sang quietly into her children's ears.

"This is where I stop, folks." Frank pulled into a snowy parking lot under a burned-out sign that spelled *PARKER OTEL*. The snow crunched under the tires of the Chevy as he rolled up next to the building and cut the engine. Then he turned in his seat toward the Lyseks. "You go talk to Morty inside. He'll help you out." He thumbed toward the ragged red and white canopy crowning the front door.

From under the wind-flapped awning a man emerged, his coat unbuttoned and his gloved hand holding his hat to his head. He half ran and half stumbled through the deep snow toward the taxi.

Frank rolled down his window. "Hey Mort," he shouted into the wind.

"This storm is a sonofabitch," Morty said and peered at the family in the back seat. "Whatcha got here, Frank?"

Zosia listened intently as Frank answered, concentrating hard to decipher the fast, casual English vernacular. "One of those immigrant families. Headin' out to Harry Klinkner's place in Lansford. Told 'em I don't go that far. You got a room for them for the night?"

"Nope."

"Shit. You all full up?"

"Bunch of truckers, handful of salesmen." Morty pointed out to a lineup of cars and semi rigs along the highway. "Chickened out in the weather. Sold the last room a bit after five tonight, before dark."

Zosia understood. They were at a dead end. The dread of panic surfaced in her again. She explained the situation to Czeslaw.

"We can drive. We just need a car." Czeslaw's raw voice was determined. He squinted out the back window. "I've driven in worse weather. We can do this. We can take one of those." He pointed to the line of stranded cars and semis.

"We can't steal a car," Zosia countered.

"We'll bring it back . . ." Czeslaw trailed off, folded his arms and sulked.

Zosia leaned forward and focused to assemble her broken English. "Mister Morty, we borrow a car? We bring back tomorrow."

"You don't want to drive in this mess, lady."

"Please? You help us?" Zosia's weary body barely had the energy to beg.

"I get the feeling these people are desperate, Mort," Frank said softly. "Refugees from the war. They seen some shit." He reached into his pocket and pulled out a pack of cigarettes. "I'd take 'em home myself, but Shirley, you know, pregnant and all."

"Yeah, I get it." Morty turned to the Lyseks. "Listen, I got some rentals out back. I can lend you one, but if you get stuck in the snow it's up to you. And it better come back without a scratch."

"They don't have any money, Mort," Frank said.

"Goddammit. Of course they don't." Morty pulled his coat together in front of him, still pressing his hat to his head. "Well, fine, I'll give them my Ford. At least it's an automatic. I'll have to answer to Dolores, but she's a sucker for these foreign sob stories. I'll call Harry in the morning. He can bring the truck back and buy me lunch next week." He turned to Zosia and Czeslaw. "You come with me."

The family tumbled out of the car. They slogged through the snow, Zosia holding Janina and serving as a crutch for Czeslaw. Morty climbed into the red Ford pickup and cranked the engine. After a few tries, it started. "You know where you're going?" He asked as Czeslaw climbed in the driver's seat.

"*Farma* Klinkner, Lansford," Zosia said.

Morty chuckled. "Yea, I know, but you're gonna need directions," he yelled against the wind while Zosia lifted her children onto the bench seat. He pointed out to the road in front of the hotel. "This is Highway 83, you're going to take it that way." He motioned north. "Turn left at County Road 26A, then take another left by the big oak tree. It's the only tree for miles. You can't miss it."

"Thank you, Mister Morty." Zosia reached out the window and patted his arm.

"Good luck, folks," Morty cheered, then his tone changed to grumpy. "You bring my pickup back just like new." He took a few steps toward the hotel. "Like new, you hear me?"

"Thank you, Mister Morty," Zosia said again out the window, then cranked up the glass. Morty jogged back to the hotel, never letting go of his hat.

Zosia kept a tight grip around Jerzy and Janina, more for her own nerves than the comfort of her children. Czeslaw stepped on the gas pedal and cringed. He crawled the pickup out to the main road, but then stopped and put his head on the steering wheel.

"What's the matter?" Zosia asked.

"I just need a break for a minute. I can do this."

Zosia bit her lip. She knew better than to argue.

Czeslaw eased onto the gas pedal, and the wheels spun. He moaned in pain. He leaned back and punched the steering wheel with his fist, making Zosia and Jerzy jump.

"Czeslaw?"

"My God damned foot is numb. I can't feel it against the pedals. I can barely move it."

He looked at her, his eyes defeated. For the first time since she'd known him, there was something else in his expression that terrified her—fear. He squeezed his bare, chapped fingers around the steering wheel and rested his forehead against it.

Janina whimpered, and Jerzy hung limply against Zosia's arm. Zosia peered out ahead through the windshield and saw nothing but thick snowflakes spinning and plunging in every direction through the headlights.

"*Muster the spirit of courage,*" Petronela whispered in her ear. A blinding heat burned Zosia's eyes at the memory of her friend.

"I'll drive," she said.

"No."

"Czeslaw," she said, rested her hand on his arm, "let me drive."

He lifted his head and stared out through the windshield for an eternity. "You don't drive."

"I do today."

"You don't know how."

"You can help me." She patted his arm, restless. Czeslaw finally turned and met her eyes. They held their gaze for a long time. "When we have no other choice, we must muster the spirit of courage."

Czeslaw's eyes softened. "That's an old Jewish proverb. Eliasz said that all the time." He bent his head. Zosia thought he'd given up until she heard his soft words: "Holy Jesus, help my wife."

Zosia got out of the idling pickup and shuffled through the snow to the driver's side. Czeslaw slid over on the bench seat to allow her room. She got back in, shook herself off, and squeezed the steering wheel with both hands.

Next to her Janina sat quiet, her wide eyes darting through the cold darkness. She was only a little older than Oskar had been when he'd crashed through the windshield of her father's borrowed car.

No. We've come too far. We'll make it there. We have to.

Frozen with both dread and cold, Zosia searched for the road between the snowflakes. Beneath her, the seat trembled with the idling engine. She willed herself to speak. "What do I do?"

"On the floor, the right pedal is the gas. The left is the brake." He leaned over and pulled the lever on the steering column down until the needle in front of her pointed to the stretched, skinny D.

Zosia blinked for a long moment. *God, help me.* She pressed her foot against the gas pedal, and the engine growled, causing the truck to lurch ahead several feet. She jumped, but gripped the steering wheel tighter. She set her jaw.

They crept along, crunching and squeaking against the fresh snow. They drifted along Highway 83, barely moving but still going forward.

"The good news," Czeslaw said through clenched teeth, "is that you don't have to worry about traffic."

By only cracking a small smile, Zosia was distracted long enough to lose control of the vehicle. The pickup slid sideways. Terrified, Zosia stood up on the brake pedal. It was as unyielding as a Wildflecken Christmas beef roast to a dull knife.

"Pump the brakes!" Czeslaw shrieked.

"What? What? What is that?"

"Left pedal! Pump! Pump! Pump!"

She felt like she was forcing a shovel into tough German soil. With all of her strength, she pushed the pedal several times, stomping in time to her heartbeat slamming in her ears.

The pickup slid to a stop, sitting sideways on the road. Czeslaw quickly threw the lever into neutral. She panted, her stomach in her throat, her eyes sizzling from forgetting to blink.

"Take a deep breath." Shaken, Czeslaw stroked Jerzy's hair while the boy wept. "Let's try again. Slowly."

Zosia lifted her hands back to the steering wheel, but they shook so badly she could only clasp them together. She brought them to her lips and bit her teeth into her finger. The sharp pain brought her back to her task.

Stay strong. Zosia pushed out her chin. She eased the vehicle back into gear and tightened her grip on the steering wheel. The pickup crept forward by mere centimeters as the engine pulled. She turned the wheel, but it didn't move. She put all of her weight into it, leaning her exhausted, aching muscles into powering the wheels back to the road. A groan emitted from the cab; Zosia didn't know if it came from her or the pickup.

The wheel surrendered. She bumped the pickup along the shoulder of the road before pulling it back between the nearly-invisible painted lines.

"Good, good," Czeslaw said. His gaze stayed fixed through the windshield, his eyes wide and bulging. Jerzy and Janina were silent, hiding their faces in Czeslaw's coat.

Zosia held her breath and guided the pickup north, taking shallow gulps of air only when it felt like she might pass out. Her knuckles were white from strangling the wheel, and her head ached from searching for the road through the snowflakes. Czeslaw stayed mostly silent, occasionally calling out directions and encouragement. When she felt the vehicle fight her death grip, she would jump on the brake like a girl skipping rope.

Straight and slow, like a needle through silk. She imagined herself pulling a fine thread through delicate cloth as she crept the pickup ahead. The rushing snowflakes were her fabric, the clanking of the transmission and brakes were the clattering Singer. *Tight, careful, perfect.* This was the most important stitch she'd ever laid.

After more than an hour of unblinking attention focused on the eternal, snowy black road, Zosia started to believe they would never find the farm.

"There!" Czeslaw's voice was hoarse. He pointed through the frosted windshield. A lone oak tree, shadowy against the charcoal sky, reached its branches upwards toward the falling snow. Zosia turned left and coaxed the Ford down a gravel road that didn't feel any different under the wheels than the snow-packed asphalt did.

Zosia leaned on the brake, and the Ford creaked to a stop. Her fingers tingled and ached as she peeled them off the wheel. Czeslaw reached over and slid the gearshift into neutral, pulled on the parking brake, and turned the key to *off.* They all sat and stared at the farmhouse in front of them. "I love you. You did it." Czeslaw leaned over and kissed Zosia on the cheek. "I knew you had it in you."

Zosia was quiet, still unable to take a full breath. The farmhouse was a two-story, white stucco building. Images of *Świński Dom,* the old, white Nazi farmhouse, flashed in her head. She looked up to where the swastika should be and instead saw only a dark window. *All* of the windows were dark. Zosia wondered if they were expected today. Or at all.

A light flickered on in a main floor window. Then another. A crack of warm, yellow incandescence emitted from the porchless front door, growing wider as the door swung in. A man wearing a red plaid shirt stuck his head out. Through the snowflakes, he waved the family inside, welcoming them.

CHAPTER FORTY-SEVEN

May, 1950.

Through the kitchen window, Sophie watched Chester saunter out to the white pickup truck parked on the street. He opened the driver's door and climbed in, slamming the door shut behind him. Smiling, he waved out the window to Sophie, shouting something about dinner and fried chicken. She waved back. The words printed on the door under her husband's outstretched arm read:

C. Lysek Construction Co.
Concrete Specialist, General Construction
Dial TE 6-4117

Chester had insisted on a telephone. "The only way Americans do business," he said. "Besides, we've spent enough time unable to reach our loved ones. We need to be connected to the world."

The black telephone sat on the kitchen counter next to the icebox. The first time it rang, Chester ran into the house at full speed from the front yard where he'd been chatting with the neighbor, Warren Spencer. Chester hurdled over George and his cars on the floor. He landed, slipped on the varnished floor planks, and caught his foot in the floor hatch that Sophie had opened to retrieve a bottle of vinegar. Suppressing her laughter, Sophie ended up answering the call before handing him the phone. With one leg still stuck in the floor, Chester negotiated his first commercial concrete job.

The hatch in the kitchen floor was a constant point of disagreement between the couple. It opened to a narrow crawl space that accessed the rudimentary plumbing and gas lines in the house. Chester called it necessary, but most often he used it only for chilling bottles of Pabst Blue Ribbon. With little children in the house, it was only a liability to Zosia. Janina stayed far away from the hatch and cried whenever it was opened, but George was curious. So far he hadn't dared crawl into the hole, but Sophie could only imagine how they would have to pry up the floorboards to retrieve him if he ever did.

Chester's stuck foot reminded Sophie of how his foot was broken when they'd arrived in America. She smiled when she thought of how far they had come in the year and a half since.

The Klinkners were kind, especially that first night after they'd arrived, cold and battle-worn from the blizzard with two fussy, hungry children. Ruth Klinkner made a pot of coffee and another of soup, and introduced George and Janina to their own twin boys, three months younger than George. Harry Klinkner set Chester's foot in a splint, then the two men came up with a plan to return Morty's Ford to the Parker Hotel the next day. Along the way, they'd stop at the local clinic to get a proper cast.

After a year of working on the Klinkner farm and several months of building Chester's business, they now had their own home—built with Chester's own bare hands, as promised. The house was tiny and primitive, but sturdy. Chester was proud of it, and Sophie was proud of him.

"Matka?"

Sophie's eyes dropped to her children, who sat on the floor in front of her husband's anniversary gift to her: a new Singer 15-91 sewing machine attached to a beautiful cabinet that Chester had made. A pile of summery cotton fabric and patterns from the *Australian Home Journal* sat on the floor, dragged off of a chair minutes earlier by an exploring Janina. Now Janina sat with her brother, paging through a picture book.

"Matka? What?" Janina pointed to a picture in the book.

Sophie squinted at the page, but George answered before his mother could. "Chicken. That's a chicken. *Kurczak*. Chicken."

It warmed her heart—George teaching Janina to be bilingual. Sophie marveled at how fast they learned. They still spoke Polish at home, but in public Sophie tried to rely on English as much as possible.

She stared at the drawing of a chicken in Janina's book. Sophie had helped the Klinkners by slaughtering their chickens, but once theAuseks had moved into the city, Sophie swore she'd never behead another. Now she bought their chickens already dressed from the butcher on Second Avenue. She made a mental note to pick one up for dinner. Maybe she could borrow the Spencers' Buick; they loaned Sophie their car when she had errands, in return for an occasional platter of pierogi or crock of borscht.

They were safe. She wished she could say the same for the children she'd left behind so long ago. She ached every day to see them again. She would never stop loving them.

Marisha and Stefek were lost in a ruined corner of the world behind a curtain of iron that had fallen across the battlefields. Chester tried his best to find them, but no one knew how to excavate the hidden layers of post-war Germany. Records were lost, paperwork burned. Her first babies, now grown, remained invisible.

Her eyes fell on a photograph perched on the windowsill.

Sophie, Chester, and Petronela Kloc all smiled at the camera in the Wildflecken chapel. Sophie held baby George, and both Chester and Petronela held her. Petronela had been the sister Sophie always wished for.

A lifetime ago.

She crumpled up a few Black Jack Taffy wrappers on the counter—Chester's favorite—and tossed them in the trash. She opened the kitchen door. "Jerzy, Janina, come. Matka will take you to the outhouse." She considered *Jerzy* something of a pet name for her son. A mother was allowed those indulgences.

Both children jumped to their feet and followed her outside. Sophie led George to the little shack and closed the door for him, letting him have the privacy that, at nearly four years old, was so important to him. The doorknob clicked when the boy locked the door from the inside.

Sophie lit a cigarette and studied the outhouse, admiring the craftsmanship. It was a shack, and would never be more than an outhouse, but Chester had built it with insulation, a gabled roof complete with shingles, a toilet seat on top of the hole, and a locking doorknob. It was quite sophisticated, as outhouses go.

While she waited, she shaded her eyes from the sun and took in the house next door. It was a two-story, pink monstrosity with two vehicles parked on the cement driveway. Warren Spencer was a welder, and his wife was his bookkeeper. They ran their business while raising three little girls, the youngest the same age as Janina.

The neighbors knew only of the prosperity of America. Sophie could rest easy knowing her children could also now reach their dreams.

At least, some of her children.

"Matka! Matka!" Janina pointed to the Spencers' driveway, where a diapered duck waddled behind the Buick sedan. The

Spencer girls had won a baby duckling at a church carnival that spring, but soon learned that adorable ducklings become full-grown ducks. By then the girls had grown attached, so Mrs. Spencer put a diaper on the duck so the girls could keep it inside the house. The Spencers owned the most civilized duck in North Dakota.

Sophie's stare fell to the doorknob of the outhouse. It worried her that George locked it behind him, but she tried to trust her young son. As the minutes ticked by, she imagined the shenanigans he was getting into. "Jerzy? Are you okay in there?" she asked through the door, keeping her voice light.

"Yes, Matka." Then, silence again.

She stared at the doorknob.

Turn.

Turn.

Please turn.

The doorknob clicked and turned. George exited the outhouse, letting the door slam behind him. Sophie sighed with relief. "Janina, come my *dziewczynka*. Potty?"

"No, Matka." The three turned back to the house.

By the time they returned, the postman had made his delivery through the narrow slot in the front door. Sophie bent to retrieve the mail: a phone bill and *Dziennik Zwaizkowy*, a Polish-language newspaper published in Chicago.

A telephone and a Polish newspaper. They didn't have an indoor toilet, but they had communication and information—things that had been missing from their lives for so long. Having the newspaper delivered to Minot meant the news was a week old, but it was comforting to read about life and times in their native Polish as they adjusted to America.

She unfolded the newly arrived edition, and another

envelope fell to the floor. Sophie opened it and read the familiar handwriting within.

> *Dear Zosia,*
> *It is good to hear my elder sister is doing so well in America. I am proud of you and all you have accomplished. We have not been doing so well here in London. Perhaps you can wire us some money? It is so easy to make money in America, I'm sure you have more than you need. I will wait to hear from you.*
>
> *Always yours, Brygida*

Sophie smirked and moved to drop the letter into the trash on top of the Black Jack wrappers but stopped. She instead stuffed it into her purse, to be thought about later.

And yet another lifetime ago.

She picked up the telephone bill and, as if an omen, the telephone rang. She absently lifted the receiver and put the bill on the counter next to Chester's notes about a supply order. "*Tak*. Yes, hello. Lysek Construction."

"Connecting to Chicago. Hold please," the operator said. A few mechanical clicks were followed by a quiet, familiar voice.

"Hello? Can you hear me?" The voice spoke to her in Polish.

Her answer hung in her throat, unable to fall into the telephone. She knew this voice, but she couldn't believe it. She swallowed hard. "Who is this?" she asked.

"Mrs. Lysek, it's Eliasz. Eliasz Kloc. Do you remember me?"

Her eyes welled. She leaned on the kitchen counter and reached for a chair to sit in. "Eliasz," she said, a gasp catching in her throat. "Oh, my God. You're alive."

The voice chuckled. "Yes, Zosia, very much so. I'm working for the Polish Consulate in Chicago. Immigrated earlier this year.

I was lucky they needed lawyers."

She smiled. "Eliasz, I'm overwhelmed." Janina climbed up onto the table, and Sophie hissed for her to get down. "Thank you for getting in touch. We think of you often."

"And I, you. But this is more than a social call, Zosia. I have good news."

Eliasz's pause was tiny. Zosia watched Janina with a sharp eye, her mind in several places at once. *The children. The chicken. Our old friend. The telephone bill. Brygida's let—*

"I've found Marisha and Stefek."

Sophie dropped the phone.

Jerzy's head turned. "Matka? What's the matter?"

"Oh my God, Eliasz." Sophie scrambled to pick up the receiver off of the floor. "I'm here, I'm here. What? How . . ." Her tongue felt like steel wool and her ears hummed. She worked to center her thoughts, to focus on Eliasz's words.

"I've been in contact with them, and I have a telephone number," he said. "They are well and look forward to hearing from you. It's going to be an international call so keep in mind the expense, but this will connect you to their home." Eliasz rattled off several numbers, along with international calling instructions and a mention of the time difference.

She jotted notes across the top of *Dziennik Zwaizkowy.* "Thank you." She tried to steady her voice. "Thank you Eliasz. You continue to be a true friend to us. Let us return the favor some day."

The warmth in his voice carried along the wires. "Not necessary of course, but I do hope to stay in touch. Please send my best to Czeslaw. Without him I would be nowhere. He saved me during those dark months in Wildflecken."

She hung up the phone and, without any thought to the time change, dialed the numbers. She waited while the staticky clicks vibrated in her ear. After the fifth ring, a female voice, still familiar from so many years before, answered.

"*Tak hallo.*"

Her little girl, her very first *dziewczynka.* Now, a woman. A stranger. Sophie hadn't considered what to say or what her daughter might say back. She took a deep breath.

"Marisha."

There was an eternal pause. Sophie couldn't choke out anymore. She brushed at her wet eyes with the back of her hand.

The hiss of time and distance filled the line. There was no answer.

She hung up.

Sophie wept into the receiver, but a gasp from across the miles restored Sophie's broken heart. The voice that returned was filled with emotion and was as familiar to Sophie as her own breath.

"Matka . . . *Oh Matka.* Stefek, come! It's Matka."

AUTHOR'S NOTE

Though *Matka* is fiction, it is inspired by the harrowing journey of my grandparents, Sophie and Chester, *Baba* and *Papa*. I based much of this novel on the stories I grew up with, but the filters of time and memory often obscure the truth. Moments considered too mundane to relay—or too difficult to relive—were never shared, and once Baba and Papa passed away, their memories were gone forever. With so many holes and inconsistencies in their narrative, I've decided to use the truth only as inspiration to weave a fantasy I hope will honor them.

Some of the stories that fill these pages have become family legends. As a child if I complained about the fatty steak at dinner, Papa would grumble about how he ate grass as a prisoner. "You don't know hungry," was his famous catchphrase. Baba anxiously puffed on her cigarettes and talked about seeing trains full of doomed Jews while she was working at a labor camp. A hand grenade destroyed Chester's first family, and my mother, Janina, was named after the daughter he lost. Chester and Sophie were in fact scheduled to immigrate to Australia before Sophie panicked about the difficult voyage across the equator, and George and Janina were stricken with pertussis just as they were about to leave Wildflecken.

It was much later that I realized the true tragedy of their experience. One can never fully recover from the broken families, the missing memories, the stolen homes. I was fascinated, and for a long time I considered writing Papa's biography. However, once I had my twins, I knew the book was to be about the love and heartbreak of motherhood. It was only after becoming a mother myself that I acutely felt what my grandmother had gone through, and I couldn't fathom it.

Life as a refugee is never easy and can—and usually does—scar a person permanently. For Baba, her experience haunted her for the rest of her days. Zosia, as a character, triumphs over her fears and overcomes her defeats. Reality, however, wasn't so forgiving. Sophie never learned to drive, leaving her more and more isolated as American culture shifted to automobiles. Throughout the rest of her life she struggled with depression, crushing anxiety, and gradual but severe dementia. She never saw her three children again after she left them in Poland; my mother arranged for the youngest to visit once in the early 1990s, but by then he was an old man, and Baba was only a shell of her former self, her mind stolen by what was likely Alzheimer's.

Papa was always the firecracker in the family, showing up at suppertime with pocketfuls of Kit Kats and hugging us so aggressively that he bent our glasses. They'd both been through hell, but Baba's demons weighed her down and tore her apart. I never really knew my grandmother; my early memories of her lucidity are foggy at best, and her mental well-being declined quickly when I was very young. But I knew the feel of her hugs, and I knew she loved me. I can still hear her voice calling my name with her deep Polish accent and rolling Rs. That's another reason why I made her my protagonist, my hero. I wanted to get to know her a little better, to be closer to her memory.

That's also the reason why it is important for me to donate a portion of the sales of this book to Alzheimer's research. I hope her story can help save someone else.

ACKNOWLEDGEMENTS

Thank you, Scott, for being my cheerleader, for believing in me, for offering the time and space to pursue my dreams. Luke and Eve, thank you for giving me the inspiration to write a book about motherhood, for showing me the desperation a mother feels when her babies are threatened. I love you all very much.

Mom, thank you for answering my questions and telling your stories, and for reading this over and over and collaborating with me. Thank you for always letting me carve my own way. You're the best *matka* ever.

Dad, I wish you could have seen this, I know how proud you would be. I miss you every day. You gave me the courage to tackle a project like this.

Supergroup, I wouldn't be writing without you. Sean Beggs, Kristi Belcamino, Coralee Grebe, Jana Hiller, Brian Rubin, Kate Schultz, and Kaethe Schwehn, you made this happen. Thank you for your advice, your support, your friendship, your honesty, and for showing up when we need each other most. I'm so lucky to have fallen in with you all. I'm also forever grateful to the Loft Literary Center in Minneapolis for bringing Supergroup together in the first place, and for continuing to offer resources and education for all writers.

Thank you to my editor, DJ Schuette, for your polish, your curiosity, your attention to detail, and especially your faith in me and this book. You pounded out the kinks and sanded the slivers. Thank you also to Colleen Schuette, for your careful proofreading eye.

To everyone who read an early version of this book and offered their priceless feedback, I'm forever grateful: Angie Guenther, Barbara Ney, Daina Sivanich, Jan Tietz, Kate O'Brien, Sally Reigel, Courtney Nelson, Mimi McDonnell Black, Kristi Ruport, Marisa Herbert, Kelly Kenley, Krysy Winden, Jennifer Nevers, Erica Drake, Kelly Perry, Staci Salls Blix, Angela Gilchrist, Ann Olsen-Samms, Barbara Poelle, Heather Herrman, and Allison Wyss. Special thanks to Sarah Wolfe for your extra attention, and for bringing it to the MoMs Book Club. I know there are others who read bits and pieces here and there, and if I missed you, please know that I appreciate every thought you passed my way.

To Amy Olson, who claims to not be a public relations specialist: you are much too humble. You're one of the smartest people I know. Thank you for your help.

Hannah Voermans, thank you for making a girl who had sinusitis and a fever look stunning. You're a gem.

To all the Hanleys, Laches and Bratbergs who have been there with kind words and encouragement: thank you, it warms my heart and has kept me moving forward.

If the story of the Wildflecken DP camp interests you, I recommend *The Wild Place* by Kathryn Hulme. It is a beautiful memoir about the author's time as a relief officer in the Wildflecken DP camp, and well worth a read. Much of Matka was inspired by Ms. Hulme's lovely prose and solid facts.

Please consider supporting the Alzheimer's Association. To donate, please visit **alz.org.**

Sophie and Janina, Wildflecken, 1949

Chester, Wildflecken, 1948

Chester and Sophie, 1980

Sarah Hanley

Connect with me to learn more and
to be the first to hear about special events,
giveaways, and upcoming releases.

sarahhanleybooks.com
Facebook.com/sarahhanleyauthor
Twitter: @sjhanley
Instagram: sarahhanleybooks

If you enjoyed this book, please consider leaving a review.
Every review means the world to me; I celebrate good reviews
and learn from the rest. Reviews never have to be long or detailed
to be helpful; any feedback or thought is encouraged.
Goodreads.com and Amazon.com are good places to start.

Thank you for reading and sharing!

CPSIA information can be obtained
at www.ICGtesting.com
Printed in the USA
LVHW090052040119
602724LV00001B/316/P

9 781732 444201